The Maredian

Susan B. Iris

Global Book
Publishing

The Maredian
Susan B. Iris

ISBN: 978-1-956193-69-5
Book Design & Publishing done by:
Global Book Publishing
www.globalbookpublishing.com

In memory of my Grandmother - Maria do Rosário da Costa Galego

For Shawna,
Happy reading,
and thanks for being
a good friend and
who helps me continue
to, or gives me reason
to express myself in
some colourful
"Portuguese"
Azorean style!
Susan Bliss

Table of Contents

PART ONE

≈

The Dawn

≈

And all my days are trances,
And all my nightly dreams
Are where thy grey eye glances,
And where thy footstep gleams

—Edgar Allan Poe, “To One in Paradise”

CHAPTER 1

Birthday Girl

Don Mills, Ontario, Canada
March 16, 2085

The megacity of Don Mills sprawled out in a glaring, kaleidoscopic arrangement of lights that converged into vertical rows of high-rises, a mix of commercial and residential structures that housed millions.

The architectural gems of Arial and Gen X harboured spiral designs with each floor glazing in purple, blue, and silver lights. Golden flames shot up into the night sky from hundred-story rooftops.

A multitude of holographs jetted sideways from their centres, flashing advertisements of the newest artificial intelligence; the Mars colony under development; a liquid food to curb ailments; a model's face filling up with subcutaneous makeup, resulting in a perfect look with no instrumentation; and the newest addition to the robot-dog and cat—robot-parrot.

Between Arial and Gen X sat a square building with an iron face and a simple Greco design. It was forty floors high with a sizable rooftop garden. No fancy name had been given to it—just an address with an inauguration date: June 12, 2025.

Inside one of its sleek, tubal elevators stood Gracie Pinto, holding her sleeping toddler, Jimmy. She had just finished another twelve-hour shift at the hydrogen-diesel plant. She should have been exhausted out of her mind, yet she remained intensely focused and dreaded what was waiting for her back in the apartment.

The elevator doors opened, and she stepped into chaos. The walls were stripped, and the ceilings torn open, exposing six-inch pipes covered in white, powdery dust. Spindly wires and cables descended from dark vaults above and light bulbs dangled. The speckled gold and black Persian carpet had been torn out, exposing smooth slabs of uneven concrete.

The renovation.

A memo had probably been emailed to Arabella, a few weeks ago, followed up with a holographic message that Gracie ignored.

She ducked around loose wires and didn't notice some slow movement working its way through the thicket of wires towards her.

Gracie halted and tightened her grip on Jimmy, who didn't stir. Her eyes took in the approaching lanky figure. He had a construction hat over a lavender turban. A nano-bug glowed inside his ear, streaming live to the network, and a two-inch, rectangular screen tied onto a Velcro strap was wrapped around his wrist, used as a voice-prompted note-taker—an archaic technology most senior citizens still used.

She relaxed. It was Mr. Singh. He'd been Gran Amália's best friend and was the property manager.

Mr. Singh smiled animatedly and waved his arms as if Gracie was a burly construction worker carrying precious stones, instead of what she was—a petite, young woman moving with caution and holding onto a sleeping child.

Oh please ... please don't talk my ear off. Not tonight, of all nights.

"Gracie, so good to run into you," he said.

She half-smiled in acknowledgment and walked around him.

"The renovation has started." He continued, "In a few days, these hallways will be wired with networks and nanobots that will create programmable architecture and holographs to change shapes and functions at your command."

"I'm sorry, Mr. Singh. I didn't ask Arabella to read out your messages yet."

Undeterred, he continued enthusiastically. "In a few weeks, you can be walking down this hallway in a Jurassic forest with *Tyrannosaurus Rex* by your side ..."

"Great! That sounds like something I always wanted walking next to me."

"You can ask the network for the Pacific—or the Atlantic—with blue whales, dolphins, or a group of mermaids swimming next to you."

"That's at least a much better scenario."

"And way above the rooftop garden, there'll be grandiose advertisements, which the corporations will pay for—so that means no additional costs to residents."

"Guess that was in the memo too, huh?"

"Generation X and Arial are fitted networks, holographs of every scenario, and other automatic conveniences. We'll finally catch up to the twenty-second century. Won't that be great?"

He looked ready to do a little jig. Gracie wasn't so enthusiastic, though. Why should they catch up? The megacity of Don Mills had become a bulging keg, bursting at the seams with overpopulation, infrastructure falling into disrepair, and slums proliferating just like their twin sister, Toronto. Those lucky enough to live in a good neighbourhood with parks and decent air quality were constantly surrounded by motion, noise, and stimulation.

Their outdated building had none of these excessive stimuli. It didn't turn into holographic worlds replete with green meadows and unpolluted lakes from centuries past. The little building wasn't anything spectacular outwardly. Inside, it had generous space and was held up by a solid structure. Suites were simply decorated with mahogany and shiny tiles. The building functioned well and didn't need all the flashing illusions of holographs embedded with alternative, healthy environmental scenes that no longer existed and were filled with extinct creatures, of a long-ago past. Gracie preferred to see things for what they were and not what holographs and their programmers wanted her to see.

"Next week, Gracie, when you come by to play chess, you'll be more enthusiastic as you'll see more progress by then."

Gracie lowered her eyes. *Ugh, chess*?

The invitation he asked you weeks ago, Gracie ...

"Come for chess next week?" she said, seemingly stalling. "How about in two weeks when my schedule is better?"

"I'll make dinner, and it'll be my specialty—mutton curry with roti. The mutton won't be synthesized meat. It'll be the real thing. It was Amália's favourite. After you taste it, it'll be yours too—or it'll at least come close to her *Carne Assada.*"

When Great-Gran Amália was alive, the focus was on her, and Gracie was the passenger, a role she was comfortable with. Gracie preferred to be left alone. The skin on her back started to spot over with hives. The excuses flowed easily.

"I don't know yet. I don't usually eat late ..."

Liar. I have many times with my hectic schedule.

"It's not good for my digestion ..."

Actually, my digestion is pretty tough.

"We can play chess for an hour," Gracie finally said. "Not any longer than that. And I'll still have to check my schedule to let you know. Sorry."

His enthusiastic smile waned.

"All right," he said. "Whenever you're free, let me know. It would be great to have you and Jimmy over. I can start teaching the little man some chess moves."

Gracie reached a white-trimmed door marked with the number nine. "I'll confirm by end of next week, okay?"

"That's fine," he said gently. "Good night, Gracie, and to you, little Jimmy."

He gave Jimmy a soft rub on the head and returned to the tangle of wires to do whatever he'd been doing before.

You bought more time on that one but eventually, he'll be back again. Why not just go? It would make him so happy ...

Gracie raised her face and positioned her left eye before the number nine. A screen sprung to life under the number, and a purple light scanned her eye.

Then, a patient, female, robotic voice greeted her. "Welcome home, Gracie."

And with that, the apartment door unlocked and slid open.

"Thanks, Arabella."

CHAPTER 2

Rose

In a slick, chrome kitchen, a pot steamed over a stove with scents of a savoury stew made from synthetic meat, tofu, grains, and root vegetables. Rose, who insisted on being called Rose instead of Grandmother, sat on a barstool. She was in town for a conference about properties for sale in Greenland and that was all Gracie knew since Rose didn't disclose much to Gracie unless she absolutely had to.

Rose watched a holograph screen filled with images of crowds trying to climb up a border wall, only to be pushed back by the flying batons of guards and sprays of fire and tear gas coming from drones above them.

A newscaster's voice reported, "... *thousands of desperate climate change refugees from the states of the Carolinas, clashed with the RCMP and with the AI border control police at the Manitoba and Saskatchewan borders* ..."

A group of politicians and their delegates emerged from the bottom of the screen ...

"... *the presidents of East and West America, the Prime Minister of Canada, and the Chief from the Assembly of First*

Nations finished their first round of talks to alleviate the ongoing climate crisis ..."

They shook each others' hands on some accord, their faces exhausted, fatigued, and filled with hopes of promises made, which nature no longer cared to uphold.

Rose wore a classical, baby-blue jacket with a matching skirt and a light-blue, silky bodice. The red polish on her manicured nails matched the rims of her fashion glasses. Her look was perfected by the lines of auburn, glossy hair that looked vinyl but wasn't. It was snipped into a perfect bowl and shaped around the contours of a youthful face with a light-olive complexion. She had smooth skin and high cheekbones that placed her in what Gracie called "the delusional age." She looked to be in her mid-forties versus her biological age of eighty-seven, all made possible by Reverse Aging Genetic therapy, known as RAG. Hideous Botox fillers that made wealthy senior citizens of the past look unrecognizable had been thrown to the wayside. With RAG, people re-aged back to their youthful states, although there was a downside for some.

The genetic therapies caused aggressive cancers in a few and activated dormant genes in others with diseases like Parkinson's. There was no pre-DNA test that could predict these genetic anomalies. It was a gamble, and for Rose and others like her, nature was on their side.

Rose sensed Gracie's presence as if she had an extra pair of eyes in the back of her head, and she swirled around at once.

"Putting Jimmy to bed," Gracie said.

Rose rolled her fashion glasses over her head. Her hazel eyes homed in, scanning the oil patches on Gracie's jean-overalls; the dark lines of shining grease under her fingernails; and the reddish-brown hair, infused with diesel fumes, pulled back into a stringy ponytail that sat in a weak, lopsided slant on top of her head.

"He's been at the children's centre all this time," Rose finally said. Gracie's posture stiffened.

"He had to stay there until I came to get him, or they would have leashed him up to a pole in front of the building until I picked him up."

"What kind of children's centre keeps them this late? Couldn't you hire a Nannybot at home?"

Gracie calculated. *Three questions. That's pretty good for her inquisition. She hadn't seen Jimmy and I for six months, and yet I thought the conversation would start something like 'Hello Gracie, it's your thirtieth birthday today. Happy Birthday. It's so nice to see you.'*

"A few weeks ago, a Nannybot malfunctioned in Belgium, beat the kid half to death, and set the apartment on fire," Gracie said. "I'd gladly pay much more for a human's care under an eyecam. My twelve-hour shifts end in one week, and I'll be back to eight hours."

Rose approached, each of her manicured toes behind transparent, high-heeled slippers, and Gracie willed herself not to recoil, watching Rose's Chanel No.5-scented hand reach out to barely touch Jimmy's back. The hazel in her eyes darkened and, to Gracie's dismay, slanted. The inevitable *tsk* followed. Each tsk intensified inside Gracie with renewed feelings of resentment.

Tsk ... Rose always knew what was best.

Tsk ... Gracie was too young to be a mother and would never be a decent one.

Tsk ... Poor Gracie can never manage anything.

Tsk ... The child would suffer and should have been flushed away.

Just like everything else Rose flushed away—wrinkles, cellulite, and her own shortcomings.

"What kind of food are they feeding him? Is it organic?" Rose asked. "He's too pale. He shouldn't be this pale. Do they even take him outside to get any sun? He's resting his face against your dirty, oily neck. Disgusting."

The rage built inside Gracie. It was moving faster just as she dreaded.

Gran Amália was no longer there to smooth things over and drive the conversation elsewhere—or tell Rose to shut it. It was just Rose and Gracie now.

Gracie's nails curled into the palms of her hand under Jimmy, pricking her skin. Long shifts, not sleeping properly, and not eating much made her vulnerable to Rose's terse words. Gracie wanted to swiftly maim Rose and completely disregard the consequences. She could understand those who had reached a fine line and ultimately snapped, committing a heinous crime.

Gracie took a deep breath and let her mouth run loose instead.

"Why do you care? Why does it matter to you?"

"He's my great-grandson. Of course, it matters to me."

"How about Evelyn? Did *she* matter? You did nothing to stop it. You let her die."

Guess I'm going there now—to the tabooest subject between us.

"You don't understand anything that was going on during those times," Rose said.

"You sent her to your celebrity doctor who was more into his rock-n-roll band than doing what was best for her. He gave her drugs that I read articles about their high levels of addiction that were worse than OxyC2. I told you about them and yet you didn't tell him to stop the prescriptions. You didn't care. You continued travelling the world to purchase international properties. That was all that mattered to you."

"Shut up," Rose snapped. "I will not defend any decision I made to"—her hard eyes fell over Gracie's dirty hair and overalls—"you."

"Gran Amália wanted to take her to the church group to try out home remedies to see if they could help the post-partum depression."

"I would never subject Evelyn to such make-believe nonsense and to remedies not based on science. It's easy for you to condemn. You didn't see what she was doing—making everyone go through. Amália protected you from it, keeping you swimming every day in your pool, swirling around in it, flapping, and dancing away."

"Yeah, well ... your science, in this case, killed ..."

"Not me. I wasn't responsible for all of this mess. You work in sludge all day. You work in literal trash ..."

"It's part of being an environmental engineer," Gracie snapped and rolled her eyes. "It's temporary and pays higher wages than working up on the glass floors of the hundred-story offices of your ilk."

"Those fumes you keep on inhaling all day ... and with the accident you had years ago ... it's damaging you. I have to dismiss whatever you tell me because you're just not well. You're not thinking straight."

Wow, she's not even going to acknowledge it. She still blames you for your mother's demise and that's it. She'll hold you accountable no matter what. You're to blame in her mind—forever. There's no fixing this.

"You're just pissed because Gran Amália had named me as the sole heir to this apartment and everything in it."

"Is that what you think?" said Rose with a chuckle, and her teeth gleamed, otherworldly in their whiteness. She took a few steps away and continued to chuckle.

"Why *should* she have left this place to you? Don't you have enough apartments all over the country and the world? Gran Amália knew if she left it to you, Jimmy and I would be out in the street."

Rose stared Gracie down. "You're even stupider than I thought. It's shameful. It really is."

"I don't care if you think I'm stupid. All I know is that I'll never be the kind of shitty mother you were to Evelyn—or that Evelyn was to me. I'll be there for Jimmy. This generational failure-selfish-screw-up-shit dies with me!"

"Such anger," Rose chortled, with one hand on her waist and feigned concern in her eyes. "Are you all right? Hold on. Do you need me to call you a doctor?"

"I'm putting Jimmy to bed," Gracie said, steadying her voice. "Tomorrow morning, get to your conference, take your bags, and get on your way. I never want to see you ever again."

CHAPTER 3

Gran Amália

In Jimmy's room, Gracie leaned against the door and collapsed. She gasped for breath as she stifled her sobs into a bleeding hand. Her shoulders trembled. She gripped Jimmy more tightly with her other arm, but he slept on, unbothered by her unravelling emotions. Tears drained out of her eyes and soaked the top of her greasy overalls.

Damn, Gracie. You fool, this is your fault. Why did you let her come? You knew this would happen and it did. It's that damned hope you have that lets you fantasize that Rose would have changed after Gran Amália's death—that she would suddenly start inviting you to brunch or the beach ... that you'd paint your nails together like normal relations. Hah! Fool.

She straightened her posture and wiped her face. Tears did nothing to change any situation.

"I won't let her ruin my day. It's my birthday. It's been a good day, and she'll be gone tomorrow. Things will go back to how they were. Everything will be good."

Gracie placed Jimmy in his bed, pulled off his shoes, and ran a hand over his cherub face. "What a good boy," she told him.

"You're lucky to be able to sleep so soundly. You barely flinched throughout that whole conversation, huh? It'll just be for one more week. Then, Mommy's long shifts will end and we'll get to spend more time together. Happier times are coming—I promise."

Her fingers brushed through his soft, flaxen curls and she stepped away. She plugged in a nightlight, a small statue of Christ the King that Gran Amália had given Jimmy. A soft, white light emanated from the statue and cut into the room's dimness.

Down the hall from Jimmy's room, the door to Gran Amália's room was partially open with the silhouette of Rose's designer, mahogany luggage by the foot of the bed. Gracie had kept the door shut since Gran Amália's death, as if she was afraid to see Gran Amália's ghost, lying in bed with a rosary in hand, a white candle burning on her lamp table in front of her venerated, little statue of the red-caped Senhor Santo Cristo, which Gran Amália's parents had brought from St. Jorge Island in the Azores when they immigrated to Toronto a hundred years ago.

The Senhor Santo Cristo sat on top of the dresser with his face cast down so Gran Amália could look up into his eyes as she prayed. As Gracie looked into the room, the Santo Cristo's face had been turned upwards, his body positioned to directly look at anyone peering inside the room. His expressive, dark-brown eyes were supposed to trigger some kind of intrinsic empathy. In Gracie, it made her wonder if something supernatural lived quietly inside the Senhor Santo Cristo. She imagined that in the middle of the night, it would come alive and make its way to her bedroom door as she slept, not to hurt her but to tell her something, although she had no idea what it would say. What even propelled her to imagine such a thing? She kept Gran Amália's bedroom door locked at night.

CHAPTER 4

Jeff

Gracie wiped off condensed moisture from the bathroom mirror. She wrapped a towel around her freshly showered body and combed out her wavy chestnut hair. She had the natural palette of a pretty girl, with a flawless, light-olive complexion, high cheekbones, plump, shapely lips, and large, brown eyes. Gracie, at thirty, with a petite frame, looked like a nineteen-year-old, at times. On her first day at work, colleagues thought she was someone's high school kid visiting the plant or worse, was an inexperienced intern. Gracie had already worked in hydrogen plants before her undergrad in environmental and chemical engineering for over three years and volunteered for extra shifts when the opportunity arose.

Gracie could take RAG therapy after she turned fifty-five, the qualifying age for the same reason Gran Amália took the treatment: to extend her lifespan. Everyone did it, and like many things that progressed, other things had to be negotiated. Referendums were held, and the majority of people voted for strict birth rates to be controlled. One-child policies became the norm. Sex education and birth control implants were mandatory and given to every child above eight years of age. As for those who had more than one child, they were disqualified from receiving RAG treatments and were tracked down and brought into a lab to permanently fix their careless reproductive tendencies.

Gran Amália, at her biological age of eighty-five, aged back to sixty years with RAG therapy and was able to take care of Gracie since birth. Gracie shuddered at the thought of what would have happened to her if Gran Amália had listened to the heated protests across the world—from zealous, religious types, environmental crusaders, and population-control fanatics who were against genetic therapies of any kind—and didn't decide to become an elderly pioneer to take on this new RAG therapy. Gran Amália told Gracie that it was her religious conviction to get younger for improved strength and health, not over vanity purposes so she could raise Gracie and get her away from Rose's and Evelyn's unrepentant ways.

Arabella's voice came through the mirror. "Gracie, you have an urgent audio message from the Synchro Sharks."

That was a name she hadn't heard in a while. "Play it, Arabella."

"Certainly."

"Gracie, it's Tatou. I've flown in from Edmonton on short business and I connected with Natasha a few days ago on Vatis. Do you remember her?"

What a question, was Tatou being sarcastic? Of course, Gracie knew who Natasha was. She was one of the base team members on their Junior Synchronized Swimming team.

"As it's your birthday tonight, I invited you both to come out to the Sagittarius Club. It'll be great to reconnect, and sorry, I know, last minute. Early this evening, Natasha confirmed that she could make it, and I was stuck in meetings working hard, so now it's time to party hard! Oh, you're going to love it. The Sage has a

1980s theme tonight, so come in costume, makeup, and teased-up hair, and we'll be jiving to 1980s hits till dawn. I reserved a car and can meet you at your place on the way at 10 p.m. Send a voice confirmation a.s.a.p."

10 p.m.? Gracie's Android wrist device read "9:34." She could go out tonight. For once, Rose's presence was useful. She could stay with Jimmy, and it had been so long since Gracie had gone out—five years ago to be exact ... a Halloween party. It had also featured an '80s theme and she dressed up as Gran Amália when she was a teenager. Somewhere in the bottom of Gracie's bedroom closet, the T-Shirt with a keyboard synthesizer printed across it, the red corduroy pants, and all the fluorescent, plastic bracelets and matching hair ribbons were still there.

She would have to let Rose know she was going out to watch Jimmy. Dealing with Rose's attitude on this one would be painful, but it might be worth the coming argument.

"Arabella," respond to Tatou. "I'm getting ready and will meet them in front of the building at 10."

"Certainly."

Eleven minutes later, Gracie twisted her hair up into a ponytail and rolled a pink, fluorescent ribbon around it. She put on the keyboard synthesizer T-Shirt and shoved its ends into a high waistband of the corduroy pants that still fit her. "Arabella, costume makeup," she said.

"Certainly."

A drawer slid open and rose up by Gracie's elbow.

Gracie injected under the skin in each corner of her eyelids blue-silver eye shadow with thick lines of black eyeliner. She injected cherry-red lipstick over her lips and brushed thick mascara through her curly eyelashes. She stood back. It wasn't the same—no era could be perfectly replicated—but it was close enough.

"Arabella, how do I look?"

"Presentable."

The Android watch flickered with a message from Jeffrey McCormick Nakamura.

"Arabella, run Jeff's message onto the mirror."

"Certainly."

The mirror split into two. On the left side, Jeff appeared. He wore a navy-blue bodysuit with a beige turtleneck underneath, a tag on the right side of the body suit, marked with black letters spelling "PervivoTech." Jeff was PervivoTech's in-house and best Robotics engineer. He graduated from a PhD program that beat out thousands to land a prestigious position that represented virtually every robotics engineer's dream job. Artificial intelligence and robotics engineering were where everyone wanted to be, right in the centre of science. Robotics engineers were in high demand, and if they were also attractive and charming like Jeff, they ascended much quicker to the celebrity coding throne.

Behind Jeff, workers tended to translucent drapes that covered the dark silhouettes of massive robotic structures, twisted and bent into rising arms, mounds, and poking metals.

Jeff ran a hand through the wavy, blonde locks that had spilled over his forehead. Not a good sign. He was uncomfortable. A faint smile.

"Hey, Gracie. Happy Birthday."

So much of Jimmy looked like Jeff—the big, blue, oval eyes, wavy, blonde hair, the tilt of his head when he smiled—little idiosyncrasies. Some of their friends argued Jimmy had some of Gracie's features too—the full lips and shapely nose, for instance.

"Sorry. Couldn't break free from this project. We plan to showcase our improved AI at the Greenland AI Global Fair. Working from the second prototype copy we have from the one stationed on Mars, we're going to be representing Canada with an improved AI version that'll be used in emergency life support operations. It's a medic AI that will do DNA sampling and carry supplies of water and medicines, basically tasked to keep the astronaut or citizen alive until a bigger emergency rescue crew dives in. We worked on the last touches over the past few weeks. It required a lot of logged-in hours, little sleep, and almost no showering. I can't remember when last I ate, and what day is it now?"

Another smile.

"I wouldn't be pleasant to be around."

An apologetic shrug.

"I hear you're getting busier in the plant, eyeing that promotion to the plant's lead engineer. Hope that's going well. I should've sent you more holographs. In Whitehorse, it's sometimes hard to do, as the satellites have been inconsistent in the past few months since I moved here. The NASA folks are still trying to figure out what's been shutting them down."

He leaned into the screen, looked behind him cautiously, and covered his mouth conspiratorially. "It's the Tristanians and the Patagonians ..." He leaned back from the screen, chuckling at his own joke, but then his smile faded, and his eyes lowered like those of a boy in a bit of trouble. He looked up into the camera. "Just a few more weeks and I *will* come down there. Get me some good southern warmth in the sunny megacity of Don Mills. Look at me ... I'm as pale as an albino Wallaby."

A chuckle.

And recently, just as elusive, Gracie thought.

"I left something for your birthday—just a little something. I hope this will provide some kind of redemption for my not being there for your big 3-0. I'll send another message in the next few days. And if you're going out to celebrate, don't overdo it. Look at what thirty has done to me. And it's only been three years." A laugh. Soft crinkles around his eyes. A fuzzy screen. A red light flashes at the bottom. A generous deposit was made.

Gracie felt numb. Jeff's career grew. He didn't abandon them financially. He could be goofy but was responsible. Still, a sinking feeling came that nudged her, telling her that he had abandoned her in other ways. He could be there with her and Jimmy if he wanted to. Yes, he could. He was Pervivo's celebrity robotics engineer. Surely, he could be let loose for a few days to fly out from Whitehorse and down to Don Mills. If the tables were turned, wouldn't Gracie do just that?

The Android wrist device vibrated...

The car is turning onto the main lobby in a few minutes. Synchro Sharks.

Gracie grabbed a leather jacket from the bathroom door and put it on.

Rose sat on her stool, and an empty soup bowl was being taken away by robotic arms that made Gracie feel uneasy. The way they moved was somehow obscene—stiff and far too quick. There was no consistent rhythm in their movements.

A news conference flashed on the holograph in front of Rose, a male voice in the background...

"... *Israeli troops inside their confiscated new territories of Jordan, Syria, and Lebanon have enjoyed relative peace for over a decade. The potential for another war has emerged as the leaders of Algeria, Tunisia, Libya, Egypt, Iran, and Turkey have reached a truce with Russian armed forces who have also vowed to destroy Israel. The Tsar Bomba has been seen mobilized in Ankara, Turkey.*"

Gracie zipped up her leather jacket, and the Android wrist device vibrated again...

`Synchro Sharks are here!`

Gracie, tell her really fast and get the hell out.

"I received a message from my friends," Gracie said, her voice steady and strong. "They're from out of town and want to take me out for my birthday tonight. Their car is already in front of the building, waiting."

Rose swirled around. Her hard eyes took in the fluorescent, pink bow wrapped around Gracie's hair, the heavy, blue eye shadow, the red-apple lip gloss, the keyboard T-shirt, the red corduroy pants and dozens of pink, green, and yellow plastic bracelets covering her wrists.

If Gracie's sight was amusing to Rose or repugnant, she kept a composed and indifferent reaction. She was silent.

Wouldn't you know it, if this was all it took to keep her quiet, you should have dressed in the 1980s whenever she was around.

"I won't be out too late."

A smear came back over Rose's lips. She crossed her arms.

"You're leaving your young child to go out to a party. Is that being a good parent?"

"The last time I went out to a club was five years ago. It's just for one night."

"You attack me and tell me what a terrible mother I am and then on a whim decide to leave your small son with me, the terrible mother. Tell me, what should I tell Jimmy when he wakes up in the middle of the night, crying out for you? What do you want me to tell him?"

Seriously, she is trying to guilt-trip me?

"He won't wake up," Gracie said, keeping calm. "He usually sleeps all night and into the morning. He won't even know I'm not here."

Rose's eyes narrowed maliciously. "That's just about the only thing you've said all evening that's truthful. He's used to not having his mommy around much, so I guess he won't fuss anyway if I do tell him you'll be coming back soon."

Rose swirled around to watch the rest of the news program.

Don't bite. Just don't. She's gone tomorrow. Turn around and leave. She's just furious because she probably didn't get any real estate on Mars despite all her work wooing government officials for the past months.

"I'll be home soon enough," Gracie muttered as she walked into the hallway and tripped backwards on something. It was Jimmy's little hairbrush. She stuffed it inside the back pocket of her pants.

The door slid shut with Arabella's voice trailing behind, "Have a good night, Gracie. See you soon."

CHAPTER 5

Synchro Sharks

The Sagittarius Club, known as "the Sage," was one of the most prominent clubs in the megacity of Toronto. The car approached the second highway above the 401. Both 401 highways were crammed with cars moving on magnetic roads at speeds that couldn't exceed the maximum legislated hundred miles per hour.

Above a smaller grass road, next to the 401 highways, was the aerial highway. A line of drones, each ten feet apart and carrying cargo up to a thousand pounds, flew toward the downtown core of Toronto, and another line came in from the opposite direction toward the megacity of Don Mills. The drones were only operational from 10:00 in the evening to 6:00 in the morning.

Gracie sat in the back seat of the car with Tatou, whose full name was Antoinette Richard, and Natasha Mitchell was in the front seat.

Tatou looked out the car window and casually twirled a toothpick in her mouth. Her jet-black hair was gelled down behind her ears and puffed up in a large curl on top of her head, falling over her forehead. She wore a white, satin bodysuit, with pants that flared open at the bottoms. Red, pinwheel-shaped rhinestones ran over the shoulders, arms, and collar of the outfit. A red chiffon scarf was tucked into her V-neck covering the opening and held in place with rows of heavy gold chains. To complete her look, a thick, gold-trimmed belt wrapped around her flat waist.

Natasha took on a different look. She had dyed the ringlets of her thick, curly hair in bright purple that ran down her shapely bronze arms. Glittering purple eye shadow covered the tops of her eyelids, and thick lines of mascara further accentuated her eyelashes, which were naturally full and curly. Her full lips shone with purple lip gloss. She wore a short, snug, pink, shiny dress with a vinyl-red, three-inch waist belt. A silver jacket was draped over her lap.

Tatou turned to Gracie and slapped her hands over her chest. "I taped them down to look more authentic."

"Elvis Presley?" Gracie asked.

"I am *the* Elvis, the king of rock 'n' roll," she said and winked. "You were always the smart one, eh?"

"That's weird. I always thought *you* were."

"Didn't Elvis die sometime in the 1970s?" Natasha asked.

"So they say," Tatou said. "The ancient people from the 1980s reported sightings of him during that era, still alive and living in Las Vegas before the big 9.0 hit and sunk all the casinos and hotels. They claimed his death was a complete hoax."

"Really? I never heard that one before," Natasha said.

"Very soon, in the next few decades, he might actually exist amongst us." Tatou continued. "I recently read an article about scientists working on resurrecting famous, ancient people. The list includes a sultan, an Egyptian pharaoh, a few European royals, a Native American chief, and the one and only Elvis Presley. Has Jeff heard anything about this from the genetics side at Pervivo?"

"They're having troubles with the satellites up in Whitehorse, so our conversations haven't been as frequent as we'd like."

Gracie leaned toward Natasha. "What about the others? Have you heard anything from them? I stopped reaching out to them over ten years ago."

"At that time, I would get the odd nudge from Ayshan and Sahara," Natasha said, nothing more. "I found out that Adrianna was in Peru dealing with some family business, Feifei was coaching the Jordanian synchronized junior women's team, and Kate was in Moscow and involved with some tycoon in the weapons defense business."

"We trained for so many hours together since we were children," Gracie said. "After the world championships in Iqaluit, the other teams that came in fifth and sixth places—they continued on."

"It was Kate," Natasha said. "She didn't want to continue, and it started to affect the other girls. Cohesion during training became difficult and when Adrianna left and then Feifei, whatever fragile crack had appeared in the team during the championship split wide open."

"Not to put any guilt on you, Gracie," Tatou said. "I felt the break up start when you left due to the accident and the new girl took over. What was her name?"

"Jasmine," Natasha said.

"The team unison just wasn't the same."

"She was a junior gymnastics champion," Gracie said. "She had stronger legs—and the experience of jumping high and twisting in the air. She was the perfect flyer that I could never be."

"You were an excellent flyer," Tatou said. "It wasn't Jasmine's fault. Unison takes years to achieve, especially in the sport we were in. We all had that advantage. With the world championships coming up so fast, we didn't have that time with Jasmine no matter how hard she tried."

"Last time I talked with Feifei," Natasha said. "Feifei said that Kate's parents decided to do RAG therapy. The therapy worked for both of them and once they were twenty-five years old again, their thirty-year relationship ended as they got together with other twenty-five-year-old RAG recipients. This affected Kate and she started to show up late to practices instead of being a few minutes early. Since we'd known her, she was always the first to arrive. There were so many other moments."

Tatou nudged Gracie. "See all the fun you missed?"

"Now that you're all caught up in that drama, why don't we start celebrating? We're together now and that's what matters." Natasha said.

She fumbled in her purse and produced a five-hundred-millilitre bottle.

"Cool, what's in it?" asked Tatou, sitting up.

"Southern Comfort."

"That'll do."

Natasha offered it to Gracie.

"Birthday girl first."

Gracie took the bottle and took a short sip. "It's nice," she said, then passed it to Tatou, who took three, long gulps.

The automatic driver's voice announced, "Arriving at destination."

Long, robotic arms extended outwards from the centres of the club's doors, and with a scanning device, they moved over Natasha's and Tatou's wrists as a light, the size of a sugar cube, came to life under their skins and a holograph with data sprang up. Gracie held out her Android wristwatch to the AI's scanning device. After the AI cleared them for weapons and viral diseases,

Gracie, Tatou, and Natasha entered the club as the song "Give Me Tonight" by the artist Shannon blasted throughout the club's high-tech system. A holograph of band members played on the main stage. Neon lights swirled around the walls and floors as if the place was rumbling inside a fiery vortex.

A slick, touch-table bar was positioned at the other end of the large dance floor. Multitudes of bottles hung down from the ceiling. Robotic arms rose from the top of the bar and moved quickly between bottles and glasses, mixing drinks and sliding them down to customers.

1980s aficionados swirled around the main dance floor. They clung to each other, yelling out lyrics in a euphoric state. As anticipated, the crowd wore all kinds of outfits—a mix of tight denim, pencil skirts that sucked thighs like second skins, thick stockings that came up past the knees, and python-sized ankle socks—as they danced around.

The men wore a variety of polyester print shirts with shiny, satin pants. Others chose heavy, shoulder-padded and double-vested suits and a handful of colourful jumpsuits.

In other corners of the dance floor, two to three smaller groups of people gathered around a holograph of Michael Jackson. All of them attempted to do the moonwalk. Others selected holographs of other icons of that era, sang along, and danced with them.

After getting some drinks, they stood in a quieter section of the club.

Tatou put an arm around Gracie's shoulder. "Guess what I got you for your birthday?" Tatou pulled up one of her wide sleeves. A small pocket was sewn inside it. She removed a transparent rectangle with two transparent circles inside it.

"You did not," Natasha said, peering down at the circles. "What type are they?"

"This is the newest development in augmented reality," Tatou said. "Which will be available to the public in the next few weeks. Throw away your smart glasses and tacky visor helmets as those are now a thing of the past. Place both of these over your eyes and voice-activate them. You tell it a code, which I've sent you Gracie, through the network on the ride here, and it comes to life. You then pick the environment you want to have the best realistic experience for the next ten, thirty, sixty minutes—whatever you want. It's not like the current AR experiences that put you inside a holograph, with a certain amount of space swirling around you while you can still register the sounds and smells outside the holograph. You wait for the nanobots to be released—completely safe Gracie, so they can locate all of your senses inside your brain so you will be able to taste, smell, and feel once you are inside the whole augmented experience. When the session is over, the nanobots return to the lenses."

"What if it malfunctions as it connects to other networks?" Gracie asked. "The last thing I want is nanobots that stay inside my head, doing whatever it wants and possibly manipulating my thoughts and ideas."

Tatou chuckled. "After all the scrutinization it's received this past decade—the testing and trials it's been put through. It's been legislatively vetted and approved—it's totally safe. The nanobots always return back once the experience is over. Guaranteed. I've been through two experiences with my own copy. It's a totally mind-blowing experience. There's nothing to worry about. So, if you want to be inside a jungle fitted with anacondas, gorillas, and jaguars, you will smell the actual nature, feel the humidity coming off the trees, see the sweat glistening off the furs of the animals, and hear the vibrating purr of a jaguar right next to you. It will make your skin crawl—literally. These animals can see you though, so whatever world or place you want to be in, especially with any kind of predators lurking, you voice-command it to supply you with heavy-duty weapons, if that's your thing, which I know it isn't, Gracie. Some of my coworkers have done the amazon jungle scene and got physically sick from this kind of augmented reality when they were attacked by predator animals even though they were sitting at their desks with nothing physically harming them."

"Oh, great. Just what I want," Gracie said.

Natasha laughed.

"For you Gracie, you'll tell it to bring you to a spa and lounge inside a hot tub. It will produce the same feel-good feelings you've had when in a hot tub without being in one. That's what's so incredible about this thing."

"Or dip inside a chlorine-filled swimming pool in the middle of a work break without running off to the pool and having to dry off," Gracie said.

"Now, we're talking," Natasha said with a nod.

"Come on Gracie, try it out, just this once, and in a few days, you can tell me I was right and that you had an amazing experience and were so silly to be afraid of, you know ... progression?"

Tatou threw a stern glance.

"Fine, Tatou," Gracie sighed. "I'll give it a try in the morning and maybe ask it to take me to that spa when I'm recuperating from my hangover."

Gracie slipped the tiny, rectangle case inside the front pocket of her pants.

The music accelerated to a faster synthesizing beat and a large crowd filled up the side of their dance floor. Tatou threw back the remainder of her beer and said, "It's time to dive in. Something caught my eye ..."

Tatou swaggered her way into the crowd and approached a girl wearing a lime-green Spandex leotard bodysuit, with red, knee-high boots and a matching boa feather scarf. Tatou moved her hips and shook her legs fast, causing the bell bottoms of her pants to flap about in a wild frenzy, trying to imitate the singer Elvis around the girl. The girl was impressed and let Tatou wrap her arms around her waist. They swung together, losing themselves inside the dancing crowd that moved to the throbbing beat of synthesizers.

"Guess she didn't need any device for that one," Natasha said and finished off her beer.

"When you're ready, you know where we will be," Natasha said. Then, she danced toward a man with silver-framed glasses, who had a thick, plastic moustache and puffed-up hair on top that came down straight to his shoulders. He wore an orange, satin, polka-dot shirt, black velvet pants, and cowboy boots. He nodded to Natasha and followed her into the crowd.

Gracie stood in a dim space against the wall and continued to sip on her beer until the heat of the alcohol flushed over her face. She should have been enjoying the moment of her temporary freedom, but instead, she thought of Jimmy. Was he still sleeping? She hoped it wouldn't be that one night when he woke up and cried, and have Rose coming to him who was like a stranger and not Gracie. What could Gracie do? She was here and Rose was there. Best not to think of it and just hope he slept the night through as he usually did. She should enjoy herself while she had the chance. How the heck did they find these costumes? What would Jeff think of this place? He would love it, no doubt. It was his kind of party, and if it had costumes, even better.

Gracie sipped her beer faster until she reached a euphoric state. Then, she stepped into the dancing crowd, finding Tatou, Natasha, and their dance partners. Gracie swayed to the pulse of a Latin-Euro '80s freestyle song as her euphoric mind didn't bring her down to the bottom of a pool—the place she most loved to be. Instead, she rose up high, seemingly out of this world, that told her everything was great—it was her thirtieth birthday, and she should be celebrating life.

CHAPTER 6

Captured

Don Mills stood flashing in the distance. Off the 401, the automated car was set to "emergency stationary driver" as Gracie went behind a group of tall bushes to relieve herself. It was almost 5:00 in the morning, and there was hardly any traffic. Tatou had brought her date, and both slumped in the back of the car, breathing heavily, intermingled in red boa feathers, amidst sounds of soft moans and smacking lips.

Natasha's partially inebriated voice rang out into the silence of the early dawn.

"Can't you both wait until you get to whoever's apartment?"

How much had Gracie drunk? Three beers and two frosted glasses of soda water. She was pissing a damn tank.

Tatou emerged from the perfumed neck of her date, and in a muffled voice, she called out, "Full auto driver mode is coming back on, Gracie ... in three minutes."

"Almost done," Gracie shouted back and listened to their continuing conversation.

"Driver, please adjust the temperature," Natasha said. "It's so damn hot in here."

"Temperature adjusting."

"Driver, what is the weather going to be today?"

"Clear, sunny skies anticipated for this morning. A chance of rain in the afternoon. Undetermined."

"Undetermined? Since when does an automated driver ever say undetermined? It's either going to rain or not," Natasha said.

Gracie listened to the night. It was silent. Automatic cars wouldn't be so common at this hour but the aerial drone highway should have been busy. Yet, it was completely empty. It had been hot since mid-March. The heat wave they were experiencing was unusual. The past week, temperatures had been between 18 and 22 degrees Celsius, much warmer than average temperatures.

A wind picked up. It wasn't a cold wind as it should have been but an even more stifling, hot, humid one.

Gracie threw the environmentally degradable wet nap into the bush and pulled up her pants.

The car lights shut off.

"A malfunction at this time, seriously?" Natasha moaned.

"Looks like the surveillance cameras along the highway have also shut off, and they may not fully capture what you were doing in those bushes, Gracie," she said.

Giggles from the girls in the back seat.

Gracie appeared, fastening the top button of her pants. "I haven't done that in years," she called out.

"Yeah, well let's just hope it's the last time you'll ever do that," Natasha said.

Gracie stumbled as she started to make her way toward the car. A crackling sound suddenly erupted. It wasn't thunder. A sharp light, the width of a street pole struck the waiting car, reducing it to shards of metal and dust. The explosion jerked Gracie backward, throwing her past the bushes and rolling her over the grass.

Smells of burnt metal, rubber, and blood filled up her nose. Sharp pains rippled through her back and shoulders.

She gasped for breath as an inferno of fire roared out from what was left of the car on the road. She was about to scream but a sharp, red light fell over her, blinding and silencing her. She turned her neck to the side just in time to watch in absolute terror as the distant megacity of Don Mills was crushed by an invisible force.

Only fiery destruction remained.

In just a matter of seconds, the dazzling rows of majestic buildings, the expensive billboards, and millions of lives went up in flames—flames that now licked the morning skies over and over again.

PART TWO

≈

Tribulation

≈

Despise not the discipline of the Almighty.
For he wounds, but he binds up, he shatters,
but his hands heal.

—Job 5:17–18

CHAPTER 1

Inside the Horror

The smell came first. It was a sweet chemical scent, petroleum-like with something putrid festering beneath it. A torrent of humid air pressed over her face as if she was inside a sweltering sauna. She tried to move her head and arms on instinct, but she was held down by something. She lay against a mushy, hot surface pulsating with low vibration. Rumbling noise reverberated inside her ears. Her eyes burned behind closed eyelids. Tears streamed down the side of her face.

She opened her eyes slowly, cringing at the discomfort of the air that was laden with an odd chemical. It was difficult to breathe. An opaque glass was ahead of her, displaying a dark abyss sprinkled with orbiting lights. Space. It couldn't be. They moved away from a small globe that was predominantly blue, greyish-brown, and white. It slowly disappeared as they continued to pull away from it. Gracie didn't understand what she was seeing and attempted to move her head, but shooting pain kept her neck still. She was positioned upright, held securely by something that sucked the back of her body a few inches deep inside the mushy wall. Her wrists were pinned down by her rib cage by something that felt like

Tough scenes in the chapter

an elastic cord wrapped around her arms a
tried to move, the cord sank into her ski
clasp down her teeth or scream and realiz
it that something was lodged down her th
She tried to swallow, and whatever it was
down her throat. The taste of blood was

What was happening?

Luminous light moved over the glass wall. A reflection formed. Gracie took in the magnitude of where she was. She was embedded against a wall full of bumps in some places, covered by glistening orange and indigo gelatin. The wall rose so high that Gracie's eyes couldn't even get an idea of the true height.

What her eyes did see were rows of people packed side by side, held immobile by elastic-like cords high above, below, and all around her. The faces were dazed, some awake and wearing expressions of disbelief; others moved their heads and shook desperately against the strange manacles. Their faces were scrunched up, and when they gaped, the metallic rim of whatever was inside their mouths reflected in the faraway glass. Their rib cages rose high and fast. No sound came from them. The rumbling noise was deafeningly loud and didn't allow any other sound to penetrate through.

Some bodies above Gracie had been driven into the wall by a terrible force that smashed their faces into it, and what was left of their heads was a mashed-up mess of crushed bone and grey matter. It dripped down the wall and fell onto people below. Bodies were twisted awkwardly into the wall, spines ruptured out of backs; legs were twisted and broken in odd angles to the side; bones jutted out of open sockets; arms were torn from shoulders and hanging, some with partially missing hands and fingers. Dark pools of blood, soaked into the orange, soft palette of the walls underneath these bodies. The lucky ones were dead. The unfortunate ones were still alive, withering like worms against the cords that welted deeper into their skin as they moved. Their eyes bulged wide open, faces hollowed, pleading to die and escape this torture.

What was happening? She was inside an augmented reality world. Did Tatou think this was funny, placing her in whatever horrid place was programmed to bring her here? Not Tatou, she wasn't mean like Kate, and Natasha, who put on a sarcastic air, was an empath at heart and wouldn't find this kind of humour funny at all. She would never agree to put Gracie here, knowing how terrified Gracie or anyone would react. Could it have been a stranger? Did Gracie tell someone about the augmented reality lenses and they had put them in her eyes and knew to program her to this place? It wouldn't have surprised her, as the world was full of nefarious people. She couldn't remember having many conversations with others at the club, though.

There has to be an explanation for this, Gracie's mind reasoned.

It was getting harder to breathe. The sharp petroleum smell threatened to dissolve the insides of her nose, making it run. She couldn't wipe away the mucus, move her hands to get those lenses off her eyes, and return back to her home. A tingling sensation rose in her throat. She quickly suppressed it. She couldn't allow herself to cough for fear she would choke on whatever device was down her throat. She focused on her breathing to remain steady. It was hard to do when her heart was beating so fast.

She had the ability to wake up from nightmares and had done so many times as a child when the stress from the fear was too much. She could do it now. Gracie closed her eyes and willed her mind to wake up.

Nothing.

Desperate, Gracie tried again.

Wake up. Wake up. Wake up.

Over the reflection of the glass, the woman next to Gracie returned to consciousness. The women's eyes took in where they were and saw the dead bodies above them—and the tortured ones, twitching in their entrapment. She became hysterical and tried to get out of the cords wrapped around her. The cords slashed deeply into her arms as she tried to pull them off. She was shaking, crying, and hyperventilating. She managed to get her hands loose from the stringy cords and yanked more of them off her. Her face was tortured in horror, wild-eyed, and she began to struggle to breathe. Her mouth gaped wide and her face looked upwards, trying to get more air—air that didn't contain much oxygen.

A loud clap and shudder next to Gracie. She immediately closed her eyes and the scent of burnt flesh filled Gracie's nose. Gracie's eyes opened to see the woman next to her had been blasted apart, torn in half, from her left shoulder down to her right leg. An arm, pieces of her lungs, stomach, and other insides shot over Gracie and dropped below. The side of Gracie's face was splattered with blood, pulp, and skin. Gracie kept still as a tremulous voice frantically chanted inside her head, *this isn't happening. It can't be. Steady breathing. Come on.*

Whatever evil entity directed the weapon at the woman, it didn't end with her. Blasts struck others along the wall, above, below, and to the other side.

Gracie shut her eyes and held her breath as the splatter of exploding bodies streamed from above her, drenching her head, face, and shoulders with blood, gore, feces, and fluids.

"*Damn Tatou and Natasha! End this stupid augmented reality crap!*"

She took in a few more breaths, trying to ignore the horrid, pungent, disgusting smells around her.

"I'm going to wake up soon. Yes, I will. I'm sleeping in my bed. Jimmy is curled asleep next to me. I can feel him. Yes, I can. Arabella is going to wake me up. Tatou said the augmented reality world wouldn't be longer than sixty minutes. It's going to be over soon. How long has it been? I can't see or feel my Android wristwatch. I can't reach my eyes to yank off these stupid lenses and check out of this place."

The wall she was stuck to suddenly came to life, trembling as if it were some kind of ... organism. Then, the cords unwrapped themselves from her arms and legs and slithered into the wall.

Gracie slid down the wall. It curved over in some places, and Gracie dug her fingers into the slippery texture to slow the velocity of the fall as she dropped about fifteen feet. She landed hard on bare feet, sinking into the mushy, hot orange-grey ground. She fell over, wincing in pain as her strong ankles and legs took in the shock of the landing. She was relieved nothing had been sprained or broken.

Where are my shoes?

She had no time to think. Other bodies that were higher up on the wall started to slowly dislodge from the wall and come down. Gracie ran to the glass wall and pressed against it, finding that the surface felt like thick vinyl. Then, she watched from a safe distance as bodies continued to tumble down the wall—some from as high as sixty feet.

The faces of the falling people were full of astonished horror and the odd grunting sounds—stifled desperate screams—reverberated throughout the chamber as they approached their final end.

I've had enough of this bullshit place. I'm checking out!

Gracie wiped the tips of her fingers on a small section of her T-shirt that was unsoiled and reached into her eyes. There was nothing in them, though.

No, this can't be ...

Her hands pressed against her eyelids, moving around them to feel for the hard, little shells. Yet, there was nothing, just soft, rounded eyes. Desperate, she lifted each of her eyelids and looked through the glass.

Come on, come on. They have to be in there somewhere.

There was nothing. Just the terrifying reflection of reddish, irritated eyes and the continuous falling of bodies behind her, splattering their remains all over her back.

She reached into the front of her pants where she had put the lenses. Some relief. There was nothing there because the lenses were still inside her eyes. Gracie rubbed her eyes faster and faster, trying to feel anything, but there was nothing ... absolutely nothing inside them.

No, this can't be happening.

Her hands twisted her T-shirt by the collar.

No, this can't be happening.

She was trapped, like an animal, in a strange place with no exit.

Others, who came down the wall unscathed leaned against the glass beside her.

They exchanged looks of petrified panic inside their eyes. Some of them were in a numbed state of disbelief and kept very still except for the tremor in their shoulders and hands.

They watched helplessly as more bodies dropped down the wall, crashing into other broken ones. Some died upon impact, and others suffocated underneath the growing heaps of corpses. Some lay there with outstretched, bloodied arms, begging those by the glass to save them. There was nothing anyone could do. In a matter of seconds, they would be killed by the other falling bodies crashing over them.

Gracie looked down at her body. She was missing her shoes and socks. She lifted the neck of her t-shirt with trembling hands. No bra. Her corduroy pants were fully intact. She lifted the waistband. No underwear. Her Android wrist device was removed—as most of the '80s costume bracelets, except for two. Those around her weren't as lucky. They'd been stripped of most of their clothing and jewellery. Some were completely naked with a sock on one foot. Others had a shirt on or just underwear; others had part of one pant leg stripped away; the hem of a dress or skirt was torn off in an uneven pattern. There were only two of them that got to keep their shoes and all of their clothes. Whatever vile thing that brought them here decided to remove whatever clothing they wanted while they were unconscious; had shoved an obscene apparatus down their throats, ensuring their silence; and stripped them of all of their personal items, jewellery, and devices that identified who they were, where they lived, and who their friends and family were.

The wall that they had been on sank into the ground, disappearing inside the folds, revealing, as far as Gracie could see, hundreds and hundreds of rows of more terrified people that had been behind the wall.

A handful of people panicked and ran through the crowd as if this place had an exit. It made sense to their panicked minds to get anywhere that might lead them out of there.

Gracie hovered in between a numb awareness and terror. From all the fatigue she had experienced in the past week, her mind was too exhausted to be strong enough to wake up from this terrifying nightmare.

No. She had to be inside the augmented world. Maybe Tatou just forgot to mention that the lenses firmed up deep into her eyes so that she wouldn't be able to feel them there. Wherever she was, it would end soon. For now, she had to stay alert, play along, and not get seriously injured or hurt, although the air quality was getting more and more difficult to breathe in.

Her thoughts were distracted by a twenty-foot-tall, one inch-thick wall suddenly rising from the murky ground, ten feet away. Its surface moved with rivulets of amber liquid that swirled in a fiery, vortex-like frenzy in its centre.

The panic-heightened, muffled shrieks and moans erupted around Gracie. She was shoved against the glass, which unexpectedly expanded and snapped back into place as more people ran from the wall, shoving others out of their way, and weaving through the crowds ahead of them.

A few had been grabbed by a burly, seven-foot-tall man with intense eyes who told them to calm down, his large hands over their smaller shoulders, giving them a hefty shake. He managed to get some of them to stop running in their sheer terror while others continued on with their panic, fighting to get away. The lasers started up again and blasted those who ran through the crowds—and the unfortunate ones closest to them. It quickly ended anyone trying to run or flee and had some of them shaking and whimpering in their spots, moving forward like everyone else.

Gracie edged closer to the burly man, acutely aware of her diminutive size in comparison to his. At that moment, being behind someone who was massive and calm was the only comfort she could get.

The smell of burnt flesh assaulted their noses, and smoke flew high in the air as the gaps in the rows ahead of Gracie quickly filled in as everyone squeezed together.

More walls rose from other points and seemed to organize them into rows, forcing them to move forward to the end of a line some faceless, evil puppet master goaded them toward.

Gracie's irritated eyes looked up into the dimness, searching, hoping to see something move ahead of them—a light, a silhouette, an inhuman movement—to get a sense of who or what was committing these atrocities.

A rumbling wall approached Gracie's group, and as the structure neared, heat emanated from it with powerful electric energy. A man, who held onto his twisted arm, which had been half-torn out of its socket, ran right into it as if it could end his pain. He got his wish. The whirling liquid inside the wall shredded his face, head, and neck, cutting him in half; the lower half of his body was flung back over the bewildered crowd. Gracie was grateful that she couldn't hear any horrible screams and heard only muffled shrieks and heavy moans as he died.

The walls moved the crowd into rows of about a dozen across, forcing them to keep moving at a steady pace. The crackling sound of lasers echoed in the distance behind them, coming through the rumbling sound—eliminating more of them. Gracie moved forward, her eyes watching the length of the bulging orange and indigo walls.

They passed by a man who was slumped against the wall. His eyes fluttered toward his forehead, blood intermittently spurted in a thin, rounded curve from his wide-open mouth, pooling down a hairy, grey chest. A metallic, coiled cylinder fell partially out from his mouth, wrapped around what was left of a torn, red esophagus.

People pressed closely around Gracie, sobbing and trembling, their bodies bloodied by the violence of the blasted bodies of victims. The pungent smell of urine, feces, sweat, and the gaseous environment made many of them lurch forward to vomit. A few of them completely fell over, turning red, shaking, and choking on their bile. They grabbed at others that walked by, begging for help, but most people moved away, as they now learned that helping anyone meant risking getting oneself blasted into shreds by whatever entity was unseen above.

Gracie focused on her breathing. She was used to pungent smells, working knee-high in disgusting sludge for long hours and days on end. The scents weren't any worse, she convinced herself, although the inside of her nose had never burned like it did now.

Of all the terrified faces around her, Gracie recognized no one. Why would she? In this carefully programmed augmented reality world, there would be no one she would know. The captured seemed to be composed of an equal number of men and women. Various ethnicities. Mostly adults.

Gracie looked behind her.

Adults. There were no children or anyone carrying a young child—just adults and perhaps a few adolescents if her attention was able to linger over their faces longer to tell. If this was an alien abduction, they wouldn't spare the lives of children or babies. They wouldn't protect them from this vile place. It had to be a programmed augmented reality world. Creators and programmers of these augmented worlds, by law, weren't allowed to expose children to this kind of heinous suffering and torture. She sighed with deep relief and with renewed hope that this would all be over soon enough.

Lost in her thoughts, she nearly tripped. Her feet recognized what she had stepped on: an assortment of fingers, hands, and wrists of victims that had been killed ahead of them. Some of the fingers had rings.

They moved around other carnage: split-open rib cages, a lone leg and foot, and strewn organs that were generally impossible to identify.

How long has it been now? Surely the one-hour mark is soon and this will be all gone.

Next, they moved into a round tunnel that opened up into a colossal dome. The temperature rose from 35 to 45 degrees Celsius. This dome had an oval ceiling with flashes of blue light rippling through it. Her eyes focused on this familiar movement, and her stressed, discombobulated mind transformed the oval ceiling into moving, blue water. She felt herself sinking down inside a place that was the most comforting and safe in the world. The warmth of the water encircled her, rising up over her body, her neck, and above her head. The tips of her feet almost touched the bottom of a pool. The smell of chlorine brought excitement to the pit of her stomach. It always did.

Gracie was eight years old. Above the pool, the silhouettes of the girls swam around; others practiced their eggbeater kicks, twirling around fast, kicking and swirling the water wildly through the quick movements of legs and arms. They wore bright, colourful, striped bathing suits, red and yellow with matching caps.

Standing by the pool's edge was Ms. Coligan in grey shorts and a red t-shirt with a white maple leaf in the centre and rising from her upturned arm was a small holograph with running numbers and underwater images of the girls practicing their skills. Gracie felt the urge to swim as fast as she could toward Ms. Coligan. She would be proud of Gracie for being able to hold her breath the longest and for her lack of fear of fainting in the pool. Most of the girls were afraid of fainting in the water when they were off with their timing—but not Gracie. She had a good sense when that was close to happening. She always timed it correctly. Ms. Coligan would tell Gracie in her patient voice to stop holding her breath and practice her warm-up exercises, which were more important. Gracie smiled, but the discomfort of the device pinching down her throat brought her back for a few seconds to the horror of the reality she was placed in.

Who was coming up behind Ms. Coligan? By the tall, slender, pale body and orange and blue striped bathing suit, she could tell it was Kate.

Kate dove into the pool and remained at the top, swimming around the other girls in a wide circle. Her body moved faster and into some odd, frenzied movement. Gracie had never seen Kate swim like that before. What was she doing? Kate swam around and around, faster and faster, shoving the other girls aggressively out of her way until her body froze. Her back hunched over and her arms wiggled around till they reached the side of the pool. The other girls and Ms. Coligan disappeared. Kate's body elongated in a strange form, and the ends of her fingertips turned into sharp points that sucked against the wall. Kate started to crawl down the wall toward Gracie.

The water of the swimming pool drained, and the comforting safety of the pool dissolved. The odd form that had been Kate became something that sparkled, and it crept down the shiny, orange-blue wall inside that horrid place Gracie was in. Gracie was transfixed—both horrified and mesmerized. More shadowy terrors had sprouted out from the walls above them and crawled downwards.

Gracie blinked as much liquid out of her eyes from the heat and fumes as possible, trying to grasp what she was seeing. Panic filled her chest, and she couldn't scream to warn the others around her. She froze in her spot and was pushed to keep on moving ahead by the hundreds of people behind her who were still oblivious to the horrors that were descending toward them.

Gran Amália's voice suddenly entered her panicked mind. Her voice was stern and confident.

"*Shhhh. Keep still. Observe.*"

Gran Amália, what's happening? Can you see what I'm seeing? What do I do?

"*Shhhh. Keep still. Observe.*"

A gust of wind moved over them, cooling and alleviating the heat. The hundreds of bodies ahead stopped moving. Some of them finally saw the glittering shapes descending ... approaching ... hovering above the terrified crowd.

Shapeless creatures of gold-amber tinged with lavender and blue sparkling colours made themselves known. Their bodies were large—over ten feet in height—yet clearly malleable, as their shapes metamorphosed into human likeness. Awkward torsos formed, followed by dozens of arms that looked like elephant trunks, which sprouted from the sides of their hovering bodies. Long legs formed, and the bottom of their feet resembled the paws of a lion. From the top of each body grew a neck, followed by an oval-shaped head, sunken sockets for eyes where there were none, a prominent chin, and two small holes mimicking some kind of nose.

They looked as if they were made out of liquid gelatin with amber-gold that moved in the same odd rivulet motion as the thin walls. Over the amber-gold of their bodies, fiery sparkles of sapphire blue, red, green, and lavender appeared. Some of them were more golden and lavender while others changed their colours from amber-gold to a flowing, sparkling blue speckled with red dots of fire—or to lavender with undertones of white gold flecked with dots of fluorescent greens.

They hovered in the weightless air, forming equal lines. Gracie counted four of them, and by the rise of moans and muffled shrieks of rows distantly behind them, there were many more. They had no weapons or devices on or around them. A low hum emanated from them—some kind of vibration—and this sound took precedence over the rumbling noise.

They remained stagnate, hovering over the rows, observing their captured humans. There wasn't an inkling of mimicked emotion on poorly-formed, human-like faces.

As the initial shock of the presence of these vile creatures wore off, some in the crowd exploded in sheer panic, and pandemonium erupted as, once again, several people frantically ran through the crowd and others fell to their knees, their bodies shaking, faces contorted, shrieking and wailing, frozen in place. Others clasped their hands around their heads, looking upwards to whatever place they envisioned, where a God or superior presence would be, begging them to take pity on them and remove them from this hellscape. Gracie looked on as if her being wasn't there. She was just watching the genius effects of talented programming in the augmented reality world, although every organ, nerve, and sense inside her quivered with terror, sensing true impending doom.

Gran Amália's voice returned...

"*Shhhh. Keep still. Observe.*"

One of the vile creatures flew over her row. Gracie lowered her head and partially closed her eyes, the panic and terror suffusing every inch of her being, stifling her breathing. The stench of sweet-scented petroleum was strong.

Without provocation, the hideous creature lashed out one of its trunk-like arms and grabbed the burly man in front of Gracie. The powerful trunk arms lifted him effortlessly, wrapping around the man's torso and thickening to an anaconda width. From the side of Gracie's eye, the terrified, desperate, wiggling three-hundred-pound man was quickly twisted into a gruesome mass of flesh, organs, and crushed bones. It only took a matter of seconds. She caught a flash of the man's face as he was crushed; his eyes popped out of the sockets, the skull cracked open—crunching like a stomped bug—and his head snapped off the shredded body, falling over the crowd ahead of them.

Gran Amália, wake me up. I can't take it anymore. Where are the contact lenses? I'm wearing them somewhere?

"*Shhhh. Keep still. Observe.*"

As they walked onward, another victim was grabbed by trunk-like arms that shot out from a side wall. The victim desperately wiggled against the immense power of anaconda coils as they were lifted upwards. This vile creature decided to strip off the flesh from this body, like pieces of meat being yanked off a kebab, starting with the top of the shoulders and down the back, exposing a spine dripping in glistening blood.

Gracie looked away, trying not to hyperventilate like those around her and focused on keeping her breathing stable and the bile stirring in her stomach from coming up her throat.

The hideous creatures moved up the rows behind Gracie, offering temporary relief, although the creatures would come back, Gracie was sure. The crowd moved faster down the curve of dim tunnels. The humid air grew heavier with chemicals.

More one-inch walls rose from the ground, shuffling and separating them into smaller tunnels. People shoved each other away to avoid the unpredictable, fast-moving walls that approached and were as much of a threat as their hideous captors if they fell into them. With the slippery ground they walked on, some of them lost their footing and did fall into a wall—at which point they were sucked right into it and shredded to pieces.

Gracie was shoved away from the glass and ended up on the left side of the tunnel. A wall suddenly rose in front of her, and with quick reflexes, she slid behind it, not seeing a dark, slippery tunnel that spiraled downwards before the wall snapped shut. The side of her thigh caught a corner of the wall and Gracie tumbled down the slippery tunnel, shrieking frantically against the device that gripped painfully at her throat. Gracie reached the bottom and hit her back against a solid wall. She flinched in pain. She was boxed in against a corner at a dead end, surrounded by walls that sweated and breathed, giving off a gelatinous shine. Up above, an overhead, almond-shaped light kept the section from complete darkness. Gracie's eyes darted over the walls, checking for any emerging shapes coming for her. Her nostrils flared from terrified quick breaths. She was alone.

She winced from the stinging pain from her injury slashed at the side of her thigh. Her hands covered the open gash surrounded by warm blood. It wasn't a serious cut, luckily for her.

Her body was awash with so much adrenaline. She wanted to run and yet at the same time fall into a deep sleep. She looked at her hands. Skin already crinkled at the fingertips.

The walls in this section, whatever they were made from, were not created from any substance Gracie had seen before and definitely were not made by the hand of humans. There was no metal, no welding, or sealing of any kind—no nails, bolts, or screws.

The walls that rose from the bottom of the organic floors also lacked such features. There was nothing to indicate a wall could suddenly rise, move so quickly and authoritatively as if it was a creature itself, expertly organizing hundreds of them in different lines.

Her pants were soaked from the stinky, damp floor, and something poked uncomfortably against her lower back. She reached down into the pocket and pulled out the culprit.

It was Jimmy's little hairbrush. She sucked back some breath as her hands trembled uncontrollably. The augmented reality program wouldn't be aware of this small detail—that she had Jimmy's little hairbrush in her back pocket.

Horror and dread enclosed her lungs as tight as the anaconda coils of those vile creatures as the truth sunk in—that she wasn't inside an augmented reality world. She wasn't inside a nightmare. This place was real and any prior staunch conviction that protected her mental well-being was replaced by the dark realization that these vile creatures had killed her friends—possibly Rose and Jimmy—destroyed the megacity of Don Mills and brought her and countless thousands of others to this place.

Her whole body trembled, and she whimpered and cried, holding onto Jimmy's hairbrush between her shaking fingers, not wanting to think of what happened to him when she wasn't there for him. Part of the terror racing in her mind wanted to drag her back into the safety of denial and convince her that no, this had to be a trick, she was still in the augmented reality world ... it would end soon, she would be back home, holding Jimmy's, warm, little body against her soon...

The tips of her shaking fingers moved over the curly, flaxen hairs that sprung out from the bristles.

Rose got them out, she reasoned. *She had to. She was a jerk but resourceful. Rose would have lived because the evil ones always do. She would have found a way and got Jimmy and herself out. They're safe. They weren't inside that fiery mess that destroyed the megacity of Don Mills.*

She had to believe that or she would go mad and panic like the others that ran through the crowds and met a painful and gruesome end.

Gracie brought the back of the little brush to her lips.

Little Jimmy is alive. Yes, he is. He is.

Gracie shut her eyes and kept on repeating this again and again like a sacred mantra, holding tight onto the handle of the little brush not noticing an amber shape starting to sprout from the corner of the wall above her. It slowly and soundlessly moved toward her.

CHAPTER 2

The Birth

It had unexpectedly been born. It was very unusual for a parent to birth something during such a crucial time. There was so much excitement, so many movements and changes. The parent would be dead soon and was the only one left with it inside the pod. No others had been birthed. It was the only one. The others abruptly left it to handle crucial matters. It had to remain there until the others returned. They were gone for too long, and it missed the heat of their bodies, their vibrations, and beautiful, comforting hums. With every hum they made, it grew stronger. It was weakened now but would be made stronger again once they all returned.

The parent was nearing the end. It told it again to remain where it was no matter what. It wasn't fully formed and was vulnerable to the environment, especially since there were other vile species that had been brought on board. They could pose a serious danger to it. It waited for the parent to finally die and the last of it was absorbed, thus providing more knowledge and wisdom. It brought the gift of curiosity. Strange that the parent wanted it to remain still yet carried within it such a strong sense of curiosity. Having that gift, it couldn't stay for long. It wanted to investigate—not too far ... just a bit away from the pod.

It moved through the warm, moist fibres of the walls. The walls were nourishing and fed it some more.

It moved down tunnels very fast, hoping to find a few of them who would allow it to curl around their body for warmth and safety. It kept on rolling through each wall until it felt an odd vibration. There they were, the vile species its parent had warned it about. There were so many of them—hundreds of thousands of little specks of them. The curiosity nudged at it. It rolled through some more tunnels. What was that? One of the vile species separated from the group and was alone. The vile specie had markings of heat inside it. It was curled up in a corner. Was it trying to move through the walls? It wasn't sure and moved toward it. The vile specie had some kind of dull light inside it. It wasn't beautiful like the lights that emanated from their bodies. This vile specie was small and had internal rapid movements of liquid that quickly moved inside tiny tunnels through its body. It had odd shapes of flesh inside it and a hard wire shell that seemed to hold it up. It would grow older in a few days and would learn what all of this was. The vile specie focused on something as if it were in a trance. Its curiosity took on a strange turn. All of them left it alone for too long. What did this vile specie feel like? What if this vile specie felt warm and was able to hum as beautifully as they could? Its parents' previous hum echoed inside it, telling it to stay in the pod. Do not touch the vile species—ever. It was vulnerable. Its outer skin wasn't fully closed yet. It couldn't touch anything that wasn't part of them. The vile specie could be dangerous.

Yet, the vile specie didn't look dangerous. In fact, it looked weak and fragile. It came closer to the vile specie. It didn't seem to be aware of its approach. It landed over the vile specie. It did not expect it to scramble back against the wall.

The liquid inside the vile species' tunnels surged fast and roared through a pumping, dark cylinder in the centre of its body that had a sound that wasn't a hum but a quick tapping. The vile specie had two rounded pools of brown amber near the top of its palette. The pools of brown amber bulged, and its outer shell made quick movements. It gave off a terrible hum. Distorted shapes jutted over the palette of the vile specie.

In that quick touch, the vile specie wasn't that soft. It was barely warm. It wasn't the same lying with its own species, in their hot, silky, warm movements, humming in song, full of security and contentment. The vile specie had no vibration—nothing. The hums that came from the vile specie were sharp, intense sounds stifled by a device that was wrapped around a tube inside it. The vile specie had no comforting hum.

It moved away from the vile specie. It wasn't dangerous. It was dull and cold.

Then it felt it. It rolled over something that was organic. It was inside it, golden strings of something, from the odd thing the vile specie had held. The fibres attached to its nerves quickly spread inside it in a swarm of hot fire, moving in a frenzied vortex, quickly breaking down and entering its cellular fibres, nerves, and molecular essence. It wasn't a good sensation. Its parent had been right. It shouldn't have left its pod. It was vulnerable and it had allowed something to get inside it that could endanger it, the others, and worse, their very important mission to the master. It had to immediately return to its pod and not run into any of the others. Yet, one of them was approaching. Its faint hums vibrated through the walls. It left the vile specie and bolted back to its pod.

CHAPTER 3

Convergence

When the vile creature landed over her hand, it happened so fast and in a flash.

In that brief moment, it felt pulsating hot with a slight electric pulse. Gracie shrieked and scuttled away from it, hitting her back against the wall. The vile creature was small—no bigger than a grapefruit.

Don't come close!

It sat there, immobile, as if observing her. Then, it came toward her again. She dug into her pant pockets to see if there was anything else she could ward it off with, but her pockets were empty. She curled her body against the wall, turned her face away from the approaching horror, and covered her face with trembling hands, screaming against the device.

From the corner of her terrified eye, the vile creature had stopped and just hovered. The smell of petroleum was more penetrating. She kept her eyes partially closed, her face to the side. If it would kill her, she wouldn't see her blood splattering everywhere. She was mad with fear, and her whole body quivered.

What the hell is it doing? What does it want?

And then she saw what had happened. To her horror, in the centre of the vile creature's body, moving in a fiery vortex, in a golden white light, was a clump of flaxen strands of hair. The plastic comb lay under it, broken into two pieces.

She swiftly turned to the creature and let out a horrid, muffled scream as her eyes narrowed. "*Jimmy!*"

Releasing her fears, she snatched the pieces of the comb that were left and was about to scream at the creature again, when it bolted high up into the air and vanished through a wall.

A brisk wind arose from above—the same wind when the vile creatures had first made their first presence known. She scuttled back against an opposite wall shrouded in darkness and watched the ceilings. To her horror, a large shadow approached from above. She had no time to think and mustered all the strength left in her and bolted up the slippery slope, grabbing at the sides of the walls, clutching anything she could cling onto—an uneven bump here and there—and pulled herself upwards as fast as she could. The wall partition had slightly moved, and there was an opening, about two feet long. Between the slant of the opened wall was the view of slow-moving groups of bewildered people walking onward. She slipped through the tiny opening and caught the other side of a hip against the fiery wall's edge. Like tiny, searing, little blades, it tore open another wound, and immediately, warm blood trickled down her leg. She didn't care, though. She was wild with adrenaline and no physical pain was able to permeate the sheer panic pulsing through her. She hunched down, hoping none of the other creatures was hovering nearby, and quickly moved in between a few people and down the rows as fast as she could. The vile creature blasted through the wall and snatched the closest victims in the strong coils of its arms—proceeding to flay them at once.

Gracie could hear their distant, agonized shrieks, and in seconds, heavy showers of blood splatter and body parts rained down. The remains of the dead bodies were flung over the crowd. Gracie didn't look down for long at the woman's dead eyes when their quick-moving feet trampled over the crushed face.

They marched on endlessly, turning into darker tunnels, for what seemed to be an hour but could have been just ten or twenty minutes. There was no way to tell time since only terror and panic gripped everyone, not knowing or understanding what their new masters wanted them for or where were they being taken—or if they were going anywhere at all. Gracie took notice of the air changing. It changed many times. She was very much in tune with her lungs since she had been a synchronized swimmer for most of her life and continued to swim even in her adult life, as swimming and being underwater was a permanent itch she could never get rid of. She was aware of her breathing capacity and of the air repeatedly changing around them. Her lungs pushed harder to take in more air. People around her began to lose consciousness and they collapsed like birds upon hitting glass. Gracie raised her arms above her head, opening more of her lungs to get in any kind of oxygen inside her. She wanted again to swim upwards as fast as possible before fainting.

Through her blurred vision, the image of Ms. Coligan's concerned face appeared above her. "Look here, right into the centre of my hand, Gracie."

Blood trickled inside Gracie's ears. She was eight years old. She had just joined the Toronto Synchronized Swimming Club a week ago.

A robotic, female voice calmly announced throughout the speakers ...

Biological contamination in the pool. Evacuate the pool area immediately until further instructions.

Ms. Coligan kept her eyes trained on Gracie and pointed to the centre of her hand, "You're okay Gracie. Look here, right here ..."

Kate and Feifei, who Gracie wanted to be her best friends, challenged her to do a high jump from the diving board during practice. Gracie, in her enthusiasm, ran onto the diving board and slipped, banging the back of her head on the edge. She hit the pool hard, numb pain immediately shot through her head as blood cut through the chorine in a wide trail of red, and Gracie sank motionlessly, half-conscious toward the bottom of the pool. A gush of water filled up her nose and mouth. She choked back on it and was too weak and powerless to keep the endless flow of water from entering her mouth. She was losing vision quickly. A great weight pushed down on her chest. She was drowning. She was going to die.

Hands reached out for her arms and grabbed her shoulders. Her limp body was jerked upwards through the heavy water, quickly moving toward the surface. The movement of legs vigorously kicked next to her, and arms pushed her higher and higher. She was pulled out of the water and laid out over the cold, wet tiles. Gracie threw up water, coughed it out, and took in long breaths as air returned to her lungs. She rolled on her back and looked up into the concerned faces of Tatou and Natasha, girls Gracie had recently met. Both girls were ten years old but were built more like twelve- and thirteen-year-olds. They crouched on either side of her until Ms. Coligan arrived with a flushed face due to having darted to get to her from the other end of the pool.

"Look at me, Gracie, keep looking at me."

Behind Ms. Coligan, the other synchro swimmers, Ayshan, Sahara, Adrianna, and others looked on. Their faces were scared for Gracie, seeing blood behind her head smudged over the tiles. Kate and Feifei appeared. Feifei looked away, hiding behind the shoulders of her friend, Kate, who stood erect, arms crossed, eyes cold, peering down at Gracie's wet, scared face with a tinge of an imperious detachment that snickered and told Gracie...

So what? It was your fault, stupid. You slipped.

Ms. Coligan looked back at them and at Gracie.

"It doesn't matter now. We're all dead. Gracie, you need to breathe. That's it, put your arms further over your head, open your lungs as wide as you can and breathe in and out. That's right. Just like that."

Gracie nodded, tears fell out of her eyes, and she shuffled along, her arms moving fast above her head. Many of those who'd been walking next to her had fallen, and there was only a handful left, with the terrifying, empty dark tunnel ahead of them.

Soon, Gracie was the only one left. She kept her focus on the image of Ms. Coligan's calm smile, continuing to hear her voice, which encouraged her to swim.

"*Swim, Gracie. That's it. Keep on swimming. Swim. Swim right to the top.*"

CHAPTER 4

Contamination

It quickly grew. To its great satisfaction, it grew into a powerful and beautiful creature more than its previous parent. All of them respected it and proclaimed their staunch allegiance to it, their new captain, and to fulfil the master's plan.

The master would come soon to meet the new captain. It was overjoyed and at the same time a bit hesitant. The singing hums of all of them were high-pitched, melodious, and incredibly comforting—truly beautiful. It had developed a hum that wasn't as high-pitched, in tune, and comforting. It was different. Odd. Dull. Not as powerful in voice as it should have been. Its parent and all the others in its lineage always had the best hums. The others may have noticed this difference just as they noticed how some moved slightly differently, metamorphosing into other beautiful forms and colours. They didn't disrespect it or treat it differently in any negative form. They accepted its dull hums and admired its immense beauty. The notion of treating their species negatively because of what they lacked in one small area wasn't part of their nature. It was made aware of these differences caused by the contact, the contamination as it called it, from ingesting human

DNA strands when its own body had been still vulnerable to foreign contact. The contamination altered its original nature, giving rise to these observations, ideas, and thoughts.

The master would come and see the contamination inside it. It had some trepidation about that. It could only prepare itself. It would practice its hums, fully expressing its allegiance, letting it pour out from every fibre, light, fire, and spark inside its body to let the master know it wasn't vile like the human species; it belonged to their species, who were powerful, beautiful, malleable, interconnected, and efficient, fully dedicated to the master and the cause. The master would accept it once it felt the powerful and pure reverence it emanated through its dull hums.

When it lay down with the group, entwined deeply inside their melodious hums and contentment, they shared visions of the glory of their powerful master and of themselves. The visions that came to it had been different. The contamination brought visions of the vile creature. The others couldn't see the visions it had of this vile creature as they did not react to seeing the visions. They did, however, react to the powerful, incredible warmth that would radiate from its body when the visions of the vile creature, with the two pools of brown-amber eyes, arose in its thoughts. It became confusing. Even though it had visions of the vile creature, it produced quick, intense vibrations inside it that were benign and felt exalting to the others.

In its current vision, a smaller creature emerged. The smaller creature ran through shrubs and green grass until it put its nose to something rough and dark that smelled musky and burnt. It was the bark of a tree. Hands reached under its arms and its nose was placed against a warm neck. Her neck. Lightly scented with something sweet and herbal. Flowers. Her body felt warm against it, the hum in her neck a thumping, oddly melodious sound.

Comforting. It mimicked the timing of the thumping to its hums. Her hand moved behind its hair, passing over the lobes of its small ears.

The little creature made sounds—a long sigh. It was content. The warmth of her lips brushed over his eyes and nose. Everything felt safe and good. The conflict rose inside it and it had to quash it fast, as the negative energy would break its rhythm. It thought again of her warmth ... the soft tresses of her hair behind her shoulders. Small fingers twirled through the tresses, and another small hand touched the side of her face. She turned to it, and her soft lips brushed over the small creature's forehead, pressing the small body tighter into the warmth of her body.

Its hum rose louder, and the waves of these visions amplified the heat that radiated out from it. It vibrated through the others, gradually bringing them into a frenzy; their bodies became a glittering sea of fire and sparkling lights never seen before when they were together. Their melodious singing reached heights of song; they hummed and vibrated, under an incredible, intense power. It went on for some time until they reached a maximum level of vibrant electric lights that entwined and formed a sizzling vortex above their withering, vibrating bodies ... until they could no longer continue to extricate extreme energies and heat and finally succumbed to an end.

Exhausted, they all compressed down to dwindling lights—a sea of gentle hums and an outpouring amongst them of deep contentment and peaceful sleep.

It was the only one who remained awake.

It slipped away from the group and wandered alone to the top level of the ship, where it liked to be, resting on the ground, looking upwards into the vast universe, filled with lights and dizzying colours from the beautiful stars, planets, and suns they passed.

Irritable thoughts came to it about this creature. It didn't want to have any benign thoughts about these vile human creatures that were abhorrent and weak, easy to break and kill. They didn't need to waste their weapons on them. They picked them up easily, twisted them into a sloppy mess, and moved on to a dozen more to emphasize their power over them.

Another thought came to it—discord. Its species rarely had discord amongst themselves and even more nonexistent was the notion of having discord within itself. Its thoughts argued that this human creature was different. She was weak and emotional like them, yet it carried visions of this little creature that were benign. The word vile, or abhorrent, was becoming hard for it to apply to her. It learned that she was a parent. It carried some parts of her inside it and equally of another male parent. It was what made up the smaller creature inside it. The strings of hair that it ingested came from this smaller creature.

The internal conflict, at times, grew intense within it, and it had to keep away from the others. It couldn't touch any of them when it was under this strange yet powerful sensation. It couldn't let these visions of the little creature interrupt it—to take it away from its primary focus and ultimate goal.

Overwhelming sensations recently possessed it—of wanting to curl up with the little creature as it did with the others ... to wrap itself around her with its melodious hums, vibrations, the warmth of its body, and bring nothing but contentment to her. What horrid thoughts and inclinations to have toward a vile species that its own species was sent to punish and kill. The turbulence moved inside it.

Yet, it wanted to find her. These sensations inside it grew stronger every moment, and just as the curiosity had found her in the beginning, it sought her out now. A flash of a memory that came to it so often ... it calculated: she was in a section of the ship—was of certain age and gender. It would narrow the search to this section of the ship. There was something else it hadn't noticed before and was now seeing clearly: A light mark on a wrist, a small patch of paler skin, where the sun didn't alter the dull colour of this section of skin. It considered this and rose with an insatiable focus. It would find her.

CHAPTER 5

Surviving

The only light they had came from stars or when they passed a fiery planet or other suns and moons. The misery of constant dimness was more common to the captured than to the blinding spurts of radiant lights.

Since their arrival on the ship, thousands had died and thousands more would die. Gracie and the hundreds that remained alive in her section were put to work for more hours than they were permitted to sleep. The vile creatures clearly demonstrated their power over them, so there was no escape. The only option was to comply or to be killed or maimed horrifically.

A routine was established. The vile creatures had no language, and they communicated through high-pitched sounds and pointed one of their trunk-like arms to what they wanted their captured humans to do, which was to walk down a long tunnel with two lines—one moving toward the right-hand side of the wall that ended with an opening, where down below, a hot sulphur pool, five feet in width, the colour of grey starch, waited for them to drop remains—the pieces of dead bodies and internal organs—inside it. It was labour-intensive work they had to do with their own hands and arms, picking up putrid carcasses already rotting, with no water to disinfect or wash with.

The second line curved and moved back with people who finished dropping the dead bodies into the sludge and returned to the end of the long row to collect more and get back into the other line to drop the bodies into the sulphur pool. A vile creature hovered above the sulphur pool. What these vile creatures would use the sulphur pool full of dissolved humans for, Gracie couldn't comprehend. Only her captors knew.

On and on this went, for hours, for days, and into weeks. Gracie had no sense of time and could only evaluate its passage based on how her body and those around her deteriorated. They went from the luxury of being well-fed daily in a long-ago lifetime to withering away and starving like animals, tortured by terrible thirst, dehydration, desperate hunger, and sickness, devoid of sunshine, breathing in toxic air and moving within a falsified gravity that didn't feel right.

The states of their minds were ravaged with fear and terror of their masters who had no reason or logic behind their killings. They would lash out at any of them for whatever reason, maim them or be merciful and instantly kill them.

They were fed a daily diet of six, fat, grotesque, worm-like creatures, about one inch in width, the colour of lime. Their black eyes resembled the eyes of shrimps, and they had small moving claws at the bottom of their mushy bellies. They were given three to eat at a time.

The rancid odour of these worms was sickening—the stench of rotted beets and cabbage magnified a few times over made her want to hold her breath and gag. Their fat bodies glistened with some kind of gelatinous substance, pearlescent in colour, slippery, and stringy, that would hang off their squiggling bodies in long lines when picked up to be eaten.

Those Gracie suspected had lived most of their lives on the top floors of hundred-story towers surrounded by a dozen tail-wagging robot-dogs and attentive robot-cats suffered the most. They'd grown accustomed to lounging in their slinky, expensive body suits replete with networks and nanobots that sucked against their bodies like a second skin—the fabric heated to their desired temperatures. They were used to watching holographs from their head devices while eating their organic, synthesized meals brought in by the best international AI chefs.

Most cried terribly at the slithering worms but there was no other choice. There was no negotiation. If they didn't eat the worms offered to them at each setting, the vile creatures would lash out and crush a hand into a limping, disfigured one. So, between quickly eating a squiggly, fat worm and walking around with a crushed, disfigured hand tortured every second with pain and no relief, the former was the better choice.

The worms had no taste to them because Gracie never chewed them. Gracie held her nose and closed her eyes as she dropped each fat worm into the centre of the cylinder device in her throat. It took some time to get used to the claws scratching the bottom of her throat as they passed it. Sometimes they'd get caught in the ringlets of the device, wiggling there for hours until they finally expired, and a bitter, acidic-like content eventually dissolved down into her belly.

For fluid, the vile creatures ordered them to drink from a basin-like bowl that jutted out from the wall and filled with lavender sludge that had a strong smell of mould and petro. This fluid never fully quenched their severe thirst.

The sludge liquid had a saline, carbonated taste to it and clumps of odd bugs swam in it, which their deteriorating minds hardly registered. They were lined up in rows to drink from these bowls and dunked their faces inside this hot liquid, some gulping as fast as they could before the person behind them eagerly shoved them off and desperately dove into the sludge to gulp away.

Gracie took a few sips at a time and was careful not to choke or spend too long drinking. The vile creatures occasionally controlled how long they could drink from these bowls and would smash anyone against a wall, causing a broken shoulder, collarbone, or arm.

Done with their drinking, they walked down another tunnel that led to their resting place with a dead end. The one-inch partition walls enclosed them until a high-pitched screech came from their vile masters and the partitions re-opened. No matter where they were, if they had been relieving themselves at the end of the tunnel, or how deep in sleep they were in, they jolted up awake as if possessed and lined up in the queue to start another tormenting day.

It was appalling to see how their whole physical selves began to change. Aside from weight loss and lower vitality, they began to lose their hair. Gracie's thick tresses, which used to fan out into a sheath of beautiful waves now fell in clumps. Only a handful was left and it was greasy, smelling horrific due to the humidity and chemicals.

In their resting place, most spent their time staring ahead, without any sign of life left inside their empty eyes and with no interest in their fate. They moved on autopilot; steady, some days a bit slower than others with complete indifference. It became too much for some of them and they fell out of their lines. When that happened, everyone ignored it and carried on as a vile creature would swiftly scoop them up, tear them to pieces, and discard them in minutes.

As their diets changed, bowel movements became a version of lime colour diarrhea which furthered their misery. Urination occurred much less. Amenorrhea happened to the women as their bodies shrank into shapeless, pubescent, boyish figures.

Whenever a row of them passed by the glass window, under some light flashing from a faraway star or planet, she would catch a glimpse of their reflections staring back, which was a new form of a cadaverous creature that she had seen inside history holographs depicting concentration camp victims in China, Eastern Europe, many countries in the Middle East, and Iowa, East America. Every day they lived under a mortifying and agonizing reign of impending death. If it didn't happen that day, eventually it would.

Gracie rested in a corner, trying to shake off the horrors that she had seen that day. Every day, the vile creatures ate, tore open, crushed, and maimed humans. Some drank blood or squeezed a human in its powerful, trunk-like arms and watched it crack and explode like a wet fruit. The vile creature often in their section, who Gracie called the Vampyre, enjoyed human blood the most; it descended a few bodies ahead of her and snatched up its victim. A lavender tinge rolled through the rivulets of its skin that was speckled over with bright, lime-coloured spots. In one extended trunk arm, it held the thrashing victim. A round head formed, and it came close to the agonized face. It spewed out bluish liquid over the victim's face, swelling it up in seconds, three times its size. The victim thrashed madly in torturous pain inside the tight grip of the Vampyre.

Gracie cursed in her mind. *Hurry up, you son of a bitch, kill him.*

Another trunk arm approached from the other side of the Vampyre's body, and Gracie was close enough to the Vampyre to notice the ends of the trunk arms had a circular ringlet, and past this ringlet lay three sets of pointy teeth that overlapped each other. The entrance of the trunk-like arms widened and stretched over the victim's head and clamped down to the base of the neck. The sharp rows of teeth crunched down as blood gushed out in a multitude of round spurts. The underbelly of the trunk arm pumped and filled up quickly with dark moving liquid that was blood, as if it was another creature of its own, wild and insatiable, lusting for blood.

When the Vampyre creature was done, the victim was nothing but a pale, outer shell, and it flung the decapitated body over them and left to take on another victim.

Gracie shut her eyes and pressed her back against the wall. The moist warmth of the wall and the undercurrent of vibration massaged the aches and pains along her back. It would be much more pleasant if she ignored the thousands of tiny, beetle-like bugs that scattered out of the walls to feed upon her flesh.

The pestering bugs loved clothes, especially Gracie's damp corduroy pants. The material swarmed over with hundreds of these bugs, and with no water to wash, it came to the unbearable point that Gracie had to remove her clothing like everyone else had. Being completely naked no longer mattered. Modesty was a distant memory and wasn't a necessity nor a marker of any person's self-dignity. Their new clothing became their emaciated bodies coated in orange grease from the humidity of the air and lines of crawling beetle-bugs moving all over them. Gracie kept the waistband with one enclosed button and the left side back pocket.

Gracie reached into the pocket and pulled out two broken pieces of a hairbrush. She rolled it back and forth between her fingers.

Those who rested against the wall in front of her tried to sleep. Their faces and eyes spoke of doom and a longing for death. They barely moved or made any emotional reaction except for a wince here and there.

Gracie coughed and sat up. Her lungs, once healthy, gave her so much pain as if sizzling lead had been poured into them and they were slowly melting away.

No one was coming for them. These vile creatures destroyed the megacity of Don Mills within seconds. There were no governments left. There definitely weren't any that were powerful enough to send a military ship to find them and destroy these terrifying creatures.

It was these same entities who'd kidnapped thousands of humans a decade before, completely disappeared from Earth with the innocents—mostly children and a few elderly souls. The conspiracy theorists had been right. These vile creatures had first taken the innocent and most vulnerable of them at that time, only to return later to take more specimens.

It was these vile creatures who tampered with the satellites before attacking Earth, which none of the advanced AI's or NASA's telescopes had detected. None of these high-powered, sophisticated technologies had been able to detect these vile creatures entering the atmosphere coming to Earth early that morning and got right down to their business of massive death and ultimate destruction.

As for something supernatural like the invention of God, some still clung to this belief even inside this horrid place. Their lips moved with prayers, they did signs of the cross, some opened their arms and looked upwards to whatever God they begged, and others knelt down. They had to do whatever they could to survive, understand this horror was happening to them, and yet had to keep on going.

Gracie's Achilles heel was always that demented, betraying hope she couldn't shake off so easily—the hope that told her she would make it back home somehow and see Jimmy again.

Whenever a small person walked by her under that common stare of wanting to die, shuffling about with an emaciated frame full of open sores, cuts, and bruises from hard labour, her wretched hope would spring alive with a small dose of alertness, and she'd observe the child closely if they could be Jimmy.

It was usually a young adult petite in structure that atrociously withered away into a smaller frame due to severe malnutrition and constant thirst.

Gracie harshly reprimanded herself. *What kind of a mother are you? Why would you want to see Jimmy in this horrible place? He's safe. He's hidden, somewhere on Earth, away from these vile creatures, eating decent food and drinking fresh water and breathing in fragrant air, feeling the sun's outstretched rays fall over his face, warming his back, his arms, his legs ...*

Gracie had to believe this to keep on going. She'd even held on to the hope that these vile creatures would use them for their labour and bring them back to Earth eventually, even if they were half alive.

Her training as a synchronized swimmer also created a spirit of persistence, never to give up and eventually win. *You will make it. You will get there, no matter how abysmal and hopeless it is.* But, as time wore on, hopelessness was quickly settling in, growing stronger and stronger.

Some of them had already given up, falling into despair and killing themselves. When they had a chance, they'd throw themselves inside the sulphur liquid. The vile creature that hovered at the end of the line over the sulphur became more vigilant and snatched up anyone who tried to cheat them out of labour, a food source, or blood. The vile creature maimed them more severely; they'd twist off an arm or rip off both hands and dropped them back in line. This must have satisfied the vile creature's sadistic pleasure, to watch the culprits be forced to work for some time under great tortuous pain until finally bleeding out and falling over dead.

This deterred others from committing suicide. It was human nature to eventually get used to anything ... especially horror.

CHAPTER 6

Mommy Gracie

It went through one million devices that were taken from humans when they were first brought on board. It wasn't a difficult task. It was fast and efficient. Most humans preferred the smaller devices they kept inside their bodies. It found it odd that these humans would put so many foreign things inside their bodies. It could understand how some of them used devices to help them see, hear, or deal with some kind of mobility or function, but to keep devices to read, write, and think for them when they seemed to be given grand cognitive capacities ... it was odd.

The little creature kept an external device on her, which was common to much older humans than she was. It worked through this smaller pile of devices, uploading each one inside it to find the little creature. It didn't take long when it came across the device with a little creature with two pools of brown-amber eyes. It was her—the face, the hair, the smile. The device was registered to a Grace Mercedes Pinto. The little creature had an offspring with light-coloured eyes and hair—the hair that had invaded its fibres when it had been recently born. He had a name—Jimmy—and he called her Mommy Gracie.

Although they learned about these vile human species—about their anatomy, behaviours, and geographical locations—many didn't care to study them further and were content to simply obey the master's orders. It, on the other hand, was intensely curious. It had its contamination inside it and although it was repulsed at that, the curiosity in it had become more of a burden and drove it to want to learn all about Mommy Gracie, Daddy Jeff, and Jimmy.

Inside the hundreds of video holographs in Mommy Gracie's device, it listened to them—to their sounds, their voices. They made ugly sounds when they spoke. It would learn in minutes their main language, English, and additional ones that were in their recent past lineages based on health DNA reports Mommy Gracie had kept in a file for herself and Jeff. Portuguese for Mommy Gracie; Gaelic and Japanese for Jeff. It learned more quickly and efficiently than her species could ever dream of being capable of without the help of any devices or artificial intelligence.

The faces of the humans moved, and they often showed their rows of small, squared teeth. It was aware that they couldn't extend their bodies and was amused that they covered their feet with materials that had two- to three-inch platforms underneath, enhancing their height. Their bodies had diverse shades, especially during the changes of their seasons, but their shades were dull and didn't glow with sparkles or fire—nor could they glisten with beautiful, internal, kaleidoscopic lights. Some of them put colours and shining gels on their faces and hair. They grew slowly from young to old. And even though the humans were one of the most physically weak, sentient species they've ever encountered, they were the most destructive.

Seeing the destruction they wreaked upon each other and the other creatures living around them in their natural world, it was clear that they were very dangerous—just as its parent had warned. It would learn much more about them and read the hundreds of private journal files Mommy Gracie had in the device that no other human could access. It already decoded the password and gained entry into the main folder. It uploaded all of the files inside it. It would see her face all the time, hear her hum, her voice, and react in that powerful benevolent recognition, as it curled up with the others. It had to find her soon, still alive amongst them. It's longing to be with Mommy Gracie was extremely strong. How would it react once it found her? If it felt nothing as it hoped—or the odd, intense sensations it had toward her abated—it would go on, relieved to finally be freed from all of these unproductive, distracting, intense feelings and burdensome curiosities.

Sometimes, it hummed out to her, like a song. The others wouldn't think anything of it, as this is what some of them did to let others know about their happiness or location. It wondered if Mommy Gracie could hear it and hum back to it. How would she? The device they marked them with when they came onboard wouldn't allow her to hum. This was another human trait it had to constantly put up with, having irrelevant, argumentative thoughts within it that distracted it from more important matters.

Maybe it was too late and Mommy Gracie had been killed already. The thought of that happening filled it with sensations that made its light movements slow down and the gravity feel heavy, making it struggle to fly faster above. A lighter sentiment would come to it that made it think no, Mommy Gracie had to be alive. She had a physically strong body—more so than most—and her mind was resilient. As it finished reading her private journals, it pondered the many bad things that had happened to her, and yet, she'd kept on going, operating with some kind of structured efficiency. She was introspective and expressed her thoughts intelligently. These were all qualities that drove her onward and made her strong, not weak, despite the fact that she didn't seem to be able to understand this. It would have to come up with a plan to find her fast.

CHAPTER 7

The Newborn

Gracie's section had cleaned up the last human bodies and remains. Walls moved around, shoveling them and organizing them toward a vile creature who pointed to the end of a new tunnel where it would lead them to their final deaths or into another hideous, terrifying place. They were brought to an open space filled with heaps of rubble and broken pieces of concrete. The heap was about thirty feet high. How had these vile creatures brought all of this onto the ship? And *why*?

The wall partitions moved again, and new faces with that same distant, disengaged stare filled up their working lines. If Gracie was more mentally lucid to count and keep track, she was sure there would be an apparent set number of workers these vile creatures kept for each section.

A terrible screech came from the vile creature that pointed at the heaps of concrete. They were to remove pieces of concrete with their weak, sickly arms and hands, hold them against their chests, walk down another tunnel, and deposit the contents into other sulphuric vaults. It was back-breaking work. Despondent looks came over those whose bodies were already ravaged with weakness and illness.

As they worked to remove the concrete in between some spaces, Gracie found a sign with Greek letters. There was a face of a girl with dark brown eyes and black hair, winking with a chef's hat. It was a shock to Gracie to find something that was made from a human during a time when things were so much different.

Treasured prizes began to be found in between the concrete: A bottle with some water in it, a small, dented juice can, a bar of broken chocolate or a granola bar. The smart ones quickly opened these treasures and ate them fast—before their starved companions realized it and tried to snatch them away, which could cause a breakdown of order. It was getting out of the line that prompted the creatures to snatch them up and maim them. If they stayed in line and disposed the concrete into the sulphur, ate their prized treasure discretely from others and yet under the vile creatures' presence, it didn't react. Gracie tried to make sense of it. None of it made sense to her.

During another resting period, Gracie leaned against the wall. Her arms and chest of bones and skin were covered in many cuts from enduring endless hours of hard labour from carrying so many sharp, broken pieces of concrete. She hoped she would hear the intermittent hum that came once in a while from inside the walls. She wasn't sure if the hum was a ship engine turning or a mechanical change, but to her exhausted, deteriorating mind, the intermittent hums sounded like a little heartbeat in a sonograph she once heard before.

The hum started up, reverberating through the wall. She put a hand over an ear to keep the bugs from crawling inside, then pressed it against the warm, vibrating wall. She closed her eyes and let the hum ring through her, pulling her out from her physical, painful misery and bringing her home.

Gracie sat on her bedroom floor, listening to Gran Amália and Rose, who stood in the hallway behind the shut bedroom door.

"She only has one shot at being a mother," Rose said. "And she'll make the same mistake Evelyn made."

Rose was visiting for a few days, and whenever she did, Gracie increased her work hours to fourteen hours a day, so that she ate out, came home, showered, and got right into bed. Today was an exception. She'd worked six hours to deal with an unexpected situation that was terribly timed, as interference from Rose was never helpful or pleasant.

"You don't know that," Gran Amália said.

"There's the illness. She's at a huge risk of getting it," Rose continued. "It will happen to her and it will drastically change her too, just like it did Evelyn. She'll be dead in the end."

"Nonsense, you're being overdramatic," Gran Amália chortled. "The illness never struck you nor I—nor any other great-grandmothers. It struck Evelyn for whatever reason. It doesn't mean Gracie will get it. There's never a right time to have a child. The best time seems to be now for Gracie. She finished her education and has been working for some time. She manages her money well, is a hard worker, never turns down a shift, and is clean and tidy despite working in filthy places. The child beat the odds of birth control, is meant to be here, and has a special purpose—as we all have."

"Her mother had the illness," Rose snapped, her impatience growing. "Gracie carries this risk inside her. The science clearly says it will come for her too. The only special purpose this child will have is the outrageous expense of pregnancy treatments and care and for what? To raise a child when she's not ready ... and what they can become in the future? A huge regret. She's better off waiting twenty more years until she matures. She has the science and the opportunity to be able to make that choice. Every intelligent woman is doing this. It's crazy and blatantly stupid of her if she doesn't take care of this now and postpone it."

"A huge regret and what they can become?" Gran Amália scoffed. "Gracie turned out fine and so will this child. Gracie is patient and has a natural, nurturing instinct in her. I have strength left in me and can help her raise this child when needed. The Lord will figure out a way and let Gracie decide for herself."

"She was already careless to not have noticed her condition get this far along," Rose said. "Didn't she notice any irregularities in her menses? Why didn't Arabella alert her to changes in her urine far sooner? They can detect pregnancy within eighteen hours. It would have been one pill and one flush, and no one would even have to know about this—especially me. I have much more important things to do ... contracts to work on, more meetings to attend across the world ... than to be standing here and having this discussion. I've even gone ahead and made an appointment for Gracie with Dr. Schloss at the St. Joseph's Health Centre, just because I know what's best for her."

Even in the brief silence between them, Gracie felt Gran Amália's repulsion tighten around the corners of her mouth. "Gracie always had some irregularities with her menses, so it didn't raise much alarm," Gran Amália crisply said. "In this home, Arabella is restricted to minimal network access. She has no business being wired inside any of our toilets or sinks. It will be up to Gracie to decide what she wants to do, as she'll have to live with that decision for the rest of her life and no one else."

"If Gracie doesn't make the best decision for herself today," Rose continued, "it will ruin her life for good, just as it did to Evelyn."

Gracie's voice cut through the distant discussion. "Arabella."

"Yes, Gracie."

"What time is my appointment with Dr. Schloss at the St. Joseph's Health Centre?"

"Tomorrow, 9:30 a.m."

"Do you have any holographs beneath the ocean with blue whales swimming above under the daylight? I read in the description section that you have something like this."

"I'll run through my network connections. Should only take a minute."

Gracie couldn't get down to the recreation centre, slip inside the pool, swim toward the bottom, and sit there while looking up to the light coming in from the windows, twinkling over the top of the pool. The next best thing would be an illusion of something similar that would bring Gracie an amplified sense of solitude and peace she needed at that moment.

As Arabella checked through her network files, another thought came to Gracie, just as unexpected as what the nurse practitioner confirmed yesterday via holograph—namely, what was causing, for the past two weeks, the heavy fatigue, migraines, and unprecedented urges for vinegar chips dipped in grape jelly.

"Arabella, stop searching."

"Certainly."

"Search your files for the sound of a seven-week fetus inside its mother."

"Certainly."

Gracie put her hands in her lap, her knees close to her chest, and waited. The sound reverberated through the network's surround system, at first a swooshing noise rumbling through a tunnel, followed by quick, successive thumping. Gracie thought of the hyperloop train that ran from Vancouver to Toronto when it would be advertised over the billboards—the train zipping ahead at great velocity, the sound slightly dropping to a pulsating thump as it bulldozed through trans-pod tunnels at 750 miles per hour toward its next stop in thirty-two minutes, Edmonton.

The sound continued, and it brought her into the pool. Her little child's feet vigorously splashed over the water, and the joy of it proved intense as ever. The smell of chlorine was one of her favourites because nothing else excited her as much. Her feet moved under the water, sinking lower, and the water flowed, swirling all around her body, covering every pore of her in one comforting hug. In between the swirling water, the heartbeats pulsated against her ears and tickled over her forehead.

Gracie listened to the heartbeats and to the torrent of voices that began to spill inside her mind.

Ruin your life for good ... just like it did Evelyn.

After Gracie was born, post-partum psychosis and depression befell Evelyn. Gracie was the catalyst that brought Evelyn into the dark descent of misery. No one said as much, but they all thought it. Rose especially. It had been always there—that accusatory look inside her eyes. She'd said it before to Gran Amália when Gracie had been a child and they thought she was soundly asleep; if only Evelyn hadn't had Gracie so young—if Evelyn had waited until she was older—perhaps the condition wouldn't have happened, and Evelyn wouldn't be suffering. If only ... if only ...

Would Gracie bend to the sickness when it came for her just as Evelyn did, gripped inside its clutches, wanting to suffocate, and driven to delusions and misery she never imagined?

Still, she might not get it. Rose and Gran Amália hadn't. Rose confidentially expected it.

Arabella shifted from the sound of the seven-week-old fetus to a holograph of the ocean. All the walls in Gracie's bedroom disappeared. Gracie was inside a murky ocean, and gurgling sounds of water moved around her as the illusion sank her down to the empty seabed. Up above swam the slow-moving, majestic beasts that were blue whales—a large one and a small one. Their sounds came through the gurgling of the water in spurts of rhythmic whistles that merged into a prolonged moan pumping with a strong thundering base underneath it. It boomed back and forth. It was the blue whale's massive heart, the beating of its heart. The blue whale turned and gently descended underneath the water, swimming toward Gracie from above. The little calf swam closely behind. Groups of two to three tiny grouper fish accompanied them, swimming along the sides of the blue whales' massive bodies.

Gracie moved her hands over her abdomen. It had twenty-three of her chromosomes and twenty-three of Jeff's. Would it enjoy technical data and analysis like Jeff or love to swim as she did? Work shifts could be shortened from twelve to eight hours. The small room used as her office could be cleared out and made into a small bedroom. Gran Amália was around to help. She was the solid pillar in Gracie's life that had been consistent. Yes, Gran Amália was a Jesus fan but didn't go on about it all day and was just as strongly faithful to the saying "cleanliness is next to godliness" and kept the apartment shining brighter than the Royal Ontario Museum. Gran Amália was a great cook, mainly keeping to her traditional, savoury Azorean dishes and often reminded her, "Gracie, when I die, you will then understand how lucky you were to eat my food."

And why should Gracie postpone motherhood like everyone else did into their fifties? Gracie didn't care to be like everyone else. Anything could happen twenty years from now. Who's to say that postponing to twenty years ahead would be better timing? Gracie could decide to change her career and Gran Amália wouldn't be around to offer her support. Relying on Rose to fill in that spot was out of the question.

Rose's voice returned, sneering more coldly, *it would ruin her life, too ...*

"Arabella, shut off the holograph," Gracie said and got up from the floor.

"Certainly."

Gracie came out of her room. Rose and Gran Amália turned around. Gran Amália had been wearing a snug pair of dark blue jeans and matching loafers and a vinyl-long-sleeved blouse stitched onto a black chiffon material, with a beaded, red heart in the center. Stripes of light-blue highlights mixed in with her wavy, chestnut brown hair that she kept cut short by her shoulders. A pair of rimless, smart glasses sat on the bridge of her small nose. Rose had worn a simple, white body suit linked with networks, flashing with colourful advertisements in the centre and along the sides of her pant legs.

"I saved you the hassle and made the appointment for tomorrow morning," Rose quickly said. "I'm telling you now: It will be the best decision you'll ever make. It will be quick and completely painless. You'll be done in less than twenty minutes, and you can return to the plant right after the procedure." A faint smile spread over her lips—as fake as the dark-red eyebrows tattooed over her eyes.

Gracie's annoyance increased and she bit down on her inner lip. Why did Rose so suddenly want to be involved in Gracie's business? There had to be something in it for her. It was as if getting Gracie to do her bidding was masking something else—perhaps Rose's own failure of not having found Evelyn in time to make the same appeal she was putting on Gracie that would somehow purge Rose of her own failures.

"Gracie, have you made your decision?" Gran Amália implored.

Gracie moved to the entranceway of the bathroom. The door slid open.

"Arabella," Gracie said.

"Yes, Gracie."

"Put on my favourite bathtime music: Tchaikovsky's Overture, the War of 1812."

"Certainly."

Gracie hardened her eyes at Rose. "The appointment with Dr. Schloss is cancelled. I won't allow *it* or anyone else to ruin my life."

Gracie was startled awake by the shriek of the call. She got up and ran with the others to immediately get in line.

In the middle of another excruciating day of hard labour, carrying a load of concrete against her to dispose inside the sulphur sludge, someone had fallen about ten people ahead in Gracie's line. No one cared because many of them expired that way now, but the person that fell had clothes on. A white lace dress draped over the woman in a rounded tent. She lay on the ground on her side, shoulders trembling. Where did she come from? Gracie hadn't seen her before. The woman's head was shaved. She hadn't lost her hair like everyone else. In comparison to their emaciated, sickly bodies, she was fat. She had some shape in her legs and arms. Why hadn't she deteriorated as they had? It was impossible that she was taken from Earth recently, as they'd moved away from Earth since the abduction and the deterioration of their bodies had been for at least six months or more.

Dark blood streamed down between the woman's thighs. The line slowed down, and as expected, a vile creature snatched up and lifted the woman in its strong coils. Her face was terribly bloated with a deep crimson red, her expression nothing but what they were so used to seeing—excruciating pain. The Vampyre creature arrived and coiled its arms around her as well. They never wrapped their arms around one victim together at the same time. They both wanted this woman and something transpired between them in their silent, face-to-face stance. Gracie never saw the vile creatures behave this way toward each other. They had always been cohesive and cooperative.

The woman's eyes widened, and her body began to convulse. A coil arm tightened around her breasts, and the Vampyre's coil arm slid further down her chest and tore the seams of the gown from under her arms. The dress swirled in a wide-open flare, falling over the crowd. Now naked, the woman exposed what these vile creatures wanted. Gracie had suspected as much. She gripped the pile of concrete against her chest that rose with exasperated breathing. Her lips quivered. The woman's belly protruded like a firm pumpkin. Spurts of blood and liquid splashed down her legs. The woman's face contorted further, thick veins stuck out on each side of her neck; the woman was shrieking but only muffled sounds and grunts were heard.

A round ball covered in blood and white foam slipped out of the woman. It uncurled itself and fell into a coiled arm of the vile creature. Their coils crushed the woman's ribs and lungs. Her face became still and was released. She dropped down into a pile of broken legs and arms. Gracie's breathing became erratic. The Vampyre creature held onto the placenta that looked like the glistening liver of a calf. The newborn looked to be about seven pounds. The rumbling noise of the ship fell silent. Gracie's ears could no longer hear any other sound but the tiny cries that emerged from the newborn. The cries were the most beautiful sound Gracie had heard since her capture. All of them in the line slowed down and listened to the newborn's cries, collectively reminding them of the humanity that had been stripped away—of the innocence and purity of a newborn's cries, which like a miracle, existed amongst all of them inside that horrid place in the midst of so much suffering and tremendous misery while being surrounded by an impenetrable and hopeless evil. The newborn was like an odd memory that reminded them of hope—like a beacon of goodness that could still exist—although Gracie knew it would be a short time for the newborn.

Instead of the newborn's eyes seeing the happy face of its mother, it looked upon shapes of the hideous things that lowered their eyeless, malformed heads toward it. The newborn must have sensed this foreign environment, as it started to struggle to breathe, and its soft cries turned into high-pitched screeching. Gracie's arms trembled.

Don't. Please ...

The long necks of the vile creatures circled around the newborn for a few more seconds before they were on it. Gracie turned her face away and tried to close her ears with her hands, without letting some of the concrete fall from her arms. There was nothing left of the newborn. Any remains of it along with its mother's body were flung inside the sulphuric acid.

The line returned to its regular pace. The vile creature flew back to its post at the end of the sulphur vault. The Vampyre creature, with its body freshly filled with newborn blood, went on its way elsewhere.

CHAPTER 8

The Keeper

It hovered over the hundreds of thousands of humans working in the centre section of the ship. It was far enough to be above them not to be noticed. It cast its vision over them. The humans had deteriorated into walking skeletons; they'd lost their hair and body shapes, and their faces were hardly recognizable. Some of them had severe injuries that would kill them soon, and most of them were weakened by hunger and dehydration. The worms being fed to them weren't enough. The alternative water source they were given wasn't enough. How would they meet the master's goal if the labour was weak and sick? It had counted their numbers. Too many of them were being killed off and injured. The numbers should have been much higher. It focused on the faces of the females. It didn't find anyone that could be this Mommy Gracie.

It flew into another section of the ship. The sharp, putrid smells were the first thing it noted. Strong smells didn't bother their species, but this was the stench of dead human flesh that had rotted longer than it should have. It wondered why it hadn't been cleared and put into their sacred waters. It followed the putrid scent down a compartment of the ship it usually didn't venture into. In a tunnel, rotted cabbage, orange peels, and wrappers of human food were strewn about. A small, tangled heap of fleshy tubes shone with blood that hadn't dried out yet.

Curiosity kept goading it forward, and it moved through a wall, entering a room.

A few mattresses were scattered around, stained with blood and thick orange grease. Huddling against the back wall in complete darkness were six females who didn't look like the skeleton humans it just had seen. They had some flesh on them. It scanned their faces for Gracie, but none of them matched.

The females were standing up, cords tied around their wrists high above their heads. Their stomachs bulged in different sizes. On the other side stood three males, staring ahead, their eyes barely flickering, with arms tied over their heads in the same predicament. Some of the females hid their faces against their arms; others shook in terror and tried to shrink further in the dark, thinking it wasn't able to see them clearly. In another far corner was the source of the stench; a dozen rotting human corpses lay with a mountain of bugs and worms devouring them.

Bowls of water were placed in different areas of the room. Pieces of cabbage leaves, banana peels, a broken chocolate bar, and dead bugs floated in the bowls. In the bowl closest to the entranceway, the smallest hand it had ever seen, smaller than Jimmy's, swam in it. It turned its focus back to the females—to the centre of their bodies. Its vision moved behind their outer shells and saw fetuses in different gestation periods. The first two had nothing inside them and were bleeding heavily, as they had recently given birth. They were very weak and losing so much blood. They would die soon. The two against the far-off wall had the largest extended centres and would be giving birth in a few days to what it estimated were offspring that weighed about eight pounds each.

One of them had strayed from the master's plan. It was a rare occurrence, but one of them had strayed or perhaps misunderstood the master's plan. The contamination inside it reacted; the fire sparked and began to swirl in what it understood was anger and betrayal.

The distant hum of the perpetrator approached. The humans sensed it coming, and they began to whimper and cry, shifting their weight against their shackles. It waited for its descent. Lavender rivulets moved through its body, and its lime speckles shone like emeralds. The keeper carried human food, a heap of fruits, raw vegetables, and granola bars. It dropped the food and the humans stretched and moaned against their shackles, their eyes over the fallen food as bugs promptly came up from the ground and helped themselves.

There was silence between it and the keeper. It finally hummed.

"What is all this?" It asked.

"The taste of their young," the keeper hummed back, "primarily the almost born and newly born, is the most exquisite meat. I bring them human food and water to keep them healthier and be able to produce this young, tender type of meat."

"This isn't part of the master's plan," it said and sensed some confusion from the keeper, who saw the flames swirling swiftly inside its chest.

"Get to the main dome," it ordered the keeper. "Tell everyone including the guardians at the sacred waters to meet there. I'll explain further."

And with that, it flew away from the keeper fast. It was aware that some of them had developed a taste for human flesh and blood—some more than others. It was told that when the human creatures were in a constant state of terror, their blood oxidized faster, making their meat taste much better. No doubt the meat from the almost-born and newborns was exquisite to taste, as the mothers were probably terrorized throughout the last terms of the gestation periods and were able to produce this kind of meat. Some of its species loved this new food source. It, on the other hand, had a complete aversion to it.

It roamed off, alone for a while, so the others wouldn't see or feel the fire that swirled throughout its fibres with sparks and flickering light. It was irritated by these sudden imperfections cropping up in its species. Imperfection is what it expected from the humans, not from them. How many more of them were failing to adhere to the master's plan?

When it had calmed down, it flew to their meeting place to address all of them.

"The master will be coming soon," it hummed to them. "The master will not approve of any deliberate breeding of humans for food consumption of their young. We were given precise instructions regarding what to do with them. I have calculated the numbers. The original humans taken from Earth are quickly dwindling, and we're far from meeting the cause. Further breeding of humans and deliberately killing them will cease. None of the captives will be slain or eaten unless they expire on their own or challenge our authority. All of these unsavory practices will end now."

They hummed loudly and acquiesced. It was their captain.

"There is only one exception—female humans. Any female, even if challenging authority, will not be killed or attacked in any way. They are to be brought to me and I will handle them."

They hummed loudly and acquiesced. It was their captain.

"Soon, new humans will need to be born to increase the labour force. These new humans will need to be as strong and as healthy as their original parents. They will need their water and food to

become almost as strong as the original humans. Newborns will need our intervention to grow into adolescents much faster than the two decades it takes them to grow within their own natural biological timeline. Those who are keeping humans gestating with young are to bring them to me to start this process. They will be the first humans to be born on this ship and used for additional labour."

They hummed loudly and acquiesced. It was their captain.

"*The original humans are to be kept working for as long as possible. They will need to be fed more and given their water source every other feeding time. They are too weak, and we cannot meet the master's cause if the humans are weak or sick.*"

They hummed loudly and acquiesced. It was their captain.

It looked over the sea of sparkling, colourful lights and vibrating hums and saw the keeper humming amongst them. Even though it could barely hear its hums, its emerald sparkles shone through it exquisitely.

CHAPTER 9

A Familiar Face

Having witnessed the newborn's death, any small hope that encouraged Gracie to stay alive died along with it. She was ready to die. She accepted that she would never see Jimmy again. If he survived, she would be with him in the next world soon enough ... or remain in a dark, yet peaceful, unconscious, eternal sleep just as she had been in during the past four billion years of Earth's existence before she was born.

It would be hard to come up with a plan. She wanted a swift death and not end up on the wall, maimed and tortured.

The horrible screech came. They rose up and got into their rows to start the day. With Gracie's newfound purpose and determination, she thought about how she was going to do this.

The quickest way to die was to slip down into the sulphur vaults. She had seen a small opening in the middle of the line, on the right side of the hill that she could squeeze in between and quickly dive into the sulphur water. She would be far away enough from the vile creature that hovered at the end of the line, to be able to realize what she was doing and catch her. All of her suffering would finally end.

She took her share of concrete and turned back into the line.

A vile creature screeched in another section, startling them. The vile creature that guarded the end of the line went to investigate. An opportunity, finally. It would be now or never.

Gracie's eyes averted sideways along the hill as they shuffled along. The middle section was coming, about twenty steps away and she would reach the place where she could quickly dive down unnoticed. She expected Ms. Coligan's voice to encourage her through this, but it was Gran Amália's voice that came, desperate and furious.

"*What do you think you are doing, Gracie, this is a terrible sin.*"

"*Sins have been happening all around me since I got here,*" *Gracie said.*

"*So many have died with illnesses they couldn't control when they wanted to live, and here you are surviving, and you want to end it?*"

"*I don't care. I can't go on, Gran Amália, I can't ...*"

"*Your body will die, but your soul will not. Only the Lord can end your life when He wants to.*"

"*The Lord should let me die then, just as He let all the others die and the innocent newborn. I'm just fast-tracking it.*"

"*Have faith. Have hope, Gracie.*"

"*Hope? I'll never see Jimmy again. I'm ready to die, maybe then I will see him.*"

"*Gracie, you will see Jimmy again. Have faith.*"

"*No, Gran Amália, You don't understand. I'm already dead.*"

Now, the lower edge of the hill was in sight and the vile creature hadn't returned yet. Gracie was ready. She dropped some of the concrete from her arms and turned toward the lower edge. The drop wouldn't be more than twenty feet. It would be a quick and fast dive.

Another row of workers made their way up the line on the other side and approached Gracie's line. Gracie's eyes should have turned back to the hill, but instead, they fell over a face, over the brown globes of a pair of eyes of someone she once knew.

She froze. His wavy dark hair had fallen out, and only stringy clumps were left. A small black beard had managed to remain, glistening with amber grease that covered over the bones on the angular face. Burns and welts covered his skin, which glistened with amber grease. She couldn't be seeing him. He wasn't here. He was another man who looked like him. Her eyes were deceiving her. A small spark ignited inside Mr. Singh's eyes. His chest moved upwards with emotion. The large eyes widened and spoke to her.

You're alive.

His eyes crinkled in the corners as if smiling. He lifted up an arm as if he wanted to wave at her or do one of his animated greetings. His arms were nothing but skin and bones and were too weak to move. Tears welled up inside his eyes. Tears Gracie was surprised he could still produce. Her tear ducts dried out a long time ago.

He saw the pile of concrete by her feet and her body turned toward the lower hill. He knew what she was going to do and he stepped out of the line. Gracie urgently shook her head. Her eyes slanted and pleaded.

What are you doing? Get back in line. They will kill you.

His face grew stern—an expression she had never seen on Mr. Singh's face. He reached out for her shoulders, a touch she hadn't felt in so long.

His stern eyes told her.

Don't give up!

Gracie shook her head at him, telling him through her begging eyes.

I can't. Not anymore. I can't ...

His grip tightened on her shoulders, surprising her with his strength.

Have courage. It's not too late.

She stood on the tips of her feet and tried to push him back to the line. He resisted and brought his face closer to hers.

You will make it. Don't give up. Don't give up.

Gracie then remembered. Her hands gripped his arms in desperation.

Jimmy! Is Jimmy okay?

Her eyes pleaded. Did he understand what her eyes were trying to tell him? She tried to speak, but it was painful to do through the device and only muffled moans came out.

His face remained still, and any previous emotion that had been in it softened.

Are they alive? Please tell me if Jimmy made it out. Do you know if he is still alive?

She shook him more frantically. His eyes stared ahead.

Mr. Singh?

His eyes remained still until an explosion of blood shot out from his chest, splattering Gracie's face and neck. She screamed against the device and scampered away. The rim of the trunk that punctured through his chest glistened in dripping, dark blood and rose high above Gracie's terrified face. The strong coil lifted up the man's torso and body with it.

Gracie was glued to her spot without any sense left in her to immediately jump inside the sulphur vault or scamper back into the fast-moving line in an attempt to remain incognito. Gracie remained transfixed not believing this was happening, directly faced with the Vampyre creature, and watched the lavender unfurl through the rivulets of its body dotted with sparkling green firelights. Its glistening trunk's mouth full of sharp teeth turned around and came toward the man's face. He should have been terrified; instead, he remained still and incredulously turned to look down at Gracie's crying, trembling face. His lips melted into a resigned smile with the benevolence of relief that, for him, it would be finally over soon, and he would be at peace.

Goodbye, his eyes said. *Have courage. Survive.*

The Vampyre's trunk arm clamped over the man's head, sucking it down to his neck, and moved back and forth as the powerful suction cracked open the skull, drained out its contents, and severed it from the body. Large amounts of blood moved through the Vampyre's gorged trunk arm. Then, it dropped the lifeless body into the place where Gracie should have been, inside the sulphur vault.

The Vampyre's body filled with fresh blood swirling inside it and ascended toward her. She scurried away until her back slammed against a wall. Even though she had been terrified, seeing the Vampyre come for her filled her with that same resigned relief the man must have felt. Finally, it would be over soon for her as well. She waited for the Vampyre to grab her and crush her.

The Vampyre creature hovered above for a few seconds. The ships' engines continued to rumble as workers around her scurried frantically away like a blur, back and forth in their lines. Gracie grew impatient. Her eyes screamed at it.

What the hell are you waiting for, kill me!

The Vampyre's arm snapped outwards and wrapped around her waist. She closed her eyes, hoping to be crushed to death or injected with poison so, in seconds, she could explode into pieces and be finished with this nightmare. Yet, it lifted her up and kept on extending her upwards, past the forty-foot walls and much higher.

What is happening? Where are you taking me?

Gracie breathed deeply. She looked beneath them, over intricate mazes of hundreds of thousands of other humans moving about in other places, doing what their group had done, moving large mountains of concrete blocks, and dropping them inside other sulphur vaults.

The Vampyre creature kept on flying higher and higher, faster and faster, and deeper inside the folds of the frightening darkness above.

CHAPTER 10

The Master

A sliver of light sparkled over a dark speck of space. The light began to stretch outwards and spread fast. Those of them that were on that side of the ship sensed the presence. Their bodies tingled. Every cell and speck of fire and electricity in their bodies bolted to life with heights of excitement and joy. Their hums started.

It did its best to hum as loud as it could. Its dull hum was heard underneath all of the other vibrant hums. They hummed with great gratitude, reverence, and love for the approaching, gleaming, and blazing light, which was the light of all light, more powerful than any sun, star, planet, or creature in existence.

The master hummed back, and the result was exquisitely beautiful. None of them could hum with the purity and power of the master. Their bodies lifted and stretched as high as they could to catch as much of the master's blazing light as it ascended over them.

Unlike the others who were deep in their feverish exaltation and reverence of the master's approach, it was aware of the master's great power. It drew back slightly in fear. The master would surely see inside it and know that it was different and contaminated by the humans. No ... the master already knew. The master was aware of everything. If the master was displeased about it, its physical body would have been removed and it wouldn't be having yet another internal debate with itself.

It hummed louder as much as it could in the most beautiful sound it could muster to override its fear. The master would be pleased by how much effort it hummed back with, and the master would know that even though it was contaminated, it was more like its species than human because its love had no bounds for the master.

The master's blazing light fell directly over it. The power of the master's heat was incredible, and its whole body sizzled with pulsating currents of electricity and roaring fire. It was almost painful. It moved closer to the master. Inside the powerful body of the master, multitudes of erupting flames rumbled. The others continued with their feverish hums to the master. The master did not change its hum.

"Do not fear me," the master hummed. "I am pleased with your work. You have carried out my plans well and corrected grievances that you understood strayed away from my plans."

The master's light grew intense. They bathed in the blazing light filled with exalted feelings of peace and contentment, feelings that were much different from the swift, powerful feelings that the images of Mommy Gracie caused its body to extract over them.

"Continue onward," the master hummed. "There's much to do and prepare. Their crowns have been removed. Others have risen. Time does not rule me. You are my captain."

Its hums were joyous. The master was pleased and accepted it despite being contaminated, and still, the master's love for it was intense. It would continue. It was all that mattered. It stretched its body further toward the master and exalted its dull hums as high as it could, full of graciousness.

"See with a vision that is clear," the master hummed. "With wisdom, you will continue to grow and not give in to discouragement so easily. Continue to follow your inclinations. I am your master—the only one. I will return again, soon enough."

The master rescinded and the powerful, blazing light faded away. The master returned back into the folds of the dark abyss of space.

They coiled happily against one another and kept the glorious exhalations going for awhile. It lay in the middle of them and watched the twinkling lights of stars and of the place the master had so quickly arrived and gone. An image of Mommy Gracie entered its vision. Her amber eyes watched over it. Her lips moved. It didn't hear any words. It knew what she said.

"Jimmy, find me. Why can't you find me?"

CHAPTER 11

A Long Ago Life

The Vampyre threw her inside a catacomb-like structure and left. Dim lighting fell into the place from a small opening high above in clear glass. The walls glistened heavily with an orange and a darker substance Gracie had seen many times—splattered human blood. The smell was strong, mixed in with the underlying pong of petroleum, filled with decayed blood, rot, and parts of dead humans. Ahead of her, about six feet away, a liquefied wall moved with rivulets of glittering amber and red hues.

Something stirred behind her. Gracie turned around and faced two dozen skeletons. This would explain the strong stench. Gracie thought they were dead, but as she moved closer to them, an eye blinked, and so did the twitch of a hand and slow movement from a chest. They sat there completely motionless, on their knees, some clutched each other's hands and arms, and others stared ahead, completely disengaged from anything that would happen to them now.

Gracie slipped behind them to the back wall and sat on the heels of her feet. She moved her eyes away from the group, back to the liquefied wall and to the dim ceiling. There were no shadows or movement. A hedge rose from the ground in front of the liquefied wall. A few whimpers. Something small lay flat on top of the hedge. With the dim lighting, Gracie couldn't tell what it was. A sharp holograph suddenly shot out from it, and the strong light hurt her eyes at first. Gracie adjusted her eyes to the image that sprang out.

Even though they were constantly under a stifling humid heat, an icy coldness prickled underneath Gracie's skin as her eyes took in the image of a symbol she hadn't seen for so long. At first, it took her a few seconds before she understood what she was seeing ... a red maple leaf behind a white background with a red stripe on each side. It was the Canadian flag. A flag she had seen so many times displayed on the side of a swimming cap, over her bathing suits, behind a jacket, beside her synchro team members' names on a holographic billboard. The Canadian flag. Home. It was home. The flag rustled in the wind, and behind it was the palette of a blue sky.

Gracie's heart wanted to race. She kept still and squashed the emergence of any nostalgic feelings, the recognition, and the bewilderment that itched inside her to react. No. She would feel nothing. She would be as emotionally dead as the others.

The image faded and was replaced by the megacity of Don Mills, glittering with exuberant beauty, in a multitude of radiant colours and lights. Arial and Gen X imperiously stood, breathing outwardly with life—their loud advertisements changing from one to another. They weren't crumbled balls of fire the last time Gracie had seen them.

She kept her breathing steady. Those vile creatures were there, observing behind the wall. She had to be still no matter what emotion tried to desperately crawl out of her.

Another holograph of a grey-blue, little, hairless dachshund-shih tzu mix with large brown eyes. Codie. Gran Amália's and her beloved, childhood, little dog posing next to a decorated, tinselled Christmas tree, his small, black nose pressed against a present shaped like a large dog bone. Her mind raced. The vile creatures were showing holographs from her Android watch that had been taken from her when she was abducted. Why were they doing this? Her breathing started to increase despite attempts to keep calm.

Another holograph: the faces of the girls, Tatou and Natasha, taken at their last outing at the Sagittarius Club dressed in their 1980s costumes and posing with holographic images of the members of Duran Duran smiling behind them. The faces of Tatou and Natasha, full of happiness as if they had won gold at the world championships, having a great time for the last time, all of them dreaming, working hard, achieving, and doing so much ... and now the two of them were dead. Gone forever.

Gracie swallowed and felt the device pinch her throat. It was better to feel physical discomfort than the constricting sadness of loss.

A holograph of a little boy—Gracie's eyes widened. A toddler's face with curly, flaxen locks, big, blue, round eyes, and red, little lips—Jimmy. He walked away from the holograph and held his small hands together. His joyful eyes stared up at the camera. He wore the silly T-shirt Gran Amália had given him that said *MOMMY'S FAVOURITE*. She remembered the day the holograph was taken at the local protected park they had gone out for a walk to do this holograph. Jimmy was looking up at Gracie, waiting for her to chase him.

Another holograph appeared. A young woman sitting with her back turned. She had beautiful, wavy, chestnut hair. It fanned out and came down her back in a thick, glossy sheath. The young woman was beautiful. She had a flawless, smooth complexion, full lips, and large, brown-amber eyes. The shock came and gripped

Gracie's chest as if the Vampyre creature's coils had seized and crushed her ribs. Sobs heaved through Gracie as her weakened eyes and mind comprehended who the beautiful young woman was. It was Gracie—what had been Gracie—on a day full of happiness ... who was in optimum health and completely free, with no fear of imminent danger of any kind.

In the holograph, Gracie leaned down to kiss Jimmy's face. Jeff entered the frame of the holograph. He sat next to Jimmy on the grass on the other side of him, a hand over Jimmy's back. Jeff smiled charmingly up at the drone, his eyes almost winking.

Another holograph followed. Jimmy stood alone. Looking around in a room Gracie didn't recognize. Where was that place? Jimmy's eyes were large, unsure, his face streaked with tears as if he had been crying for some time. Jimmy turned to the camera, and the holograph froze and zoomed in over the face, which was full of uncertainty.

Gracie looked at the discomfort inside Jimmy's eyes, not realizing that her meticulously controlled breathing had spilled out through her heaving chest and she had stood up with trembling legs and slid past the rows of the others. She reached toward the holograph and held out her hands to Jimmy's crying face, wanting to comfort him, hold him, do something, just do anything under a horrible sense of powerlessness. Why was he distressed? Where was that place? Her panicked voice called out to him behind the device.

Jimmy, I'm here. Mommy Gracie is here. I'll come to you. Tell me where you are?

The rush seized her more than she anticipated—a sense of deep, horrid loss and pain. The emotions unfurled and released themselves from her shaking body in an explosive rage. "Jimmy, where are you? I'm here!"

Her face distorted uncontrollably. Gracie's weak legs gave out from under her. She dropped to her knees, and her neck bulged as the torrent of screams gushed out of her, one after the other. She was lost under so much pain that nothing mattered. She didn't care how her screaming made the device grip at her throat. She didn't care about the partition rising behind her, pushing all the others behind it, and that she remained the only one, with those vile creatures hovering somewhere behind the wall.

She shoved her face against the slimy ground and clawed at the skin at the back of her neck, tearing the skin open and blood running down her broken fingernails. She screamed and screamed. Blood spurted out of her mouth as the device constricted tighter around her throat with each raging scream. She didn't care. Every scream rallied against these vile creatures—against the unfairness of everything ... the fact that she was robbed of her son, from Jeff, her friends, her home, her life and was placed here, living in this horror, a place she didn't deserve to be, and those vile creatures had no right to do this, to her or to any of them. Her own voice implored her, *Gracie, stop this madness*!

Gracie raged and punched madly—like a screeching, ferocious animal—at the slime-covered ground. She tore at it, ripped at it, and pulled at it until her fingers hurt and felt like they were going to break off. Pain shot throughout every inch of her body. Everything in her weak body was telling her to stop this—to remain still. Yet, there was nothing to stop this maniacal rage; it was freed and there was no end to it. She sat up and grabbed the device and threw it at the amber wall. The device bounced away and landed on the ground by her feet. The holograph of Jimmy floated above.

Why did I go out that night of all nights and left you alone to face so much horror and pain...

Gracie looked up to the dim ceiling through the glass, at the tiny specks of stars inside the palette of the vast space and let out a bestial scream. Her nostrils flared, her arms became rigid, and her bleeding hands pressed deep into her palms until her weak body could no longer stand the outrage and she collapsed into the stinking, petroleum-scented mush in a heap of bones, trembling and heavily sobbing, her forehead pressing against the hot gelatin. Spurts of blood continued to come up her throat and she coughed back on the device, barely being able to breathe, wheezing any air her fragile lungs forced her to get into them. The only comfort she had was that she would be dead soon.

It didn't take long for the breeze to fall over her trembling body and heaving shoulders.

The vile creature landed with a heavy thud in front of her. A soft humming sound came from it. A sound she had heard before. She opened her eyes. Its feet—lion-like paws—were the largest she had seen on any of the vile creatures. It had a golden, bright, amber colour speckled with fiery reds, sapphire blues, silvers, and white gold. It would crush her soon.

Yet, it remained there and waited.

Exhausted and barely able to move her body weakened by her outrage, she rolled halfway onto a side and looked up at it.

The vile creature extended large, coiled arms that sprouted from its sides. A small head formed on top, with two small holes mimicking a nose. In the centre of its body was Jimmy's face, with a smile, his eyes staring down at her. She blinked and struggled through shooting, agonizing pain to get onto her elbows. The vile creature's head came toward her, and the image of Jimmy fluttered faster inside the vile creature's chest. A handful of golden strands of hair appeared and rolled together, beaming in a swirling, fire white-gold vortex. In her deteriorating, sickly mind, she remembered the strands of hair that were taken from Jimmy's comb, so long ago by a much smaller creature. The strands of fire white-gold dissipated into tiny, fiery specks and moved throughout the rest of the creature's body.

What the hell are you? her eyes asked.

Arms reached out to her, but she had no strength to fight them off. The hot, moist, gelatin-like creature rested a side of its body against her and sunk into her as it wrapped its arms around her. It smelled of petroleum and the faint smell of iron. A heavy feeling swooned over her with a numbing sensation. Her physical pain was gone and all she could do was listen, listen to its intermittent humming.

A heartbeat, she thought in her deranged, intoxicated mind.

Little Jimmy's heartbeat!

She lifted up a hand and rested the back of it against the nape of the creature's formed neck. The warmth of its body was comforting and brought her back to the warm pool.

The girls and Ms. Coligan were waiting for her. Behind them, a holograph announced *Welcome to Iqaluit, Nunavut*, the World Junior Synchronized Swimming Championships. Gracie hadn't missed it. She was there. She was right there with the girls and Mrs. Coligan.

Out in the audience sat Mr. Singh, Gran Amália, and Evelyn, dressed in a peach, pale jacket and matching long skirt. Her hair was washed. Her nails were trimmed. She had a clear complexion. Her face wasn't pock-marked. Her eyes were alert, lips glossed in pink. Evelyn was there. She was there for Gracie. Finally. Gracie trembled against the warm, vibrating, humming creature and let her eyes close.

CHAPTER 12

The Captain

The device flashed. It and the others stood behind the wall watching the group of female humans. The images moved. The vile humans didn't stir. No reaction from them just like the thousands before them. An image of little Jimmy flashed. There was a reaction from a human in the far corner. It could see her shrivelling lungs move, trying to get more air, and her eyes fixated on the holograph of Jimmy. Lights, although much weaker, exploded throughout the little creature's body, and something broke in the human. She stood up as if in a trance, wanting to touch the image of Jimmy. Her face twisted, her arms flayed and pounded ...

There was no fear in her but immense anger. She screeched terribly loud, causing the others surrounding it to grow with great hunger in response to her sounds.

It moved closer to the screen. It could see the dull, near-lifeless eyes. And it was her. Mommy Gracie. Only she would react like this toward seeing the holograph of Jimmy. The device bounced off the screen, and Mommy Gracie's frail body slumped into a heap of protruding bones and skin.

The white strands of fire inside it reacted, and it hummed in response. Its body tingled with heat, and the fire moved in rapid succession. Its hums grew louder and louder. The others near it forgot their great hunger and recoiled, not understanding its reaction. She was barely alive and would expire soon. A heavy sensation entered it. It didn't want her dead. It wanted to take her away. It would take her away.

It was the captain.

It emerged from the wall, showing its power and that little Jimmy was inside it. She would remember who it was. It hummed and called out to her. She had no fear—just weakness and sickness. She remembered. She was cold to the touch—skin and bones, no softness, no warmth—and her body was ravaged under so much pain. It wanted her terrible pain to end. It would take her to a place that would bring her joy and comfort.

It was the captain.

PART THREE

≈

Revival

≈

Sleep that no pain can wake
Darkness that no day will break
A soul shines through the wind
Visions of pain, full of tears
To overcome a deluge of fears

—Terrence Wolfstad, 2028

CHAPTER 1

The Santo Cristo

Strong coils tightened around her body, and she could barely breathe. She swirled inside a powerful force of the wind that howled against her ears and contorted her body. She wasn't in any physical pain and couldn't feel much of anything except for terror raging through her mind. Pressure over her eyes. She couldn't open them if she wanted to. Sharp scents of petroleum assaulted her nostrils. Intermittent humming chirped against her ears. A hot, fleshy, gelatinous body wrapped itself around her, fully enclosing her up to her neck.

In the eye of her terrified mind, she plummeted downwards and dropped inside her bedroom. She sat underneath the window. A vibrating sound boomed behind it, and white lights flashed across it. Gracie stood up with trembling knees and took in the streets below. They cracked open, buildings swayed on their foundations as if made out of toothpicks, crushed into disintegrating pieces and clouds of dust in their final annihilation.

Gracie gripped her ears. The vibration sound was painful. She sat against the wall. Thick coils, black as licorice, moved over the tops of her legs. She frantically tried to pull them off. Sparks flew and her burnt fingers pulled back. The coils spread out in a thick sheet over her lap. At its centre, a pair of orange-green eyes, animal-like, glowed up at her.

"*Gracie*," said a low, coarse voice and hot air came from its invisible lips, brushing the tops of her ears, "*you will ruin its life as your mother ruined yours. You are broken inside. You know it. Everyone knows it. A quick drop from the rooftop garden will end it quickly for both you and Jimmy.*"

The voice was right. It was right.

"*Rose said the darkness would come for you. The darkness has always been with you. You will always feel like you don't belong. You will always feel like the small, insignificant, little cog left abandoned under a dusty pipe out of millions that make up a grandiose machine. You fight for things that you can never win. Give it up. Now is your chance. And Jimmy has the darkness inside him too. He's inherited it from you.*"

No, Gracie, don't listen. Fight it... You can. You're fine as you are. You aren't always alone. Being alone brings you more comfort than not. You don't need to belong. You are your own person. Don't let the darkness ruin you as it did to Evelyn. You can fight it for Jimmy. He deserves a chance to live and have his mother.

Laughter from the voice. "*A chance to live? And where is Jimmy now? He could've been spared all the pain, the tears, and fears you've placed inside his eyes and little heart when he faced death alone.*"

Gracie heaved into her chest, shut her eyes, and shook her head rigorously.

"I will not listen to you. I won't ... I won't ..."

"Gracie, *querida*, are you home?"

Gran Amália! The dark mass disintegrated inside Gracie. It curled inside her abdomen and inside her lungs.

Gran Amália stood in the kitchen with her back turned, stirring a pot of mint soup.

"The darkness," Gracie breathlessly said. "I have the darkness. It's inside me. It's telling me to hurt myself and to take Jimmy with me. I don't know what to do. Help me, Gran Amália. What do I do?"

Gran Amália turned around with a stoic expression on her face and her glasses at the bottom of her nose. Her large brown eyes penetrated Gracie's flushed face. "It's okay, *querida*," Gran Amália, calmly said. "It's going to be all right. I have a remedy that will remove the darkness."

Gran Amália took a spoon and scooped up some meat broth soup, which was tempered with mint leaves and soggy bread pieces. She blew air on it to cool it off and shoved the spoon inside Gracie's mouth.

"The *holy spirit* soup," Gran Amália said. "It will remove the darkness. Eat *querida*. Eat it all up."

Gran Amália shoved another spoonful and nodded reverently. "The *holy spirit* soup will cleanse you of the darkness."

Gracie shook her head. "It's still inside. I feel it moving, Gran Amália. It's hurting me. It's at the back of my neck. It's clawing toward my head. It's going to crack open my skull when it comes out."

"Then, drastic measures must be taken, *querida*," Gran Amália said assuredly. "Go to Him. He is the only one who has full power over it."

In one second, Gracie faced the Santo Cristo, whose porcelain arms began to metamorphose into flesh covered with blood and Jerusalem sand. The little statue creaked as it quickly rose, stretching outwards, and growing rapidly.

Panic gripped Gracie. She backed out of Gran Amália's bedroom, horrified, and scrambled into a hallway full of bright light. The kitchen and Gran Amália were gone.

"Gran Amália, where are you?"

Behind Gracie, the sound of two feet dropping to the floor startled her, and the whole floor let out a terrifying rumble. Gracie gripped the cracked walls and stumbled inside her bedroom. She slipped down the wall, listening to the rumbling storm of destruction continue to batter the exterior. She hugged her knees to her chest, quivering and feeling a tightening pain move around her throat.

Footsteps pounded down the hallway, and each step ruptured every tile as if they held enormous weight. The steps inched closer to the bedroom door until a shadow came underneath the door. The door should have automatically opened, but instead, it remained shut and began to crack and splinter apart, powder concrete blowing out from the sides of the doorway and into the room.

Gracie exasperated with fear shut her eyes and covered her head with trembling hands.

The door exploded open. Parts of flying wood fell into the room, a few nearly hitting Gracie. Within the clouds of white dust dissipating, stood the Santo Cristo, the size of a tall man, who looked down at her with sympathetic dark, brown eyes. He had typical Portuguese features given to him by Azorean hands, of olive skin and dark brown hair and a neatly trimmed beard that was caked over with blotches of blood, sand, and dirt. A luxurious red velvet cape was wrapped around his shoulders, untouched by the explosive particles of dust and wood. The cape was intricately designed with golden olive tree branches on each side of it, carefully hand-stitched with embroideries and precious jewellery. A thick gold rope hung from around his neck with a golden medallion that came down a thin chest. A beige tunic was tucked around his hips above bruised knees. His ankles were punctured with gaping holes.

Strands of long brown hair plastered against the sides of his face, soaked with blood that dripped from sharp pointed ends of the crown of thorns that pressed into his temples and across his forehead.

"What do you want from me?" Gracie's trembling voice asked the Santo Cristo. "Please leave me alone." Her hands shook, still covering her ears.

The heavy medallion around the Santo Cristo's chest moved to the side of the cape, revealing an open cavity with a large, glistening bloodied heart. A crown of thorns made out of white gold swirled around it. A flame of fire roared above it.

The Santo Cristo stretched out a hand toward Gracie's terrified face. Scorching heat emanated from the hand that didn't have any gaping holes in its centre. Deep wounds could be seen on each of his wrists.

The heat from his outstretched hand penetrated Gracie's nose and mouth with a hot powerful vibration. And something moved within her at once. The darkness had grown into a large lump at the back of her skull and moved into her throat. Gracie felt it growing inside her neck, causing it to hideously bulge. Some parts of the darkness that lay dormant inside her chest coagulated into thick licorice, forming another lump that joined the first.

The emerging pain was horrible. She desperately gripped at her bulging neck, trying to breathe, and frantically kicked and squirmed on the floor.

"Please stop!" she begged the Santo Cristo. "You're making it kill me!"

The Santo Cristo pulled his hand away, goading the darkness to come out of every pore of her body and from her mouth.

Blood. So much blood filled up her mouth. It spurted out from the corners of her mouth and down the sides of her face and neck.

"I'm going to die!" She cried to the Santo Cristo.

The licorice mass was plucked from her mouth, shimmering and coated and dripping in blood. It was a massive thing, the shape of an eggplant and weighing at least ten pounds. It was impossible for Gracie to have had that thing inside her.

Gracie collapsed against the wall, breathing heavily, relieved that the excruciating pain was gone. There was no more taste of blood inside her mouth.

The eggplant wiggled and screeched while under the grip of the Santo Cristo's power. Red fur grew on top of its wiggling body, covering large gills that gasped for air. A long snout formed on one end and three stumpy pairs of reptilian legs, each foot with three claws, sprouted along the sides of its body. The creature spun around slowly, its orange-green wolf eyes glowered over Gracie's terrified face. With one loud screech and desperate wiggling, the Santo Cristo directed the creature into the roaring flame above his heart. The fire grew and its flames quickly disintegrated the creature into nothing.

What was that sensation? Soothing, cool gelatin coated her throat. It filled up her chest.

Hums against her ears.

The scent of petroleum.

The Santo Cristo arranged his fingers into a peace symbol. In his right hand, swirling above it, in a quick vortex was a small globe.

A choir sang in her head...

He's got the whole world in his hands, he's got the whole wide world in his hands...

Walls disintegrated behind the Santo Cristo. Water filled up the room, engulfing Gracie until bubbles formed underneath her nose. The water didn't touch the Santo Cristo nor put out the fire above the heart. He rose upwards through the water as if flying. He didn't remove his soft eyes from hers and in a distinctive voice, told her, "Arise, Gracie."

Gracie lifted her arms to start swimming toward the Santo Cristo, but a burst of strong coils came through the wall behind her, gripped her down, and overpowered her.

"I can't!" She screamed to the Santo Cristo gurgling through the water. "I can't swim to you!"

The Santo Cristo kept a sympathetic look over her as he continued to flow farther upwards and into the shimmering rays of the sun. His voice urged her on.

"Swim Gracie. Keep on swimming. Swim right to the top."

CHAPTER 2

What the Heck...

Sounds of howling wind coursed against her ears. She descended fast, deeper into the watery abyss as if she were dropping through the air.

Her body jolted upwards and everything stopped. Every sensation drained out of her. There was silence. No smells. She felt nothing. She was dead. She had to be. She was still breathing fast, in wheezing successions. Behind her shut eyes was a dim light. Disappointment. She wasn't dead. She was still alive. Her ears searched where she was. No other sound but the pounding of her heart against her ears. Her back was moist. Something stuck to it. She lay down on her side over something flat. It was soft and familiar. Nothing crawled over her skin. Hunger and thirst returned, just not as severe. Wherever she was, it was set at a comfortable temperature and wasn't terribly humid. She breathed in dry air. There was no terrible smell in it. No chemicals; it wasn't laden with any substances. Just clean air. Her mouth was dry—not as parched as before. There was a numb ache inside her chest, and she had a mild headache.

What's happening? Why am I not dead?

She slowly opened her eyes, terrified by what she would see, either a scene full of the vile creatures hovering silently in front of her, waiting to pounce on her with their trunk-ends full of shiny pointy teeth, eager to tear into her flesh, rip it off her skeletal frame and drink her blood as she awoke or...

A dim light shone from behind the cloth of a beige lamp. The lamp curved into a dome like the cap of a mushroom. A beaded brass string dangled down its side. It sat on a glass round table. Her eyes darted around, adjusting to the shapes and shadows in the room. None of the shadows moved or crawled in a menacing stalk. The shapes in the room looked like furniture...

Furniture?

Her fingers pressed into the soft material under her. Blankets. She was lying on her side, over some kind of blanket on a ... bed? The thought was incredible ... *a bed?*

Her eyes moved upwards to the ceiling as they further adjusted to the surroundings. The room was decorated in white floral mouldings that looked like puffed meringue. Still, there were no dark menaces lurking about. The side she was lying on felt heavy. She got up, slowly and made little noise.

She sat up and held on to her chest as her lungs inhaled an agonizing deep breath. They ached as if they'd truly been burnt. She gasped for more air and looked down at her body. She was clothed in soft material—a blue satin robe. Between the slits of the robe, a lace gown came to her knees. The layers of amber grease, grime, dirt, scabs, and multitudes of bugs were gone from her legs and skin. They were clean and dry. She'd put on some weight, though nothing close to the weight she'd maintained on Earth. Her legs weren't skin and bones. It had some flesh to them, not much to form a curve to the calves but it had something.

Her fingernails, which had been cracked from terrible labour, dehydration, and poor nutrition, had grown out. They were short and clean. She shuddered, *What the heck is happening? I just wanted to be dead. Why didn't they kill me?*

The bed she was lying on had a quilt with a pattern of dark flowers that matched the pillows and additional throw pillows. The round glass-top bedside table had a matching floor-length ruffled skirt. There was a large dresser with an expansive mirror sitting on it. The dresser was against the wall facing the bed. A large cupboard or an armoire, Gran Amália had called it was on the other side of the bedroom. In front of the armoire was a chair made out of tiny braided rows of some kind of wood, the same material ancient baskets were made out of.

Am I hallucinating? Or is this some kind of purgatory?

Gracie touched her face. Her nose and lips were intact. Her lips were smooth and not chaffed. She put a finger inside her mouth. The device was gone. Her teeth were all there, and her tongue—it wasn't a coarse, dying, shrivelled piece of meat. She could move it, and it had some moisture under it. The insides of her cheeks, too. Her nose twitched, and the smell of petroleum was there, although she had to really smell it, as the scent had become more of a light undertone. There was still a pulling sensation of continued movement. She was on a ship of some kind.

Fear wanted to return, but she felt more exhausted and impatient than anything else.

Those things surely can't be far off. They'll come to get me soon enough. Oh, hell! Why didn't they just kill me? I should be dead and finally at peace. Those bastards kept me alive, with more horrible suffering to come. If I had a shred of luck, death would have ended this all.

A memory, the image of Jimmy fluttered inside that vile creature. It had her Jimmy inside it. It was mocking her. Or had it just been a terrible dream?

Gran Amália's voice suddenly rang in her head. "*Get up, querida. Only the dead can lie down all day and do nothing.*"

Gracie moved her legs off the bed and flinched when her feet tingled over the soft fibres of the beige carpet. It had been so long since her feet were on the dry ground instead of the fleshy, slippery pulsating ground of the alien ship. Gracie stumbled with the first steps and drew close to the dresser's mirror.

A very thin, pale girl, with prominent cheekbones looked back at her. Her hair had grown into a dark fuzz. A faint round mark like a light burn was at the bottom of her neck. Her large amber-brown eyes were the only things reminiscent of the woman she once had been before the abduction.

Gracie turned toward the door. Her skin prickled. Her fear increased.

Come on, Gracie, her fear whispered, *stay in the warm, dry bed; pull up the covers; and if those vile creatures come back, so be it.*

Gran Amália's voice wouldn't stand for it. "*You can't stay in this room all day and do nothing. You have to do something. Anything.*"

Gracie nodded to Gran Amália's voice. There was no point remaining in the room. Those vile creatures would find and kill her anyway. Hunger and thirst plagued her. Maybe there was something to drink and eat in this place.

Gracie expected the door to sense her approach and slide open. Yet, the door remained shut, unmoveable. It had a gold knob on it. It looked ancient.

Gracie came closer to it. No movement. She listened for any sounds behind it. Nothing. Her breathing trembled, and for the first time, her teeth clattered in her mouth. She reasoned with herself, *If those vile creatures are waiting for me behind the door, ready to snatch me up and finally give me what I've been wishing for, so be it.*

She steadied her shaking hands and turned the doorknob. Her inner voice encouraged her, all the while. *If they wanted you dead, they would have done it back in the death pit. There would have been no hesitation. They cleaned you up and dressed you instead. They want you alive.*

The door clicked open. Cool air fell over her face. She hadn't realized she was perspiring. There was an icy cold floor under her feet. Ceramic tiles. It was dark. No automatic lights came on. Digital and red, the number "1:23" was displayed on something about twenty feet away.

Gracie's eyes darted over the dim ceiling. No moving shadows. There was a row of switches on her right. Gracie had seen these in films from past centuries. A shaking, finger pressed over a few switches.

If those damn things wanted me dead, they would have killed me already, she kept on telling herself.

Lights came on, glaring in her eyes, which adjusted to the brightness after a few seconds. She stood in a spacious foyer covered in shiny, ceramic tiles. To the right was a kitchen. Gracie was stunned and exasperated.

What the heck, a kitchen?

It was a kitchen with rows of wooden cupboards, plain countertops, a beige two-door fridge, and an electric stove with a small appliance over it that displayed red digital numbers—seemingly a clock.

On the left side, the ceramic floor continued down a wide hallway with a few closed doors on either side. No vile creatures lurked about anywhere ... yet.

She pressed a finger over a few more light switches.

The lights went on past the kitchen and into the next room on the right side that looked like a dining and sunken living room area.

Her mind tried to understand. She was inside an ancient-style apartment.

Oh why, oh why am I not dead ...?

She shuffled into the kitchen. Soft hums came from the appliances. Two large storage freezers stood against the wall next to the kitchen, which connected to a small dining room area.

Large gloves hung from the back tiles of the kitchen wall. Every other tile had a rose in it, the colour of harvest brown, matching the wooden kitchen. A paper calendar with the month of May lay on the countertop with some kind of writing apparatus named magic marker, attached to it on a string.

There was a double sink with a chrome faucet. A glass was next to it. Her attention homed in on the glass and onto the faucet. Her breathing deepened.

Could the faucet actually produce water?

Gracie had dreamed of this moment for so long, under a constant scorched throat, an endless, desperate longing for water, that overrode all thoughts, even those of Jimmy—to have this incredible, precious, and vital commodity ... *water*.

There were no sensors, no sign of any robotic arms tucked into the countertop. The sink had two knobs—a red one for hot water and another blue one for cold. Gracie turned the blue knob.

At first, a gurgling sound, then a few drops of water or something transparent that looked like water came out of it. The drops became quick spurts and then flowed into a thin stream of clear liquid.

It's water ...

Gracie's dry eyes watched as if something magical was transforming before her. She took the glass in both of her trembling hands, not wanting to waste any more water and placed it under the nozzle. She filled it more than halfway and shut it off. She swirled the water in the glass for a second. Nothing assaulted the liquid. There were no bugs—and no odd colour. It was clear and had no scent. The tip of Gracie's finger touched the top of the water. It sparked chills through her body.

It was cold water!

She wanted to lose it. Her whole being came alive, and every ache and pain she felt was swiftly overpowered by the greed to drink many glasses of it.

Sip slowly. You might have difficulty swallowing.

Gracie held the glass tightly with both trembling hands and brought it to her lips. The cool water ignited her mouth into a beast that wanted to gulp down the whole glass of water in seconds. Yet, a stern voice kept her eager sips in control so she wouldn't choke. She didn't know how much damage the device had done to her throat. She chanted, "One Sip. Two. Three. Breathe out. Another Sip. Two. Three. Breathe out. Again ..."

She drank another glass of water in the same controlled fashion, and even though she could have drunk three or four more glasses, she stopped at two.

You don't want to get sick. You can drink in a few hours. That digital clock is working. It's now 1:27.

She put the glass on the counter and felt the cold liquid gurgling in her stomach as if entering old, rusty pipes that had been turned off for years and were getting used to processing water again. If the vile creature came for her now, she didn't care. She would die very happy.

Her attention turned to the yellow fridge.

If there was water in the faucet, could there be food in the fridge?

She grasped the fridge door with both of her weak hands. The door had a rubber substance that sucked it tightly shut. A small light turned on inside it. Its shelves were clean and empty. In the freezer compartment, an empty ice cube tray.

Check the cupboards.

Inside a cupboard, next to the stove, were rows of rectangular packages covered in aluminum foil. Gracie pulled out a few. Each package was marked in black letters and in English, Vegetables. Proteins. Polyphenols.

Being able to read anything in English, in her current environment was shocking. The packages had no other writing on them.

Gracie struggled to tear open the packets.

You need a slicer or scissors to open these packets. Kitchens have these kinds of tools—remember?

It had been so long since her mind thought of such things.

Right. Check the drawers.

Gracie opened a top drawer that organized each compartment into various pieces of cutlery. A pair of small scissors lay at the bottom of the organizer.

Gracie cut open three packages. Each bar inside the packages was similar in colour—a brownish speckled thing that was completely unappetizing—but the gnawing and ravenous hunger in her didn't care for looks and sought to be quickly satiated.

Gracie took a small bite of the vegetable bar. An over-powering rage awoke her senses, urging her to shove the rest of the bar in her mouth. She restrained herself and chewed. Her jaw ached in discomfort with each slow bite and her mouth tingled as if her saliva glands were struggling to work again. Her mind recalled flavours of mildly salted carrot, celery, parsley, and onion that seemed so foreign and distant to her memory and yet proved delicious at that moment. Her teeth shivered, and the urge to cry overwhelmed her. She couldn't produce any tears yet. Instead, her face instinctively scrunched up as if mimicking to cry, after swallowing each pleasurable bite. She filled up the glass halfway with water and got into an eating rhythm: small bite, chew slowly, face scrunch, sip water, chew slowly, swallow, and repeat. She did this with the two other packages until all that was left were empty aluminum packages. She sipped the remaining water and took three more packages of each flavour. She snipped off the tops and shoved them into the pockets of her robe.

I don't know when those vile creatures will return. If I wake up alive, I'll still have this amazing food.

She refilled another glass of water almost to the top and took the calendar. Then, she cautiously moved into the hallway. Her eyes darted ahead, around her, and down the hallway. No signs or sounds of the vile creatures. She pressed on the light switches, and the darkness rose behind her like a discomforting presence.

Gracie shut the bedroom door and placed the glass of water on the bedside table. She threw the calendar over the quilted bed and removed the stash of packages from her pockets. She hid the packages underneath the bed and lay back against the pillows. Her mind swarmed in confusion and fatigue. The questions that she didn't want to ask came to her mind, why was she here? What did the vile creatures or the one that brought her here, want?

She took the calendar. Her hands had never felt a paper calendar before. Her Android device scheduled everything for her. The paper felt smooth and slinky. Gracie uncapped the magic marker and turned the pages to the front cover of the calendar.

A cartoonish picture of a fluffy bear accompanied by bold blue letters, floated above it: *Snuggle. A fabric softener*. Someone or something had snipped out the bottom corner of it—perhaps the year? Gracie turned the page to the month of January with no year in it or anywhere else in the calendar. She held onto the marker that felt odd between her fingers and crossed in two shaky lines, the first day of the month with a red X. She placed the calendar on the glass table and pulled on the brass bead string.

She lay in the dim room with a sense of detached calm. Whatever those vile creatures wanted to do with her now, she was ready to die. She was no longer afraid.

Happy New Year, Jimmy, whatever year it is now.

The meal continued to digest inside her, causing her eyelids to close and her body to fall into a heavy sleep that offered her some temporary peace.

CHAPTER 3

The Arrival

A few hours later, she woke up with a start, leaving behind the sound of little girls laughing and phantom images of synchronized swimmers standing above her in a pool over the transparent glass, looking down at her, edging her to come up through the glass and join them. Their faces and bodies had been crumpled by smoke and fire until they were just skeletons standing, dripping, and gleaming with dark blood.

Gracie's wide eyes stared into the dimness of the room with a heavy dismay that she was still alive and not dead. She sat up and turned on the lamp. She was relieved to be alone. She got up and approached a two-door closet with wooden knobs.

Nothing jumped out at her from inside the closet. Instead, it was filled with rows of clothes packed together on hangers, some neatly folded and stacked atop built-in shelves. The clothes had bold colours and odd prints.

What the heck ...

1980s-styled jackets hung on hangers, some in tweed, others in bold colours, jutting outwards with soft shoulder padding. There were acid-washed jeans and shirts with company logos—names that Gracie never heard of. There were hanging rows of skirts of all lengths, dresses, stretch pants with stirrups, velour navy and dark-green one-piece jumpers, ruffled blouses, lace tops, and lace dresses with silk waistbands. Nylon bodysuits in many bold pastel colours were neatly arranged on some of the shelves. At the bottom of the closet were boxes of shoes, sandals and boots—coincidently in Gracie's size. She pulled out a few dresses and pants. They looked to be in Gracie's small size, before the abduction.

What the heck ...

Gracie's head swam. She closed the closet door without having taken anything. Water and food took precedence. She would leave her stash alone under the bed in case she wanted to snack at night. Night? When was night? It was never night or daytime. There was no sun to regulate her sleeping patterns or internal algorithms—just the numbers on the digital clock in the kitchen that kept track of time until it stopped functioning.

She took the glass in her hand and noticed the colourful cartoon figures on it—a frog, a pig, a fuzzy bear, an odd blue avian creature of some sort, and more. They sat in a two-storey open-air car with a sign in the front that read "The Great Muppet Caper" and another sign along the side "Happiness Hotel."

Happiness for her was to sip the remaining lukewarm water and get to the kitchen. She hesitated before she turned the doorknob of the bedroom and listened.

If those damn things wanted me dead, they would have killed me already.

She repeated her feeding schedule a few more times, making trips to the kitchen and back to the bedroom until bodily demands for a bathroom urged Gracie to further explore the left side of the complex.

Behind one door, was a small storage room with tiles and a sewage drain. It had an industrial sink with a hose attached to it and shelving with cleaning supplies, hanging brooms and mops, and an ancient AI vacuum cleaner. A small closet next to it had shelves filled with bedsheets, blankets, colourful towels of all sizes, and a pile of crochet dollies.

In front of these closets was what she was hoping to find a bathroom, only this one was spacious and designed mainly in pink. It had pink tiles, a pink bathtub, a shower curtain with a floral pattern, matching pink rugs, custom fitted around the base of the pink toilet, and a pink covering over the toilet lid which made Gracie wonder, who in their right mind would have rugs in a bathroom around a toilet, and cover a toilet lid with it.

On top of the pink toilet tank sat a tiny doll. She had shiny blond hair, black glass eyes, and a little hat with a pink satin ribbon tied on the side. She had a crocheted white skirt that covered a toilet roll under it.

What the heck ...

The pink countertop on the sink had a brass faucet. Underneath it were baskets filled with shampoos, conditioners, bars of soaps, hairpins, ribbons, combs, hairbrushes of all sizes, facial pads, toothpaste, mouthwashes, and moisturizers.

Inside the drawers were transparent packages of eye shadows—in sharp silvers, blues, lavenders, and beige. There were tubes of lip glosses—pinks, corals, and translucent hues. These were items Gracie hadn't seen on the market for at least a decade since the advent of subcutaneous makeup products.

In a bottom drawer: a hair dryer, a curling iron, and an electric shaver. Behind the glass cabinet: a first aid kit filled with boxes of various bandages, ointments, menstrual pads, and tampons.

The walls in the bathroom were painted the same pink with a floral border of flowers that matched the ones on the shower curtain and the bottoms of the hanging towels. The walls, the tiles, and every corner of the bathroom were meticulously constructed. There were no cracks or ruptures in any tile or corner.

The toilet flushed. It surprised Gracie for a second before she dismissed it. She dismissed any feelings the minute they arose. Perhaps the vile creatures were doing some odd experiment on her, learning to see her reaction to things.

The faucet, bathtub, and shower had water, both cold and hot. The water pressure in every faucet was strong.

What the heck ...

Gracie moved into the kitchen and tried to open one of the large freezer doors, but she was too weak to do so. The sunken large living room was fully carpeted in dark brown. A rectangular glass table rimmed in brass gold was in the centre. Beige, upholstered, elongated couches with seats the length of small beds adorned the right side of the wall, which was covered in thin slabs of wood. A solitary chair, which matched the upholstered couches, sat by the end of the glass table.

In the centre of the room was something Gracie had seen from films of the twentieth century: a television apparatus encased inside a walnut-oak dresser. Gold-plated letters shone over a few dark knobs that read RCA. TV. On top of it was an odd-looking AI, a black box of something. The name on it, in gold letters, read, Sharp 2600 VCR. Gracie followed the wires behind the VCR and found they were plugged into electrical outlets just like the ones in the kitchen appliances. Everything was powered. The creatures managed to recreate complete, functional living quarters with the right amount of gravity, temperature, and oxygen for her.

Panic.

But why?

Filling up brass shelves were things that looked like ancient paper books, encyclopedias, and rows of plastic hardcovers. Written along some of the spines of the plastic hardcovers were: *The Best Southern Cooking. Twenty-Minute Workouts. Learn American Sign Language Series. Martial Arts for Beginners.*

It was shocking to read things in English, and Gracie was at least grateful that whoever these items belonged to, English had been their primary language.

On the left side of the wall, another AI stood. This one was about four feet in height and had many knobs and buttons. Two speakers of the same size stood along each side. This AI was called Stereo HiFi. It was some kind of musical box or radio, as it had volume buttons, frequencies, and radio channels. Stationed on top was a round swiveling player like a turn table. This giant music box had two glass cupboards, with stacks of paper-thin coverings. Gracie knew what the coverings were. Gran Amália had owned a few of them.

Records.

Over the glass table in the centre of the room, heaps of magazines were laid out.

Harper's Bazaar. 1982.

Vogue. 1983.

Country House. 1985.

TV Guide. July 1986.

Gracie approached a line of paperback books on the shelves. It was amazing to see such relics. She'd grown up with holographic-digitalized books and network audiobooks. An actual book would have been extremely rare and fetch a hefty price when sold on the network.

Gracie picked out a paperback book entitled *Great Stories of Anton Chekov*, edited by David H. Greene. The little book was encased in a transparent plastic cover, and the pages were rimmed in a faded teal to match its cover. The pages had a smell to them, similar to the box of wood matches Gracie found in one of the kitchen drawers.

She sat in the upholstered, solitary chair and turned to the first page. She read it out loud, surprised to hear the sound of her voice after so long. It crackled a bit. With more reading out loud, her voice would get back to the strong voice she once used to have.

"Misery, to whom shall I tell my Grief?"

When she finished reading the story, she placed the book on top of the rectangular glass table.

"That was a very good story," Gracie said. "Touching." She leaned back in the chair and looked up at the beige lighting in the ceiling and addressed the main character in the story, "Mr. Iona Potapov. I'm going to tell you a story about Jimmy, my little son. He was almost two years old when I saw him last. Along with his daddy Jeff, we planned a vacation together for the coming summer and ..."

Her voice fell silent. She sat up. The tips of her fingers dug into the upholstery of the chair. Every cell in her body sparked with terror as she immediately sensed it. Her breathing shot up through her lungs, air quivering through her open mouth. Blood rushed to every surface of her skin. She scrambled to her feet. Deep in the near silence of the room came a low intermittent chirping-hum that instinctively belonged to a vile creature. It was distant at first, but it grew every second.

The voices in her head became a desperate torrent of demands.

Get to the bedroom and hide under the bed!

No! Stay put!

The back of the bedroom closet—lock yourself in and pile blankets over yourself!

It'll find you anyway. It has no eyes but it has some visual mechanism.

What use would it be to hide?

It's going to tear into your skull and screech out to its buddies to finish you off!

You should have eaten the canned pecans and molasses earlier today.

Pay attention!

She remained transfixed in the kitchen. Her body trembled. She was wild-eyed as she looked behind her down the hallway, then up at the ceiling. The digital clock read 3:49.

I can't even try to kill that thing. With what?

Kill it, Gracie? What a laugh.

To her relief, Gran Amália's voice came.

"*Stay calm, Gracie. Face it. Look right up at it. Don't fear it. If it wanted you dead, it would have done that a long time ago.*"

Gracie nodded and tried not to relieve herself. She held her arms tight against her sides. There was a tightening inside her lungs. She had to calm down.

That's right. Breathe. One. Two. Three. If it kills you, at least it'll be all over.

There was great comfort in those last remarks. There was nothing to lose anymore. She would fight it if she had to ...

The vile creature arrived from the corner of the hallway facing the kitchen. Gracie stood back, trembling, hearing her teeth chattering against each other. She tried to breathe steadily. Her eyes didn't dart away from it.

Its large amber body descended like melting caramel that condensed into a thicker substance and snapped upwards.

The sound of its hums vibrated through every cell in her body. She moved away from it until the sharp pain of the kitchen counter sunk against her back. The scent of sweet Kerosene was strong.

Oh my God, this thing is massive.

It's alone. There are no others.

I'm going to die, Gran Amália.

"*No, querida. If it wanted you dead, you would no longer be here. Hold still. Keep your eyes on it, try not to be afraid out of your mind.*"

The creature formed into a rectangular shape. Trunk arms sprouted out from the sides. A small rounded head formed from the top. Under the light of the kitchen, its amber colour flecked over with fiery golden sparks and a swirling of other glittering colours. If it wasn't such a terrifying, vile creature, it would be considered something fascinating and even beautiful to look at.

Arms dropped down its sides and then came toward Gracie, who was frozen in place, her ribcage rising and falling in fast but long breaths. Gracie wanted to close her eyes and detach herself from this situation as if she was observing from another Universe.

Meanwhile, Gran Amália's stern voice insisted, "*Look at it. Right at it!*"

Its trunk arms reached out to her shoulder and touched her. Its touch was light and ticklish, although Gracie's panic barely felt anything at all. It gave off light vibrations like an electrical current. Its texture was stern, smooth, and pliant. It moved its trunk arms over her collarbone to the top of her head, then down the sides of her legs, and pushed her toward it.

Gran Amália, it's going to stab me in the heart!

It could be curious.

It's waiting to strike.

If it wanted to strike you, it would have done so by now.

A trunk arm moved over her abdomen. Her hands blocked it, like a shield under it, following wherever the trunk arm touched her. There were too many trunk arms, though.

Another wrapped itself around her neck, and a few others around her waist and hips. Her body stiffened. Her legs resisted. But she was no match for the thing. She turned her face as it pushed her into its chest.

The smell of kerosene was strong, and the creature's hot skin vibrated and pulsated against her. Her terrified mind succumbed to an odd sensation that brought her inside a vision, looking at the glittering lights of a vast galaxy surrounding her. She floated toward a small twinkling light that was a planet, entering the dark, windy atmosphere, hovering above a gigantic black ocean with massive tides that glittered with multitudes of sparkling jewels throughout it. Chirping hums elevated against her ears. The creature's trunks held her tighter. She should have been terrified out of her mind, but instead, she began to feel comfort, safety, and the sensation of incredible happiness overpowering every other emotion that tried to rise within her. The creature was intoxicating her. Her mind grew groggy, she wanted to fall into a deep sleep, remain inside this strange warmth, comfort, and security of the creature's embrace. Then, it suddenly ended.

Trunk arms reached out behind her. A loud click and a bang. Something cracked open. The creature released her from its embrace. She felt the coolness of the apartment air fall over her face.

Returning to her senses, she scattered away from the creature and banged her back against the counter. The creature had unlocked one of the freezer doors and left a metal box on the counter.

The creature's hum rose. Gold specks swirled and came together in the centre of its chest. A vortex of golden strands of fire formed, and behind the strands of golden fire came to the image of Jimmy's face.

Gracie, mesmerized, fear watering out of her, reached out to it like a fool.

Jimmy ... my Jimmy ...

The creature hummed.

"Jimmy. Where is he? Do you know where he is? What happened to him?"

The creature shrank back inside the wall in a strong suction that pulled it through until it disappeared. Intermittent-chirp hums grew distant and then went completely silent. Gracie was left with heavy breathing, her heart pulsated in her ears and she collapsed onto the tile floor. She glanced over to the stove. 4:19.

It was here for almost thirty minutes. It held her for that long. It felt like five minutes at most.

The corner in the ceiling where the creature arrived and departed from, had no marks or residue to indicate anything massive emerged from there.

Relax Gracie. You're safe.

Tense muscles in her body relaxed. Her gown clung to her back like another layer of thick skin. Her arms and the right side of her body, which she'd been pressed against it, were clean. No residue was left, and nothing assaulted her. She ran her hands over her face and found that it was clean.

Whatever it intoxicated you with isn't permanent. It didn't harm you.

It went back to collect its buddies to finish you off.

Jimmy is inside it.

What does it want?

Gracie lay on the kitchen floor, her eyes shut for some time, her knees tucked into her chest and arms around them, feeling the shivering through her shoulders calm down.

The questions continued to roll through her head.

What is it planning to do?

Jimmy, my Jimmy!

Does it know anything about Jimmy?

Suddenly, Gran Amália's voice returned. "*Querida, do you know how much the electricity bills are going to cost if you just sit there and leave that freezer door open?*"

Gracie nodded to the voice.

Gran Amália, you're right. I've been sitting here long enough.

Gracie wiped her face and eyed the top of the metal box left on the counter. No sounds came from it. It wasn't sealed shut. The lid was larger and wider than the bottom part. Gracie carefully grabbed the end of the lid and flipped it off.

Seriously? It must have some sick sense of humour ...

A heap of lime-coloured fatty worms, swarmed over each other like larvae, covered in their pearlescent, syrupy texture. The disgusting smell of rotted beets and spoiled vegetables assaulted her nose. Gracie held her breath and shoved the box inside the freezer compartment in the fridge.

That takes care of that.

She turned toward the wide-open door of the freezer room and placed a chair in the entranceway.

It would suck if I got locked inside the freezer with no network to unlock the door. I'd die frozen stiff, surrounded by frozen food that I couldn't even sink my teeth into.

Despite the freezer door being modest, behind it, was an expansive room, stacked with hundreds of shelves filled with boxes. The boxes closest to Gracie were labelled in bold letters, *mixed vegetables, tropical fruit, grade-A beef meatballs, frozen eggs,* and *chicken nuggets.* She was getting cold and hungry. She took one bag of mixed vegetables, tropical fruit, and chicken nuggets. She placed them on the kitchen counter, and the freezer door clicked shut.

In a partial daze, she looked at the three bags of frozen food that she would be eating soon.

Chicken nuggets with vegetables and tropical fruits. I'm going to eat like the elite.

An uneasy feeling crept over her ...

But why?

"*Never mind, querida,*" Gran Amália said. "*Get a small pot and fill it halfway with water, boil one cup of the vegetables, one teaspoon of salt, 8 chicken nuggets on a baking sheet in the oven at 400 degrees for twenty-five minutes. Eat up. You might not have a chance ever again.*"

Gran Amália's last words didn't sound cold or like a prediction. Rather, they were a statement of steadfast warning. Gracie had no time to be amazed at the wonder, that she was in a kitchen finding pots and kitchen gadgets inside cupboards and drawers on an alien ship when just a short time ago, all she'd hoped to find was her own death.

CHAPTER 4

Getting Better

Strange. For creatures that caused so much destruction, they were easily frightened. It wanted to touch her. Feel her. Listen to her heart. It was one of the most beautiful hums she made. It wondered if wrapping itself around her would be like resting with the others, peaceful, safe, and happy. She was terrified. She quivered. Yet, she kept still. Blood coursed through her. The thumping shadow in the centre of her chest—the heart—contracted just as fast. Yet, a warm feeling came over it. Every fibre in its body reacted. It wanted to keep itself wrapped around her body for a very long time. It brought it to places it had seen, and her negative energies dissipated. It summoned the image of Jimmy.

She expressed another emotion, overriding fear and making her approach to touch it. Jimmy brought her courage. She had the inklings of a warrior—only, she didn't know it.

She was still full of bones and wasn't soft. Her body needed more nutrition, and inside the freezers lay more nutrition. When it had infused her with elixirs that repaired, healed, and gave her water, it was able to see her dreams. Odd and interesting dreams. It couldn't let her die even though the contamination inside it asked a pressing question: if she died on her own, would it still have these feelings of wanting to be with her, or would they be erased?

It read her journals ... how the death of a mother parent who had rarely been present in her life and never knowing a father had caused many emotional difficulties, as if it imprinted serious psychological damages in her, making it very difficult to overcome when she aged. Would similar negative feelings and energies arise inside it if she died?

These human emotions could affect its logical senses and put the master's cause and everyone else in great danger. None of its species had been contaminated with a human before, so it had nothing to compare its experiences to—nothing to help it predict the risks.

She almost did die. When it saw her heart weakening, blood slowly moving through organs, air leaving her lungs and her body struggling to breathe, negative energy filled it. It couldn't let her die. It wanted her to live. It worked hard to ensure she lived. The master was aware of its contamination—it wanting to be with her—but didn't seem to mind. It was to continue doing its work.

The contamination did allow it to experience a lot of feelings its own species didn't normally experience. It felt loneliness as Gracie described in her journals when she was surrounded by thousands of cheering humans inside a recreational pool centre. It felt the same loneliness when it was smothered and coiled around the thousands of warm bodies of the others, vibrating and humming safely and contently. Strange. All of these conflicting emotions. It would have to wait to be with Gracie again. It was very patient.

CHAPTER 5

Getting Busy

After the creature's visit and the fact that it didn't physically harm her, some of Gracie's trepidation waned. She was sure this wouldn't be the last visit from the creature. In the meantime, as Gracie crossed off days on her calendar, aluminum wrappers grew higher in the trash can, and she felt stronger. She could even open the freezer by herself.

A feeling of amazement rose in her for one second and then the fear—*but why?* lingered in her mind. She spent more time in the freezers to see what other frozen food was available to her. There were boxes full of all kinds of steaks, pork chops, and other cuts of meat. Gracie would have to figure out how much meat she should be eating. She hardly ate any meat in her previous life, as it was rare and very expensive.

Other boxes were filled with packages of chicken drumsticks, breasts, thighs, whole chickens, Cornish hens, and pieces of turkey. There were boxes of frozen fruits and vegetables, frozen milk, egg mixtures, and juices. It was difficult for Gracie's brain to fathom all of this incredible food. Some she had never heard of before. She would have to learn how to cook things.

The second freezer was filled with boxes of dessert and meat pies; cheesecakes; various kinds of ice creams; processed foods like pizza; french fries of all shapes and sizes and onions rolled in thick batter; boxes of seafood such as shrimp, scallops, and lobsters; and of frozen bread in various rolls and long sticks. There were cans of frozen juices of all varieties.

How the heck did this creature bring all of this food here? How long has it been here?

And the burning question that terrified her more than any other question ... *but why?*

What if the creature left her for good and never came back?

Not a chance. It will come back. It wants or needs something from me. I have to keep busy. Conform to a daily schedule. I can't live this new life, harassed by my own questions. I'll go insane. I have to keep busy.

Gran Amália's voice agreed. "*Querida, a life without work and purpose is a complete waste.*"

My mind isn't as foggy. I should learn how to use ancient AI. Let's start with this VCR and television first.

There was a manual on top of the Sharp 2600 VCR.

It's in English. We're going to do well. First step: press the POWER ON button ...

A small green light and a rolling sound came from within the machine.

Next, this television AI ... the nozzle, pull it out so it goes on.

Okay.

A blue light sparked in the centre of the television and turned fuzzy over the screen. A knob on the side read "volume." Gracie turned it to number five, and a sizzling sound came through its speakers.

Channel should be on number three. What's a channel? It must be this circular thing on the TV numbered from zero to ten. She turned it to number 3. This seems a bit complicated. Complication is good. It's much better than having to think about the creature and why it kept her alive and put her here.

Gracie learned inside the plastic covers were video cassette tapes that were extended parts of the Sharp 2600 VCR. Gracie pushed one of them inside the slot of the VCR as per the illustration in the manual.

Press play.

The sound of wheels churned. The screen on the TV sizzled with blue lines and then became clear. A generously muscled man appeared. Thick sunglasses covered his eyes; he had long wispy hair and a short beard; and he spun around in a pink and blue sequenced cape, with letters that spelled *Macho Man* over the back of the glittering gown. A heavy white feathered collar ran down the sides of the cape.

Gracie's ears tingled and her body felt heavy. She sat down on the edge of the chair facing the television and listened to the muscled man's voice entering the room ...

Ohhhhh yeah, Macho Man Randy Savage, Intercontinental Heavyweight Champion, who was in a state of shock when Ricky the Dragon Steamboat came back ... yeah ...

Gracie's brain registered her own state of shock ... a human voice. She was hearing a human voice that spoke English. How long has it been since Gracie had heard a human voice? The voice of the man, Macho Man, Randy Savage, was excitable with a raspy voice as if he struggled to breathe behind each word, but it was still a human voice, not a screech—not a terrifying hum or vibration. It was the sound of a human voice that formed words, although a bit strange, as she wasn't sure what an intercontinental heavyweight champion was—perhaps a boxer—but they were words spoken in English, reverberating here, inside this space, reaching her ears, making her nearly cry.

Gracie pressed the rewind button on the VCR until the cassette stopped. Then, she pressed "play." Some lines on the television set for a bit, and it cleared with a steady scene of thousands of people cheering, over three levels of a stadium, and the letters at the bottom of the screen appeared: *Pontiac Silverdome, Pontiac Michigan.* A ring in the centre. It wasn't a boxing match; it was a wrestling event.

Gracie sat there amazed and watched the program for twenty minutes.

I have to see the rest of this wrestling show another time. There are hundreds other cassettes. That's a lot of viewing time. Time is what I've got, isn't it?

She turned her attention to the door at the far end of the living room, nestled in an odd corner. It was like all other doors, off-white colour with a fake gold doorknob.

Gracie's body temperature dropped. Her hands started to sweat.

No need to panic. It's just a door to another room and nothing more.

Gracie approached and listened. No sounds. No movement behind it.

Just open it and get it over with. If that creature wanted you dead, it would have seen to that when it visited ...

She turned the knob and stood inside a colossal room. Three opulent chandeliers hung from high ceilings, spread out evenly.

Gracie pressed a few light switches on her right.

What the heck ...

A ballroom?

The temperature was much cooler inside this room. Gracie walked on slick, shiny hardwood floors. To her left, were four columns of full-length mirrored walls decorated with floral arches on top. They slid open to reveal hangers and compartments filled with multitudes of opulent ball gowns in sequence, satins, silks, velvet fabrics, faux feathers, and wools; fur coats and jackets of all lengths in a variety of colours; chiffon dresses; and military-style coats with crested gold buttons. On the top shelves were rows of boxed shoes next to pairs of boots, and slippers with glittering gems.

At the end of the last mirrored closet, were three compartment closets with glass windows. Behind each compartment were elaborate gowns that hung over wires that mimicked a human body. There were smaller display pods next to the dresses, with glittering jewels; gold and diamond necklaces; and bracelets with inlaid rubies and other jewels Gracie had never seen up close before.

In the last compartment was a Royal Crown on top of a pod. A faded red velvet cape that was now closer to orange, dotted with brown dots that once had been vibrant black, hung over a wire. A heavy gold scepter leaned against it. The crown glittered in sparkling colours that danced under pod lights along its walls, and it was almost as beautiful as the sparkling, fiery colours that swirled inside the creature.

The kaleidoscopic glitter of all the clothes and jewels overwhelmed her. She'd seen enough. She would have to revisit this place again and not think much about what this meant ... if it meant anything.

There was another section of the apartment that she hadn't explored yet—the other end.

Maybe it'll lead me back to Don Mills, Ontario, Canada.

At least her sense of humour was getting sharper.

Behind the door was a small foyer that led to another heavy metal door with a thick round glass window, which was too high for Gracie to look directly through.

Then the smell came ... the smell of that dark, inhumane place filled with chemicals, filth, and death. Gracie pinched her nose. If she had ever imagined that she was on a different ship, she was terribly wrong. The stench told her that she was still on the ship from Hell. Her shoulders started to tremble, and yet with an unspoken determination, she tip-toed to the metal door and tugged at the chrome handle. She yanked hard until her arms ached. The handle didn't move and was secured in place. Her relief was temporary.

Are you dense? You think that door will keep any of them out? It won't. They move through walls. You saw that creature easily get in here. Just get the hell out of here now.

She spun around and slammed the outer door shut. She leaned against the shut door, catching her breath, hands trembling uncontrollably, trying to shake off the horrible smell and everything dark and evil that it brought.

Never walk through this door ever again.

Gracie dragged a chair from the kitchen table and pushed it under the doorknob.

Still shaken, she took the portable record player and placed it over the glass table in the bedroom. She looked through the records and found the song that Gran Amália would sing to her after she woke up from a distressing nightmare.

She breathed out a few times before the record needle was steady in her hand to let it fall on the moving record. She turned off the lamp and lay in bed, blankets over her head, and listened to the scratchy sounds of the record player as the melody of a piano started.

She mouthed the song verses, hearing Gran Amália's voice in her head singing along ...

Peace is flowing like a river ...
Flowing out from you and me ...
Flowing out into the desert ...
Setting all the captives free ...

CHAPTER 6

Communication

Gracie filled the blender halfway with unfrozen milk, added one cup of frozen fruit, and one tablespoon of honey. Then, she closed the lid and pressed the frappé button.

The ancient appliances were actually quite simple to figure out. They didn't have many buttons to press or other complex features. They did their jobs just fine. No wonder there were no networks yet to do anything for those ancient people living during those times.

She filled the Great Muppet Caper glass in hand, then she sipped the sweet substance while reading some of the sprawled-out piles of 1980s magazines.

There were sixteen magazines in total. She read them twice, and this time, she would go through them again and circle words and phrases she wasn't familiar with.

"*What's your damage?*"

"*Don't have a cow.*"

"*Your mullet is looking choice today.*"

"Mullet?"

She circled it twice.

"Is that a type of food? I'm sure the encyclopedia will tell me what this mullet thing is."

The sound of approaching chirping hums. Gracie's body reacted immediately to it, and every cell inside her vibrated in terror and panic.

I can't continue to live in fear of it. I'm tired of this. If it wanted to kill you, it would have done it already. I have to communicate with it. If this creature could create an ancient apartment from the 1980s, complete with utilities, there has to be a way to communicate with it.

Her eyes turned to the ceiling, to the corner where it came from last time 3:49 on the digital clock.

She watched the creature descend from the same spot and waited for it to mutate, forming its head, mimicking a human face, and sprouting lion paws while multiple trunk arms flowed out of the sides of its body.

When it was fully formed, trunk arms reached for her, warm pulsating coils of its slinky smooth skin moved over her shoulders, down her collar bones, and over her legs. She held up her hands and arms to it.

"I know you won't hurt me."

Behind her, a trunk arm held onto a small metal box, which it dropped on the countertop. She kept her eyes on the humming creature, looking over the glittering, multi-coloured, fast-moving rivulets in its skin. The tip of its trunk arm flipped the lid and picked up three slithering worms. Lines of pearlescent slime fell from their wiggling bodies and hung in the air like syrupy strands. She wanted to turn her face in disgust, but curiosity kept her watching what the creature was going to do. It dropped the slithering worms with their syrupy lines into the blender.

"You want me to eat those things?" she asked it incredulously.

The creature hummed, and its trunk arms wiggled over her back, producing a ticklish sensation.

"Okay. Fine. I'll hit frappé and drink. There must be a good reason why you want me to eat these disgusting worms."

Once the worms completely disintegrated inside the drink, Gracie poured it into her glass.

"Cheers," she said and took one sip.

It didn't taste bad. The fruit mix and the honey did a good job of masking the fact that three wiggling lime worms with dark shrimp eyes and curled nails had been added to the mix. If Gracie really searched for a slight difference in the taste from before, it was the hint of beetroot.

"Is this good? Are you happy?"

The creature hummed, and two trunk arms shot out to coil around her waist.

Her hands sprung up as if the creature was putting her under arrest. She didn't hear the glass crash over the tiles, splattering cold liquid over her feet and legs. Her heart thumped wildly in her ears.

"That was just a joke. I'm sorry ..."

Trunk arms pushed her toward the centre of its body. She pressed her lips tightly together and turned her face away, not wanting to breathe in its kerosene scent.

A trunk arm lifted the broken glass and dropped it into the sink with a loud clank. Gracie managed to push away from its coils and stumbled into the living room, to the sprawling magazines over the table.

Try to communicate with it, Gracie.

The creature's coils inched toward her.

She took a notepad from amidst the magazines, and with the red marker, she scribbled out her name as best she could. She didn't know how to write, technically. Nobody in generations Beta or Gamma handwrote anything. They occasionally typed on devices and more often dictated commands into them. The only handwriting she came close to doing was scribbling the initials of her name over a device.

She tore the sheet of paper and held up the scribbles she made in round broken circles and a few lines.

This creature must be able to see.

Gracie pointed at herself and back to the image on the notepad.

Gracie Mercedes Pinto. That is my name.

The creature's trunk arms retracted back to itself.

Is it actually listening?

She pointed to herself and repeated, "Gracie."

"Do you understand?"

A low hum echoed from the creature.

"Okay, let's try this."

Gracie rummaged through the magazines and found a photo of Earth. She showed it to the creature.

"Earth. Home. What has happened to it?"

The creature's coils reached out for her, running over her eyes, nose, and the side of her face. She stepped away.

Fool. It can crush you in seconds.

At the back of the magazine was a Pet Corner page with a handsome cream-coloured Afghan hound—clearly a mother—sitting next to a woven basket with two of her puppies. She held up the photo to the creature.

"Dogs. Animals. This is a mother dog."

The creature didn't react, change its colour or the movements of its trunk arms.

Gracie pointed to one of the puppies.

"Puppy."

Gracie pointed to herself. "Mother. I am a mother. Puppies are babies of this mother. My baby is Jimmy. Do you know where Jimmy is?"

The creature reacted. The glittering colours swam faster inside it, gold specks shone brighter, in the centre of its chest, golden spirals of Jimmy's curls lit up in fire; and in its centre, the image of Jimmy appeared—the big ambiguous eyes, the little smile, the red rim of the collar of his T-shirt against the tiny neck.

Gracie drew back some breath.

What the heck ... it understood me.

She eagerly nodded at it.

"Yes. Jimmy. That's Jimmy. Do you know where he is?"

How is this creature going to answer?

The creature moved back to the place from which it had arrived. She followed it.

"If you understand me, please bring him to me. Is that why you have him inside you? Is that what you're trying to tell me?"

She pointed at Jimmy's image flashing.

"Please, find him. Bring him to me ... please."

She stood frozen in her spot as the last glittering piece of the creature's skin sunk through the ceiling and its hums faded into silence.

Gracie crumbled onto the cold tiles of the kitchen floor, exhausted by having so many emotions course through her—sheer terror, then courage, then desperate excitement, and now ... emptiness.

She stood up and noted the time. 3:49 arrived. 4:19 departed.

Seven days apart from the last time it visited. It arrived and departed at the same time. It's consistent.

CHAPTER 7

Where is Jimmy?

She looked different. Her hair had grown. Her body had put on more weight and muscle. She was less afraid. She hummed more slowly. She raised a paper with a funny picture that said her name. It already knew her name. Gracie Pinto. It was what everyone else called her except for Jimmy, who called her Mommy Gracie. She showed it photos of other species and objects. She was trying to communicate with it. It was already fluent in her primary language—English. It understood her completely. Communicating with Gracie would have to wait. It wanted her stronger and healthier—and for her to lose her fears of it.

As it came down toward her, her internal organs and blood were calmer. Her warrior heart was getting stronger. Her body was warmer and softer, and the hums she made were getting more refined.

"Jimmy? Do you know where he is?"

Of course, it knew where Jimmy was. Jimmy was inside it. Right there, in front of her ... in another form, but Jimmy was there. It flashed the image of Jimmy. Her heart hummed faster with another energy that tightened her organs and made her breaths shorter. She didn't understand. It didn't want to touch her under this excitable, negative energy. It retreated back to the wall. Her amber eyes glistened with tears, and blood pumped quickly through her veins. The humming sounds she made caused every cell in its body to churn in discomfort. It felt her emotional pain despite her physical body getting better. It would find her something to help ease some of this emotional pain that made her heart, eyes, and lungs react. Perhaps, it would help her become less fearful of it. It had an idea.

CHAPTER 8

A Surprise

Physical injuries in synchronized swimming included dislocated shoulders, broken hips, broken teeth, knee dislocations, and hip injuries. Gracie had been lucky; by the age of thirteen, her list of injuries wasn't that bad. They consisted of one-time events, a broken finger, pulled hamstrings, and a sprained ankle. The concussions happened twice. The second concussion at thirteen was a devastating one that removed her from competitive synchronized swimming. The incident happened so fast, during routine practice, less than five weeks before the Junior World Championships.

One of the girls—no one really knew who because being kicked in the head happened so often during fast-paced, powerful routines—knocked Gracie out, not with just a debilitating concussion but a misaligned vertebra, followed by a year full of relentless headaches, bouts of vertigo, mental fogginess, sleepless nights, and limited visual stimulation.

Not to mention the disappointment—something so important to her and along with it Gracie's sense of control being taken away. For most of her young life, she put in many hours of training, making great sacrifices, and she was so close to being an international champion with her team, representing Canada. All of these dreams were gone because of one misplaced kick. What was the point of having trained as a synchronized swimmer if the goal of standing on an international podium, would never come to fruition?

By the time she made a full recovery, she was approaching sixteen, and a new team was in place. Why was she having these dreams about those times? Hadn't she experienced happier occasions in her life, meeting Jeff, graduating from her engineering program, holding Jimmy right after he was born?

It was the brokenness. What would it take to finally mend it, if there was anything at all that could do it?

Thirteen-year-old Gracie lay in a hospital bed, a holograph behind her detailing numbers and images of her heart rate, blood pressure, breathing, and other functions. Mr. Singh sat on the right side of her.

"Gran Amália is coming in an hour to visit you," he said. "She's making a creamy potato and codfish bake, bean and collard soup, and pudding caramel flan, your favourite." Mr. Singh shrugged. "You know how she is; she doesn't want her Gracie to eat any mud soup and cat treats called hospital food."

Despite all of this attention, kindness, and love, the emptiness and the desire inside her couldn't be erased. On the left side of the bed, the two chairs were empty as if telling her...

They still chose the drugs over you. Your father's been dead for twelve years. Evelyn is lost and should be here. Mr. Singh is here. Gran Amália will be here soon.

She still longed for Evelyn to be there, and it was that endless hope that Gracie couldn't break off from.

Mr. Singh pointed to her left side.

She's here, look at her ...

"I don't want to. The last time I saw her two years ago, she was terribly beaten and emaciated; she had a heavily pockmarked face with sunken cheeks; and her hair was stringy and missing in some places. Who wants to see their mother like that?"

"It's going to be all right," Mr. Singh reassured her. "Go on, look at her ..."

In a bed next to Gracie, Evelyn slept, eyes closed on a face with a clear complexion. Her hands rested on top of each other over her chest. Dark brown hair fanned out over the pillows and in between them. She wore a white lace gown, surrounded by her belongings: street trash, rolled up papers, crunched-up cardboard boxes spotted over with pigeon excretions, ruptured plastic bags caked in mud, and empty vials—hundreds of them—by her feet, along with subcutaneous applicators. These were the only things she owned.

A shadow fell over Gracie. It was him. Gracie knew *what* he looked like. She found the article. A homicide. Shot dead. 2056, inside the slums in Toronto. He was tall and slim. Short dark hair. Dark olive complexion. Five o'clock shadow beard. Heavy eyebrows and his eyes, amber like hers, the only physical characteristic she inherited from him, the amber eyes. The expression in his eyes was considerate, pensive, and nothing dangerous as she assumed. He slumped against the wall, in a loose gabardine jacket and blue pants. He pulled out a cigarette from inside the jacket pocket and lit it.

"You shouldn't do that here, Kevin," Mr. Singh said.

Kevin Pinto. That was the name he went by. Dead at twenty-five years.

He kept his amber eyes on Gracie as he sucked on the cigarette.

"Tell him, Gracie," Mr. Singh said.

"Tell him what?"

"What do you want to say to him."

"I hate him. I hate her too."

"I don't think you really do."

"How do you know?"

"You would have woken yourself up from this dream or nightmare as you have done many times. Instead, you remain in it, quivering with emotions, wanting to see as much of them as you can, even though he's dead and she'll be dead soon. What do you really want to tell them?"

"They didn't fight to get better for me. We could have been a family—a complete family."

"Is that all? And why should they have fought for you? The only person that can fight for you is *you*, Gracie. Why keep on returning to them, looking for something they aren't capable of giving you but only letting you down? They themselves never cared to fight for themselves."

"Mr. Singh?"

"Yes?"

"I'm sorry to say this, but do you know that you are dead?"

Mr. Singh shrugged.

"That *is* the cycle of life, isn't it?"

"Mr. Singh, I saw you on the ship. You were here with me on the ship."

"Was I?"

"I'm sorry, Mr. Singh."

"For what?"

"Putting off chess and dinner with you. I should have come over. It would have made you happy. Now, I don't have that chance ..."

Mr. Singh took her hand in his. "Gracie, you weren't ready. Amália had passed away less than six months. Perhaps I was in the wrong to pressure you. It was too soon. It's all right. You don't need to worry about that again. It looks like a visitor has left something for you in the kitchen. Better wake up now."

She woke up with a start and scrambled off the bed. She entered the kitchen. Nothing dropped from the ceiling where the creature normally descended and there was no sound of any chirp-hums. However, sitting on the tile floor by the table were two cardboard boxes. One had a lid; the other did not.

She peeped over the box with no lid. A row of hardcover books—four of them. She read their titles along their spines.

Practical Techniques in Figure Skating.

"Sure. That will be quite practical in this place."

Best Stock Investments for 1986.

"I don't think an alien ship made it on that list."

Kings of the Iberian Peninsula: Fourteenth to Sixteenth Century.

"At least this could be an interesting read."

How to Become a Beekeeper.

"Out of luck with this one, too. No bees here or any bugs for that matter, and I'm definitely not complaining about that."

Scratching sounds from the other box distracted her. She remained calm and listened intently. The scratching stopped for a second and then started up again, faster.

Gracie grabbed a long spatula from the countertop.

"Whatever you are, you don't sound big."

With the tip of the spatula, she lifted the top flap of the box. The scratching stopped. It was replaced by a quick tapping sound against the box. She cautiously stretched out her neck and peered inside. Her eyes met a pair of rounded black eyes. Gracie lowered the spatula.

"What the heck …"

"A puppy here, in this godforsaken place?"

The puppy was about three months old, well fed by its mother, and kept clean, as its black fur shone with no signs of any bugs. It was a sturdy puppy, with a pair of floppy ears and a small white patch on its chest and over the tips of its paws. It sat patiently in the box, and its black tail with a white tip continued to thump against the box. It showed no signs of being distressed and wasn't afraid to see Gracie, something that it may have never seen before.

Gracie brought the puppy to her chest. It felt surreal to touch another living thing that was tangible, mammalian, made out of bone and muscle, and had an earthy scent that could only come from a puppy. The memory of Codie flashed in her mind. The puppy was male and its tail slapped against her arms. It snorted in excitement as it sank its black nose under her ear and gave eager licks. Gracie looked around the kitchen floor. No other boxes were left.

"Where's your mother and your siblings, huh?"

Gracie put the puppy on the tile floor, and it sniffed her legs and the other box.

The creature had understood her. She didn't ask for a puppy. It saw the dogs she had shown it and brought her one—not an Afghan puppy, but it brought her a dog. It was the same species, a mixed breed of some kind. Judging by the puppy's strong jaw, handsome nose, and muscular body, one of its parents had likely been a pit bull. The puppy was full of excitement, thrilled to grip at the tops of her socks with its small teeth, yanking them down.

"What should I name you?"

The puppy ignored her and tugged off one of her socks.

"How about Laika, the first dog in space? It was a girl dog, though."

The puppy shook the sock in a frenzy.

"Guess you don't mind."

Gracie brought the puppy into her arms, its tail thumping fast as it went back to licking the side of her neck.

"Laika didn't survive very long in space. It looks like you've been doing just fine, huh?"

Gracie looked into Laika's eyes.

Finally. A creature with a soul.

Laika made Gracie do one thing she hadn't done in such a long time ... smile. It almost hurt her face.

CHAPTER 9

A Breakthrough

The next couple of days, Gracie spent her energies on Laika, training him with simple commands and getting him to relieve himself in the storage room with the tiles and sewage drain. The hose attached to the industrial sink and the spray cleaning products helped her do a quick clean-up with liquids and scoop up anything substantial to flush down the toilet.

"*Cleanliness is next to godliness,*" sang Gran Amália's enthusiastic voice.

Yes, Gran Amália, I will keep everything hygienic. I will never take my health for granted.

Gracie wasn't sure when the creature would return. She almost wished it could tell her its schedule. She never slept soundly. If she managed to fall asleep, it was for only a few hours at a time, hounded by nightmares and terrified that one of those things would come for her while she slept and kill her. Did the other vile creatures even know she was in this section of the ship? How did this creature keep it from them? These were questions that nagged at her.

She spent most of her time watching ancient films from the 1980s and a few from the 1970s. She had the luxury of frozen, authentic food available to her; she learned how to cook, fry it, spice it, bake it, or boil it, using a thermometer for meats, reading carefully each step-by-step instruction in the Good Housekeeping Illustrated Cookbook. It was tiring for her mind at first. She spaced it out throughout the day. Kept to simple recipes—the ones with the least steps and illustrations—before graduating to higher-level ones.

On the left side of the outer bedroom door, in the hallway, stood a heavy punching bag on a boxing stand. Next to it, a half-door cupboard with two shelves containing a dozen board games, a pair of boxer gloves, and on the bottom shelf, an iron, stacks of unused paper, and an ancient writing apparatus, a Smith Corona typewriter.

As a pot roast, similar to Gran Amália's *Carne Assada*, simmered, Gracie watched Chuck Norris and Bruce Lee films. She put on the boxing gloves and practiced upper cuts, side punches, and kicks on the solid punching bag, just like they did. She completed the Chuck Norris Fitness System, the Martial Arts for Beginners, and combined it with twenty-minute workouts. She scheduled time to watch the American Sign Language video series and started to learn how to sign the alphabet with her fingers. All of this hand coordination brought back some familiarity to her brain. It wasn't synchronized swimming, but boxing and the martial arts exercises were fast and powerful movements, and she felt her body muscles begin to develop. She was careful not to overexert herself. She paid close attention to any aches or pain, as there was no network standing beside her, with a hologram showing data of her breathing and muscle exertions, telling her to take it easy.

She found plastic sheets of paper called stencils and with a pencil, she practiced printing each letter by tracing each letter shape over a transparent paper until rows filled up and her finger muscles ached.

She did miss the network. She couldn't deny that. Her hands and fingers tired out fast when she began to write daily journals in notebooks. With her Android device, she filled up many journal pages in minutes as she dictated to it.

At least she wasn't alone. She had Laika, who she ate meals with, and with his puppy energy, enjoyed runs with Gracie in the ballroom. She wrapped a pair of socks in a knotted ball and would throw it across the spacious ballroom, so Laika could expend more energy, retrieve it and bring it back to her.

Although Gracie grew physically stronger and healthier every day, her mental well-being was a challenge.

Gloom and doom crept into her mind when she wasn't occupied. She chastised herself in the beginning. How lucky she was to be alive when others perished, subjected to harsh cruelties. How lucky she was that this creature kept her alive, although she still didn't know why, and she was surrounded with luxuries—water, food, and living quarters of an ancient time that were fully functional, replete with entertainment, books, videos, and music—excellent classics.

Aside from often thinking about Jimmy, still with hope that he lived, her mind wandered over other losses. She thought of Tatou and Natasha, killed the night of her capture, of Mr. Singh ... promising to meet with him in a few weeks—a promise never kept—and of coworkers at the plant, who told her numerous stories about their families, how they grew up, and the frustrations and triumphs in their lives. She would never have the chance to tell them how much she liked listening to their stories and thank them for sharing them.

She thought of the other people that made an impression on her during a time she never paused to think much about but now did being completely alone. A stronger sense of appreciation for them and their memories crawled out of her subconscious. Gracie thought of Jessie, the talented young artist who layered Gracie and Gran Amália's hair; Mr. Cortez, whose flower shop provided beautiful flower arrangements for Gran Amália's Santo Cristo altar, and Ms. Wong, who delivered their groceries every two weeks ... all of their lives snubbed away. Nothing left of them.

There was Rose, who still brought dark feelings inside Gracie. In this new world of terror, death, destruction, and chaos, Rose would have been hysterical and wretched. Or she would have been in denial of the horrors—a denial she had mastered toward others not wanting to see their own suffering and dying.

Still, Gracie hoped more out of desperation than benevolence, that Rose survived, took Jimmy, and got out of the city, although Gracie wasn't sure if they would be better off. Gracie had to keep this hope that they survived. She just had to ...

And there was Jeff … his smooth face, charming smile, bright eyes, and enthusiasm. The gentle feel of his hands running along her arms, down her back ... his lips over hers, the silk of his hair brushing against her closed eyelids ... their cheeks sinking against each other ... breathing in scents of his cologne—spice and musk—and the feel of his warm, smooth, chest pressed against her soft breasts. She hoped the city of Whitehorse was spared and he had survived.

She was snapped out of her thoughts by the sound of the approaching chirp-hum. She sat up from the couch. 3:49.

Laika sensed the creature's arrival and jumped from his bed, which was a plush pillow covered with blankets in the entranceway to the kitchen. Laika ran up to the corner the creature arrived from and sat down attentively.

Gracie had no time to grab Laika as the creature descended in a fast-moving pool of glittering amber and colours, quickly solidifying into its regular shape. Laika moved a few feet away. His nose moved with a partially raised tail. He didn't bark or growl, seeming more interested in the creature's scent than anything else.

The creature formed its usual long trunk arms. Laika approached one and sniffed it. His tail wagged.

Gracie exhaled.

If Laika isn't afraid of this creature, then maybe it's all right ...

Trunk arms reached for Gracie. She moved away and entered the living room when a thought came to her. She pulled out the board game Scrabble from the cupboard closet in the hallway.

"Let's play a game," she told the creature.

The creature didn't react. It remained still under a steady chirp-hum.

She laid out the letters on the board, trying to keep her hands from shaking. She spelled ... G-R-A-C-I-E.

"Gracie." She told the creature and pointed to herself.

This creature could build a 1980s replica apartment; it surely must know language.

Trunk arms coiled around her shoulders, vibrating and ticklish. Gracie kept on with this game of spelling for ten minutes, her fear merging into desperation for answers.

"Where is my son, Jimmy?"

Would the creature even tell her if Jimmy was on the ship?

The creature's trunk arms pulled her into its warm, pulsating flesh. Her skin began to prickle over with a euphoric sensation; quick heartbeats slowed down, and her knees grew weak. She nearly lost her balance, but the creature's coils held her firmly. Her mind swirled in dizziness; the sensations of comfort, belonging, and security pulsated inside the warmth of the creature's body against her. Its hums matched the same rhythm of her heartbeats.

Where was this euphoria coming from? It was intense, goaded on by an adrenalin rush of excitement similar to when the team had won the Junior Canadian Championships.

Her voice warned her, *pull away from it. It's poisoning you. That's what it's doing. It smells like chlorine. It's poisoning you. Don't be fooled.*

Gracie's arms trembled as she reluctantly withdrew from the creature.

The cool temperature of the apartment evaporated the dampness on her face, and she leaned back against the kitchen counter.

"Why do you keep me here?" she asked as the euphoria drained out of her. "Am I safe? Do the others know? I can't sleep soundly without knowing that I am safe."

Something cold pressed into her leg. Laika removed its nose and looked up at her with concern in his eyes.

A trunk arm reached out to the board and moved letters around, making some of them fall onto the brown carpet.

Gracie bent down to pick up the letters and placed them in the box when in the centre of the board were the words, *Yes. Safe. They do not know.*

She stared at the letters, neatly placed in the centre of the board and tightly together. Other letters were thrown around the corners, off the board, and onto the table. The message was clear and couldn't have possibly been a matter of happenstance. The blocks of letters were put together, deliberately and it answered her question.

Filled with incredulity as opposed to fear, she looked over the creature's head. The cynical voice in her arrived. *This thing is fooling you. You're never safe from them. It's keeping you alive for some purpose, and whatever it is, it's not going to have a positive outcome for you.*

The creature hummed and moved its trunk arms over her shoulders. She shuddered at the glimpse of rows of dormant teeth lying flat behind the rims.

"Do you have a name or something like a name?"

Trunk arms moved over the board. She watched intensely as the letters swished around. The trunks moved from the board and coiled around her shoulders and waist. She drew back the trunk arms to the board as if gesturing to a young child, to focus.

"If you don't have a name, I'll give you one."

Gracie moved the letters around the board, emulating what the creature had done, and let the letters merge.

Before she could even question herself why she would choose such a name, she stood back from the board and pointed to each of the letters.

A-M-I-G-O.

"Amigo, that is your name."

The creature's trunk arms moved over the board and mixed the letters.

"You don't like your name?"

Trunk arms moved over the board and spelled ...

"Amigo. A nice name."

Gracie's heart raced. It can communicate.

This human killer is playing with you—as a cat does with a mouse ...

"You understand me?" There was no hiding the quiver behind her words.

Trunk arms moved over the board again.

"Yes."

Gracie, breathe. One. Two. Three.

"Are you that tiny creature I met a long time ago?"

Letters moved under the tip of its trunk.

"Yes."

"Jimmy, my child ... do you know where Jimmy is?"

A trunk arm pushed a question mark to the centre of the board.

"Is Jimmy here on the ship?"

"Yes."

She clasped her hands over her face.

"Can you bring him to me? Is he safe?"

"Jimmy is here."

Amigo showed her Jimmy's image over its chest.

It's toying with you, her cynical voice said.

"What about the actual human child, Jimmy, my little son?"

The question mark was shoved again.

"Earth. Is anyone or anything left?"

The swishing of letters ...

"Earth exists. We are far away."

"Why did you come to Earth?"

"An important mission."

"What kind of important mission? Who sent you?"

"Seek and you shall find Him."

"What does that mean? I don't understand."

"You do know. Seek inside."

Trunk arms moved letters over the board.

"The master."

"Who is your master?"

Trunk arms slid to the underside of the round wood table and a few others reached over her head. She flinched, and let the trunks run down her arms, over the chair behind her, playfully, as if purposely evading her questions.

Desperate for answers, she gripped the ends of two trunk arms, not caring if she felt the outline of the rows of teeth through the gelatinous skin and brought them back over the board.

"What do you want from me?"

"Stay here."

The rivulets in its skin spun quicker, and its colours sparkled.

"What type of species are you exactly?"

"A complex one. A simple one. A better one."

"Okay. How long will I be kept here?"

"Some time."

Trunk arms effortlessly lifted up the kitchen table a few inches from the floor. Laika ran up to the table, sniffed it, and started to hop around playfully.

The table dropped with a heavy thud, scattering the letters off the board and table. Amigo's trunk arms coiled around Gracie and tried to push her against it. Gracie held onto the coils and didn't move.

You're crazy. It's going to crush you in a few seconds.

Amigo's trunks uncoiled from her and sank inside its body. Amigo moved upwards toward the ceiling.

"Where are you going? It's only 4:14. We have five minutes left." She grabbed at its' side. The skin was scalding hot, and she jerked back.

You fool. Don't forget what this creature is. It can poison you.

The rivulets in Amigo's skin moved faster, to show her in the centre of its body, the golden spirals of Jimmy's curls swirling in golden firelight. In its centre was the image of Jimmy.

Amigo remained in that position until the digital clock turned to 4:19, then moved up the wall and disappeared.

Laika sat by her legs and watched, not perturbed by the events that just unfolded.

An uncapped red marker rolled over the centre of the board. To the right of the board was the notepad Gracie used to practice her printing. In red bold letters, which Gracie didn't write, were the words "*a new start.*"

CHAPTER 10

Answers

Two days had passed since Amigo's last visit. She wasn't sure if Amigo would be coming that day—the third day or on the seventh day as last time. For now, she had to keep her mind off Amigo. She opened the book *Kings of the Iberian Peninsula: Fourteenth to Sixteenth Century* and read the next Iberian Royal.

King Sebastian of Portugal

King Sebastian was born on January 20, 1554. His father, João Manuel, the Prince of Portugal, died two weeks before his birth. His mother was the Princess Joanna of Austria. King Sebastian was described as tall, slim, and very strong. He grew into a fearless, ambitious, and arrogant king. Was a huge enthusiast of martial arts and war and he sought nothing else but to gain glory for his kingdom by conquering most of Northern Africa and—what the crusaders failed to do—return Jerusalem to Christian control.

In 1576, Abu Abdullah Mohammed II Saadi lost his Moroccan throne and fled to Portugal where he met with King Sebastian and asked for his help to defeat his Turkish-backed uncle and rival, Abu Marwan Abd al-Malik I Saadi.

On August 4, 1578, King Sebastian set sail for Morocco and marched his army under extreme heat and Sun at Alcácer Quibir, where he suffered a crushing defeat. King Sebastian was lost during the battle and was last seen riding headlong into enemy lines. His body was never found. He had no heirs for the Portuguese throne, and this led to the accession of Felipe II. Portugal thus lost their independence and remained under Spanish domination for the next sixty years.

Gracie turned the page to Cristóvão de Morais painting of King Sebastian.

Not a bad-looking face. Very fair. Oddly full lips. Long, slender fingers decorated with black diamond rings—I've seen a few of them in the ballroom jewellery case. I have to take another look. Your bluish-green eyes certainly are intense.

Gracie closed the book and sat up. 3:49 and immediately the chirp-hums arrived. Her heart raced for a minute.

It's back to three days. And still punctual.

Gracie stood by the Smith Corona typewriter she had earlier placed on the kitchen table with a stack of paper beside it.

"If it can create a 1980s apartment, I'm sure it knows how to type on one of these things. Wonder where the paper goes? I really do miss Arabella."

A trunk arm came from behind and rolled a page of paper into the typewriter. A bell chimed.

"First, let's have a conversation. Can you tell me who is this master? Is the master something like you?"

Gracie held her breath and watched the tips of two trunk arms form a one-inch pointer at the ends. They moved over the typewriter keys, and in a flutter of seconds, Amigo responded ...

The master is nothing like us. The master is more powerful than the Sun, the Universe, and all things the master created.

Gracie stared over the neatly typed letters that ran across the top lines of the paper. "Does this master have an actual name?"

A flutter over the keys.

The master is infinite. Reigns overall. Submits to no one. Is wondrous, and beyond comprehension.

The words sounded familiar. She had heard them before ...

Gracie looked over Amigo's indented spots—where its eyes should have been—and the two punctured dots in the centre of its small head for some kind of breathing mechanism, only assuming that it breathed at all. The rivulets of its skin moved with sparkling ruby-red, blue-sapphire, and white-gold sparkles that swirled through glittering amber syrup.

"Is the master God? Or something like God?"

Yes.

"God sent you to massacre everyone on Earth?"

Not everyone. You are here.

"I saw the city I lived in before my capture. It was flattened in seconds. Millions of people were killed. There were innocents ..."

Most weren't innocent.

"My little son—if he died in that massacre, he was innocent."

The innocent souls kept others alive. They are the ones who pleaded for the master's mercy and He has provided it.

"I don't understand this."

Gracie! her inner voice intervened, *you're debating with a human killer. You saw what it could do. It's lying and deceiving.*

A flutter of keys under the points of its trunks. It typed within seconds half a page.

Humans have created incredible things on Earth and around space. They did not command the formation of the Universe, nor plant the seeds on millions of planets for many forms of life to evolve, nor did humans create the dwelling of light and powerful energies that would reduce humans to particles beyond what the human eye could see. Humans are in no position to scrutinize the master, how to run His planet, His Earth that He has deemed the most beautiful of all His planets. The master is the master of all. He submits to nothing. Everything submits to Him.

Amigo ripped out the paper and rolled in a fresh page. A flutter of keys followed.

Come close. You are safe.

"Would you hurt me?"

I can't seem to. I won't.

"You've tried?" Fear crawled up her neck.

I can't harm you. The contamination. It's inside my cellular structure, DNA, genetic sequences, what you humans call it. Part of Jimmy lives in me. I see him. I hear him. There's a strong pull toward you, which is the same as I have with my own species. I want to be with you.

Gracie took this in.

"You don't know my Jimmy and what do you mean you want to be with me?"

I feel intense warmth for a parent. It's not sexual.

Gracie let out a breath.

"Are you a male or female or ..."

Asexual species. United as one.

"Do you live long?"

What you really want to ask, Gracie, is how they die or what can kill it?

Gracie rolled her eyes as Amigo typed. *Right, and I'm sure Amigo would tell me,* Gracie thought.

We have one offspring during our thousand years of life.

"You live to a thousand years?"

Some less, others a bit longer. My parent lived for 1,200 years before I was born.

"Where is your parent now?"

Dead. We die shortly after we birth. The offspring ingests some of the parent's nervous system and skin as their first food, helping them to form cells. If the parent had a propensity for curiosity, they would pass on those structures to the young before they die. It's what we do.

"Are you bound by the laws of nature?"

We are bound to an extent by some of these laws of nature. We aren't fully defined by them either.

Gracie, that doesn't make any sense ...

"Can you be more specific?"

We are a very complex species. I don't want to continue to type. I want to curl around you and hold you. It's what we do.

Amigo's trunk arms shot out and wrapped themselves around her shoulders. She flinched, and her hands shot up to protect her face.

"Just a few more questions, have you seen this God, your master?"

Amigo kept his trunk arms around her while two others typed.

`Yes.`

"Has the master seen our suffering, the deaths, horrors, the cries that couldn't be screamed because of that thing lodged down our throats?

`"Yes, the master is aware of everything."`

"Why didn't He stop it?"

Amigo's trunk arms released her.

And a flutter of typing followed.

Are you insane? Don't piss him off; you're playing Russian roulette with this human killer.

Why should He? Your species has murdered much more of you in so many wars and countless other creatures on your Earth, so much more than the master could ever catch up to. Most of you have ignored, ridiculed, and convinced yourselves that He doesn't even exist.

"Amigo, my son was innocent; all those people killed, murdered, tortured, even eaten ... and what about the woman with the newborn baby eaten alive? Doesn't this God have mercy? Isn't He loving, kind, and fair? How can He be those benign things when He commanded the murder of those innocents?"

Gracie watched sentence after sentence run over each line across a new sheet of paper as Amigo typed.

The master did not command the murder of the woman and newborn. That shouldn't have happened. They were both innocent. The others who were maimed, torn apart, and eaten were not innocent.

Believe nothing of what you hear and only half of what you see.

Gracie, this human killer is throwing information at you that it took from your device, in your journals, sayings Gran Amália would tell you ...

Amigo continued to type. It was 4:06.

The devices in your throats were marked where we could see who were the evildoers and those that were marked as innocents, although they weren't completely innocent but they were not evildoers. The evildoers are the unrepentant murderers; rapists; killers of children, animals, the infirmed, and the elderly—violent, sadistic abusers who thrive on the deliberate death and horrific suffering of others. The cries of the innocents reached the master. This time, He gave us permission to do what we wanted with these evildoers. A few innocents died, yes, including the ones who fell to the darkness, giving up and losing themselves upon facing their despair.

"They killed themselves because they suffered from severe hunger and thirst! We were being tortured with no reprieve."

Mistakes were made. Many didn't want to learn about your species. Just wanted to kill the evildoers. I wanted to learn because I was contaminated with a part of you, so I wanted to learn more about humans. Not enough nourishment and water were given to the humans. I rectified it and atoned for it. The master has forgiven me.

Why would the master forgive you for those mistakes?

For once the typewriter keys didn't move or flutter. All that followed were the sounds of Amigo's hums in her ears, slow and careful.

Does your species have a rank of some kind? Do you have a rank on this ship?

The tips of Amigo's trunks positioned back over the keys and typed ...

`I am a servant of the master.`

Typing ...

`I am the captain.`

"You are the captain of this ship?"

Faster typing.

`Captain of this ship. Servant of the master. I serve the master, above all.`

"Was your parent the captain of this ship before you?"

`Yes.`

"Your parent brought this ship to Earth, destroyed the place where I lived, killed my friends, possibly my son, my grandmother, my neighbours, and coworkers, and took me?"

`Yes.`

It was a sickening feeling. She sat down on the recliner. This was worse than seeing another vile creature. Those ones were vile, but they didn't have a parent who killed her own—everything she had known and brought here to suffer horrors ...

Gracie, are you kidding yourself? This human killer could be making all of this nonsense up. It's entertaining itself, getting off on your reaction to it.

Gracie was deep in her thoughts and didn't hear the keys clacking away. She didn't want to read anymore.

Go on and ask it how many humans this human killer has skinned alive, torn apart, and eaten.

Amigo pulled out the sheet of paper and let it fall over her lap.

You were marked as being one of the very few innocents. Not an evildoer.

"Is that supposed to make me feel better?"

She threw the paper away and stood over the kitchen table. "Have you killed any humans or eaten any?"

She drew in her breath as Amigo typed.

The smell of human blood, flesh, and extremities is repulsive. I stopped the killing of humans, as the number of evildoers has gone down. A very few of them, humbled by great suffering, turned their hopes back to the master. They are kept alive along with others as labourers.

Sure, if you can believe whatever this human killer tells you ...

"Labourers for what purpose?"

To full fill the master's plan.

"*What is the master's plan?*"

I can't tell you.

How convenient. It can't tell you. It's toying with you, Gracie. You know it's toying with you.

"What do you eat then?"

We have our own nourishment on the ship. Not humans. This was an acquired taste. As I said, they are no longer consumed.

"Is your master really God?"

Gracie was startled by the sudden flurry of typing across rows and rows of lines.

The master has made Himself present not just to humans, to our species, and to thousands of other intelligent species created in His vast galaxies. It has been humans and a few other species that turned from Him. He's come to regret creating humans, who in the beginning, He hoped would be His most esteemed creation but instead have been the weakest, proven to easily succumb to the forces of evil. You have sensed it. Seen it multiple times. Felt it. The darkness.

You don't know what this human killer's intentions are. Keep to practical questions.

"What will happen to me? Can you bring me back to Earth? Is it safe to return?"

It's not time yet. We must wait.

"Wait for what?"

I can't say.

"How do you keep the others away from this place? Keep them from finding me?"

They don't wander around the ship. They have tasks to do and are assigned to positions and leave their positions only to rest together, united as one, in a designated area, away from this part of the ship. The captain is the only one who roams and has access to all areas of the ship. That is our way. You can sleep soundly; you are safe.

Gracie wanted to believe Amigo, but her cynical voice was adamant. *You are crazy to believe it. It's still toying with you.*

"Where do you go on the ship when you rest with the others?"

Far. At the bottom of the ship.

"Will I ever return to Earth?" she pressed.

I can't say.

"Is there enough water and food to keep me here that long?"

`For a very long time. I will take care of it.`

At least this part of the conversation was somewhat comforting.

Amigo's hums turned into a higher-pitched chirping sound. 4:59. Almost a half hour over time.

Flashing in the centre of its massive chest Jimmy's image.

"Jimmy, my little Jimmy," tears filled her eyes. Amigo didn't embrace her or reach out for her. It drew back up to the corner it had descended from and disappeared.

CHAPTER 11

Silenced

A strange feeling inside it. It found the word for it. Regret. It was being careless. It had revealed too much. It could be endangering the mission and betraying all of them and the master. The master was everything to it. It was its life source. It didn't betray the master. She was beyond wanting to believe anyway. Its mission wasn't to convince her either. They had received the master's holy books in many forms and writings—others through verbal teachings and stories. It was up to them to understand and believe. It wasn't its mission. It would keep its communications with her extremely limited, no matter how much enjoyment it felt communicating with her. It would spend more time coiling around her, bringing her close to it—as one. This was what its species did. Coiling around her made it extremely powerful. When it returned to the others shortly afterwards, the exaltation in energies that pulsated through them was incredible, explosive, and intense.

Gracie's amber eyes shone with health. Her hair flowed in longer, thick waves with a dull, reddish-brown—though not as beautiful as its species skins that glittered and sparkled in multitudes of colours, lights, and energies.

Her skeletal frame was stronger. A thin layer of fat, which her body needed, filled out her legs, arms, chest, and back, forming her almost into a shape that was considered healthy for humans.

For the first time, Gracie wasn't afraid of it. She was a bit wary but not trembling afraid. Her organs and blood remained steady inside her for the most part.

It even felt a positive feeling. Enjoyment. It enjoyed communicating with Gracie. It was a strange thing—communication. Overwhelming amounts of humans enjoyed communicating verbally or through their devices. Communication was one of their ills, one of many roots where evil lurked—whence it was unleashed, blossoming into so much pain and destruction. It wouldn't dwell on it. It didn't have many positive feelings for humans in general. It felt warmth, toward Gracie, though—only Gracie. If it wasn't contaminated, would it still feel the same way toward Gracie? It would never know. There were no other species like it before. The master accepted it, and nothing else mattered.

CHAPTER 12

The Darkness

The full hour of the last meeting wouldn't happen again. Amigo kept its visits to every three days at the same time and for thirty minutes—no more. It refused to type much after their last heavy conversation about the master, itself, and its species. It became this silent thing, humming, observing, tickling her with its trunk arms, holding her against it, intoxicating her into euphoria, feeding her with visions of expansive galaxies and planets she suspected Amigo had travelled to. Some were frightening places covered with waves of roaring, endless fires ... others devoid of Suns, Moons, and stars but filled with wind torpedoes and rains, some with just swirling, gases.

Finally, Amigo would take her in the vision to her favourite place, the large flaming Sun, full of beams and radiant light that sprang out from its sides. Gracie couldn't look directly into the Sun's extremely powerful light, but the heat embraced her, and the sounds of many flames and fires roared inside it.

The burst of comforting warmth, the sense of safety, amidst the roar of fires, flowed through every cell inside her as her whole body dissolved into an airless entity. She had no skin, no bones, no muscles; she was lightweight, and this essence that she transcended into, vibrated in a joyous rhythm in tune with Amigo's hums. Soon, it would be over.

Amigo unwrapped its coils from her shoulders and placed her on the cold tiles.

Laika rested in his bed and immediately seized the opportunity. He galloped up to her and eagerly licked the side of her flushed, perspiring face.

She opened her heavy eyes in time to see Jimmy flashing in the centre of Amigo's body as it disappeared through the ceiling.

This went on for weeks and for months. Soon, the Snuggles calendar reached the month of August.

During each visit with Amigo, she probed it with questions. The Smith Corona's keys remained still. Amigo refused to respond to her questions. Before she got further frustrated, Amigo would whisk her into the warmth of itself, and the euphoria and visions would last for the rest of their visit.

She collected all the typed pages from their conversations in a folder. She reviewed them numerous times, writing the questions she had asked above Amigo's answers. She added a few follow-up questions in the margins to keep asking Amigo ... just in case it ever decided to answer.

In early February, Amigo did answer one question.

Gracie asked, "Amigo, why do you keep bringing me these disgusting worms for me to eat?"

`Have you been eating at least three a day?`

"With my fruit shake every morning."

`They are rich in Vitamin D. Eat your worms. They are good for you.`

In the last two visits, Amigo must have grown tired of her probing, and it answered a number of questions.

"Amigo, that grey sludge, that we would dump dead bodies and concrete in—what is its use?"

Any essence of other species and things that it absorbs strengthens it.

"I don't understand."

You wouldn't. Come to me.

"Did you set up this apartment?"

Yes.

"I don't understand how?"

I told you before. I am a better species.

"What about all of this food in the freezers, where did you get it?"

From Earth. Where else would these things made by humans, belonging to humans, farmed and produced by humans, come from?

"Do you know anything more about what's happening on Earth?"

Earth is still there. Changed, it's there.

"Are there any humans left?"

Not as many as before. There's enough of them left.

"Do you know if the city of Whitehorse in Canada was attacked?"

I'm not sure.

"Does the master know that you keep me here?"

The master knows everything and everyone.

"What about Jesus, the Christ?"

Yeshua lives inside the master, with the Holy Spirit, the powerful force and essence of the master. They are one. All of the master's loyal creations will eventually return and become one with the master. No one will be alone or left behind.

"What's going to happen to those who aren't Christians or don't believe in God but are righteous people?"

The master decides. The master is the master of all. He submits to nothing. Everything submits to Him.

"If you find Jimmy through whatever networks, will you bring him to me or tell me?"

Yes.

"Promise?"

Yes.

"Amigo, are you being truthful about everything?"

You can believe it or not.

"Why are you helping me stay alive?"

Everything that has happened was not just coincidence or chance—my parent, pushing well into their inability to birth anything, being away from home, yet managing to suddenly birth me on its ship during a crucial time, chose to give me the gift of great curiosity, above all its other gifts, which in turn propelled me to meet you shortly after, while you held something genetically of your son, that I accidentally contaminated myself with and fused my vulnerable cells with. Was this all just a chance? Both of us didn't choose to be born. We had extremely limited chances of being born. But we exist. We are here. I want to be with you. Together. Why is this difficult for you to believe?

Shortly after, their time was up, and Amigo departed as always leaving her alone with her inner cynical voice ... *Gracie, seriously, does this thing want a standing ovation for all of that nonsense it's typed out? It's insulting your intelligence. It's feeding on your vulnerabilities. It has access to your journals, and it knows your weaknesses. It's exploiting you.*

Gracie's mind wandered to her purpose. What was it now? What was left for her to do and become? She was looking at a frightening future, living the rest of her life here in this 1980s retro apartment with a creature visiting her every three days, tickling her with trunk arms, intoxicating her as if she was injecting opioids for the very first time—minus the addiction—and delivering visions of vast galaxies, and other planets.

Her days became nothing, but routine twenty-minute workouts accompanied by women in tight pink leotards, matching leg warmers, and white sneakers. Then, in the afternoons, a few hours of practicing martial arts moves, putting on boxing gloves and venting all of her frustrations on the punching bag, with Chuck Norris and Bruce Lee on the television, mimicking and memorizing every move of theirs, her execution almost as fast as those administered to their victims.

For months, she was aware of being locked up inside an apartment and had nowhere to go. Trapped, like a sea lion, put in a wooden box and left in a small tank to swim the rest of its days instead of having the freedom to follow what its own natural instincts craved: endless exploration of the vast ocean, mating, and hunting for its own food.

She learned to do everything manually with no network hovering, waiting for her voice to activate it to life with holographs of daily news, traffic, weather, and various entertainments.

Gracie thought about the People Against Network Surveillance, who for decades rallied against the governments of the world, to end networks being implemented everywhere in public spaces, automatic cars, inside and outside people's homes. At that time, it was hard for Gracie to understand their fight as Gracie had grown up like almost everyone else, surrounded by networks; their presence was imprinted in her since she was sent to preschool.

Gracie did terribly miss the network and she didn't think she would ever get used to not having them around. At first, it felt as if something was missing … then the lack of being under any network surveillance, made her less conscious of the network and she never realized just how conscious of the network she had been, until being inside an apartment with absolutely no networks monitoring or analyzing her every move.

Now, Gracie had humans of an ancient past, their images rolling through VHS cassettes, displayed across the screen of the television, their voices coming through speakers—in the same scenes again and again ... mad, shirtless raging wrestlers running around with the previous flag of the United States of America and a two-by-four, chanting, "USA! USA!" to cheering crowds. She watched 212 VHS tapes with 1980s films a few times over and other recorded shows, including a show, Gracie wished she had more episodes of called, *The Littlest Hobo*.

A voice inched its way into her thoughts.

You can end it. You have more options than ever.

The voice wasn't her cynical voice. It was deeper. Gracie could almost feel its hot breath against the sides of her face as if hovered over her.

Gracie sat up and dug her fingers into the couch. The darkness.

Drown in the bathtub, the darkness said. *Cut your wrists. You would be at peace finally. Isn't that what you wanted? This deceitful creature has only kept you alive to serve its own sickening purpose—imposing its slithering self all over you, bringing you into it, poisoning you like some heinous lover ... as if you belong to it. That is how they copulate with one another. It nourishes their bodies to eventually replicate themselves. That's why they rest with one another. Sickening.*

"I won't listen to you," Gracie said, covering her ears. "I never did, and I won't now."

She scampered off the couch and went through the closet to pick out something to wear. It was the third day, and Amigo would be arriving in an hour.

Gracie dressed in navy blue velvet trousers that flared in an open wide curve by her ankles. She wore a silk white blouse and a gold rope belt around her tiny waist. Her hair had grown down to her shoulders with volume and waves. Her cheeks had filled back out, along with other parts of her body that bloomed into small curves turning around her hips, filling out her buttocks, and forming small but firm mounds of breasts over the fading outline of bones on her chest. Her lips were fuller and pinker. The golden amber flecks in her eyes grew more golden, the whites in them clearer, and even her handsome eyebrows formed into expressive arches.

In the bottom cupboard in the kitchen were six bottles of alcohol. Gracie took the crème de cacao and poured a generous amount into her instant coffee.

She started with one drink. The flavour was very sweet. She hadn't had chocolate in so long. She refilled her cup to the top with the crème de cacao.

She brought the stand-alone record player into the ballroom and a few records under her arms. She turned on the volume and played a Casablanca Record from 1977. The song, fitting for her growing inebriated state, was called "I Feel Love" by Donna Summer and George Moroder.

With the music blasting on the record player, she swirled herself into a dance, her eyes closed, as if she were in the water, pushing out her arms, channeling the routine they had done at Canadian Juniors. She became quickly lost in the music, feeling the water all around her, swishing against her ears, over her cheekbones, over her eyes, embracing her whole being, kicking her legs as high as she could, her body shooting up through the water, toward the bright light glimmering over the pool, her arms swimming fast, to the beat of the music: "*I feel love. I feel love.*"

The tendrils of her hair swung wildly over her face, back and forth. She stopped and stood, panting, the blouse clinging to her back. She took another gulp of her drink, put it down, and remembered the faded velvet yellow-green gown. She pulled it off the wire bodice. The colour of it must have been a deep green colour as found in a few patches that didn't get damaged over time. It was extremely heavy, like a velvet drape, and yet fragile, as the sleeves and bodice easily came apart. There was a label sewn in a seam.

Gown of Miss Scarlett O'Hara.

Gracie shrugged. "I don't know who the heck Scarlett O'Hara is?"

Gracie put down the gown and stumbled to the glass to the opulent crown and the other vaults of grand jewels. She placed the heavy, bejeweled crown on her head. It sunk down to her eyes. It was a crown made for a king, not a queen. Maybe she shouldn't mess with these things, especially since she was drunk.

She shouldn't be disrespectful. There was no one or any network there to tell her otherwise. This was all hers to do with as she pleased; that's why it was brought for her—to enjoy all of it. She could wear it and parade it around if she wanted.

She took the king's wrap, a stiff article with a faded orange colour that once had been a bright red, bearing black dots that mimicked a leopard pattern.

"I proclaim this cape belonged to the ancient Polish king."

Gracie had no idea who that would be, but in her inebriated mind, the royal cape, the crown, and the scepter belonged to an ancient Polish king.

The cape felt soft in some places and rough in others. She wrapped it around her shoulders and held it against herself. The other glass vaults contained sparkling rings with large gemstones, ropes of thick gold necklaces, and bracelets. They were worth millions on Earth. In this place, they had no worth. They were ugly, stiff, faded fabrics—way past their glorious time—glittering gems with bright colours, and embroidered chains that didn't offer much to Gracie.

Worth was having water, food, then Laika, and the entertainment that kept the human mind and emotions in a good state—the books, music, videos, and films of the ancient people. Even writing, tracking things, organizing, and cleaning every nook and cranny brought tranquillity and a sense of accomplishment. Dust didn't grow anywhere, and she was always grateful that there were no bugs around.

She put on a few glittering necklaces and rings with black rocks.

The rings of King Sebastian. They fit my fingers perfectly.

She reached down to finish the rest of her drink, and despite the music thumping away; it couldn't drown out the sound of the distant chirping of the hums as if they were right next to her ears.

Excitement ran through her. She grabbed her glass and ran into the kitchen to fill up another with the Crème de Cacao.

Remember Gracie there is no aspirin or ibuprofen in this place to deal with a hangover.

Amigo arrived. Gracie stood in front of Amigo, drunk out of her mind, careless, bursting with love for Amigo, wrapped in a Royal Cape, a crown holding her tresses back from her flushed face, and rows of glittering necklaces filled with rubies and diamonds hanging down her neck.

Amigo's trunk arms reached out for her. She grabbed two of them and swung them up and down.

She placed Amigo's trunks over her heart.

"Feel it, feel this, Amigo."

She closed her eyes and sent Amigo all of her feelings of love.

"Love. Love. Love."

She turned the ends of Amigo's trunk arms and felt the rows of flat, sharp teeth lying dormant inside the skin of the trunk arms. The outer edges of the trunk arms were double-ringed with skin speckled with indigo dots.

"Can they shoot out poison from these ends?" she asked Amigo. To her pleasant surprise, Amigo's trunk arms reached the typewriter and responded.

`Yes.`

The texture of the trunk arms was stern, mushy, and pliant. She wrapped the trunk arms around her neck, completely drunk and fearless. Amigo continued to hum and other trunk arms reached out, tickling the side of her face and neck. They moved over the large crown, feeling the necklaces, then moved down her chest and coiled around her waist.

The rivulets in Amigo's skin glittered in fast kaleidoscopic, colours, making her dizzy.

"Those are beautiful, Amigo. Are you singing? Is that how you sing?"

Amigo didn't answer and kept its fast-moving trunks tickling over her.

"I just got a thought! Amigo, can you bring another human here ... like a friend for me? I'm getting lonely doing everything alone. You would be able to save someone else. You're the captain of this ship; you can do whatever you want. There's so much food and water here."

Trunk arms over the typewriter...

`Not a good idea.`

"Why?"

`You would hate each other. One of you would eventually kill.`

"We wouldn't. No way! That wouldn't happen. How?"

`It's what you humans end up doing under these circumstances. Laika is a much better companion. Laika is loyal with a good disposition and can't talk. Hate needs words to bring it to life and attach it to emotions. Won't happen with Laika.`

She let go of Amigo's trunk arms, and her inner voice entered her mind. *Amigo is right. Being stuck here with one another, being confined to this space every second of the day, not being able to just leave ... it would happen. It starts with bickering, and the words would grow harsher, more agitated, then abusive, moving on to screaming and ultimately violence ...*

"Amigo, what's going to happen to all the humans on this ship? Will they return to Earth?"

`I don't know.`

"Will I die here, alone?"

Amigo's trunk arms moved away from the typewriter. She grabbed the trunk arms and pressed them over the typewriter keys.

"No, you get back there and answer me, mister. Answer ..."

The keys clacked slowly.

`We all die.`

"No kidding, Einstein, but am I going to die here, eventually? Is that the plan?"

The voice of the darkness quickly took advantage of Amigo's hesitation.

Of course, it will. You think it's some kind of saviour, with all its nonsense about being contaminated with Jimmy's DNA ... about this master that doesn't exist ... but it will let you die once it tires of you. You thought that of all the lives here, yours would be so special? That it chose you? To save you? Your own parents didn't choose you over their drugs. They never even chose to make an effort to get well for you. You were never their choice to change. You weren't good enough for them. This human killer will puncture a hole right through your chest as you sleep, then suck out your heart and twist it between its rows of teeth-daggers!

Typing ...

`Seek the master. He's the only one who will decide. I will do whatever I can to keep you alive. Should you die, you won't die alone. I will be there. I promise.`

The voice of the darkness was elated. *It's telling you, exactly what you told Jimmy. You promised to be there for him, always. This human killer will be there when you die because it's the one who will take your life. It's better for you to take your own life in your own hands, on your own terms, instead of being docile prey, waiting for this human killer to wipe you out.*

Gracie was conflicted. She wanted to believe Amigo, but she wasn't sure. A headache was coming.

"I guess that's good news. Amigo, can you leave? I'm too drunk. I need water and rest and to silence the voices in my head."

Typing ...

`The darkness inside. I understand.`

"You're aware of it?"

`It's been inside you since I brought you here. I will go.`

Sparkling colours inside Amigo swirled together, then separated, and in the centre, the golden strands produced Jimmy's image.

She clasped her hands together. "My Jimmy ... bring me back to Earth so I can be with Jimmy."

Her happiness drained out of her, and she was filled with profound sadness. Tears overfilled her eyes, and she leaned in close to Amigo's chest.

"He's the only child that I was permitted to have," she said. Four trunk arms held her back. She wiped away tears.

Amigo moved up to the ceiling and was gone.

On the bed, she lay looking up at the meringue, swirling pattern on the ceiling.

"Keep my little Jimmy safe, Amigo."

She turned onto a side and wrapped herself tightly with the ancient Polish king's cape. She hoped to sleep for the next few hours, not puke over the bed, and definitely not over the ancient cape.

CHAPTER 13

Terror Descends

Gracie woke up thirsty with a numb headache and was very grateful for the minimum side effects. She tried to remember what had happened a few hours ago.

Where is Laika? He wasn't on the bed. Gracie stripped the heavy jewellery and the ancient Polish king's cape from her neck. His crown was on the basket chair.

In the kitchen, she gulped down a large glass of water filled with ice cubes and called out for Laika. She found him in the ballroom sleeping in the centre of the velvet folds of the yellow-green gown. He ran up to Gracie, tail wagging.

"What a beautiful boy you are," Gracie cooed. "Bet you liked the disco party, huh?" She gave Laika some rubs behind the ears.

"With Donna Summer and Giorgio. We should do this another time ... maybe not invite crème de cacao to the party though."

Laika gave Gracie a few more enthusiastic face licks and stepped back. His large head turned to the side. Gracie heard it too.

A low hissing sound.

Laika's body grew tense and backed away from Gracie and stared intently past the doorway to the ballroom. The horrible smell came, like death coming to find them. Gracie stood up, not wanting to see what the horrible smell warned her of, and yet she could clearly see in her mind, the approaching giant mass crawling behind the walls toward them.

Gracie scooped up Laika and immediately ran inside the voluminous closet behind hundreds of hangers of long gowns, fur coats, and other clothing. Laika, sensing the impending danger and Gracie's terror, wanted nothing but to protect its mistress.

Laika wriggled his muscular body out of her arms and bolted to the entranceway of the ballroom, aggressively barking and snarling at the terror that Gracie could mentally see descending from the ceiling. A lavender hue speckled with lime dots filled up large, engorged trunk arms that stretched out from its body, gleaming from the rims of the trunk arms were sharp rows of teeth.

Inside the deep corner of the closet, Gracie hid behind sparkling, opulent flowing gowns. Her shoulders shook violently, and perspiration coated her arms. She couldn't find her voice to scream or make any sound, simply watching in horror as the Vampyre's head reached down from its massive body close to Laika, observing him lurch aggressively, barking and snarling. The Vampyre didn't strike Laika, simply floated away to the other end of the closet, to the opened vaults and to the royal jewels that remained. Its trunk arms moved over the jewellery as if sniffing out the scent of a human that had been there.

Laika didn't give Gracie away and kept on barking and snarling behind the demon Vampyre.

Gracie's eyes darted over the hanging costumes, clothes, capes, and furs above her. There were no weapons that could even injure this thing, let alone kill it.

An explosion of clothes, hangers, jewellery, and shattered glass rained down as the Vampyre's trunks effortlessly ripped out a closet, stripping away the racks of clothes and costumes from their stands. Its trunk arms tore at the walls easily like peeling the paper off a package and threw it behind in a heap. One of the giant chandeliers disentangled from the ceiling and crashed onto the floor, sending thousands of crystals skittering all over the place. Laika managed to scurry away from any thrown or falling objects and was right back behind the Vampyre, wildly barking and biting the air.

With the tearing of the first closet and glass vaults, the closet door in front of Gracie slid down in its rail, leaving enough space for Gracie to bolt through it.

Four massive trunk arms grabbed the poles of clothes, from the two closets next to the closet she hid inside. Laika bounced around, his barks growing indignant, furious.

Behind a hanging gown, one of the Vampyre's trunk arms came into view. Lavender rivulets moved through its body; its speckles of lime dots shone like emeralds; and the smell came along with it—rotten beetroots and the familiar putrid, stench of that place.

The clothing bar creaked, and with it, another explosive blast of costumes, fur coats, clothes, and pieces of the cracked, torn closet doors rained down. Within the explosive chaos, Gracie bolted through the small opening in the closet and scooped up Laika, nearly missing a trunk arm coming her way. She shut the ballroom door and clicked the inside knob. It would have little effect, though; the Vampyre would be coming through the door or through the ceiling any second.

Adrenaline was wild in her veins, and before she could run to the other side, trunk arms erupted through the thick wood of the door as if it were made out of foolscap paper.

The Vampyre remained in the centre of the ballroom, motionless for a moment. Then, its massive body turned to Gracie as she regarded it, breathing erratically. Heavily. Four more trunks on each of its sides floated back and forth, waiting for its master to direct them forward. Gracie ran toward the other end of the apartment, but before she could reach the end of the hall, a trunk tried to grab her arm. She was amazingly fast and ducked. In doing this, Laika wriggled out of her arms and jumped high in the air to grab the trunk arm, in its powerful jaws.

Gracie screamed. "No Laika! Don't touch it! Release!"

The Vampyre floated into the room and joined its elongated trunk that was inside Laika's jaws. Laika furiously shook it and tugged at it. Another trunk arm seized Laika and coiled around Laika's ribs and neck. Laika kept on fighting, snarling, and twisting its muscular body in a firm grip.

Gracie horrified, pulled open a drawer and threw the butcher knife at the Vampyre's centre. It sank into it as if were made out of gelatin and popped back out ineffectually, falling onto the tiles with a loud clank.

Laika howled in pain as purple dye spurted over the side of his body. A trunk arm with white sharp teeth at its ends raised over Laika's shoulder, prepared to take a huge bite.

"Leave him alone!" Gracie screamed, then snatched the tray of ice cubes she had left on the counter and threw it at the Vampyre. Sizzling sounds and steam rose out of it.

It released Laika. Gracie jumped over the countertop and reached for the fire extinguisher that hung by the side of the cabinet and sprayed it over the Vampyre, who flared its trunk arms and let out a hideous soul-shivering screech. Gracie grabbed Laika, who whimpered, a patch of skin missing from his shoulder, purple liquid oozing out from it.

There was nowhere else to run or hide. She was trapped with Laika. She placed Laika down on the couch and held on tight to the fire extinguisher, keeping it pointed at the Vampyre.

The Vampyre's body turned a deeper purple-blue as if it had summoned all the poison it could muster.

"Come and get me, you son of a bitch. I will fight you to the end!"

Gracie stood tall, her breathing loud, getting raspy. She kept her intense gaze locked on the Vampyre, waiting for it to come at her. As she stood there, a tight pressure moved as if untangling itself inside her chest. There was the sensation of something flapping open inside her lungs. It quickly rose up her throat, and the fire extinguisher dropped from her hands. The intense pressure forced her arms to spread wide open to accommodate the rumbling, loud, grotesque sound—a sequence of guttural hums that came out of her mouth. Each vibrating hum directed at the Vampyre almost lifted her up from the floor.

The Vampyre remained still, some of its deadly trunk arms engorged with poison lowered back to its sides, seeming to listen.

What the heck is happening?

Gracie's legs—as if they had their own mind—walked fearlessly toward the Vampyre, which hissed, moving away. Instead of rushing at her or directing one of its trunk arms to tear off her head in seconds, it shot back to the wall and moved upwards. It was almost out of sight when its body suddenly jerked as if another force had grabbed it. Gracie heard the chirp-hum and saw a flash of amber and gold specks that belonged to Amigo.

The Vampyre was gone.

She had no time to think about Amigo or how she was able to make those ugly guttural sounds. She put down her arms, ignored the discomfort inside her lungs, and brought Laika to the bathtub, turning on the shower, washing as much of the lavender poison off him as possible. She towel-dried him and put him on his bed, covering him with blankets. He still whimpered.

She checked the sores on his shoulder and found that the bleeding had stopped. Gracie rummaged through the medicine cupboard, in case there was something that could help Laika. What did dog medicine look like? Gracie had no idea. Her panicked mind ran to the encyclopedia.

Surely there's something on vet care? There was nothing. Her trembling hands moved pages and pages, finding nothing until she began to cry and tore at the pages in a fury. She flung the book at the ceiling and screamed, "Not Laika!"

Then, she ran back to him.

Get a grip, her voice told her. *Calm down. You having a fit is not helping.*

On the side of her arm, a small chunk of skin had been removed, and a line of purple dye ran down it. She wiped at it, and the wound swelled up and some more purple dye came oozing out of it. She squeezed the purple dye out of the wound until only her blood was left. She turned her attention to Laika.

You can't force Laika to puke. He didn't eat poison, that bastard injected poison into him. Get him to eat and drink something. Be calm and wait it out.

Laika refused to eat any cooked chicken, his favourite, and drink any water. Gracie pulled a blanket over Laika, held one paw in her hand, and sat next to him. She ignored her own body temperature rising with its possible infection and her eyelids becoming heavy. She would continue to fight off sleep for the next hour and not succumb to it at any cost.

CHAPTER 14

Betrayal and Shame

It held the keeper tightly within its powerful coils. It couldn't escape. It wouldn't let it escape. The keeper was confused—afraid—and the others who watched them rolling together inside a furious vortex of fire sparks and sizzle flew away.

The fury that roared inside it was massive.

It hurt Gracie. It hurt Laika. It hurt them. It was not permitted outside its designated territory. It should have watched the keeper more closely. It was defective. It was right about it. It had strayed from their ways before. It was defective.

The rage that flowed through it brought them inside the working quarters and over the grey, steaming sacred waters. It shoved the keeper inside of it and watched it immediately disintegrate. The top of its head was the last to float before it disappeared inside the sludge. The guardians scampered away from the scene to join the others at the bottom of the ship—those who gathered and felt the death of the keeper. The human labourers barely moved from the scene, keeping to their lines while others watched this interaction.

Amigo bolted high up to the top layer of the ship. Its body pulsated with blinding fury. It felt fear and confusion from the others. One of them had died, and no other had been born to replace the parent. They were incomplete.

As the anger and rage simmered down, the realization of the horror that it just committed against its own species brought on a terrible sensation of shame.

Immediately, a radiant powerful light flashed over it.

Despite the abomination it had just committed through the weakness of the human contamination—their emotions, where evil easily grasped and overtook them—the master's light offered it warmth and comfort.

"Why is my captain full of forlorn and shame?" the master *hummed.*

It could not hum back. The shame and shock of what it had just committed paralyzed it; even the rivulets of its sparkling beautiful lights were dull and moved slowly through it.

"A life has been taken away before it birthed a new life and not during a battle," the master hummed. "That is not the way of this species. Why did you do this, succumbing to evil and committing this heinous act against your own species?"

"Master, the keeper, tried to hurt her," it weakly hummed back. "It would have killed her."

"The keeper was about to return to its post before you arrived and made the choice to kill it."

"The human contamination inside me made me do this. Master, I beg you, please heal me from it. Make me like my own species and not be what I am ... this kind of species."

"I created both of these species. You are what you are. Respect it. Nothing makes you do anything. Because a life has been taken without being replaced, another life must be taken."

"Master, I beg you ..."

"I will give you the choice, this human contamination that you blame weakened you to kill; that came from the human, Gracie, bring her to me so that it will be her life that is taken. Or if you choose, you can offer your own life. One life to replace the other that was killed. You are my captain, and we have reached the end of this phase and will be ready to move on to the next. I would choose wisely. Go and make your decision before the next Sun beams over this ship."

The master disappeared, filling it with heavy sensations of regret ... and it couldn't even find the will to hum gratitude back to the master.

CHAPTER 15

The Confrontation

Gracie awoke a few hours later. Laika was still asleep. His rib cage moved with slow and steady breathing. He no longer whimpered. Gracie got up. Her fever was gone. Her own wound had stopped bleeding.

She entered the ballroom and surveyed the destruction: heaps of clothes, plaster, shattered glass, and crystals were strewn across the ballroom floor.

Under the wreckage, the record player remained. All of the records had been crushed under the weight of the racks of clothes, parts of the closet doors, and the glass vaults.

"Disco nights are over."

Around the collar of a pink blouse still in its hanger, hung a beaded rosary, intact and not broken. Each bead was delicately carved into a flowery design. Small red rubies were aligned over the gold crucifix and each bead. It was beautiful. Gracie took it off the hanger and placed it over her head.

At least some things can be salvaged.

It would take weeks if not months, to organize the mess. That was the least of her worries. She hoped Amigo had taken care of the Vampyre.

The darkness arrived. *None of them were supposed to know about this place. They were supposed to faithfully keep to their posts. It seems like the human killer's story is not so truthful.*

Amigo will explain. There must be a reason ...

She pressed her fingers against her throat. No swelling. She took a few deep breaths. Everything felt the same although Gracie, being extremely attuned to her lungs, knew they never felt the same since the abduction. The terrible chemicals she breathed for months and now this ... something was inside her lungs. She was sure of it. Only what was it?

The sound of a chirp-hum.

Amigo is back so soon? It's never done that before.

Laika barely moved his head as Amigo descended. Laika's tail, which usually wagged with so much enthusiasm remained eerily still.

"Laika is very sick. Is there anything you can do to help?"

Amigo kept on humming and didn't move.

"Help Laika, Amigo. That bastard poisoned him. I don't know what to do."

Amigo remained still.

"What's wrong? You usually reach out to me. You don't want to touch me?"

Amigo's trunk arms typed.

`Laika will die soon.`

"Can't you help him? You helped me get better; you can help Laika too?"

`Amigo cannot.`

Why would the human killer help? You're getting pathetic ...

"You can help, Amigo. Of course, you can."

`I cannot.`

"You just don't want to help. You're going to just let Laika die? Would you do the same to me?"

Of course, the human killer would.

Amigo's trunk arms went back to resting by its side.

"You aren't going to answer me? Why, because is that the truth? How did that monster get in here? You told me that they keep to their posts and don't wander around the ship. How did that son of a bitch get in here? Did you lure it here?"

Amigo moved away.

"No, you don't get to move away from me!"

Gracie's rage rose.

"If you lied about this, then I guess everything else was a lie. Pure bullshit! This master, whatever you are, and this mission—whatever it is. How convenient that you've been so reluctant to tell me much about yourself. Yet you help yourself to my device, read my private journals, know everything about me, and I don't know shit about you. And everything you've told me has all been a lie!"

Gracie grabbed the typewriter.

"You don't want to talk? Fine. I never want to talk to you again!"

Gracie smashed the typewriter over the tiles, cracking the case, keys flying all over the place, and the roller hurled under the table.

She stood in front of Amigo's chest, the heat emanating from it covered her face uncomfortably like hot air flowing from a 400-degree oven. She didn't care.

"Why did you bring me here? You gave me false hope to live. You brought Laika in the guise of a companion, only to let him die, to hurt me so I lose something else that I loved so much again. You want to keep me here, alone, with no human companion, to slowly go mad. Well, fuck you! I'm better off dead. You should have killed me before you brought me here. I wanted to die. All you had to do was wait, just give me ten minutes tops and I would have finally been dead, and away from all this bullshit!"

She grabbed one of the trunk arms, pulled back the rims, and forced some of the sharp teeth to stand like tiny daggers, bringing it against her neck.

"You know about human anatomy; it's right next to my artery. All you have to do is slice, in two seconds and it will soon be over for me. As for your pathetic story of not being able to kill me—bullshit! You can kill me. Go right ahead and do it."

The glittering lights inside Amigo's chest grew brighter and swirled faster.

"What are you waiting for, do it!"

Amigo's hums intensified. A trunk arm came behind her and grabbed her wrist, forcing her to let go of the other trunk arm. The trunk arms retreated to its body and Amigo started back up the wall.

She screamed, "You aren't leaving until you kill me!"

She grabbed the fire extinguisher and pointed it at Amigo. She expected her inner voice to tell her to stop this now! Or Gran Amália to scream, "Santa Maria!" Or the darkness to encourage her to fight Amigo. Yet, all of the voices were silent.

She sprayed the fire extinguisher over Amigo. A terrible hissing sound screeched. Amigo's body rose higher, inflamed; glowing specks moved inside it frantically, and the sound of crackling electricity coincided with sparks of fire.

Amigo's trunks tightly coiled around Gracie and brought her close to the centre of his chest.

"Go ahead, kill me. You're going to let me die just like you're going to let Laika die."

A trunk arm snatched away the fire extinguisher and flung it across the living room. Other trunk arms moved over her wet, sobbing face, underneath her eyes, behind her neck, and through her hair. Amigo's trunk arm lowered her down.

Gracie looked at Laika. His eyes stared ahead, his rib cage still, blood seeping through the blankets and pooling in a semi-circle over the white tiles.

Laika was dead. Gracie fell to her knees, covered her face in her hands, and cried.

Amigo rose upwards and disappeared through the ceiling.

CHAPTER 16

A Solution

"*You have made your choice, the master hummed. Where is she? Wouldn't it have been a wiser choice to bring Gracie, the human you accused of having contaminated you and had you kill?*"

"*Master, I couldn't choose her.*"

"*Why not?*"

"*For most of her life, she has been blamed for things that were never her fault. It caused her to be broken, and she has just started to mend this. I killed the keeper in my rage. That was my fault. It is my life that should be chosen to balance the species, but I have another solution that can restore the balance.*"

"*You have kept them strongly unified like none of the other captains had been able to. How will you restore the balance?*"

"*Master, it is true that humans are prone to hatred and anger, but some are prone to a powerful emotion of love. Gracie has a powerful, deep love for her son, more powerful than the version of love my species is able to express. The contamination has enabled me to experience this human love from Gracie. I never felt this kind of power before. I can bring comfort to the others with this powerful love that Gracie has given me, overriding their fears and confusion and bringing them back to a state of safety, security, and balance."*

The master was silent, except for the flames that roared inside.

"The mission is complete," The master finally hummed. "I need my captain to move into the next phase immediately, which will be quick to complete."

"Yes, master."

"After, you will rest with them, do what you proposed, and show them this powerful gift of love, the purity of it, that I have given the humans, to unify all."

"Yes, master. What about Gracie?"

"If you come up with a plan that doesn't stray away from the finality of my plan, you have permission and free will to do what you want with her."

"Yes, master."

As the master departed, Amigo exploded in hums, full of gratitude and reverence for the master.

CHAPTER 17

Finding Amigo

Gracie, exhausted from grieving, stood up. She placed each of Laika's paws in a criss-cross fashion against his chest and wrapped his body in his blankets inside large plastic bags. She brought Laika into an empty compartment in the freezer. Gracie couldn't think of a prayer to say and instead spoke to his soul.

"Laika, I'm sorry you died. You should have lived much longer. Despite being a dog, you reminded me how to be human again. You made me laugh. You gave me companionship and were easy to train, for which I am very grateful.

Even though you never experienced the joys of running through the grass ... or in rain ... or felt the sunshine, chased squirrels, or a ball, had some ice cream from a cone, seen the light of a moon, or just breathed in the air from Earth like all of your parents had done, you also didn't experience being shunned for who you are; you were never abandoned, unloved, unwanted, or neglected. Every single day of your life, you were loved, wanted, and welcomed. I loved you. Even an alien liked you and not many pit bulls can claim that."

"Goodbye, Laika. I will never forget you. I hope your soul lives on into the light until we meet again."

Gracie shut the freezer door behind her.

The lights of the apartment shut off. Gracie wasn't alarmed. She felt numb after everything that had taken place.

A tremble ripped through the floor, cracking a thick line through the tiles up to the hallway. An earthquake came to mind. *Earthquake? I'm not on Earth. Was that an explosion?*

She listened. There were no other sounds—not the low buzzing of kitchen appliances working or of the ship moving. Gracie's sense of gravity felt it. There was complete stillness. She tried the light switches. Only the light switches went on in the hallway and bathroom. Water still ran in the bathroom faucets.

The darkness was back. *Amigo, the human killer is shutting off the apartment.*

In the bathroom, Gracie removed the rings from her fingers and threw cold water over her face. She should sleep all of this away.

She entered the coolness of the bedroom and lay over the soft quilt, holding onto a pillow against her, staring into the darkness. She was almost asleep when another tremble came, knocking the mirror from the dresser over and shattering the glass. Gracie sat up and went into the hallway.

On her left side, to her horror, the doors to the apartment were wide open, including the large metal door with the round, thick glass window, as if the power that held it securely had been released.

Gracie's numbness turned into fear.

What is happening?

Gracie, trembling, walked down the hallway. The horrific smell and the memory of those walls breathing with their own life terrified her. She held her breath.

No matter how much she tried to shut the thick round glass door, it kept on popping open.

This can't be happening. No.

She shut the inner door of the apartment. There was a sound of water drizzling somewhere. She retrieved a flashlight from the storage room and turned it on. The freezers were thawing out.

How can this be? I'm having a panic attack. This can't be happening.

Gracie touched one of the freezer doors, and her hand jerked back. The door was scalding hot. A stream of water flowed underneath the doorway, and the smell of cooked things, all the frozen meat, vegetables, cakes, pies, and ice creams.

Another tremble came through the apartment, splitting the floor open in explosive spurts. Glasses and dishes shattered behind the cupboards, falling out and smashing over the countertop and tiles. A few cupboards got loose and crashed over the kitchen counter.

Gracie put a small knife that could fit in the pocket of her pants and grabbed a hard-plastic miner hat in case the small flashlight she held ran out of batteries. She took the fire extinguisher, which didn't have much left in it.

I have to find Amigo. Amigo will tell me what is happening.

A memory came to her. Amigo, where do you go on the ship when you rest with the others?

`To the bottom of the ship.`

Another tremble. The kitchen sink faucet popped outwards, a stream of water gushed out, and lights in the bathroom flashed. The pink toilet was cracked in two, and water spurted out in a quick flood from the bottom of it.

Gracie took a pair of walking shoes from a shelf in the closet and put them on. She couldn't stay in the apartment. It was falling apart. She had no other choice but to get out and find Amigo. After the last conversation she had with Amigo, she wasn't sure it would want anything to do with her now.

You don't have to go anywhere, the darkness said. *You can stay right here and call out for Amigo. It will come for you.*

"I have to go and look for Amigo. There is no other choice. I'll be dead if I stay here any longer, and no doubt, that's what you want."

She took a deep breath and mustered all the courage she had. Then, she pushed against the large metal door and stared down a pitch-dark, putrid-smelling tunnel.

The fleshy walls were humid and hot. The putrid smell was nauseating. Tiny beetle bugs came out of the pores of the walls to pounce on fresh blood as her hands held on to keep her balance. Walking over the uneven, slimy ground was no easy task.

She turned on her flashlight and hoped not to see any of the vile creatures ahead of her. She came around the tunnel, which suddenly dropped sharply into a slippery slope. She lost her footing and fell down it. The flashlight and fire extinguisher she was holding popped out from her hands as she desperately grabbed at anything on the walls to slow down her fall. Her eyes darted above her, into the endless darkness, where horrors could be moving, ready to scoop her up and twist her into a merciful and quick death.

She reached the bottom of the slope and faced another tunnel where four other humans appeared. She was just as startled as they were to see her. The humans were running from something, but their faces weren't afraid. The humans were muscular, with strong bone structures and wide unsymmetrical faces. Their eyes bulged and were slightly wide apart on their faces. They had hairy arms that gleamed over with the orange greasy humidity of the air. They all wore plain beige and short capes. Two of them had bushy beards, and they had damp hair that swarmed over with bugs.

The tallest one of them, approached her, with a wide smile and odd gargling sounds that he wouldn't be able to make if there had been a device down his throat. He was trying to say something. He had a mouth full of straight, phosphorescent teeth—just like the others when they flashed her enthusiastic smiles.

The man pointed to her wrists. A gold bracelet. Gracie stepped back but he grabbed her wrist fast. His strength was incredible. He held some kind of instrument and pointed to her bracelet. The others hunched all together, smiling as they looked on.

Gracie had been terribly afraid to run into vile creatures and would never have thought of running into humans that didn't severely deteriorate were strong and could be dangerous. Where the heck did they come from?

The man clipped her bracelet, and they watched it fall onto the dark ground. The man nodded as if he had accomplished something and made a sound that Gracie thought was the word: *Free*. The others nodded and repeated, "Free." The man let go of her wrist and they all raced together into the entranceway of another area. Gracie watched, perplexed, and followed.

Inside this large oval-shaped room, it was like she stepped into another world. Charred carcasses of what looked like the creatures, littered the corners of the place, heaps of them. A group of humans dragged out a creature, no longer a massive gelatinous form but a solid one—a smaller one. A woman from the group came forward, and from a pail, she showered the creature with what looked like the grey sludge they had dumped remains of dead humans and blocks of concrete inside.

The creature made no sound when it struggled and wiggled as the substance burned it down into tiny dark wisps of dried husks.

The humans excitedly stomped the remains with their feet in great glee. They danced, bellowed, and screamed. It was a war cry.

The man that had clipped her bracelet came out of the group and pointed at Gracie. Everyone stopped rejoicing and turned their heads toward her. Surprise and shock came over their faces to see something like her that looked something like them yet looked very different than them, dressed in a silk white blouse, and navy-blue velvet pants with white shoes. They probably thought she was some other kind of human from another planet or an odd illusion.

Gracie, terrified, not knowing how civil they would be, backed away and darted into the dark tunnel that kept on sliding downwards to the bottom of the ship where she hoped to find Amigo. She looked over her shoulder for a second and was relieved that none of them pursued her.

Those humans found a way to kill the creatures. The ship belongs to the creatures. It would be a battle that they were positioned to lose. They were probably sick and suffering. Lost in their delusion to experience something they never had their whole lives—the chance to fight back and kill a few creatures. Amigo, where are you?

She turned on the flashlight of her hat and breathed in slowly; the chemicals in the air were starting to irritate her eyes, which already had enough sweat that poured down her forehead, into them. She wiped the tears quickly away. The tunnels curved sharply and kept on going down and down.

Amigo, where are you?

She swallowed and moved faster. The tunnel opened into an oval room filled with greasy, steaming water. This place had more light in it. She cautiously entered through the opening. Her eyes looked over the walls and ceilings; there were no creatures but endless rows and rows of huge rockets ... missiles. She couldn't fathom how many there actually were. She recognized a few flags imprinted on the sides of them as she quickly shuffled by—Japan. India. Israel. Russia. The previous flag of the United States of America and the new flag of United Korea.

She got back inside the dark tunnel that began to tremble.

She knelt down and held herself against the wall for a minute then got back up. Above, shadows quickly moved as if they had a purpose. The creatures were up there, and she was walking right toward and underneath them.

Just keep on moving, her voice encouraged. *Keep on moving.*

Yet, her legs wanted to stop. The horror constricting inside her lungs made it hard for her to breathe.

Amigo, I'm sorry. I'm sorry for being angry at you. I was wrong. Amigo, come find me. Please don't leave me here.

Her body trembled violently. Her legs wanted to fold under her. Her voice rose in her head, strong and persistent.

Keep on going. Don't give up. Hurry!

Hissing, hot steaming air descended behind her. She could see it as if she had a clear vision behind her head. It wasn't just one but a whole pack of them. She wondered how fast it would be before she was lifted and finally killed. She kept on moving fast until she was inside another curved hallway. Her breathing was erratic. The things behind her swished above her. Something hot brushed the side of her neck, and the extreme heat it gave off burned her. Why didn't they attack her? Maybe she was imagining that they were there. She ran faster until a sharp pain in her lungs, made her stop. She collapsed against the wall and gripped her abdomen. She was struggling to breathe. She should have focused on the rhythm of her breaths. She couldn't go on. The pain pierced through her ribs. She sank onto the wet, hot ground and awaited her fate. The flashlight over her hat flickered and burned out. Complete darkness surrounded her. She was alone, left with terror and the sounds of hissing and threatening movements swishing by her.

A chirping-hum, in three quick intermittent beats, reverberated down the pitch-black tunnel in front of her.

Amigo. Was that Amigo or was she dreaming it?

The chirping-hums continued.

Her legs sprang to life, ignoring the sharp pain in her lungs and holding onto the side of her ribs, she entered the dark tunnel.

"Amigo, I'm here. I'm coming."

She followed the sound, which grew stronger and stronger. She turned into another tunnel, and Amigo's chirps dimmed.

"Turn back!"

She entered the adjacent tunnel. Amigo's chirps returned, and she scrambled down the extremely slippery tunnel where the temperature had further risen. Amigo's chirps were the loudest there. She slipped and let her fatigued body fall down the slope. She reached the bottom and standing ten feet in front of her was a colossal wall that covered the whole width of the spacious room. The wall was bubbling with rivulets and covered in kaleidoscopic, twinkling lights, and sizzling colours. Rows of creatures above crawled toward it, swooped down, and slithered inside it, disintegrating into the swarming colours. Hundreds if not thousands of creatures watched her through this massive wall. The smell of kerosene was horrible.

Gracie cautiously approached the wall.

"Amigo," she called out in a firm voice. "Don't leave me behind. Take me with you. I have nowhere else to go."

Amigo's chirp-hums continued. She couldn't see Amigo inside the mass of glitter and sparkling lights.

"Amigo. I want to live. You told me, that you wouldn't let me die. If that's true, take me with you. I'm sorry for what I said to you. I didn't mean any of it. I was angry and so sad about losing Laika."

At the top centre of the mural, swirling golden strings beamed. They slowly swooshed down to the centre of the wall. She came closer to it and waited.

"Please, Amigo, take me with you. Don't leave me."

Trunk arms shot out from the gelatinous wall and wrapped themselves around her shoulders. She stifled her scream, and at the same time nearly cried from relief. Amigo's trunk arms coiled around her body and turned her around to face where she had entered the room. Strong coils lifted her twenty feet above the ground and pulled her inside the warm, pulsating gelatine.

A gentle voice she didn't recognize encouraged her ... "*Breathe, Gracie.*"

"*Yes,*" her mind answered it. "*I am breathing. One. Two. Three.*"

She was inside the massive gelatine wall, inches in. Her eyes were shut.

"*Don't be afraid. Calm your heart. You are safe.*"

"*Okay, I'm trying,*" *she answered.*

"*You can open your eyes. You won't be harmed.*"

"*Okay ...*"

She opened her eyes and despite the feeling of a heavy mass over her eyes, there was no irritation, and her eyes could see right through the wall as if it were made out of water. Her lungs inhaled. Her mind was too terrified to be able to think logically about how she was able to breathe while inside whatever gelatin substance this was. Vile creatures swarmed around her, above and below. She could hear their hums and gurgling movements close by her ears.

Amigo's strong coils and body covered her well. She held onto the coils as if they were the buckles on a monster roller coaster ride she was about to embark on.

A glass wall rose from below and covered the outer wall like a sealant. A frightening rumbling sound came to life. Gracie watched, wild-eyed, as they dislodged from the ship and hurled into space.

The ship that she had been held captive and brought onboard looked like a meteorite. As they pulled away from it, the outer parts of it began to dissolve and break into multitudes of fragments. Gracie could almost hear the terrified screams of the humans who were left behind as explosions ruptured throughout the ship, finally silencing them and their hopes to find the freedom they dreamed would be theirs. Gracie wanted to cry, but she held back.

Little by little, the meteorite ship disappeared from her view until a final explosion of light gleamed from all the hydrogen missiles that completely obliterated it. The explosion rippled through space, and even though they moved as fast as they could, the ship shook violently. Tiny rocks and grains of sand hit the transparent glass in front of her. She shut her eyes and held on to Amigo's coils tighter.

Minutes later, the ship stopped shaking, and they continued on a smooth journey to wherever they were going, which Gracie was too terrified to even consider. She just knew the destination wouldn't be Earth.

Amigo's chirp-hum continued against her ears amidst the sounds of lower hums, hissing, and gurgling. These creatures were all speaking, and communicating with each other. A sedated feeling washed over her, thanks to her renewed trust in Amigo, and she let her eyes close. Instead of having visions, Amigo mercifully induced her into a safe, deep sleep.

PART FOUR

≈

Extrication

≈

A person devoid of hope and conscious of being has ceased to belong to the future.

—Albert Camus, The Myth of Sisyphus and Other Essays, 1955

CHAPTER 1

Abandoned

She roused from sleep. The safety of Amigo's tight coils loosened their grip. She slid through gelatinous sludge, pressed by the scalding heat emanating from the others.

A blast of cool air fell over her face. It bolted her awake as she fell onto a mound of sand. She didn't register any pain from the fall as sheer panic erupted through her.

She stumbled on her feet and waved her arms in a frenzy at the oval-shaped ship that flew away.

"Amigo, come back! Don't leave me!"

The wind blew her hair around her face. The ship rose higher. She could hear Amigo's chirping-hums become faint.

"Please don't leave me, Amigo!"

Grey skies twinkled with stars and with the dim light of two distant moons. She stood on a low sandy hill.

The ship flew higher until it was a tiny speck, it's rumbling sound weakening.

She threw herself into a frenzied panic. "Come back, pleeease! You promised not to leave me, Amigo! Please come baaaack ..."

She jumped up and down and vigorously waved her arms.

But it made no difference. The ship remained in the air for a minute and, in a flash, disappeared as if it never had been there at all. She stared up at the empty skies, her mind not wanting to comprehend what was happening.

Amigo will come back. Amigo has to come back.

She wrapped her arms around her shoulders and repeated in consolation, *Amigo said he wouldn't leave me. Amigo will come back. Yes, Amigo will.*

Her resolve returned. She'd survived this long and come this far; she could ride this one out. She had to. There was no other choice.

She faced the reality of not having basic necessities again. No water or food. Maybe there was water and food source on whatever planet Amigo had left her on. She reached into her pant pocket, and the dagger was still there.

Panic returned. She spun around and waved back to the empty skies.

"Amigo! Please hurry back! Pleeease ..."

CHAPTER 2

Unity

The last vision it had of Gracie was a little speck moving up and down and the sound of her cries, vibrating inside it ...

"Amigo, come back! You promised not to leave me!"

The sensation of pain was as terrible as the sensation of shame. It had to rid itself of this negative energy immediately. It had to bring them together.

It released the most powerful hum it had ever produced. It would fulfill its promise to the master and send love to the others, unifying them.

Strong heat amplified inside its body. Then, it shot out Gracie's love—the love she'd given it—suffusing the others. It quickly escalated them into a frenzy, and their bodies swirled, entwined around each other, coming together, forming a glittering sea of fire and sparkling lights. Their hums and electrical sparks reached an incredibly intense power.

"Feel my love ..."

Gracie's voice was inside it.

Love heals. Love brings everything together.

The essence inside them was permutated and their incompleteness began to be destroyed as a new essence flexed and grew to replace it, eradicating memories of having been incomplete. Sizzling vortexes rumbled and shook the ship, almost as powerful as the hundreds of hydrogen bombs that had exploded in the galaxy. The vortexes alleviated above their withering, vibrating bodies until they could no longer continue to extricate any more energy or heat from themselves.

Love protects. Love does not divide. Love Mends.

They succumbed to an end, unifying as one, confusion and fears gone. They were filled with peace and tranquillity again.

They are complete. Now they can rest.

The master's voice arrived...

"*Sleep my captain, peacefully inside the warmth of the others and under my divine light until the time comes when you hear my voice calling you to, rise my captain. Rise.*"

CHAPTER 3

Forgiveness

Gracie leaned against an alcove of rocks, sheltering herself from the wind and debris. Her eyes watched the skies for the sudden appearance of the ship. Winds continued to howl, and the sound of skittering, pestilent little red bugs that lived inside the rocks, would come to investigate what she was. Luckily, they had no interest in her.

Amigo will return but not anytime soon. Get up. You have to find a water and food source before you get really thirsty and hungry. You have the dagger to fend yourself from any predator or kill something to eat.

Winds grew stronger, and the debris made it hard for her to navigate her surroundings. She pulled out her shirt from her pants with the edge of the dagger and tore a long strip from the bottom.

She climbed onto a mound of rocks and tied the strip of material around the highest peak. The material was blown in the wind like a flag. It would be her locator to come back as she ventured out to find water or food.

The ground of the planet was mostly flat. The sand sparkled, silver with tiny charcoal pieces from the twelve- to fourteen-foot-high rocks that sprung all over the planet. It was as if the pathways were filled with confetti.

Her eyes darted from the glinting pathways to the curves and crevices of the rocks. She kept the dagger tight in her right hand. Every so often, she would look back to ensure the flickering flag was visible.

She followed around a bend of rocks that curved into an open space. Down below was a small pool made out of thick, dark sludge.

This could be a water or food source. Please, Amigo. Hurry up and come back ...

Gracie tried to ignore the dryness of her mouth. She climbed down a cluster of rocks to investigate. The smell from the sludge was just as bad as the terrible sludge the vile creatures had made her drink back on the ship. She dipped a hand into the sludge. It was warm, sticky, and thick like fudge with granular bits of charcoal rocks swimming in it.

Gracie bent further down when the rock she stood on came loose. She plummeted into the putrid sludge, and her body sank deep inside it. She immediately closed her eyes, held her breath, shut her mouth, and frantically swam to the top of the sludge, feeling the massive weight wanting to hold and pin her down. The sludge reeked of ammonia and rot.

Her arms brought her to the edge. She gripped at the rocks and lifted her body, which weighed double, out of the rotten mess. She frantically shook her hands to be rid of as much sludge as she could before wiping it away from her closed eyelids and lips.

As she did this, she wasn't aware of what had gathered underneath the pool. One of them popped its head up from the warm depths that had been its home for millennia.

Gracie saw it in her mind—the bubbling on top of the sludge. She opened her eyes and searched for her dagger. It wasn't in her pocket. She had it in her hand just before she fell into the sludge. Gracie took a loose rock with a sharp point and spun around.

The creature's head was small, no bigger than a hamster's. It was a fish of some type, with round eyes rimmed in yellow and green pupils—its dark body camouflaged well inside the sludge.

More bubbling movement in the pool. Silhouettes of countless others, swimming near the top of the sludge.

The creature popped back down, along with the others, and disappeared.

Gracie lowered the rock.

This could possibly be some kind of adequate food source. It better taste like cod. As Gran Amália would say, beggars can't be choosers.

She looked over the rocks in hopes to find the dagger. Nothing. She kept the sharp rock and looked at miles of glinting silver sand and the low mountains of charcoal rocks that in the distance glittered like black diamonds. All of a sudden, there seemed to be so much glittering and flashing in Gracie's eyes that she had a hard time focusing on which pathway to turn into.

In the distance, a funnel formed. The sludge over her clothes began to harden in the blowing wind. She turned back toward the tiny flag fluttering in the distance. She had a bad feeling that the funnel could turn into something much stronger. She wanted to be as close as possible to the place Amigo left her.

Amigo should be showing up soon ... she hoped.

Winds grew stronger and the sludge condensed into a hard surface that slowed down her pace. She took off the velvet pants and left them over a flat rock. She quickened her pace toward the flapping flag. In seconds, the winds gained a velocity that told her she had to get under an alcove of solid rock soon.

She reached the flag just before the winds flung it away, along with the top of the rock Gracie had secured it around.

She wiggled her body between two large rocks, deep inside a crevice. The sharp edges of the rocks tore at the skin by her ribs, but she couldn't worry about it as the funnel quickly turned into a fast-approaching tornado.

Her hands gripped a piece of rock that jutted outward in front of her face. She lowered her head into her chest. Above her, the top of the rock provided some shelter. The sludge over the back of her blouse secured her further like glue against the rock. She couldn't move.

The tornado arrived. She closed her eyes and called out to Amigo in her terrified mind.

Amigo, come back. I'm going to die. You left me here to die!

With the sludge pinning her and being pressed tightly between two solid-rock crevices, the powerful force of winds couldn't pull her into its clutches and hurl her inside its massive vortex, which roared with debris, taking chunks of rocks around her, including the rock above her head. She shrank her trembling body further inside the fissure.

Meanwhile, the tornado dumped mounds of debris on top of Gracie. Her legs were completely buried in it—almost up to her neck. She was only able to breathe through a tiny slit in her mouth. She spit out any tiny debris that tried to stick to her lips. Her eyelids were covered in thick crusts of debris and sludge. She could only see through a tiny sliver.

The storm roared above and around her, covering already grey skies in a palette of complete darkness.

Even though I walk through the darkest valley, I will fear no evil, for you are with me; your rod and your staff, they comfort me...

I am going to make it. Amigo, please come back.

She rode out the tornado for what seemed to be an eternity. Once it left, another kind of suffering was brought on. Hundreds of bugs, the size of hummingbirds, that looked like roaches with fanged teeth crawled out in droves from underneath the rocks. They swarmed over the warm blood that dripped from her scraped skin. They rubbed the length of their coarse bodies along the cuts.

The weight of debris and chunks of smaller rocks kept her immobile and pinned down. Her wrists rested on top of a jutting rock, her hands upwards, underneath, and covered by debris.

Her mouth was extremely dry, and soon it would be parched. Hunger came too, in stabbing pangs. The temperature of her body increased. The storm had taken chunks of larger rocks and deposited them in clumps over the pathways near Gracie.

A few feet away, a mound of rocks began to stir. Rising upwards from it was a woman. Her back to Gracie. Long, brown hair unfurled with the winds. Gracie tried to open her eyes wider under the heavy debris that covered her eyelids and face. The woman turned around. She bled from the eyes and held out her arms with a desperate expression on her face.

"No, not here ..." Gracie whimpered.

Evelyn's gown was shorn in places, and the track marks on her arms looked like measles.

Evelyn approached, sobbing and crying.

"Gracie, Mama's come back for you."

The wind picked up the tattered gown, revealing more track marks down the front of spindly legs.

"You're dead," Gracie told the apparition.

"I've come back for you. I'm here for you now. Please, Gracie."

Her crying increased.

"Gracie, please ..."

"I forgive you," Gracie said. "I understand. The sickness was strong. Completely controlled and overwhelmed you. You still fought the darkness and didn't kill me. You left me with Gran Amália, who was the best mother you weren't able to be. Gran Amália gave me a life rich in values, love, hard work, and good food. Thank you for that. I forgive you. You can be at peace. I'm at peace. I also offer you the same ..."

To the left side of Evelyn, Kevin Pinto stood, wearing the same gabardine jacket and blue pants, his hands inside the deep pockets of his pants.

Gracie shut her eyes. "I forgive you both. Be in peace. I'm at peace now. I forgive."

The bugs started to gently gnaw at her bleeding wounds. Physical pain was a welcomed distraction.

She opened her eyes. The apparitions were gone. Mounds of dark rocks remained. Her face trembled. The cold increased. Her temperature rose. The damn bugs were making her sick and weakening her. She couldn't move her arms or her legs.

"Amigo, please help me ..."

The winds became calm, and there was another disturbance. It came from deep inside the sludge of the pool. Thousands of creatures rose up to the top of the sludge. The storm was over. It was time for them to feed.

Their long, powerful bodies plopped over the rocks and slithered onto the sand. The spines of their backs were robust, their sensors fully awoken, alerted by the scent of something odd, something new yet familiar. It was the prey that had fallen into their pool. They smelled the perfect prey—the kind teeming with fear, writhing in pain, weakening, and not too far away.

Her eyes shot open. Her body tingled. She saw the soundless predators in her mind, coming in droves down the sand pathways, tracking her scent. It would be a few seconds before hundreds of them descended over the mounds of rocks that hid her from view. A few of the clever ones slithered over the rocks behind her and came down close to her face. A fever raged through her body. She was weak due to dehydration, incoming starvation, and severe infection. Moreover, at least two pounds of debris covered her.

The rest of the creatures arrived and slithered over the mounds of debris, grunting, some pressing against her ears, their strong, warm bodies investigating her neck and veins, smelling the dripping blood and moving down the sides of her body.

They moved all over her for a few more seconds and didn't yet attack. Perhaps the smell of the dried sludge underneath the rock—glued to her body and clothes—made them hesitate.

One of them with the largest head—it was the one Gracie had seen come out of the sludge—slithered up the mounds of rocks that covered her chest, its powerful body pushing away some of the rocks that had buried her. Their eyes met.

The creature saw death and sickness in her. Its head stiffened, and the gills on each side of its neck shuddered open like a fan springing to life. Hundreds of others gathered behind it and had the same reaction.

As the creature prepared to attack, it cocked its head to the side. The other creatures heard it and so did Gracie. A whizzing sound ...

Amigo! Amigo has come back!

The creature took one last glance at Gracie, promising that it would return, then it slithered away, along with the thousands of the others. They moved obscenely fast, down the pathway of sand and back into the safe depths of their warm sludge.

A flashing light fell over the rocks near Gracie.

Gracie tried to speak, but she couldn't. She was trapped underneath mounds of debris and couldn't lift up her head, being so weak. The beam drew close and flew over to the other rocks nearby. It was a small drone. It kept on flying in the opposite direction from Gracie, it's whizzing sound distant.

"Come back! I'm here Amigo!"

She awoke again, delirious with fever, her breathing weak. A few critters entered a gaping hole in her right side. She felt their claws clutching at her sticky skin and incisor mouths, used to breaking open the rocks of their natural environment to eat other prey, continued to gnaw at her flesh, creating a wider hole, in which some of them snuggled inside and rubbed their bodies against the open wound.

The moons reappeared over the skies, which the storm had covered with debris that lingered in the atmosphere. The whizzing sound returned. The drone was back, high up in the sky, passing over Gracie.

She shouted in her mind, *I'm here, Amigo! I'm still alive!*

It whizzed over her a few times and was gone.

It was over now. Gracie would be dead soon. If this was how she was going to die, so be it. She didn't choose to be in the world, and she wouldn't get to choose how she left it.

A beam of light suddenly shot out over the rocks near Gracie. The drone returned soundlessly. It hovered above nearby, its beam focusing on something that caught its attention.

The beam swooped down to a small opening made between the mounds of rocks over Gracie's chest. Gracie saw the reflection over the drone, perceiving what had intrigued it. A tiny red diamond glinted back through an opening in Gracie's shirt. The beaded rosary necklace she had worn under her shirt—for which the creatures unknowingly moved some debris away when they slithered over her.

The red diamond found the light of the moon and responded by glinting, something most creatures wouldn't notice nor care for, but to the hypersensitivities of the drone, it was enough to grab its attention—a red glint instead of the usual glitter from the silver sand and black rocks. The drone homed in on the red glinting light and moved closer to explore.

This was Gracie's last chance. She had to do it. She had to work through the sickness and misery of death coming to her fast and find whatever ounce of strength left inside her to fight, even though she needed all of her strength just to keep herself breathing. If Amigo sent this drone to find her, she had to do something to let Amigo know she was still alive and under the debris.

I used to be a synchronized swimmer, and what has it taught me? We train together, but we fight alone in the depths of the pool ... through the cold water, through the pain. When we're close to losing consciousness, holding our breath for so long, suffering concussions and sprained bones, we fight through it. We're one of the strongest, toughest, persevering athletes. We don't give up. We fight. We always rise.

The voices of the girls, Tatou, Natasha, Ayshan, Sahara, Feifei, Adrianna, Kate, and Ms. Coligan, enthusiastically cheered her on.

"Swim, Gracie! Swim right up to the top! Do it now!"

With all of her strength, Gracie moved her fingers under the debris, near the drone and signed ...

S ... O ... S.

The beam of the drone fell over the slow movement under the debris—made by her long, thin fingers, which looked like tarantula's legs.

Gracie could feel herself begin to lose consciousness.

"Once more!" the girls and Ms. Coligan shouted. "This one is for the team—the Synchro Sharks!"

S ... O ... S.

She barely finished signing the last S when her fingers became still and she lost consciousness.

When she awoke, her body was still hot—feverish—and something scraped away the dirt stuck to her face. Rocks and mounds of debris were yanked away. Warm water sprayed over her forehead, and another over the wound on her side. She should have flinched in pain, but the fever was enough to numb any pain. Clumps of dried debris were scraped off from over her eyelids, mouth, and nose. She wanted to take a deep breath, but she was too weak to do it. A plastic tube entered the side of her mouth. Semi-sweet water trickled down her parched throat. Then, it stopped for a few seconds before continuing. She felt pressure on the side of her left arm and prickling sensations. She was too weak to lift up her head and further open her eyes.

Amigo came back. Amigo kept its promise.

When she awoke again, the fever had abated. She could open her eyes. The drone rested on a mountain of debris next to her. No lights or sounds came from it. To her left was a much larger drone, shaped with more intricate compartments. Wires came out of it and pumped liquids into Gracie's arms. A multitude of wired hands came out from it. A hand brought the tube with the semi-sweet water back into her mouth. A tent was above them, shielding the wind and debris.

Amigo. Where's Amigo?

A hose slipped down her back and washed her with a warm substance that smelled like chemicals, cleaning the dried blood, dirt, and residual bugs away. The open gash in her side was cleaned out, sprayed with something red, and covered with a soft cloth patch that clipped shut.

"Isn't it wild, Gracie?"

Jeff stood behind the drone, wearing his signature navy-blue bodysuit and beige turtleneck with the tag on the right side of his chest marked with black letters spelling PervivoTech. The curls of his hair moved with the wind. No debris over him. It was another… apparition. Only, Gracie was feeling better after the last one and could see more clearly, taking in his infectious half-smile, the twinkle in the oval blue eyes, and the kindness and love in them as he looked down at her.

"I designed and created this Medic-AI, Gracie. This one here is my baby girl."

He nodded to the AI that had cleaned, patched her up, fed wires into her, and kept fluids running through the tube in her mouth.

"Things take time and a lot of patience. It was worth it, Gracie. It's helping you, isn't it? Yeah. Glad it's helping you."

He leaned down to Gracie.

"Gracie, I know I let you down a lot. I shouldn't have taken that job in Whitehorse and left you alone with Jimmy, so close when Gran Amália had passed… I didn't realize… it was selfish ... arrogant. I was behaving like—you know, the typical successful robotics engineer type. I was totally caught up in my career ... the endless work hours."

"We both thought we were doing what was best at the time," Gracie said.

"Man, I just wish we'd gotten to Nagasaki to meet my father's family," Jeff said. "I would have practiced and improved my Japanese, learned to make sushi the real way ... and we would have made Gran Amália's filhós, those doughnuts for them to try. I kept on delaying the trip and all our other trips, again and again ..."

Jeff ran a hand through wavy locks from his forehead and sighed. "I should have made a few more trips to see you and Jimmy."

"When you were there Jeff, every minute mattered. We always had a good time, didn't we?"

"Yeah, that we sure did."

He took her hand and kissed it.

She placed it over his face. "I'm going to miss your beautiful face," she said. "I wish I kissed it more."

"Yeah, that makes two of us." He winked, patted her hand, and stood up, looking around the surroundings. "This is an odd-looking planet. Wonder which solar system this is?" He looked back down at Gracie, his eyes turning serious.

"When an earthly man disappoints you, Gracie, remember that there is only one man who never lets you down or disappoints you."

"Jeff? What the heck are you saying?"

Jeff disappeared, and Gran Amália replaced him, hovering above the shield of the tent. She sat in a chair, blue glasses at the bottom of her nose, her fingers busily tapping over a device strapped onto her wrist, playing a game of solitaire chess.

"*Querida*, He is always with you, every second of the day." She pushed up her glasses over her nose.

"The Lord Jesus was the only perfect man to live on Earth. It's not fair to judge mortal men against the Lord. In the Lord, you have the truth. Comfort. He will never abandon you, Gracie. He's with you now. You will see."

Her image faded and was replaced by a distant blinking light. Gracie thought it was a star, but it wasn't. The blinking light was fast approaching. It was a ship—a large one. Gracie choked back on the water in her mouth. The tube moved away. Gracie tried to speak and call out with a voice that crackled and was barely audible. "Amigo! I'm here Amigo!"

The ship neared, and the rumbling sound was deafening. It didn't look like a meteorite. It didn't look like a transparent oval ship. It was angular and metallic. It flew down, close to them, and the winds ripped the tent from its poles, sending it flying. The ship came close enough for Gracie to see a symbol over the side wing: five blue shields with five bezants in white. Gracie had seen this symbol before.

"*Listen carefully Gracie*," Gran Amália's voice explained. "*The five bezants in the flag represent the five wounds of Christ.*"

Underneath this symbol, in bold dark letters, Gracie thought she read the words *O Quinto Império.* The Fifth Empire.

In the distance, the ship started to descend.

PART FIVE

≈

The Fifth Empire

≈

But no, it is not moonlight: it is light ethereal.
'T is a day, and, in the sky ample with desire,
The unreal dawning of the Fifth Empire
Gilds the banks of the Tagus.

—Mensagem, Fernando Pessoa

CHAPTER 1

The Rescue

She was wheeled down a ramp. The air was musty. Something was inserted inside her nose, pumping air through it. The warmth of lights fell over her face. Gracie couldn't open her eyes.

Amigo, are you here?

No humming or intermittent chirping sounds—just the movement of wheels rolling down a tunnel.

You came back, Amigo ...

Her body was lifted up and placed over a cold surface. Gracie instinctively started to coil into a fetal position, but something pulled her shoulders back against the cold surface.

Amigo, wrap yourself over me. I'm so cold.

The tearing of material snipped around her. Her clothing was removed, and she was dropped inside a tub filled with warm, swirling water that came up to her neck. The scent was pleasant, with berries and vanilla.

Fast-moving scissors snipped some locks of her hair that were heavy and wet. Her body was lifted again. She embraced her body, which was gleaming wet like a newborn baby. She was placed over a cold hard surface. Her body trembled and her teeth clattered.

I'm so cold. Amigo, why aren't you wrapping yourself around me?

Lights whirled above her in a frenzy of flashing behind her closed eyes. Her wrists were strapped down. Instruments worked over her, peeling away the cover of infection on her side. She cringed as the section was further cleaned, probed, and covered again. A torrent of strong warm air blew over her body, hair, and face.

Gracie woke up and sensed a presence looming over her. She felt warm material covering her shoulders, legs, and arms. She was able to open her eyes and looked into a pair of light-brown eyes that belonged to a human on a face that was filled out, not sunken, not crawling with bugs, or marked with scars. The human wore an oddly shaped helmet that came down to their neck and a matching body suit.

The human adjusted the light and dimmed it. Their eyes met. The human looked over their shoulder. Gracie's eyes grew heavy. The sound of another human approached, and Gracie listened to their whispers.

"Tudo bem?" a female voice asked.

Lingua Familiae.

The human adjusted something in Gracie's arm and both presences lingered for a few minutes before their footfalls disappeared through the swoosh of a door that opened and closed shut.

Gracie awoke again. A holograph sizzled and appeared by her bedside. A woman in her mid-forties with an olive complexion, large dark eyes, and a pleasant face greeted Gracie. She looked like a benevolent aunt Gracie never had. It was no doubt to keep her at ease. A polite smile on the holograph's face. The network introduced itself.

"*O meu nome é, Maria Augusta.*"

Gracie sat up and found that she was in a hospital bed.

Maria Augusta gestured for Gracie not to move. The back plate of the bed lifted up.

"*Melhor?*"

Gracie nodded.

Maria Augusta wore a beige jumpsuit and matching leather loafers. The symbol of five blue shields and white bezants was on the right side of her suit.

"*Há fome?*"

"Do you speak English?" Gracie asked.

Maria Augusta nodded her head. "I can speak English if it's better for you," she said with a British accent.

Beggars can't be choosers.

Gracie's eyes adjusted to the room and made out a ceiling-to-floor glass screen along the left side of the wall. It was the entertainment centre to flash social media. By the foot of the bed and near the wall was a rounded table with three chairs. On the right side of the room, was a compact kitchen and beverage cabinet with multiple folded robotic arms. Floating next to her bed were holographs that ran read-outs of her blood pressure, heart rate, temperature, and other data points.

"Where is this place?"

"You're safe. Do you think you can try some light food?"

"Am I on Earth?"

Maria Augusta turned on her polite smile again. "You're on the Imperial Majesty's ship, *Navio Militar do Quinto Império*. Tomorrow, you will have visitors. They will tell you everything you need to know."

"Humans."

"Of course. How about something like ..."—Maria Augusta searched her electronic files—"chocolate pudding or a vegetable soup?"

Gracie leaned back against the bed.

"Pudding. It's made with real milk and not powdered milk?"

Maria Augusta smiled. "Real milk, of course."

Maria Augusta's holograph disappeared, and robotic arms in the kitchen sprang to life. Gracie nearly jumped. Gracie had cooked and fixed her meals for so long, watching wired arms and hands work on command, manoeuvring a pot, taking and mixing ingredients, heating them over a hot plate ... it repelled Gracie.

"You okay?"

"I'm just getting used to the new environment."

And getting used to a network being able to read every molecular movement I react to.

Gracie pulled up her short gown and touched the thin transparent sheet that covered the area of her injury on her right side. A laser had closed up the skin, and the cicatrize wouldn't be very noticeable at all.

"How long have I been here?"

"Sixteen days."

It felt as if Gracie had been there for one day.

"You suffered some dehydration and had a terrible infection—sepsis. You were sedated for a while as you healed. You're much better now. Your visitors will debrief you tomorrow. I'm here to make sure you're able to eat, drink, and feel comfortable."

Wired hands stretched out from the kitchen countertop and brought her a bowl of chocolate pudding, which was placed on the overbed table tray. The smell of chocolate was incredible. Wired hands poured some cold milk over the top of the pudding. Gracie waited for the hands to return to the kitchen and dutifully start cleaning up.

Maria Augusta re-appeared.

"Perhaps wait five minutes before eating it. You don't want to burn your tongue.Would you like to have a holograph of people sitting near you to eat with you?"

"How about a holograph with me sinking to the bottom of a swimming pool?"

"I'll see what I can do," Maria Augusta answered politely and vanished.

A few minutes later, a holograph turned on, dropping Gracie into a peaceful pool. This would frighten most people, but in Gracie, it aroused feelings of safety and sublime security. She had forgotten how the network could amazingly produce such a realistic illusion.

She lay against the pillow, forgetting about the chocolate pudding. Up in the ceiling, rays of sunlight gleamed over the pool. There was no scent of chlorine—just chocolate.

Gracie imagined the water pressed around her, the tips of her feet pointed outward as if she were floating off the bed and standing at the bottom of the pool. She held her breath for a few seconds and exhaled. She shut her eyes. She didn't expect the empty feeling to suddenly brew. Her mind drifted back to the meteorite ship, deeply ensconced inside the safety of hot pulsating gelatin as multiple trunk arms coiled around her and a sense of euphoria rushed through her. A glittering stream moved through the dimness of the walls, flowing upwards.

A sense of loss ... Amigo had left her, and the suffocating grief filled her, evoking the question she was all too familiar with ...

Why didn't you come back for me?

CHAPTER 2

The Briefing

Gracie turned off the warm shower. She was dressed in a beige bodysuit with a small emblem—the green and red flag of Portugal stitched on the left side of the uniform. Above it marked in small black letters, *5º Império.*

At least this synthetic cotton is much better than having to wear polyester.

Gracie reached out for a golden doorknob. There was none. The door automatically slid open.

Maria August appeared. "Good morning. Your guests have arrived. Is it okay to let them in?"

"Sure."

Three humans walked in—soldiers by the look of their black heavy boots, stiff postures, and how one of them held a weapon across her chest.

Two soldiers, a male and a female in their late twenties, stood behind another male, who looked to be in his fifties. The younger soldiers wore light olive uniforms with the Portuguese flag on the left and 5º Império above it. Stitched on the right side were their names, J. Mendonça and K. Mendes.

K. Mendes's gun packed the kind of heavy artillery that would blow something easily to smithereens. At least its nozzle was pointed to the floor. Her fingers were on every trigger. She remained by the entranceway.

The older man with the initials E. Da Costa had an authoritative presence with a hard expression on his face that was as stiff as his unwavering posture. Gracie suspected he was a Commander Chief or a General of some sort. His uniform was dark olive green. He sat at the round table and gestured for Gracie to do the same. A polite smile smeared over his lips similar to Maria Augusta's smile; only, he was a living human, not a pre-programmed image made to mimic human emotion as best they could. His eyebrows were thick and as black as the crewcut fuzz on his head. Small scars punctured his face and the underside of his jaw.

He pushed a transparent container toward Gracie. Inside it was the gold, ruby-beaded rosary. Next, he placed a circular device in the centre of the table, the size of a 1980s poker chip she had seen in the film *The Gambler* with the actor Kenny Rogers.

J. Mendonça stood a few feet away from Gracie. She had seen those light-brown eyes before, peering down through a small slit of a transparent visor as the wheels of a fast-moving gurney churned.

Humans. Humans in her presence. How often during her captivity did she yearn to see healthy humans again? Those who were free from terror...

She had often dreamed of being rescued by them, jumping into their arms, full of relief, thanking them graciously over and over again.

Surrounded by these humans now, there was no enthusiastic inclination for her to do such a thing. Instead, she noted their physiques. They were tall, muscled, and athletic as any well-trained soldier should be. They were weak and could be easily broken, torn apart, smashed against the room's walls ... Coils could snap away their weapons, easily tearing their arms and legs from their tendons and sockets while spewing poison down their mouths, causing their necks to bloat up like the underbelly of a fat dragonfly, then burst open in seconds, killing them.

"You prefer to speak English?"

E. Da Costa's firm voice brought her focus back to him.

"Yes."

"Are you from north of the Empire or from the First Empire?"

"What empire?"

"The United Kingdom is from the north of the empire. The First Empire consists of Greenland, Canada, and East-West America."

"I'm from Canada."

Stoic faces.

"I'm General Eduardo Da Costa, from the emperor's elite military forces. These are the emperor's elite soldiers, Jorge Duarte Mendonça and Katarina Mendes. They are two out of hundreds of elite soldiers on this ship. What is your full name?"

"Grace Mercedes Pinto. I go by Gracie."

"Gracie. What is your date of birth?"

"March 16, 2055."

General Da Costa's eyes darkened and searched her face for deceit.

"I'll get right to my question. How did you end up on that planet? The drone investigated every area for miles and found a pair of pants that belonged to you, and yet there was no sign of a crashed ship. You couldn't have just appeared on that planet. How did you get there?"

"What planet was I on and how was I found?"

General Da Costa didn't have a disposition that would tolerate anyone avoiding his question and even though he remained unmoving, something in him propelled him to answer her question. "The small planet was located on the fringes of another galaxy," he said. "A storm aficionado on a nearby ship noted a storm brewing on that planet and sent out his drone to investigate. It brought back images of a large storm that had passed and of something else that glinted outwardly from a pile of rocks. This glint was made from a different kind of rock that wasn't indigenous to that planet. The drone homed in on it and sent film footage back to the aficionado's network. Grainy images showed movement from the rocks that formed shapes which the network traced ... belonging to an obsolete language, indicating there was some kind of intelligent life under the rocks. The aficionado had a medic-drone onboard and sent it out to take blood samples and genetically map this species, which was confirmed to be human with the DNA of 75 percent Lusitanian blood, therefore, considered a citizen under the Fifth Empire. *Our* Empire."

General Da Costa leaned into the table. "There was no device in you or on you. Nothing to identify you. We were orbiting nearby and diverted our route to reach you in approximately three weeks. You were close to expiring upon our arrival, suffering mainly from severe infection. Now that I've answered your question ... how about answering mine?"

Gracie proceeded to tell them her story, the night of her birthday at the '80s club, her captivity, the vile creatures, the torturing and murder of humans, and how they enslaved them, forcing gruesome labour upon them. She recounted Amigo ... how it rolled onto Jimmy's locks and became infused with his DNA. She told them about the '80s apartment Amigo had constructed for her, how she passed her time, and how she escaped in another ship as the primary ship exploded, leaving her on the planet they found her. She wasn't sure why, but she didn't tell them about Laika, the Vampyre, the ballroom or all the riches in it, the groups of non-communicative humans, or the missiles she saw.

They listened intently, under unmoving expressions.

"Those vile creatures are called Maredians," General Da Costa said. "They are a highly intelligent species that used massive weapons to annihilate cities all over the world, depopulating whole countries and remaining on Earth for twenty years, continuing their destruction and ceaseless murder." General Da Costa's thick eyebrows squinted tighter together.

"Amigo. That's the name you gave it, despite having witnessed so much death and horrors caused by it?"

Gracie remained silent. How could she answer the General's question? The general's hostility continued to mount. The thought of her being safe in the midst of humans waned. She forgot how they too could be unpredictable and incredibly cruel.

"If you were able to communicate with this Amigo creature, did it tell you more about them?" Jorge asked.

"It didn't tell me exactly what type of species it was—only that they're asexual, live to a thousand years, and give birth to one offspring, dying shortly afterward. I asked, who brought them to destroy us, and it said ... their master. God."

"God?"

A half smile spread over General Da Costa's face, verging on disgust. "It doesn't make any sense," General Da Costa said. "Why would these Maredians keep humans alive, work them to death by dropping human parts and broken concrete into a sulphur stream, only to blow up their entire ship? These Maredians aren't fools. Then again, there haven't been any accounts of anyone returning alive from a Maredian ship to tell us what happens on their ships ... until now."

"You were born in the year 2055. Are you sure?" Jorge asked.

"I celebrated my thirtieth birthday the night before my capture. You would never forget that day. What is the date today?"

Jorge exchanged a glance with General Da Costa.

"October 2, 2221," Jorge said.

"2221," Gracie barely repeated, trying to understand that number and what it meant. Her mind calculated.

"I've been away from home for 136 years? I'm 166 years old? How is that possible? I should be thirty-two or thirty-three years old. I should be dead. Maria Augusta, what is the age of my biology?"

"Approximately twenty-eight years of age," Maria Augusta dutifully responded.

"That can't be ..." Gracie said in a disbelieving whisper.

Jorge's lips moved, and the centres of his eyes softened. She turned her face away and couldn't hear him or see the general's hard stare observing her. She looked beyond their faces to another place—a place painted with light-blue walls. A Christ-the-King nightlamp was turned on, and a little boy was sleeping soundly in his bed, pudgy little arms hugging a pillow. A little boy who would wake up to horrors around him without his mother to protect him ... and if he survived, he'd grow up and hate her, a woman he barely knew or remembered, the same as she had hated her own mother, who hadn't been there for her. If the Maredians and their attack didn't kill Jimmy that night, it was time that did.

Gracie shut her eyes.

Maria Augusta's voice rang in her ears and grew distant as if she spoke inside a whirling tunnel. Tightness tingled behind her neck and crawled over the sides of her face as if something invisible stretched outwards and squeezed the backs of her eyes, flicking them open to see the room and the humans transform.

The humans lost their shapes and became silhouettes of colours. Above them and behind the walls were rows of alleviated levels. Perched on each level, clumps of soldiers looked down into the room and watched them.

What is happening?

General Da Costa moved away from the table. Jorge and Katarina flanked him, and although their faces remained stoic, the veins in their arms pulsed with intensity. A sensation flowed inside Gracie, making her body want to rise up from the chair. Her hands gripped the sides of the chair to pin her down.

Maria Augusta's voice rang clear, asking her again ...

"Gracie, answer me. Are you okay?"

"Maria Augusta, something to drink please," Gracie managed to mutter.

"This is hard to hear. Very hard. I need a minute, please." Gracie willed the pressure behind her eyes to relax and let go of whatever caused her to see these transformations. The pressure obeyed, weakened its grip, and drained away.

She opened her eyes. The room reverted back to an off-white colour. There was nothing behind the walls with alleviated levels filled with soldiers watching them.

The humans relaxed. Katarina stepped back from the general, and Jorge removed his hand from a pistol that was hidden inside a side pocket in his suit.

"Where is my little boy and my family?" She asked. "Is there anyone ... what happened to my home?"

What stupid things to say. They were all dead. Everything was gone. There was nothing left on Earth to return to as when she left it. It was all radically changed.

Jorge's face softened, and she imagined the General's eyes, too, if only for a second.

"I can't be 166 years old. How is that possible?"

They would have expected her to break down and cry, but no tears came. They said nothing. What could be said? She was now in this time and place, alive but ultimately alone. No family or friends. No acquaintances or familiar faces. Only their memories being resurrected 136 years later. The tears suddenly wanted to come, but she hardened and willed them away. Unfortunately, the network caught onto her stress levels, and Maria Augusta appeared, programmed with mild concern on her face.

"Gracie, the juice is coming shortly."

A polite smile.

At least Gracie was grateful the network didn't ask what was wrong, or worse offer help—as if there was anything the network or anyone else could do.

Perhaps Amigo, when he took her from the work quarters had incubated her and preserved her like a pickled vegetable in such a way that allowed her to bypass cell degeneration.

"The goal of these Maredians was to wipe us out. That no doubt was their plan," General Da Costa continued, cutting into her thoughts. "Over a hundred years ago, that all changed when two major events unfolded."

Robotic hands placed a cup with a straw in front of Gracie. Gracie drank the cold semi-sweet liquid. Passion fruit.

"The first was in the year 2105 when a missile went off somewhere in United Korea. No one knew whether the nuclear blast came from the alien spaceship hovering over those parts or a nearby country had foolishly sent their own missile which the Maredians hadn't confiscated yet, against the spaceship. No one could possibly know what really happened, as that side of the world folded up in complete destruction, including the west coast of the First Empire, where your country resides.

This nuclear blast caused the climate to drastically cool off in many countries closest to the destruction. Survivors in nearby areas, far away enough from ground zero, noticed the Maredians leaving in droves. It seemed the Maredians didn't like the cold."

"The second event," General Da Costa continued, "occurred in the year 2110, when Portugal, which had suffered the least damages from the initial Maredian invasion for reasons most still argue about, developed a weapon against the Maredians. The tides soon turned, and we were the ones who drove the rest of them back to whatever hell they'd emerged from."

"Yet, there was little to celebrate. They had left a message behind about their return ... with millions more of them and with their master. This would happen between the years 2220 and 2222. They would carry out their plan."

"We're in that year range," Gracie whispered.

"That's right," the General said.

"Why empires on Earth? I don't understand."

"There are 10 empires in total," General Da Costa said. "We are the Fifth Empire which consists of the Iberian Peninsula, France, Morocco, the Atlantic islands, the UK, and Iceland. You can hear about the formations of the other empires on this device. You already know which countries constitute the First Empire."

"Many say Portugal was lucky. The country doesn't have an excessively cold climate and yet no Maredians remained to continue their killing, unlike in neighbouring countries. We don't know if it was the Tagus that they didn't like or maybe it was because of an ancient prophecy about the 5th Empire coming to fruition. The main focus is that everyone in the empire is prepared to fight alongside all the other empires—with the Global Council and the supreme leader—to annihilate the enemy when they return."

The General stood up.

"We didn't expect to find you alone on an unknown planet, left there by an enemy. You can understand how my officers upon learning about this, have concerns. I don't want any of them to face any distractions from their obligations and operations. You are very lucky to have survived and happen to be under the care of what I consider the best of all empires."

He meant it, and the way his dark eyes burned into her face, he expected her to appreciate that very quickly.

"Jorge isn't only a trained soldier but a medic. He's assigned to you and will remain by your side, closely monitoring your health and progress. Katarina is the leader of this section of the ship. She too will keep you safe."

"Tomorrow morning, you'll meet the emperor," the general continued. "This is his second mission on this ship, and he's very curious about you. There's never been anyone found alive that's been in the presence of a Maredian. We've recorded this conversation and have sent it to his advisors."

"Will I ever return back to Canada?"

"You can dictate to the network more details of where you lived, places, full names of your family members and if your son lived, you may have living ascendants. Jorge can help you do this, but it could take weeks, even months before we hear anything back from the first empire as all of the empires are getting ready for this last stand against the Maredians. They most likely won't spend their time on a research project about someone who showed up in a remote part of space, who claims to be a citizen of theirs and who's 166 years old."

General Da Costa straightened his back and strode away. Katarina followed behind.

Jorge pushed the chip device toward her.

"As General Da Costa had said, this has more information about the invasion, how we rebuilt and came so far, the formation of all of the empires, who rules them now and how emperors were elected."

"When will we return back to Earth?"

"About six months."

"Six months? I want to go home ... even if there's nothing left. I just want to be home, in my city, in my country where I belong, and help rebuild it like the general said. My little son could have also survived, and I may have living ascendants."

"You will get home eventually," Jorge said. "In the meantime, you will stay with us until we reach Earth." A faint smile brushed one corner of his lips.

"I promise we're not that bad."

"The emperor. What's his name?"

"He's called Your Majesty, Emperor Sebastian."

CHAPTER 3

The Emperor Sebastian

Down a shiny hallway, Jorge walked by Gracie's side. Katarina was ahead of them.

"Nervous?" Jorge asked.

"I've met other things much worse than an emperor."

Groups of soldiers passed by, dressed in the same olive-green uniforms as Katarina and Jorge. They nodded in acknowledgment and kept their stare trained on Gracie until she was out of their view.

They stopped in front of two massive doors.

A masculine AI voice greeted them. "Welcome citizens, stand back, please."

Jorge and Katarina positioned themselves two feet from each other.

A blue beam fell over each of them, and a holograph appeared, displaying their names and rank. *Jorge Duarte Mendonça. Elite Medical Officer. Katarina Mendes. Elite Lieutenant. Grace Pinto. Citizen.*

Then, the holographs disappeared.

"Permission granted to enter," said the AI.

"Thanks, Alfonso," Katarina said.

The vast doors parted, and Gracie was brought inside an atrium that was raised a few stories high. A grandiose banner draped down from the ceiling written on it, in bold letters she had seen along the underside of the ship's wing the words *O Quinto Império*.

They escorted her down a level that opened into a court full of network tables, which jumped out with holographs of maps, dimensional graphs, and charts. Groups of soldiers hovered around—each a flurry of activity.

It was a sight to see—so many humans together, fearlessly talking to each other, chortling, smiling, and pointing to the rolling information on the holographs as if no invasion had ever happened. As if time had moved on.

No one yet took notice of them. Gracie slowed down. The pressure behind her eyes returned, and the same sensation crawled over the sides of her face, stretching outwards and squeezing the backs of her eyes, flicking them open to experience the same visual phenomenon—the room transforming into a klaxon of moving colours, lines of wires running through the walls, under the shiny floors, and under the tabletops.

Each distinctive face, along with their uniforms and their medals became nothing but moving organs, highways of veins pushing blood through a throbbing heart, throat boxes rising as they spoke ... and beyond that, a palette of a misty black substance intertwining with a white opaque substance.

Gracie placed a hand over her eyes. Nothing swelled and nothing felt odd.

"Doing okay?" Katrina asked.

"Just trying to get used to having so many people around. I'll be fine," said Gracie, removing her hand from her eyes.

The pressure dissipated, and the holographs and images of soldiers in their olive-green uniforms returned. Soldiers fell silent as Katrina, Jorge, and Gracie approached.

Unmoving faces. Some curious. Eyes lingered on Gracie as she passed by a few of them.

"Damn, she's pretty," someone whispered.

"How was she not maimed?" someone else said.

"She couldn't have been with any Maredian. She'd be dead."

Gracie walked past a man and woman, names stitched on the right side of their suits S. Dias and M. Lopes. They watched her with cold eyes. Other soldiers wore expressions of impunity and suspicion. She had no friends here.

General Da Costa stood up from behind the centre of a console. He nodded to someone, another man, who could easily be mistaken for his brother—only, he had a thick beard and wore a navy-blue military uniform. He immediately waved a hand at them. "Do not approach," he snapped.

The air was tense. Gracie could hear their breathing, hands slipping inside the side pockets of their suits, seeking a weapon—except for the nearest soldiers, who already had their guns across their chests and their fingers on the triggers.

Behind the man, sitting in a leather chair, in the same navy-blue attire, deeply immersed in a holograph of a boxing match, was a youthful man with light-brown hair that bore a ginger undertone. Gracie assumed this must be Emperor Sebastian.

General Da Costa leaned down to his ear. The holograph froze and the emperor swirled around to look at Gracie. His eyes were steel blue-green.

Gracie had seen this face before ...

Emperor Sebastian had a pale, hairless face that was beautifully freckled, his lips were small but full. His steely blue-green eyes scrutinized her, as if she was the inconvenience that interrupted his boxing match, despite the fact that he had asked to meet her at that moment. A cold and reserved vibe emanated from him.

Then, the memory came. She was inside the apartment, turning pages to the book she had read more times than she could count, *Kings of the Iberian Peninsula: Fourteenth to Sixteenth Century*, the Cristóvão de Morais painting of King Sebastian poised in green armour with his faithful hound by his hand seemed to leap from the volume.

And now, before her was the same face ... the same long fingers tapping the swerving chair. "Your Majesty, her name is Gracie. She was the one that was found in the environs of Canis Major Galaxy," General Da Costa said. "You asked to meet her today."

"I've seen your face before," Gracie said, "In a book—"

The advisor pounced.

"It's your Majesty, Emperor Sebastian, and you do not address his Majesty without permission."

The emperor kept his hard eyes on Gracie and waved a hand at his advisor. The lines in the boyish face softened. "Easy, Gilberto. She doesn't know our customs. How could she? She's been in captivity for 166 years. You don't look that bad for someone that age."

A few soldiers chortled.

"I've read your report this morning. It's a fascinating story about survival on a Maredian ship where no harm came to you. You've also provided us with an interesting insight into these Maredians, who are an interchanging, malleable, species with one parent who lives up to a thousand years before their own death, and if they're young enough, they can ingest human DNA, show images of that child across their bodies, and are quite fond of the twentieth century, communicating on a board game or a machine type-writer, to let us know that it was God that sent them to destroy what's left of us."

His smile widened, and light crinkles appeared in the corners of his eyes.

A few laughs in the chamber.

Gilberto's dark eyes slanted with disgust.

"Whose face is similar to mine that you've seen inside a book that is just as rare as that ancient, bejeweled rosary that was around your neck when you were brought onboard?"

"Your Majesty," Gracie said, gaining a slight nod from General Da Costa. "It was inside a history book recounting ancient kings of the Iberian Peninsula. A painting of King Sebastian."

"Yes. I am familiar with the painting and that King. You aren't the first that has seen similarities between that king and me. Take a good look at me, though. I don't have what was called a Hapsburg chin, and I'm freckled. I'm not inbred, so don't even go there." A wide smile.

"Your Majesty," Gilberto intervened, "she's still recovering from extremely traumatic events. I'm sure she doesn't mean to offend."

"She's more amusing than offensive," the emperor said. "I'm quite impressed that she's able to recall this information about Portugal's ancient history while recovering from extreme traumatic events."

The emperor stood up. He was six feet tall with a strong upper body knotted with round, firm muscles. He had a lean midsection and hard, muscular, thighs. He had the physical body of a soldier. He stood in front of Gracie, hands behind him.

"I am the Emperor Sebastian of the Fifth Empire," he said. "I fought hard and earned my station in this empire. The coming and final war against the Maredians will be a battle that I also win. It will be the ultimate victory for me, for this empire, and for all of humanity."

The soldiers behind him nodded in solidarity.

"There's no time to make up fictional stories. Those who keep idle rust into irrelevance and will never belong to the glorious Fifth Empire, understood, Gracie?"

She hadn't made up any fictional stories … considering the tension around her, it was best not to argue with the emperor.

She nodded.

"I'm glad that our medic and staff helped you get better. Whenever you're ready to contribute to our cause, I hope you will do so. Your companions will help you figure it out. It was interesting to meet you, Gracie."

The emperor didn't wait for her to respond. He sharply turned his back and said, "Take her back to her quarters."

Then, he sat back down in his chair, as if Gracie had never been there, and activated the boxing match, returning to where he had left off.

CHAPTER 4

Prophecy and the 5th Empire

Katrina and Jorge were escorting Gracie down the hall back to her quarters when a group of soldiers caught up to them.

"Hey there ..."

Gracie recognized a couple of them. S. Dias and M. Lopes. S. Dias, who was well over six feet and brawny, extended out a hand.

"My name is Sergio Dias," he said.

Gracie stared at it, as if forgetting basic etiquette.

"Gracie is still recuperating, and her arms are weak," Jorge said.

Sergio nodded understandingly, then turned to M. Lopes, attractive, in her twenties, almond-shaped dark eyes with short-cropped, jet-black hair.

"This is Miranda Lopes." A smile of exchanges.

"And this one here…" Sergio said and turned to a short, sturdy, muscular soldier, "is Manuel Pontes. We wanted to meet you, as we heard about your remarkable survival story. We've never met anyone who survived a Maredian before. You seem almost ... unreal."

"I'm quite real," Gracie said.

"We wanted to meet our new companion," Miranda said. "Gilberto advised us that she'll most likely be assigned to our section."

"Gracie is under our supervision for the next two weeks, orders from General Da Costa," Katrina said.

"That's right, but after those two weeks, she'll be assigned to our section. Check the network log. You have permission at your rank. The emperor has agreed to that arrangement." Miranda moved her eyes over Gracie's face and down her clothes, noting how they fit her. "It looks like she's feeling better?"

"I am, thanks," Gracie said.

"Medic Mendonça, don't you worry," Sergio said, putting a heavy, muscled arm around Jorge's shoulder. "She'll be in good hands with us. We'll introduce her to the twenty-third century and show her how things are done."

Jorge pulled Sergio's arm off his shoulder, distastefully.

"She's in our custody for the next few weeks, and it will depend on her progress. She's been through a lot," Jorge said. "She needs to get stronger."

Manuel who stood behind the muscular Sergio had a boyish face and short brown hair. His dark eyes looked over the waves of Gracie's hair, which flowed down her shoulders. His heart pounded quickly, not out of fear but excitement. Yet, his face was emotionless.

Gracie could smell Manual's scent, a mix of ammonia and iron.

"If you're done with your introductions," Jorge said, "you can return to your sections now."

"Maybe in a few days, Gracie can join us for breakfast in the dining room. Would you like that, Gracie?" Sergio asked.

"When I'm feeling better, sure," she said.

"We'll be seeing you soon then," said Miranda with a friendly smile. "Just ask your network by our names, Sergio or Miranda."

They departed and continued down the hallway, eventually disappearing around a corner.

Jorge shook his head. "General Da Costa certainly has his hands full with these soldiers."

A moment later, they stopped in front of Gracie's door.

"My quarters are just down the hall from yours," said Katarina, "and Jorge's is right in front. Although those soldiers were being friendly, if you do need anything, contact me or Jorge first before anyone else."

"I will," Gracie said.

Katarina exchanged nods with Jorge and walked toward her apartment.

Jorge filled up a needle from a vial full of clear liquid.

"This is a concoction of vitamins and other sedative molecules to aid you in deep sleep," Jorge said. He positioned the tip of the needle against a vein in her arm.

Gracie looked away.

"Are you more of a medic or soldier?" Gracie asked.

"I'm fully trained as a combatant soldier and have pretty good aim. I much prefer to shoot medicine inside veins, do blood transfusions, and provide emergency care, though."

"Who is Gilberto?"

"Gilberto Menezes is a governor from the Global Council. Each empire has a representative from the council. They serve their emperor directly."

"Yesterday, General Da Costa mentioned something about a prophecy coming to fruition and the Fifth Empire. I'd never heard this before."

Jorge pulled out the needle and opened a small package with an alcohol swab, proceeding to press it over her vein. "Most consider it all hearsay."

"What is it then?"

Jorge put the vial and the needle into a kit, closed it, and sat on the edge of the bed. His hair wasn't cut as short as the other soldiers. It was parted on the right side and curled slightly by the lobes of his ears. It was a light brown, as were his eyes, with slivers of hazel, most likely caused by the light in the room. He had a lean smooth countenance, with shapely lips, the bottom lip being slightly full. She wondered what his own story was—how he and his family survived. She leaned against her pillow.

It's best not to know. Nothing mattered anymore.

"I'll recount this prophecy," Jorge said. "I will do my best to tell you as much as I can remember."

Gracie nodded.

"The prophecy of Fifth Empire is a messianic and millenarian belief," Jorge began, "which in the seventeenth century, a Jesuit priest by the name of Father António Vieira popularized."

"The idea of the Fifth Empire was mentioned in the book of *Daniel II*, when King Nebuchadnezzar had a dream, of a statue that featured five different kinds of materials, which Vieira interpreted, were five Empires. Four of these Empires had already occurred: the Assyrian, Persian, Greek, and Roman Empires. The Fifth Empire, he believed would happen in the distant future. It would be the Portuguese Empire."

"The myth of the Fifth Empire was connected with the supposed death of King Sebastian, who disappeared in battle and whose body was never found."

"People at that time believed that King Sebastian would be resurrected in the future and establish this powerful Portuguese empire that Vieira envisioned."

"The Fifth Empire is a coincidence. Many today don't know about this myth, and those who *do* know regard it as an artistic flourish in the poem by Fernando Pessoa called 'O Messagem."

"The Fifth Empire isn't some prophecy coming to fruition. It was the Supreme Leader who put the empires together about a decade ago."

"We, who happen to be Portuguese, and the emperor who comes from a Portuguese line of descent and, yes, has the same name as King Sebastian, and similar physical attributes, was selected based on a democratic system of votes accounting for military successes, physical strength, and immeasurable courage. He joined other territories to bring back a devastated world to some semblance of civilization and order again. He holds the largest numbers of "fake" Maredians killed during combat exercises. His numbers have remained undefeated by any other emperor, general or soldier across all the empires to date."

"What about the First Empire? I haven't yet activated the General's chip to learn about the other empires."

"The First Empire had a lot of survivors in the Northern Hemisphere after the first invasion. Survivors who made it to the north, settled in Inuit communities, along with other first nation communities who later joined them. They banded together with the focus to build new communities and learn the skills of the northern peoples, allowing them to survive, unbothered by Maredians who terrorized other countries in warmer climates for nearly twenty years. English and I believe the other language is called Inuktitut, are the main languages spoken today by all citizens of the First Empire, which is made up of survivors from Canada and East-

West America. Alexandra Arvalukk is the current emperor. This empire is numbered as the first, as the Maredians had first attacked it while nuclear war broke out between Russia and their Arab allies against Israel. The Maredians entered the scene shortly and wiped-out troops from all parties and destroyed what was left of any city in the Middle East—no one was spared. Their ships continued to attack the rest of the world from then on."

"After the Maredians left Earth, for the next hundred years, countries started to rebuild. They aren't the same as before the initial invasion. There are no gargantuan or megacities, as the world suffered drastic drops in populations. Most of these cities today, remain heaps of crumbled dust from initial blasts that burned them down day and night. Some are still full of human ashes."

"Do the other empires have networks and spaceships like the Fifth Empire?"

"In the 2060s, Portugal was becoming a leading nation in technology advancements, space programs, and AI. At that time, they had a motto that went something like 'In the ancient past, we navigated the vast and precarious seas of the world. In the twenty-first and twenty-second centuries, we navigate a new sea—the seas of space.' Space programs and technologies were very important, and having many survivors, they quickly revitalized these programs, as satellites weren't damaged like everyone else's. This allowed them to monitor the movements of the Maredians with operational drones and networks. It helped them efficiently organize and gather survivors and rebuild the military with every citizen participating. Although the Maredians left Northern Portugal unscathed, the city of Lisbon and the beach towns in the south were devastated and they were cleared out as much as possible. Then, using the operational drones, we began to search for other survivors in nearby nations."

"Couldn't our weapons kill the Maredians?"

"Nothing could. Not even explosive rockets. The bodies of the Maredians would fall apart to only quickly fuse together. There were accounts of Maredians removing missiles and nuclear plants—wiping them off the face of the Earth, completely disarming us."

Gracie thought of the thousands of missiles she'd seen back on the ship before leaving it.

"Strange that these Maredians were on a mission to remove every nuclear plant and millions of weapons from every continent. In addition to missiles, they removed aerial-attacking fire systems, war helicopters, on-the-ground semi-automatic systems, grenade launchers, cruise-missile submarines, war tanks, you name it—any weapon that was developed for war against other countries, which didn't harm the Maredians in the slightest ... they took them."

A faint smile as he ran a hand over the side of his head. "Ironic isn't it, that something so simple in nature had deterred the Maredians from harming survivors. The cold weather. How are you feeling? Do you want to rest now? You must be getting a headache listening to all of this."

"No, please continue ..."

Gracie didn't think Jorge understood how listening to him speaking, sitting by the side of her bed, the light playing over the mild expressions over his smooth face, the intonations flexing through his voice as he recounted the past felt comforting.

"Prior to the nuclear attack," Jorge continued, "our drones already observed the lack of Maredians in the northern parts of Canada, Iceland, Greenland, and Russia, and some of them suspected the Maredians weren't fond of the cold. This idea hadn't been strongly supported yet due to the fact that the drones also observed that there weren't any Maredians roaming inside

Portugal or the western parts of Spain where temperatures are extremely hot."

"Once the nuclear blast occurred in the east and the cold came, Maredians in those areas immediately left. The idea that Maredians didn't like the cold got the support it needed, and scientists, biologists, and the military began working day and night to develop the current successful weapon we have, a chemical that turns their gelatinous bodies into rock, giving us the advantage to blast them into annihilation. We packaged it and gave it to the rest of the world, from Portugal with love since 2110."

"And the Supreme Leader, who is he?"

"His name is Anton Abaddonovich, he resides in the city of Jerusalem, a place where the Global Council also resides. He came from the city of Nur-Sultan in the country of Kazakhstan. He brought all the leaders in territories across the world together and with him at the helm, established global Empirical territories across the world, who report to a Global Council which he is the leader. It wasn't an easy feat to do, and there is some strong opposition toward him."

"Why would anyone oppose someone who's brought so many together?"

"He wants to organize all of the empires to eventually merge into one global empire, with one flag and currency where he remains the leader at the helm. Most survivors across the world had agreed to merge into one of the ten Empires, as they were given the opportunity to select their emperor and most at that time wanted to be brought back into the civilization of governance where they would receive adequate health care, food, water, safety, protection and be organized to rebuild their devastated communities. To convince them now to merge into one single empire, many countries primarily in Asia, Africa, and South America, who worked hard for centuries to cast off the shackles of colonialism, won't be so easily convinced to surrender their sovereignty peacefully to one Supreme Leader. Hundreds of languages have been already wiped out as the Global Council only recognizes a handful of official languages. They are also vehemently against any religious dogma. The empires aren't permitted to recognize any single religion as being part of their cultural identity. This doesn't sit well with believers of many faiths that reside in the various empires, especially since when the Maredians came and left, a rise in the belief in God returned with many survivors even today. It's a complex thing, fighting over religion as this is something that will never go away. Right now, I'm a bit disappointed that my vitamin mix hasn't made you drowsy?"

"I'm starting to feel it," Gracie assured him.

"I'll make my usual rounds after breakfast tomorrow and check in."

"Yes, I would like that," she said, her eyes growing heavy with sleep.

Jorge held out a chip to her. "Press twice, right in the centre, for this red light to turn on. It's for emergencies and as your medic, it's connected directly to my network. Of course, you can always call on Maria Augusta if you need anything." He placed the chip on top of the overbed table tray.

"Thanks," Gracie said.

"Good night," Jorge whispered and turned to leave. Automatic lights dimmed behind him as the door slid shut. Gracie turned onto her side and pulled a blanket over her neck. She began to drift into sleep when she heard a familiar soft thump. Her eyes shot open. A cold shudder spiraled down her back.

By the foot of her bed, its glistening, grotesque body silently rose upwards. She immediately began to shiver uncontrollably. The smell of it, the stench of rotted beets doused in Kerosene. It was the smell of evil, the smell of hell. The chip Jorge left on the overbed table tray was far from her reach.

Her mind tried to reason, how could a vile creature be here in the safety of her room and on a military ship?

She stared wide-eyed at the shimmering emerald rocks that swarmed inside the rivulets of amber skin. Gleaming rows of sharp dagger teeth dripped with lavender poison, sprouted from inside multiple coils of swollen trunk arms. The trunk arms came toward her trembling face, the rows of teeth, clamped together like hungry saws wanting flesh, splattering poison over the blankets.

Gracie tried to scream but her voice was frozen. She tried to scramble away but the weight of its massive body crushed her legs and pinned her down.

A trunk arm stretched open its mouth wide enough to take in her whole head and snap it off her neck. There was nothing Gracie could do but surrender. She lay against the bed and closed her eyes. It would be over. Finally. She felt nothing, not even the pain that ruptured through her legs, underneath the massive, vile creature's weight.

Deep inside the trunk arm, a horrifying screech came along with a stream of pulsating hot, poisonous lavender that fell over her.

Seconds later, Gracie snapped upright in bed. Trembling hands covered her face. Sweat soaked her shoulders and back. There were no putrid trunk arms or any vile creature coming for her. She was alone. Her eyes darted around the walls. No shadows. Just dim lights running along the walls in the kitchen on the other side.

Where was Maria Augusta? Gracie's maniac heart rate would alone have summoned her.

"Maria Augusta?" Gracie's weak voice called out.

No response.

"Maria Augusta?" Gracie called more forcibly.

No response. The usual holographs that flickered with Gracie's vital signs behind her were gone. The ship continued to move at its usual pace, but that evil smell ... it still lingered.

Gracie moved to the end of the bed cautiously. Her shaking hands took the chip Jorge had left on the overbed table tray. She pressed the centre twice. No red light turned on. It was as dead as any actual 1980s Las Vegas chip.

Her eyes ran over the corners of the room. The pungent smell returned, putting her pulse in overdrive.

"*There's nothing there*, Gracie," she told herself. "*You're safe. There's a temporary malfunction with the network. That's all.*"

Even as Gracie tried to calm herself, the smell was too strong to let her accept that. She had to get to Katarina and Jorge. They would tell her why the network wasn't functioning and what had caused that smell. It was impossible that a Maredian was on board, but every sensation and nerve shook with alarm inside Gracie, telling her that a Maredian *was* on board.

She cautiously approached the door, which automatically slid open. Gracie peered down the hallway that was eerily dark and quiet. There was no human patrolling it or anything crawling on the ceiling coming down from it. The shining floors were solid, and nothing sprouted out of them. She heard a low hum—more of a groan. It could be some unknown machinery that Gracie hadn't paid much attention to before.

Gracie inhaled deeply as she'd done many times to keep herself calm and her senses fully alert.

She kept close to the wall and walked fast toward Katrina's door. She didn't anticipate a small hallway that cut into hers.

In the darkness of the hallway were shuffling sounds and as Gracie focused on reaching Katarina's door, it was too late. A hand came behind her, and a flash of something followed. She barely felt the zap at the base of her head as her body promptly dropped to the floor in a heap.

CHAPTER 5

The Game

Pain erupted in the back of her neck. Sounds of distant laughter echoed as glasses clanked together. Gracie opened her eyes. A flow of lights shone behind a glass wall, over the back of soldiers' heads. They sat around each other, drinking and enthusiastically conversating. An occasional female let out a high-pitched laugh.

Gracie sat up from a chilly concrete floor. She was in a pit with little light. The smell of rotting kerosene was strong. She breathed out whirls of smoke in the air and felt something warm resting against her. An arm. Another human was with her. Gracie's eyes adjusted to the dimness and saw three other humans lying still over the concrete ground.

Resting against Gracie was a burly man with curly grey hair, an unshaven face, and a round belly, who smelled of alcohol.

A woman nestled against another sleeping burly, red-haired man. The woman had a wide, flat face with dark, greasy hair stuck to her head. They wore the same clothes: green-yellowish jumpers that were the same colour as the velvet drape gown Scarlett O'Hara wore. Grease smudged their faces and arms. Although their plump faces indicated they at least ate well, they looked aged, sunken, with cracked lips, or ravaged by some kind of harsh manual labour.

They stirred awake, and a loud groan erupted. Gracie scrambled to her feet. A Maredian was twenty feet away. It bobbed up and down in a strange swaying motion. The Maredian was encased behind glass. This didn't give Gracie much comfort. Its colouration was different. No sparkling amber rivulets moved through it. No gold. No lavenders, reds, silvers, or blues. This one had a dull, eggplant hue.

Its smell was nauseating—a sweet smell like moonshine that hadn't fermented properly. The Maredian was about seven feet tall—not like the powerful ten-foot specimens she'd seen. This one could be sick, but that didn't make it powerless.

Gracie looked around. She was in a concrete pit with high glass coverings on the left side. Behind it, a handful of soldiers casually smoked cigars and drank beer. They sat around tables on an elevated level so that they could look down into the pit.

They played cards, snickered, laughed, and nudged each other. Gracie recognized their faces.

There was Manuel, twirling a cigar around the side of his mouth, the top of his suit open, revealing a white undershirt over a broad chest, displaying a mop of dark curly hair that sprouted like the Chia Pets, Gracie had seen advertised in one of the VHS tapes.

Next to Manuel was Sergio, whose long bronze arms rippled with at least twenty-four inches of solid muscle. He dealt out cards to Miranda and another female soldier.

The others in the pit were now fully awake. They moaned and scrubbed their dirty, greasy faces. Miranda sensed Gracie's stare and a wide smile spread over her lips.

"They're awake!" Miranda cheerfully announced and stood up, nudging Sergio and the woman next to her. Their heads turned toward the pit. They clapped and cheered and turned their chairs to form a line behind the glass as if a show was going to start.

The others around Gracie looked on apprehensively. The woman licked her dry lips. The burly man with grey hair coughed heavily. His eyes sank against the side of Gracie's face, down her neck, and over her waist and legs.

"The degenerates, the enemies of Emperor Sebastian, have awoken," Miranda continued. "We've got the rapist," she said, pointing to the burly man with grey hair. "The pervert thought that he could get away with the rape of two female soldiers while they were unconscious and recovering from sudden surgeries. Then there's the couple who foolishly tried to poison the governor and his staff."

Jeers from the group.

Manuel clamped down on the end of his cigar with his teeth. His eyes shone with excitement. Sweat dripped down the side of his red neck.

Miranda pointed at Gracie. "And our recently arrived star, the one who claims to have lived with a Maredian and who happened to never harm her. We hacked into the files and read everything. She spent so much time with the enemy that she eventually became the enemy and is no better than any criminal."

The Maredian hummed deeper. It was rising.

Gracie moved her eyes to the Maredian. The sound of its hums changed; it was guttural. It planned for battle.

"Go on. You're all free to do whatever you want before you die."

The burly man with grey hair immediately came for Gracie. She shot out a hand that grabbed his punch in mid-air that came toward the side of her skull. Although her hand was much smaller, her grip was remarkably strong and her hand began to snap his wrist and crunch his knuckles as if they were a bunch of walnuts inside the centre of her palm.

The man's eyes bulged out of his face, and he choked back on his spit.

The soldiers went berserk, cheering and banging on the glass. This agitated the Marediam, and its humming grew faster and lower.

Gracie let go and swiftly executed a hard kick between his legs, sending him high up and crashing into the glass. Blood splattered from his broken back like splashed paint from a Jackson Pollock abstract painting Gracie had seen in one of the encyclopedias. He dropped onto the concrete floor, unconscious.

Perhaps that will help fix his problematic tendency, Gracie thought.

Hands suddenly seized her waist. She grabbed the left hand and snapped two fingers as if they were dried spaghetti and threw a back kick right against him. She turned around and sucker-punched him in the face, feeling the nose break under the powerful impact as yellow teeth flew out of his mouth like kernels of corn and blood dripped down the side of his thick neck.

Yet, the fool, got up with a broken nose flopping over his face, cartilage exposed, eyes brimming with rage and feverish hate—the same look seen on the faces of several of the soldiers behind the glass, who jeered, screaming for someone to hurry the fuck up and rape that bitch to death.

Gracie recognized the voice. It was Manuel. A sick feeling emerged, nauseating her. This allowed a dangerous distraction that worked to the enraged man's advantage. He grabbed her neck with his powerful right hand—each finger thick as a bratwurst.

Gracie thought her neck would surely crack. She was losing air. Her arms automatically flayed as if swimming. She stopped fighting for breath and instantly held it in, helping her to focus. She delivered a punch to the right side of his rib cage, causing the man to immediately let go and fall forward, screaming in excruciating pain as his face went beet red and his eyes rolled up to his head.

Gracie flexed her hands in tight fists in front of her and with a boxer's dance, moved around the man, waiting for him to catch his breath and come at her.

Soon enough, he did, and with an enraged roar, he stumbled toward her. Gracie punched the side of his head, confusing him, then delivered another one—an undercut punch that brought him to his knees.

Cheers and whistles from the onlookers.

Gracie kicked him in the gut and grabbed him by the back of his greasy hair. Remembering a move made by one of the wrestlers at Wrestlemania 3 that she was fond of King Kong Bundy when he sent his opponents flying through the ring, she did the same with the man and rammed his forehead right into the glass, leaving more streaks of blood and spit behind. His limp body rolled over the burly man's.

Gracie's eyes homed in, on a tiny sliver of a crack left in the centre of the glass. Soldiers ran over to inspect the mess, partially fascinated by it.

"Incredible. No one has done this to an opponent ever before!" Sergio said.

Gracie suddenly sucked in some air. Sharp pain exploded in her shoulder, and she stumbled forward, turning around to face the smiling woman, who held a dagger deep inside Gracie's shoulder. The woman gritted the few teeth she had in her mouth, crunched up her face, and twisted the dagger deeper inside Gracie, taking some sadistic pleasure in doing such a thing.

Sergio's voice protested.

"That's not fair! No weapons allowed!"

Gracie calmly grabbed the woman's wrist and looked into the pale-brown eyes. Gracie pulled the dagger out from her shoulder, never flinching, and without a word, threw it behind her. With a hard punch to the side of the woman's head, the woman flopped onto the concrete floor like wobbling jelly, out cold.

The sound of sliding glass released the Maredian from its encasement.

Gracie moved to a back corner of the room, sinking down on her hands, knowing it would make no difference, as eventually, it would come for her, but Gracie knew, if this Maredian was starved, it would first feast on the humans closest to it.

Her onlookers mistook this as a cowardly move and booed at her.

She summoned her other sight to turn on. The ceilings were concrete, with no vents and only had a simple network wired inside. It seemed to be dormant. The walls were coated with an odd substance—like school glue—and long tables were folded inside. Perhaps this place was some kind of lab. She wasn't sure. Next to Gracie, the entrance door was solid and locked, featuring a small glass window. Her eyes searched for sensors around it. Nothing.

The soldiers became quiet as the Maredian left its confinement, screeched, and pounced on the grey-haired man. It lifted him up in its trunk arms and coiled around his body. The man moaned, realizing what had lifted him upwards, and he let out a horrific scream. Even though he was in great pain from Gracie's violent kick, the horror in him overrode the pain, and he desperately wiggled against the tight coils with the hope to be freed.

Gracie trembled as she looked on and begged in her mind, as she had done so many times before.

Please don't ...

A powerful trunk arm mercifully tore off the man's head and shoved the neck sprouting with streams of blood, into the centre of its body. The Maredian moved back and forth as it sucked out blood, veins, and guts from the man. The Maredian made gurgling sounds, hums, and subdued screeching as if this feeding gave it so much pleasure and relief.

Manuel was the first to cut into the heavy silence, cheering. He waved a fist in the air. Sergio joined him, and Miranda looked on happily, enjoying the man's death. The other female soldier cheered on nervously.

The unconscious woman moaned and looked disoriented for a second until she became aware of the Maredian monstrosity gorging and feeding next to her. She hollered and started to scamper away, but it was too late. A powerful trunk arm coiled around her flailing body and quickly planted its monstrous body over her, smothering and devouring her alive.

Gracie's eyes saw a flash on the mechanism on the side of the panel of the Maredians' enclosure. It was a manual latch. It might be connected to another network on the ship. Gracie made her move and sprinted toward the enclosure. A trunk arm shot out in front of her, but she saw it coming, jerked away, and scooped up the other groaning man. The trunk arm instinctively coiled around him and squeezed the bulging gut into an explosion of yellow fat and geysers of blood.

Gracie reached the manual latch and tore it off.

Sergio and the others went ballistic.

"What the hell are you doing? You broke the enclosure! How is that thing supposed to go back in there!" Miranda hollered. She pulled out a gun, clicked it open, and unlocked a side door. She aimed the gun at Gracie with a smug smile. "I can kill her now," she told the others.

"No, the Maredian eats her alive," Sergio said.

Miranda was suddenly knocked backwards. The gun was thrown out of her hands behind her.

Maredian trunks pounded at the small crack made in the glass until trunk arms completely smashed through. Gracie watched, as horror descended on their faces.

Sergio grabbed his heavy gun from under the table and shot toward the Maredian. The Maredian, having been generously fed, was quicker than they expected, and it bolted away from every attempted shot. Multiple trunk arms swirled around, causing some kind of confusion as one reached him from behind, snapping off his arm easily. The gun blasted shots into the air.

Next, a trunk arm grabbed the female soldier by her neck. She screeched and kicked as the Maredian easily pulled her toward it. Sergio grabbed her hand with his remaining arm, trying to help her.

Miranda and Manuel were frozen in horror. The screams of the girl quickly stiffened when coils wrapped around her waist, forcing anguished Sergio to let go of her hand. The Maredian dragged her like a rag doll, right through the glass into its body.

Gracie couldn't discern whether it was the girl's screams or Sergio's that rattled through the glass as the Maredian ate her alive.

Sergio, enraged, reached for another gun with his other arm and blasted one of the Maredian's trunk arms into a splatter of gelatin. The Maredian screeched and backed off. It sunk its body downwards. It was amassing poison inside itself.

Sergio came for it, ready to blast endless rounds into it, and lost sight of a trunk arm that came around to the left side and spat poison into his eyes. The gun blasted rounds into the air as he hollered and stumbled backwards while other quick-moving trunk arms silenced the weapon and formed long sturdy daggers composed of razor-sharp teeth. They wildly tore into Sergio's massive frame, easily dismembering him in seconds and silencing his pitiful screams.

Manuel bolted out from the side door, drunk and delirious with fear, desperately banged on the main, door and shouted, "Code 09. Alphonso! Open the door! Code 09!"

The door began to slide open, and Manuel being short, squirmed through it, just before a trunk arm reached out, latched onto the door, and rammed it shut into the concrete wall.

The Maredian, satiated and drenched in blood and guts, its hums loud and rapid, brought its attention to the remaining two women.

Miranda stood next to Gracie, her eyes wild in their sockets.

"What are we going to do?" she asked shakily. "It took the rest of our weapons."

The Maredian screeched and stretched larger, pumped up by the generous feedings—extra servings—instead of the planned four degenerates. A pool of blood, fragments of skull, bones, locks of hair, and excrement formed underneath its mass of what was left of the others.

Faces behind the glass in the doorway. Urgent shouts and banging on the door.

Miranda was relieved.

"Manuel got help."

The arrived soldiers distracted the Maredian. Gracie thought, what would happen if the soldiers blasted open the door and the Maredian, sprang up above them and got out, moving silently through the ship and disappearing through walls. How would they find it and kill it?

Without any sense, Gracie waved her arms at the Maredian.

"Come to me! Right here!"

The Maredian turned its body toward Gracie.

"Get inside the enclosure, to a back corner," Gracie told Miranda. "I'll follow you right after and shut it closed. Its glass isn't damaged, and it might not know how to open it. It can buy us time until the soldiers get in here."

Miranda shoved Gracie toward the Maredian. She entered the enclosure and shut herself in. Maredian trunks reached out for

Gracie. She ducked and bolted through the side door back to where the soldiers had been. Gracie leaned against the shut door and saw a few feet away, a rectangular device flashing with a green light … Gracie grabbed and pressed it, thinking it might open the entrance door. Instead, it opened the Maredian's enclosure.

The Maredian's attention moved back to it and found its prey exposed. Trunk arms coiled around terrified Miranda, whose face filled with terror and pain as she squirmed in its tight grip. She screamed and screamed, frantically fighting it off, punching and kicking it.

Blasting noises at the back door.

The soldiers were almost inside.

Miranda's screams became gargled, and she threw up spurts of blood as strong coils crushed her ribs. Her anguished screams grew louder and louder, ringing inside Gracie's ears. Heat rolled inside Gracie's chest, intensifying and rising up in her lungs and throat. Her lungs swelled up and flapped open, forcing Gracie to stand erect and spread out her arms. Guttural hums came out of her, vibrating deeply.

Gracie ran through the side door and approached the Maredian fearlessly, just like when the Vampyr attacked her and Laika. Gracie kept her intense, maddened eyes locked on the Maredian as her rib cage rose with each guttural hum.

The Maredian dropped Miranda, knocking her out of her misery, and moved away from Gracie. It listened to the odd hums; Gracie made from the depths of her human chest.

Gracie kept on approaching the Maredian, forcing it to move around, its trunk arms paralyzed at its sides until it was back inside the enclosure.

An explosion sounded behind her. Soldiers swarmed in, yanking Gracie back, and weapons exploded in a quick succession of blasts inside the glass enclosure, tearing the Maredian apart. Hands pulled Gracie's arms behind her, snapping her wrists together in handcuffs, and a nozzle pressed against the back of her head. A flurry of humans in front of her tapped her face and gripped her shoulders.

"What the hell is happening here?"

Gracie couldn't find her voice to answer them. Her eyes were still fixed on the dying Maredian, listening to its odd screech and agonized cries. The humans didn't hear it and went about assessing the carnage around them. They grabbed Miranda, who came around.

Gracie stood over the burnt body of the Maredian that shrivelled into the size of a doll. The Maredian watched her as it died, burning down into a shrivelled crisp. Its screeches and cries fell silent.

A soldier came into her face. "Step away, now!"

Gracie acquiesced.

General Da Costa entered the pit. He had no apparent reaction while assessing the body parts and broken glass strewn all over the place. There would be a hefty price to pay for whatever happened, and no doubt, he would be held responsible for what his soldiers had done, if he was aware of it.

His stern eyes moved over the patches of blood smudged over Gracie's suit from the stabbing. His face darkened. "Take her to the courtyard immediately."

The burnt remains of the Maredian was put inside a metal box and snapped shut. A soldier carried it out.

Gracie followed behind, flanked by two soldiers. Her eyes fell on Manuel, who stood by the doorway, trembling, tears streaming down his face. She stared at him contemptuously as she walked past him. He smelled differently this time. He had completely pissed himself.

CHAPTER 6

The Tribunal

In the courtyard chamber, groups of soldiers formed a circle around Gilberto, and Emperor Sebastian. Jorge and Katrina stood next to them, expressionless. A holograph moved with sizzling lines in the centre. It became terribly quiet as Gracie entered the room. Intense eyes over her. Gracie had just gone through a kidnapping and a Maredian attack from their soldiers and yet sensed that she was in danger.

General Da Costa entered the courtyard and stood by Gilberto.

A group of soldiers brought Miranda and Manuel in and shoved them into chairs next to Gracie. Their hands were cuffed.

Blood drenched the sides of Miranda's suit. Her breaths came in slow and raspy. Her eyes stared ahead. No medical aid was provided to her; no one fretted over her condition nor took into consideration that she could be in tremendous pain, having suffered at least a few crushed ribs. Miranda remained unperturbed by any terrible pain she felt.

Manuel's shoulders shook as he sniffled. He kept his face pressed against his chest, unable to lift his head and look up at anyone in the room.

Miranda's eyes shifted to Gracie. Gone was any hate or smugness. Even imminent death could sometimes touch the heartless in its own way.

From his chair, the emperor looked over them expressionless, his arms folded across his chest. Gilberto's face grew intense and approached Gracie.

"We heard Manuel's testimony. It was you who released the Maredian from its confinement, by breaking the latch that kept it secure."

Gracie kept calm. "They released the Maredian to attack me and three others, who I assume were prisoners. I broke the latch, hoping it would alert the dormant network that there was a problem in the area. I didn't know where I was. I was taken to that place by force."

"She wanted to be back in its arms," Miranda said, a laugh behind her voice, blood smudged over her teeth. "Her intentions are very questionable."

"She should be eliminated along with those traitors," a crisp male voice said behind Gracie. "It was a bad idea to bring her onboard."

N. Valentim. He was average in height with dark curly hair and intense green eyes.

"It's not a coincidence that she was involved. Her allegiances could be to them if she did release that Maredian. She's unstable ..."

"She passed the quarantine policy, Nuno," General Da Costa said. "Nothing was detected. No lethal virus. Nothing harmful. Otherwise, she would never have made it here."

"Why was there an expensive rescue mission sent out for her? We could have been home by now."

They were perspiring, bathed in fear. Gracie could smell it. Gilberto's dark, cold eyes watched her.

"Recede, soldier," General Da Costa said.

Nuno didn't hear him, and he started to tremble in fury.

"On Corvo Ninety-Eight, in less than two months, fifty-two crew and military staff were wiped out just like that. It can happen again." General Da Costa's eyes intensified. "Human errors were made, which everyone on that ship paid for. We learned from their reports left behind. It's not the same situation here. We obey orders from the Global Council and adhere to their policies. Or are you of the belief that we should not obey the Global Council and their own directives?"

"She spent a lot of time with the enemy," Nuno said. "Yet, they didn't kill her and left her on a planet for us to find. We could be bait, and we still don't know the truth; why would that Maredian let her live and leave her on that planet? She's a Trojan Horse and a liability more than anything else. There should have been a vote on this."

"A vote?" General Da Costa said.

"Elimination of the enemy posing a potential threat."

"She's no threat to anyone. We will get to the bottom of how she ended up in that section of the ship with the Maredian. Be patient. Now, return—and I won't ask you again."

Nuno backed away and tightened his hands into fists, casting his burning gaze at Gracie as he walked by.

Gracie partially understood their sentiments. She had spent almost two hundred years with their enemy—most of it unconscious—and yet the enemy had spared her from harm, providing her with food and water in a functional apartment useful to her every basic whim ... while hell erupted on Earth, ravaging their great-grandparents, grandparents, their own parents, and themselves. As they prepared for another battle with the Maredians, she'd been with them all along. It was incomprehensible for them to believe that Gracie, too, had suffered. There was nothing useful to be offered up by the human condition—only feelings of jealousy and resentment directed toward those who were lucky enough to be spared during the horror of times. And Gracie knew how dangerous these emotions were—how they led to blind hatred, begetting division, civil unrest, and then war, resulting in untold death and destruction.

"How did you get into that section of the ship?" General Da Costa asked.

"I was lured out of my room," Gracie said, "by the smell of kerosene—the scent of a Maredian."

"You were able to smell the Maredian from your quarters?" Gilberto sternly asked, exchanging a sidelong glance with some of the soldiers. "The location of where the Maredian was kept is quite far from your quarters on this ship. There are no vents in that place; therefore, it's impossible that you could have smelled it. Answer the question truthfully; what lured you out of your quarters?"

"I thought I smelled a Maredian," Gracie said, not wanting to argue as they were already tense and nothing she could say would be believed anyway.

"The network in my quarters was dead. Maria Augusta wasn't responding when I called for her. I went to get Katarina, whose quarters are next to mine. While I did that, I was attacked from behind, knocked out by something ..."

Gracie pulled up her hair and turned her face to the side.

General Da Costa approached.

"A taser," he said.

"I awoke in that cell—whatever it was. They brought me there, to be killed by the Maredian along with the other prisoners, who also tried to attack me before the Maredian was released."

"How was the Maredian let loose?" Gilberto said. "How did it manage to break a specifically designed Maredian-proof glass encasement and kill one of our lieutenants and another elite soldier?"

Gilberto swiftly moved in her face.

"If anyone died, it should have been the degenerates and not any of my esteemed, elite soldiers!"

"Your esteemed elite soldiers wanted one of the degenerates ... let's just say more nicely ... to 'violate' me to death," Gracie said, keeping the rising anger out of her voice. "They eagerly cheered for it and wanted to see it happen. The dangerous Maredian just kills. It wouldn't violate me slowly for some kind of sick pleasure. This is a unique evil known to humans like your esteemed, elite soldiers."

A profound sense of hopelessness came over her.

"After so many years, the human species still functions as many other generations before, allowing evil to dominate and rein over their senses? Is this sick game accepted as part of today's society?"

She expected Gilberto to be enraged and pounce on her—to curse her out for such an insidious notion. But instead, he said nothing and half-smiled as if her words amused him and nothing more.

"Is there any humanity in this century?" asked Gracie, still brimming with anger.

The disgust on the soldiers' faces flared up, especially over Nuno's face as if Gracie's criticizing of the actions of the soldiers made them think that she was defending the Maredian.

Emperor Sebastian remained emotionless, swivelling around in his chair, contemplating everything that had been said.

"The behaviour and actions of these soldiers, if true, is indeed unacceptable," General Da Costa said. "We do not agree with these sentiments. That is why Miranda and Manuel will be dealt with and be an example of, demonstrating what happens when we allow ourselves to get out of control and decide to let our baser emotions rule us." General Da Costa shot a hard glance at Nuno.

Gracie was somewhat relieved. It might be an event not supported by them, but she still wasn't sure if General Da Costa meant it or was just attempting to save his own hide from the disaster that happened under his watch.

"What would have happened if that Maredian had escaped? Then what?" Gracie said.

"That area is highly secured. The walls are coated with a substance a Maredian cannot move through. Alphonso would have tracked it down in minutes, and it would have been dealt with immediately," Gilberto said with a nonchalant shrug.

"How is there even a Maredian onboard? Keeping a horrid thing in the same place where you sleep, eat, and drink? And where did you get it? Didn't they leave Earth in the year 2110 or so?"

"This one was captured in Morocco," Gilberto said, "and placed in a special freezing encasement. It's been ours for over a hundred years with no accidents, no problems, or anything getting out of control ... until you got close to it. We were the only empire with a captured Maredian and the only ones attempting to study one—to discover more of its weakness so we could kill its kind more efficiently. The supreme leader will not be very happy about this loss," he said, his eyes lifted toward the emperor.

"However, with the Maredians coming back very soon, we may be able to replenish this loss with a fresh one. If we can catch one again. They're not so easy to capture."

"Who is your God?" Gracie suddenly asked. "What moral compass do you seek guidance and virtue from?"

Gilberto's eyes slanted. "The God of War," he snapped. "The scientific, evidenced-based God of War that advocates fighting these Maredians when they arrive—until none of them are left. That is our God."

An artificial male voice, Alfonso, interrupted them. "*Images restored. Holographs being generated in twenty seconds.*"

General Da Costa's stern eyes rested over quivering Manual and Miranda.

"Although the old lab was shut down years ago with networks removed," General Da Costa said, "all who had restricted access to it, as Lieutenant Dias, mistakenly thought it was just a cold room with concrete walls covered in Maredian-proof substances and nothing else. But there was one network that still remained. Every lab in use or not, on this ship, is networked. Anyone tampering with the network will suffer a very bad fate as Lieutenant Dias learned."

"*Holographs generating,*" Alphonso said.

A holograph displayed the scene of Gracie fighting the degenerates. The emperor leaned forward in his chair, his eyes focused on Gracie's strength—how she crushed her opponents swiftly and easily. Voices from Gilberto's elite soldiers were heard in the holograph, jeering, cheering ... then Manual's outburst. The Maredian was released not by Gracie as she had recounted, clearly exonerating her. If she had to be nervous about anything, it was the next scene.

The sound she made was hideous—like a loud, croaking frog. It didn't seem that loud to her at the time, but listening to it on the holograph, it was terribly loud. She entered the holograph, with her arms wide open, her neck bulging in tune with each sound she made out of her mouth, her ribcage rising quickly as if something lived inside her lungs, her eyes penetrating, unflinching at the Maredian, as she inched toward it and it backed away from her, something everyone in that room knew a Maredian would never do when encountering a human.

The expressions on their faces were a mix of surprise, disgust, and concern hinging on fear. The emperor's expression changed to one of deep focus.

Gracie shut her eyes, despairing. This was the evidence that would no doubt deem her a threat, and she would suffer the same fate as Miranda and Manuel.

All waited on the emperor to react. He leaned back in his chair with a hand under his chin.

Gilberto smiled at Gracie, which was more frightening than his usual frown. "Looks like you spoke the truth," he said patronizingly. "And you didn't release the Maredian. You also have an interesting ability to make a disturbing sound that sounds something like them."

Gracie herself didn't understand it. "I'm human," she said. "I'm not one of them. I can assure all of you of that."

The faces remained cold and unmoving.

Gilberto snapped his fingers at two soldiers and gestured to Miranda and Manual. "Alphonso has clearly shown the evidence regarding who the mutineers are. No further waste of time. Remove them and incinerate them immediately. As for her—she remains just a bit longer."

Hearing this command, soldiers snatched up Miranda and Manual. Miranda let out a whimper, and a stream of blood ran down her chin. She could barely hold her head up, but no sound of protest issued from her as she was dragged away.

Manuel's whole upper body heaved in time with uncontrollable sobs, and he kept his eyes down as he was shoved away.

Gilberto leaned down to the emperor's ear, and Gracie read his lips: "*What do you want to do with her?*"

"Send her to lab seventy-four. I want to know what is inside her," the emperor responded.

A look of slight surprise fell over Gilberto's face.

"Your Majesty, with all due respect, the MXT will take up quite an amount of energy to run tests. It's much easier to turn our attention to the enemy and handle her in the same way her traitorous companions will soon face."

The emperor contemplated this for a minute, then said, "I want to see what the MXT will tell us about what's causing this sound. Afterwards, I will make my decision."

Gilberto nodded in acceptance. "General Da Costa," he said, "bring her to the lab as per His Majesty's desire."

"Before she's taken, the emperor said, "I need to ask her a question. Alfonso," he demanded, "roll section thirty-eight."

The holograph sprouted above the console in a large frame, and the emperor stood up and moved around the holograph with his hands behind his back, watching Gracie fight off both of the men, moving around them, dancing like a boxer, delivering solid punches to the side of one man's thick face, side-kicking him easily—effortlessly.

"This is what many fear, your Majesty," Gilberto said. "Her strength and how she easily subdued those strong men. She can easily kill one of us if she gets out of control."

"Yes, Gilberto," the emperor agreed. "She's very strong, especially for her small size. Yet, our soldiers are always armed, and so far, in the past week that she's been in close contact with her medic and guard, she hasn't displayed any outward hostility."

"None, Your Majesty," Katrina confirmed with a nod from Jorge.

"Not *yet*, your Majesty," Gilberto gently said. "We want to avoid any potential hostility, considering the coming war and our complete dedication and focus to its urgency."

The emperor approached Gracie and looked over her physique as a lion would stare down a rhinoceros.

The soldiers' fingers slipped over the triggers on the firearms.

"You fight well," the emperor said. "You've been trained in boxing and martial arts."

Gracie nodded.

It was best to say very little considering she was still in a precarious situation.

The emperor gestured to Jorge and Katarina to escort her away.

General Da Costa followed closely behind.

"I'm just curious to know," the emperor continued, "who was your master in martial arts? Did you have a league name?"

"Chuck Norris and Bruce Lee, Your Majesty," Gracie answered. "They belonged to the League of VHS."

The emperor nodded and said, "The Emperor of the Fifth Empire congratulates Chuck Norris and Bruce Lee from the League of VHS, for having trained you well."

The doors of the courtyard chamber slid open ahead of Gracie. A smirk should have been on her face, but instead, her eyes followed a shining, endless hallway that would lead her to lab seventy-four, which would tell her soon what exactly was nestled inside her lungs and behind her eyes.

CHAPTER 7

The Discovery

After a hot disinfectant shower, wearing a thin covering, Gracie was brought inside a stand-up machine that was circular and semi-opaque.

A tall man in his forties with a dark complexion and a transparent mask over his nose and mouth entered the room. The name Dr. Campos was stitched on the right side of his uniform.

Dr. Campos nodded in acknowledgment to Gracie. "I see that the patient is ready."

"She is," Jorge said.

Katrina remained with another soldier recessed in the entranceway. General Da Costa stood next to Jorge.

"Don't be afraid, Gracie," Dr. Campos assured her as he read holographs, which ran her heart rate and other indicators.

"The MXT will run a complete scan over you. I'll need you to stand with your feet a bit apart. Hold onto the two handles on the sides of the machine and keep your posture straight."

Gracie did what she was told. Lights inside the capsule dimmed, and blue lights moved through the walls of the capsule.

"You'll be all right, Gracie. Close your eyes if it will help you relax. This will be over in a few minutes."

Close her eyes? Sensations had already begun to move behind her eyes, and she saw beyond the capsule, over the faces of Dr. Campos, Jorge, and General Da Costa.

Blue light fell over her feet and rose up in short intervals. The beams were hot, and Gracie's skin prickled. A holograph formed in front of Dr. Campos and displayed the outlines of bones; muscles; digestive, reproductive, and internal organs.

Although they kept their voices low, Gracie could hear them.

"Things appear normal," Dr. Campos said.

The scanner moved up her stomach and lungs.

The holograph changed, and in the darkness of what had been organs, the MXT magnified and turned other features that displayed something that coated the walls inside her lungs like a veil that moved gently with each breath. Behind each branch of air sacs in her lungs, tiny sparkles of gold, red, and blue glistened, flowing through a viscous amber fluid.

"What's inside her lungs?" General Da Costa asked.

"I'm not sure. It looks like some kind of breathing mechanism," Dr. Campos said, "that has merged inside and around the lungs."

"A double breathing mechanism, maybe?" Jorge asked.

The blue light inside the MXT moved up her chest, over her throat and head.

The amber fluid continued in a steady, glistening flow from her throat into the pituitary and penal glands.

"Is it dangerous? Will it cause any disease that will jeopardize us?" General Da Costa asked.

"It seems to have an ability to infuse and embed itself inside the inner lining of her lungs, windpipe, throat, and even inside the brain. It's not a solid lump that can be simply surgically removed."

Dr. Campos turned his attention to Gracie. “Gracie, how are you doing?”

“What are you seeing?”

“Nothing concerning.”

Nothing concerning? Whatever had been put inside her was *very* concerning. Amigo, what have you done? Yes, this respiratory system Amigo put in her probably allowed her to breathe in the getaway aircraft, see through it, and even survive the atmosphere on the planet Amigo left her. This discovery would send most humans into a terrified panic, and she may not survive what these dangerous humans would decide to do with her now.

The MXT moved along the sides of her throat and concentrated on the tissue there. The sides rippled, and gills appeared underneath her voice box.

“That might explain the strange sound she’s able to make,” General Da Costa said.

“Why would the Maredian create this kind of breathing mechanism or whatever it is inside her?” Jorge asked.

“Perhaps some kind of experimentation. Who knows,” Dr. Campos said. “The good news is that it doesn’t seem to entail any growth. It’s not replicating, and there’s no presence of anything else such as a contagion causing any other serious illnesses in her. I would recommend keeping a close eye on her—under guard to be sure. Give her no reason to hum and frighten the others with it, and things should be fine until we get to Earth, and she’s transported to a much better medical facility for further observance.”

The doors to the lab slid open. The soldiers made way for Gilberto.

“Report, Dr. Campos,” he said, looking at the MXT’s holographs.

"She has some kind of respiratory system inside her that's most likely the cause of the odd sound she makes when stressed. There is no contagion detected that can spread—nor does anything appear to be evolving inside her. This Maredian system connects to her pituitary and penal glands, which may account for her inability to age at a normal rate. This is my speculation. In the meantime, I recommend she be closely monitored until we return to Earth."

The MXT turned off. Jorge helped Gracie out of the MXT and sat her down.

"How are you feeling Gracie?" Dr. Campos asked.

"Fine," Gracie said, although she was far from feeling fine. She couldn't look up at their faces—faces that she knew would stare at her with expressions of discomfort ... perhaps disgust or fear. A few minutes ago, she had been a human like all of them, and now they saw her as something horrific—human and Maredian fused together.

"Load these holographs into her device and increase all security sensors in it," Gilberto said.

Gracie broke out of her thoughts and weakly stood up.

"What device? There's a device in me?"

"It's behind your shoulder," General Da Costa said.

"I want it out of me."

"That's our security policy," snapped Gilberto. "Everyone here has a device."

"I don't want it. I never asked to have a device put in me."

"That's unfortunate for you. As I said, it's our security policy."

"Advisor Gilberto," General Da Costa said, "we *do* have some soldiers who are permitted to wear the device as a bracelet, in instances of allergies or any other kinds of discomfort. The emperor has authorized this option."

"Take it out. I want it out."

"Is it hurting you?" Dr. Campos asked.

"I don't want any device inside me."

"It won't matter," Gilberto said. "Very soon, the emperor will decide your fate and whether you have a device or not won't matter."

A smug smile.

"I can just freeze the area and remove it," Dr. Campos said. "It won't take up much of my time and will keep my patient calm—as I recommend, to keep her calm as much as possible, irrelevant of any upcoming ... events."

Gilberto intensely stared down Dr. Campos.

"Fine. It's your time, Dr. Campos," he finally said and leaned down to Gracie's ear. "What are you so worried about? It's too late. Looks like the beast has already marked itself inside you."

He straightened up and strode away with his guards behind him.

CHAPTER 8

The Advantage

Gracie stood in the courtyard. She wasn't handcuffed, but her hands crossed in front of her as if she was. Soldiers stood behind her with their fingers in their usual position, ready to fire at will if commanded to do so.

Emperor Sebastian's face bore its usual stoic expression. Most of the soldiers eyed her with inner disgust just as she had feared as if they were looking at a Maredian and not at what she was determined she still was, a human just like all of them.

General Da Costa, Jorge, and Katrina stood to the right side of her. They were expressionless. Perhaps neutrality was better than showing disgust or sympathy toward her.

A middle-aged man, bespectacled, with short spiked, white hair and with the physique of a soldier, approached the emperor. Dr. Ferreira addressed the court.

"As his Majesty's personal medic, I've closely reviewed the holographs and the reports. After some time of deliberation, I recommend that it is best for Your Majesty to have the subject removed, in the interest of the mission."

"It's just some kind of breathing mechanism," Gracie blurted, "I won't hurt any of you. I don't have a contagious virus. This condition I have isn't harming anyone but me. It makes my breathing hard but doesn't hurt anyone else. I alone suffer with this condition."

"Your Majesty, I wouldn't call what has shown up inside the subject—"

"It's Gracie!" she sharply said. "My name is Gracie Mercedes Pinto."

"Suffering or not from this condition," Dr. Ferreira continued, "she has something unknown made from a Maredian put inside her for reasons we aren't sure of ... while we're waiting for a war with them to begin at any moment. We *cannot* have anything on this ship that may pose a problem."

"I'm human still. I'm human like all of you with a different breathing system—and I still have my human lungs. I am not a Maredian and I don't pose any threat!" Gracie said, exasperated.

The emperor remained quiet, staring at the holographs with the amber viscous liquid that flowed through the lining wall of her lungs—and the gills swirling back and forth along the sides of her throat.

How could she convince him? The majority of them in the courtyard, guided by pure terror, looking at a human-Maredian hybrid, wanted her immediately exterminated. She was going to be murdered not by a Maredian as she always thought but by her own species.

The painting of King Sebastian in his green armour flashed in her memory. The steel blue-green eyes ...

Tatou's voice from so long ago echoed in her ears … *they are working to resurrect ancient people. The list includes European Royals ...*

Alfonso's voice reverberated through the courtyard: "Subject reacting."

Clicks and the sizzling of weapons came to life.

"You will be making a big mistake if you kill me, your Majesty," she said, her voice calm.

Hearing this, he turned to look at her.

"I am the hope that you've been waiting for—that you finally have—Your Majesty. I am it. I am that elite soldier that will bring back your empire to a glorious victory, over all the other Empires when the Maredians return. No other Empire has something like me—heightened senses, fighting skills, and this sound I possess, renders the Maredians weak, no other soldier has this ability."

"Yes, the Fifth Empire has been a *glorious* Empire. Yet, the Third Empire has quickly advanced its space programs and combat missions, despite having suffered a devastating nuclear war. They have dramatically impressed the supreme leader in the last few years. Train me, and I will bring back the glory of your empire that you so desire and so deserve. The Global Council and everyone in all of the empires will revere you like no other emperor in the history of human existence."

Her eyes burned into his, and she could see his body behind his suit, intensify with excitement, pupils dilated, long fingers curled into fists, his heart beating wildly in excitement. A flush of pink came over his cheeks. If the emperor was anything close to a personality like King Sebastian, then every word that she said would resonate deeply and prove that it absolutely meant everything to him.

"Do not hastily throw this unique opportunity away because no one here can see what you can—the importance of winning at all costs. You sensed this before when you wanted to see the MXT results. You knew, instinctively something was telling you to have that checked and not just dispose of me then. Now you know why, your Majesty. I will bring you to victory. I am it."

Gilberto remained still and didn't pounce with his usual condemnations. He watched Emperor Sebastian closely.

The emperor didn't remove his eyes from hers. "You are an excellent fighter," he said. "You do have the foundational skills to fight. I still have a small problem. What assurance can you give me, that you will be ultimately loyal to me and not to anything else?"

"I can assure you that I have no allegiance to any Maredian. I am devastated by what they did to me. I have suffered. I am still suffering, and I also believe strongly in and follow an ancient philosophy of allegiance," Gracie said.

The emperor faintly smiled. "What does that mean?"

"My Creator comes first," Gracie responded, "after Him, my emperor, king, and governor. As you are my emperor, I faithfully obey you if you lead me to what is righteous, which is to fight and defeat the Maredians."

The emperor approached Gracie, and she felt the horror inside the others in the room. She sensed them recoiling. Yet, the emperor's cold eyes scrutinized her face and the side of her neck, where the odd sound emanated from.

Then, he turned his back.

"Take her to the training combat section," he finally said.

Gilberto's eyes met the disbelieving look from Dr. Ferreira and from most of the soldiers.

"Sire, you don't know what she's capable of. None of us do," Dr. Ferreira said. "It's not my professional recommendation. I ask for you to respectfully reconsider."

"Enough!" Emperor Sebastian snapped. "All of you aren't understanding what we have here. All of you are blind by your own pathetic fears. I am disgusted. All of you can't see it. The

Maredian showed fear when she made that sound. It lowered its defences and backed away from her. That is our new weapon against the Maredians! I want that sound immediately captured, amplified, and uploaded in Alphonso, and inside every soldier's helmet. She has an ability that will help us defeat the Maredians and the empire will rise back to its glorious days from when our surviving great-grandparents first defeated the Maredians and when I ascended as emperor."

He snapped his fingers at a soldier behind Gracie. She quietly exhaled, feeling a sense of relief but it was short-lived.

"Sergeant Nuno Valentim is one of our best trainers," the emperor said. "After recording your unique sound, he will start your training immediately. Bring her to the combat zone."

The Emperor Sebastian strode out of the courtyard, flanked by soldiers, leaving behind Dr. Ferreira and Gilberto, whose lips mutually tightened with displeasure, as if they both had just tasted the vile Maredian sludge Gracie and thousands of other souls had once drunk to stay alive.

CHAPTER 9

The Proposal

Gracie was put on a daily twelve-hour on-the-ground combat course filled with traps. Holographic gelatinous Maredians would ooze out from rocks and materialize in front of her. Gracie put on her other sight, which she began to call the Maredian sight when she sensed movement coming from underground, far behind or through a mound of rocks before any of the more experienced soldiers were aware. She practiced moving from one sight to the other until it took her only a few seconds to perform the switch.

"Stay alert, soldier!" Sergeant Valentim's voice barked inside her helmet.

A group of soldiers was with her on the trail, their faces covered in special silicon. Slits for eyes behind a transparent screen. Helmets fitted with a hard shell around the top and backs of their heads.

The machine gun she held on to was remarkably light, despite its size. Her perception was high, and she would hear movement before any of the others did. She turned instinctively and shot down Maredians before they pounced or grabbed her with their trunk arms.

As the days passed, her skills steadily enhanced. She easily defeated Maredians but allowed herself to lose to other soldiers and to Sergeant Valentim if she was in a scenario that put her in that position.

She was much stronger and faster than she let on. She held back, as demonstrating her full potential would never allow them to lose their fear and suspicion of her. Her strength and movement had to be kept at a level close to theirs—and not by much. She always let go of any human opponent and walked away when Sergeant Valentim barked at her to release them, even if it meant the opponent would kill her. It was imperative she obeyed.

A creature suddenly sprung from the top of a rock, and Gracie shrunk down and shot at it with quick successive shots. Pieces of gelatine splattered all over the rocks and on the ground ahead of her.

As weeks went by with this intense training, Gracie grew into a solid killing machine, destroying hundreds of Maredians. She moved over rocks, sensing movement from behind her, above her, and by her feet. She sensed it all and destroyed each attacker. She gritted her teeth, and perspiration formed on her face. Her lungs at times would flare open. But she focussed, keeping the guttural hum that wanted to move up her throat and release itself closed. She paid attention to the breathing inside her human lungs ...

"One, two, and three."

High above the training trail on an elevated level and behind the glass, the emperor, Gilberto, and an entourage of elite soldiers watched. A satisfied expression came over Emperor Sebastian's face; he had watched Gracie navigate the last course and observed the carnage she caused—the mountains of shredded Maredians and the suits of her soldier companions drenched with Maredian matter ... her own suit being mostly clean.

Sergeant Valentim's orders came inside her helmet. "Course completed."

They formed a line for him to inspect.

Sergeant Valentim glanced sternly at their posture and their uniforms. He stood in front of Gracie. "Shower up," he ordered everyone but remained in Gracie's way. "When you're done, immediately report to lab 368," he said.

Gracie nodded.

Lab 368 was a lavish apartment with a varnished-wood bar to the side and a sunken living room area full of modern slick couches and a holograph of a large moving galaxy that swirled in front of Gracie.

Gilberto came out from the folds of the holograph. The expression on his face was calm—not his usual stern expression.

The two soldiers who'd escorted her now left.

"Don't be alarmed," Gilberto said. "You're safe here. The soldiers are outside the door. Would you like a drink?"

"I'm fine," Gracie said coolly.

"I won't keep you long. I just wanted to have a conversation."

"You can have a conversation anytime with me on the training course."

"There's a time and place for the kind of conversation I want to have with you," Gilberto said. "Congratulations. You've been receiving good feedback from the Sergeant and your colleagues despite them not having much faith in you. The emperor is quite pleased by your progress and consistent cooperation."

Gracie nodded. She had no interest in saying much to him.

"I wanted to make a proposal. You are unique. No human has ever had your level of contact with a Maredian and been physically altered as you have. The supreme leader and the council know about you, and to my surprise, it's generated great enthusiasm and interest from them. The supreme leader wants you to join the Global Council in our fight for a better and just world."

"Join you? I promised Emperor Sebastian to help him win the war. My allegiance is to *him*. And after this war, I want to go back to Canada."

"Gracie, do you comprehend what you will be going back to? Canada is no longer the country you remember. It has changed. Emperor Alexandra Arvalukk and her council may not *want* you back. If they do, what will you return to? Terrible memories of a past that no longer exists."

He approached Gracie, his eyes softening, making her cringe. "You're still young. You can have a second chance. Leave the past and start fresh. We can give you a new identity. You can have a new family. There are no ridiculous restrictions on the number of children a woman wants, and yet, can have a lustrous career working with the Global Council. You and your new family will be well taken care of for the rest of your lives. You will have few worries and will be very happy."

His dark eyes dropped to the centre of her neck. "Moreover, we can provide you with medical attention and remove parts of the Maredian from your lungs so you can swim again."

"Dr. Campos said it can't be removed; it's infused inside my cells."

"With the kind of medical facilities we have, anything is possible. Don't you want to swim again?"

Gracie nodded.

Of course, she'd want to swim every day if she could.

"The supreme leader and the council will build you an indoor, Olympic-size pool at your home in any empire you choose to live," Gilberto said.

"Our citizens have been developing unimaginable technologies that will merge us with AI, as was only just starting in your time. Now, there's full support from the supreme leader and Global Council to proceed. No more worldwide protests. The few billions of people left on Earth—the vast majority of them—are focused on rebuilding their new cities and lives. They aren't thinking about progress in AI and other advanced technologies. Soon, we will achieve things never imagined possible. We will be able to live for over a thousand years in our youthful forms, where we will never rot or become diseased for a very long time. Our minds will have heightened senses and sharper focus inside modified brains, thanks to our progressive work on gene editing. Why would anyone oppose such remarkable opportunities to never suffer from sickness or any disease and have incredible cognitive abilities?"

Gracie kept quiet. An anxious feeling grew inside her. *Brain modification*. It had a lot of potential for mind control. She calmed down some of her unease. The network no doubt was analyzing every part of her.

"As for the Maredians, we *will* defeat them, Gracie," Gilberto continued. "They don't stand a chance. It was a good argument you made to the gullible emperor, feeding into his own weaknesses. His insecurities. His yearning to be grand and great. I was impressed by your speech. Rest assured, the global armies will destroy the Maredians and the opposing enemies of the Global Council that has started to gather in Jerusalem, who are a threat to a peaceful world and want to bring back their backward traditions and religious dogmas to the empires. Yes, even in these great times, on the cusp of a better civilization, there are still those who want to remain living with superstitions under an imaginary superpower, following ancient texts written by madmen, who used their holy books, bound by rules supposedly attributed to a God to control a populace into submission, simply serving themselves while committing the worst atrocities against human beings. Who in their right mind would want to bring that back? We have this immense opportunity to start afresh, and it has been working well for the past couple of decades. All registered citizens in the established empires have access to protection, medicine, and food. Poverty is only for those who chose it and foolishly refuse to live in the empires that offer these advantages for everyone. Fools who want to keep their so-called freedom."

His dark eyes shone with a strange glee.

"Freedom, Gracie, to fall prey to criminals who want to keep their freedom too, terrorizing those wandering inside neutral territories, and fall sick to illnesses, injuries and death with no help from any empire, as it was the choice they made and their price to pay for their so-called freedom. Education, science, and technology are what rules every present-day empire and comes with true accountability, equality, peace, and order for everyone. Why wouldn't anyone want that?"

He stepped away. "You have been offered a great opportunity. Think about it for a few days."

He walked to a cabinet and opened a drawer. "Before you go, take these with you as a sample of bigger and much better things to come—if you choose wisely."

He removed three rectangular packages covered in aluminum foil from each compartment and offered them to Gracie. Each package was marked in black letters: Vegetables. Proteins. Polyphenols.

"Thank you," she said, keeping her emotions still as she took them from Gilberto.

"Don't be fooled by their appearance," Gilberto said. "They're packed with the highest nutrition and are eaten like meals in between council meetings. They're especially made and are only available to council members and their families. This is just a sample for you to enjoy."

"I want to go now."

"Of course. Think about what I said. You know how to reach me."

He pressed a button on the side of the cabinet, and the same soldiers who escorted her to the apartment escorted her out.

CHAPTER 10

Arise...

The master's hum arrived, strong and undeterred.

"Rise, my captain. Rise. It is time."

The master's divine light spread over all of them, causing their bodies to tingle and spring to life. They began to hum in great gratitude and reverence. They stretched out their bodies toward the hot, blazing light that emanated from the divine master. Fire and electricity sparked through millions of them as their excitement and joy heightened.

"I have deployed the others to the four corners of Earth," the master hummed. "The 144,000 have received my seal. Very soon, we will descend over Jerusalem where I will make myself known and defeat the iniquities of evil that have plagued these humans since I've made myself known to them thousands of years ago. Take your forms and shapes and follow me."

Their hums turned into a feverish pitch, filled with gratitude and reference for the master.

CHAPTER 11

Ashes from the Past

"We've heard back from the First Empire," Jorge said. "A student researcher from Emperor Alexandra Arvalukk's office heard about your case and took it upon herself to get a drone out to the previous Don Mills megacity and research the names you provided."

Gracie stopped running on a moveable mat and turned it off.

Jorge activated the device, and a holograph appeared.

A razed-down city Gracie hardly recognized, buildings reduced to piles of concrete, similar to those inside the Maredians domes she once carried sprawled before her. One of the columns of her residential building remained, partially bent, somehow still standing. Gracie recognized the parts of iron—now a faded orange colour—that had decorated the outside of the building she once lived in. There were no billboards or high skyscrapers. Nothing was left.

"Very few survivors made it out alive from the initial attack," Jorge said. "It was quick and deliberate for the victims. Accounts from those survivors described a powerful vibration that tore through the cities, disintegrating everything and anything in its path to dust. Their pain was likely minimal. Most didn't know what was happening and were gone in seconds. They were the lucky ones."

Gracie stayed silent. There was nothing to say. She had been told the story, but to see it for herself was something else. Gilberto was right. There was nothing left for her to return to. Perhaps it was wise to erase those haunting memories, start again, and take this second chance.

She brought a hand over her chest and lowered her face.

"You okay?"

"Just an ache in my lungs. It will pass."

"They checked records of survivor lists to find out if there are any ascendants of the people you knew. The robotics company, PervivoTech, in the city of Whitehorse, where a Jeffrey McCormick Nakamura worked and lived, was obliterated in the initial attack. I'm sorry. You okay? Should I continue?"

Gracie nodded.

"A few medic-bots and other AI's kept in the company's storage facilities underground were the only things that survived. As for the building where you lived, almost everyone including Mr. Kirpal Singh was lost. Also, one James Pinto Nakamura. I'm so sorry."

Gracie nodded, held back tears and looked away. A part of her had always known but the relentless hope had kept her going and made her blind to accept it. Hearing it now at least offered her closure.

"Still okay if I continue?"

"There's more?"

There was one person who *did* survive.

A shiver ran through Gracie. Jorge didn't need to say her name ...

"A Rose Monteiro Silva," Jorge said.

Gracie stared back blankly. Jorge mistook her reaction as this possibly being a mistake. "Isn't that the name you provided? It's her, considering the location and her age during the initial attacks; there was no one else with that name in that entire building. There's no mistake. She arrived along with a few survivors in a place called, Moosonee."

"Moosonee?" Gracie said, seeing a map in her mind of the Great Hudson Bay.

"That's over five hundred miles," she said. "How did they get there?"

"There aren't many details in this hundred-year-old report. The report *does* mention that a ship was taken to the North West Passage and that they settled in Resolute, a small Inuit community in Nunavut. They reached that place about a decade after she left the city. I'm impressed that she managed to survive the initial attacks and Maredians along the journey toward the North. She passed away at 103 years old from heart complications. They have a photo of her standing outside a house with a few of the survivors she picked up on the way to Resolute. You might recognize her."

A digital photo sprang up. A group of twelve people with sombre faces stared into whatever device captured the image. Faces of ghosts trapped in time. Gracie found the familiar eyes and the twirl of faded red locks that fell down a tired old face. Those eyes—they were the same eyes. A face could change—grow old—but the eyes usually stayed the same. This older woman wore dark slacks with a mustard-coloured sweater and a matching wool hat. Her hands cupped over each other in front of her, as she had done many times. Only, there were no exuberant rings on the long fingers and no bright-red nail polish adorning each perfectly manicured nail.

Gracie had never seen any resemblance between Rose and Gran Amália before. In this photo, though, with all egocentric vanities stripped away, the resemblance was there, behind the furrowed brow, the tense curl of the bottom lip, the bone structure of the face, the reserve in her expression, and straight posture.

Even so, the thought of Rose gathering others along the way to make it together to the North was incomprehensible to Gracie. The Rose she knew would have left everyone out to dry, found a car, blasted out of there, and hitched it up North on her own. It conflicted with the memories Gracie held of the original Rose, and not surprisingly, old simmering anger spewed inside Gracie, hotter than the Maredians' coils. Even with Rose being long dead, it managed to rattle Gracie into deep-seated resentment that turned her insides. Gracie's chest pulsated in discomfort. The Maredian respiratory system tightened.

"When they reached Churchill," Jorge continued, "she left behind a note as was the common practice for survivors to do, in some places, with names of loved ones they hoped would be alive. She left your name, Grace Mercedes Pinto, her granddaughter, hoping that you had somehow survived. She left some information about where she was heading, and she signed off each note with 'Love, Grandma Rose."

An image of the note appeared. It was typed, but her name at the bottom ... she had digitally signed that herself. The shape of the "R" and the way the "e" was dragged halfway on the line, was precisely the way she digitally signed her name.

"Your Grandmother left the same note in every community she reached, every four hundred miles or so. Once she settled in and networks were revived after the Maredians left, she often searched for you, reaching out to survivor networks. It seemed she really wanted to find you as if she sensed that you were still alive."

Gracie stared at Jorge in disbelief.

"Find me? She never wanted me to acknowledge her as my own grandmother. She didn't want me alive. She hated me so much because I turned out decently and not some drug addict like her own daughter."

Jorge wasn't sure how to react to Gracie's sudden terse words.

"She hoped I was dead. She would never put my name on any list asking if I survived, wanting to find me. That's absurd! She let my mother die because she turned a blind eye to it, as a typical sick, spiteful, narcissistic person would. She was full of jealousy and lies. You don't understand. This is wrong. All wrong. She would never search for me or hope that I was alive! No. No. This is a fake report. It's all wrong, completely wrong!"

Jorge put down the device and placed his hands over her trembling shoulders. "Gracie, understand, when the Maredians came to Earth, anyone who survived the attacks, the earthquakes, and endless floods ... their whole way of life drastically changed. In this new world, they had to adapt to survive. Your Grandma Rose possibly changed like many other survivors, because of the new circumstances they faced."

"Those survivors dealt with hardships we can never understand. They had to bury their dead if they even found them while hiding from approaching Maredians. They had to quickly get out of the cities and to places they thought were safe. Without having any authority or government in place, they also had to fight off psychopath humans during their journeys and the wild beasts that swelled in numbers, as the only animal the Maredians cared to kill was ... us."

"These survivors learned to defend themselves against all odds and kept on moving to the North as she had done. Her old persona, no matter how nasty she remains in your memory, died the day the Maredians came. In the place of horror, destruction, and the imminent threat of death, emerged this new woman we read about—courageous, with a fighting, strong will, with hope, to keep on moving, who lived to 103."

"Perhaps she came to her senses, reflecting on her own wrongdoings because she chose to leave messages behind quite often that survived in different communities and daily messages she sent through the network, up to the last day she was alive, never giving up the hope that she would find you. If she was that same unkind person you mentioned, she would never have bothered and would just continue to live her life. The past is the past. You can only move forward now."

Gracie kept holding back tears, but she couldn't anymore. She let them stream down her face. Gran Amália was a strong, sensible woman but it was Rose that had endless hope and determination. Gracie realized she had gotten that propensity from Rose. It was Rose that passed on this endless hope, to never give up. It was her all along.

Now, there will never be the opportunity to make amends, all of that time having passed away so long ago. The sudden pain and devastating losses—of her son, Jeff, Mr. Singh, and Rose wanting to find her and would never know Gracie still lived, rushed at Gracie.

Gracie cried quietly, wiping away tears from her face. If Jorge had still been questioning Gracie's kindred nature, her tears proved that she was just as human as everyone else.

He brought her against his chest as she sobbed.

"Be calm," he said against her ear. His heart moved in a similar rhythm to Amigo's hum. Blood coursed through his veins, and heat rose from his chest. She further pressed against him, and her mind drifted to an odd nostalgic sensation, the warmth of Amigo with a sense of security, tight body coils wrapped around her; only, it was Jorge's muscular arms that came around her back and held her.

"It'll get better with time. It always does," he whispered.

"Has there been someone ... have you lost anyone?"

"Three years ago. In a blast near the Atlas Mountains on a mission to bring supplies to a few survivors there. The Maredians left Earth, but unfortunately, ravaged humans remain in many places around the world." Jorge's hands stroked up and down her spine. "We can only look forward to a better future," he said. "That's all we can do."

She lifted her face and gazed into his eyes. The browns in his eyes shone with flecks of green, and the olive complexion of his smooth face transformed into a deep, harmonious male beauty. There was a pull between them that relaxed all remaining intensity in her upper body. His hands ran over the sides of her arms and held them still as his face came down to place his lips against hers. His mouth moved back and forth across her soft lips.

Gracie pulled back and leaned into his chest, her nose pressed at the bottom of his smooth neck that had a scent of light, musky cologne that she was starting to like more than chlorine. His lips brushed over her forehead, and they stayed together, holding each other, lavishing in the warmth of their bodies pressed together, barely paying attention to the sudden alarm that reverberated from Alphonso's deep voice, overriding all other network voices. "*Enemy ships detected and fast approaching. Prepare for immediate confrontation. Enemy ships detected and fast approaching. Prepare for immediate confrontation ...*"

It took two full repetitions before they heard it, unlocked from each other's embrace and ran out into the corridor.

CHAPTER 12

Evacuation

In the courtyard, holographic images of galactic maps, the Earth, and aerial maps swirled around Katrina, General Da Costa, and Emperor Sebastian. A clump of large Meteorites hovered in space with their centres spinning like crackling fire.

"Earth is in view," Katrina said, "and we are approximately twenty-five minutes from those Maredian ships."

"The First Empire has destroyed Maredian ships trying to get through their side of the hemisphere," General Da Costa said. Some Maredian ships have entered, and the satellites have tracked them landing in the Levantine Sea, near Tripoli, Libya. Fourth Empire troops are making their way to that area.

"We have mobilized land troops in Lagos and our air fighters have received permission from the Fourth Empire to enter Jerusalem to defend the Supreme Leader and the city there."

Huge beams suddenly shot out from the Maredian ships, easily shattering fighter ships from the other empires. Broken debris and a burst of lights shot outward. Numbers whirled around on the screen: six ships down.

"Their weapons seem to be more powerful than previously recorded," Emperor Sebastian said.

Empire ships pounded the largest of the Maredian ship, and although a side of the Maredian ship started to rupture, it turned away and managed to pass through the last defence and entered the sphere of Earth.

A massive Maredian ship advanced in front of them, and in seconds, a terrible rumble exploded through the ship.

Alphonso's voice reported the damage. "*Fire and severe damage in sections twenty-eight to thirty-one. Severe deterioration of extremities.*"

"I'm on my way to attend them," Jorge said dutifully, throwing a quick glance at Gracie, telling her, he'd be back soon.

She nodded.

Emperor Sebastian's eyes filled up with hard hatred directed at the looming Maredian ship. "A full attack," he ordered, slamming a fist over the console.

Red lights shot out from the ship, banging against the meteorite, chipping away at it. Despite the enormity of the Maredian ship it swooped upwards and released a flaming beam that hit the side of the emperor's ship, producing a horrible tremble that threatened to knock the ship right out of space. Gracie was thrown under a table of consoles by the impact. Distant screams and clouds of smoke rolled inside the courtyard. Everyone became quick-moving shadows.

A high-pitched alarm rang out. Alphonso's calm voice announced, "*Severe Damage. Immediate evacuation. High probability of ship destructing in ten minutes.*"

The emperor shouted, "We must evacuate now! We'll destroy them all, soon on Earth!"

General Da Costa added, "Get to your emergency pods immediately!"

Gracie slowly crawled out from underneath the bottom of the console table, holding on to the back of her head. Heavy smoke made her gag. She covered her mouth and tried to pull herself together. They had spent months training for battleground combat and never went through an actual evacuation.

She tried to see through the thick smoke and the flashing lights of the holographs with images that sizzled and shook, to search for the emperor, for General Da Costa, and any other soldier nearby.

Distant frenzied shouts of soldiers rang through the smoke clouds, "Get to your emergency pods now!"

Alphonso's calm voice returned. "*Severe Damage. Immediate evacuation. High probability of ship destructing in less than seven minutes.*"

Gracie stumbled into a corridor. A fire was nearby, and as extreme heat fell over her face, she ran, calling out, "Help! Is anyone here? Emperor Sebastian! General Da Costa!"

Another rumble reverberated through the ship.

Horrified, distant screams.

Alphonso's voice: "*Proceed to immediate evacuation. Proceed to immediate evacuation.*"

Gracie ran down another corridor and wiped away the sweat in her eyes to turn on the Maredian sight. A dark hallway. No one was in it. Next to her were walls and walls of empty corridors. Across the ship were heaps of shattered, burning metal, and in between were the flailing arms of trapped soldiers. Unconscious bodies of soldiers were strewn across the floor and over consoles. It would take her twenty minutes to reach them, which Alphonso clearly told her she didn't have.

She turned into another corridor and a pair of hands grabbed her shoulders.

She was face to face with Gilberto.

"My emergency pod is large enough to accommodate you. We must hurry."

"I have to get onto the emperor's emergency pod."

"They've evacuated already and so must we, as this ship is going to blow any minute."

She ran with him down a hall and into an elevator shaft that brought them down a few levels. The elevator doors opened to a short ramp that led to a small waiting ship, with engines fully blasting.

The doors snapped shut behind them.

"Strap yourself into the seat. Hurry."

She did as instructed and held her breath. Her heart rate was wild. She placed her hands over her ears as the ship blasted out of the dock, as tunnels and walls collapsed around them, melting into flames.

Her Maredian sight turned on, and she saw inside the emperor's torn ship—through the thick smoke—and observed the remaining soldiers, injured by previous blasts, who didn't make it into their escape pods, trying to get up, only to fall into whirling, fireballs that began to roar throughout the tunnels. Others fell into open pits and oxygen-deprived spaces.

Finally, the emperor's ship erupted into an explosive geyser of torn metals and materials. The force of its destruction reverberated into space, shaking their getaway ship as it sped, toward Earth and avoided beams from other Maredian ships.

A crackling sound inside the getaway ship. The pilot announced, "*Entering the atmosphere.*"

The turbulence shook Gracie in her strapped seat, thrashing her around and making her fear that her neck would dislocate. Gilberto's hands held onto the metal straps in front of him, turning his fingers white as bone.

A flash of strong light. Gracie held her breath, it was the Sun.

The pilot's voice: "*Dropping 45,000 meters ... 30,000 ... 20,000 ... 10,000 ...*"

A grey, body of water sprawled out majestically beneath them. A distant coastline, empty and endless. The ship landed in the water with an enormous splash. They were slightly deep inside the water for a minute until the ship shot upwards and rumbled over land and water, toward the shoreline.

The pilot's last announcement: "*Fifth Empire emergency pod landed at 14:44:00 hours, in the Dead Sea.*"

CHAPTER 13

The Supreme Leader

Despite the Sun being out, rain rolled down the glass. Through sprinkling rain, a few tanks and trucks waited along the beach, surrounded by soldiers.

The door latch lifted, and a gush of chilly air entered the ship. A ramp was pulled down. Gilberto unstrapped himself and lifted the metal arms from his seat. Gracie followed. A soldier helped her down the ramp.

She landed over rivulets of sand covered by inches of water that surrounded the lower calves of her boots. She breathed in cool misty air that filled up her lungs—air that her lungs hadn't filled up with in so long. Rain pelted her forehead and dripped down the sides of her neck. Drones whizzed above, reporting back to their commanders any potential threats.

Feelings of gratitude surged through her as she breathed in more air from Earth that she thought so often she would never breathe in again.

Her mind tapped out the sounds of soldiers around her, shouting at each other, others speaking inside the units in their helmets. She waded through the water toward the shoreline, still in disbelief, her mind swirling under an elevated emotion, as if inebriated, continuing to experience something of a miracle, taking in earthly scents of wet sand and damp air. She was back on Earth. She was home. Home.

"Put on this helmet, soldier," said a stern voice from behind her. A soldier wearing a uniform of black and dark grey patches, with a bright-red emblem on the left side of the uniform—*SL Elite Forces*—handed her a helmet.

"Get in the grey Jeep, and the supreme leader's soldiers will take us directly to Jerusalem, where he's waiting to address his armies," Gilberto said coming up to her. "There, you will see only good things happen."

Gracie sat next to Gilberto as the Jeep roared onto the road. The rain had weakened, and in some places, the Sun slanted toward the east, its golden rays playing over the empty stretch of land that was mainly made out of clumps of rocks and sand.

"How did you find me on the ship?"

Gilberto pointed to her wrist. "Your bracelet device. I checked it before I was about to leave and saw that you were still on the ship and close by. The others must have quickly left you. I couldn't just leave you behind." An empathetic shrug.

Gracie looked over the skies, and the Sun stretched outwards, intermingling between distant white and grey clouds.

"What do you think of this place?"

"It's not Don Mills, Canada," Gracie said. "But beggars can't be choosers. It will do."

Gilberto partially smiled. "The coming of the Maredians did humanity a favour. Across the globe, it finally brought people together to fight for one cause. Then, people began to rebuild their communities and old tribal sentiments rose—human against human as expected."

Gracie looked over the barren sand, as they drove by two army trucks, covered with plastic sheets. With her Maredian vision, Gracie saw they were mounted with four nuclear cruise missiles.

"After the battle is won against the Maredians, we will erase any opposition left on the ground and move onto the next phase of repopulating the Earth with a new generation of people, Gracie."

"If those nukes on those trucks are dropped, it won't just wipe out your opposition, but any resources left on Earth to sustain your population. Hasn't there been enough war in this region?"

"It's been carefully and strategically planned," he said with a smile. "This will be the final war. Some of us will live on the supreme leader's space station for a few decades. It can hold thousands of citizens. There are many countries that are empty in the world—countries that won't suffer the harsh effects of a nuclear winter or the environmental aftermath where millions of our faithful across all other Empires will live."

"Arrangements have been made for them and their families, right after our triumphant war with the Maredians. These arrangements could be made for you too, Gracie."

He leaned close to her. "We have a whole team of medics and higher-ranking officials, who are just as attractive as Jorge for you to choose from. Difficult memories can be erased. We have the facilities for that. You can be free from painful memories from your previous life, of your family, friends, and little son. It will be as if they never existed. You can choose of course, to remain on the Earth and die or live to emerge a truly new person in a world, under the Supreme Leader with the help of AI, united together in peace, just like the Maredians, and we've seen how efficient they've been working toward their cause. United as one, as your Amigo had told you."

"We are not like the Maredians, we are a completely different species," Gracie said. "Every human is born unique with different talents and abilities; no human is the same. That uniqueness should be celebrated, not deliberately manufactured and modified, turned into some kind of one hive ideology."

"That human uniqueness, Gracie, is what always leads to the ideas of supremacy between groups of people as it's always been the driving force for war since time immemorial," Gilberto said. "Unlike the ancient past where these one hive ideologies have failed, AI will help us truly achieve solid unity, where misery and the atrocities associated with war will never happen or be experienced again for future generations. Join us Gracie and you will see."

"What about Emperor Sebastian?"

Gilberto's amusement smudged off his face. "Emperor Sebastian will enjoy fighting his war with the Maredians. That's all he's obsessed with. So be it."

They drove close to the city of Jerusalem, where next to the partially torn temple stood an expansive white-stone castle with six columns and twenty or so steps in front of it encased by what looked like Maredian-proof glass walls.

In the centre of the castle was an enormous statue of a male figure—a replica of the supreme leader.

Further inside Jerusalem, Gracie was able to see the physical features of the supreme leader, Anton Abaddonovich, plastered everywhere in the city. He was an attractive light-olive-skinned man with short wavy brown hair. His brown eyes were soft, and his smile was gentle and kind—someone you could trust. He stood in every poster, dressed impeccably in a tailored suit or military uniform, alone or surrounded by young, happy families or soldiers.

The Jeep dropped them off in a crowded area full of thousands of gathered soldiers facing a stage.

"Don't be self-conscious about your uniform. It doesn't matter. Everyone here belongs," Gilberto said. "The supreme leader will be addressing the crowd soon. Stay here and I'll send someone for you in a few minutes. They'll give you a proper uniform and other items."

Gilberto disappeared into the crowd.

Every soldier around her was dressed identically in military uniforms, which Gracie had seen earlier, with black and dark-grey patches and a bright-red emblem on the left side of the breast. *SL Elite Forces.* It didn't matter if they were male or female, tall or petite, or from a different ethnic origin. They all reported to the one supreme leader and his generals.

Gracie turned on her Maredian sight and saw Gilberto at the back of the stage talking to a few soldiers. Appearing amongst them was the supreme leader dressed in an impeccable navy-blue suit. The Maredian sight in her jerked forward, showing the insides of the supreme leader: a conglomerate of shadows ... and then a thick, sludge of darkness that engulfed his whole being. Others around him had different shades; no one was solely filled with dark moving shadows.

She pulled back her vision so she could see the organs of the others, but the supreme leader had no organs. The dark sludge inside him swirled into a circular vortex. It was alarming. That wasn't possible. He wasn't AI. Gracie saw no circuitry, chips, or devices. It was as if the supreme leader had a human outer shell and inside, he was something else that wasn't human.

Gracie shuddered.

What the hell are you?

The supreme leader's eyes turned to Gracie, although he was at least a mile away, and inside the brown pupils, familiar orange wolf eyes shined. The Supreme Leader nodded acknowledgment at her.

Gracie took a few steps back and turned to walk through the crowd.

On their ride there, she had seen blue shields with white bezants over a truck on a side street. She quickened her pace toward it now. Behind her, a few soldiers came through the crowd toward where she had stood. They looked around the enclosed crowds. She moved quicker hiding behind clusters of bigger soldiers walking by. When she reached the side street, she was relieved that the truck was still there.

A young woman talked into a device in her arm in English accented from someplace in England. She wore a light blue uniform with letters on the left side, W. Ding. Her black hair was pulled back into a long ponytail. On the left side of her suit was a small emblem of the union jack and above it 5º Império.

"Hi," Gracie breathlessly said. "I need to find the emperor's ship. Do you know where they've landed?"

W. Ding was caught off guard and hesitated.

"My name is Gracie Pinto, and sorry to bother you, but this is an emergency. Do you know where I can find Emperor Sebastian's ship? They were supposed to land somewhere here."

W. Ding nodded. "Along the beaches in Tel-Aviv," she said. "They've already landed about ten minutes ago."

Gracie gestured toward the name.

"Wendy Ding," she said.

"Wendy, I need to get there. Can you take me there, please? It's urgent."

Wendy looked unimpressed and unmoved.

"I can't leave my post yet. I just finished making an important delivery, and I have to track it."

"I'm an elite soldier directly reporting to Emperor Sebastian himself," Gracie asserted. "Our ship was attacked by Maredians, blown to smithereens, and I got on an emergency pod with Gilberto, who is his Majesty's advisor. We landed in the Dead Sea, and I lost sight of him. I need to report to Emperor Sebastian immediately."

Wendy looked over Gracie's uniform—over the letters of her name, G. Pinto. Wendy shot a glance behind her and over Gracie's pleading face.

"You're with us, the Fifth Empire?" Wendy asked.

"Yes," Gracie responded. "They don't just give out these uniforms to anyone, do they?"

Wendy tilted her head. "I suppose not." She jumped off the side of the truck and flung open a door "All right. Get in. I'm heading back to Tel Aviv anyway to pick up some more soldiers into the city."

Wendy didn't drive; she flew the truck as if it were a drone, zipping through narrow side streets, barely scraping the sides of the truck. Gracie wasn't sure which ride terrified her more, the ride in the getaway plane hurling through heavy turbulence as they entered Earth's atmosphere or Wendy's driving skills on the road out of Jerusalem, toward Tel-Aviv.

"Aren't these highway roads magnetic with their speeds regulated?" Gracie asked, hanging on to her tight seat belt.

Wendy's face squinted.

"What century are you living in? These roads haven't been magnetic for over a hundred years."

Gracie shrugged. "Sorry. I'm new to this place."

"There are police drones that do come around, but right now, since the war has started, that's the last thing on their drones' radar."

Gracie nodded and was more worried about the drones Gilberto would send out to track her down since her bracelet made it so easy to do. She relaxed when the roads and the aerial highways remained empty for some time.

As they drove through streets nearing Tel Aviv, they were filled everywhere with ten to twenty feet mounds of broken white and dark rocks that once had been beautiful complexes of buildings, hotels, and restaurants. Smells permeated the cool air of something familiar of rot, dead carcasses, dried-out animals, and cinders of ancient people. Singed palm trees dotted the roads, here and there. Gracie saw an occasional flyer or a torn T-Shirt stuck between broken rocks. A faded image on a T-shirt of a once luxurious hotel in the background: Herods Tel-Aviv.

Along the Tel Aviv coastline, Fifth Empire ships floated in the distance in the Mediterranean. Aerial drones flew above, and thousands of soldiers gathered in straight lines, waiting to enter another line of trucks to bring them into the city.

Gracie got out of Wendy's truck and ran toward the shoreline, asking Fifth Empire soldiers in Portuguese along the way, "Where is Jorge Mendonça? General Da Costa?"

She asked about twenty soldiers until one of them pointed to a large red tent that had been set up further down the beach. Gracie sprinted toward it.

To her relief, she found Jorge and leapt into his arms. They crushed their lips together and held on tightly.

"I didn't know if you made it out of the ship," she told him.

"I'm so glad you're here," he said.

He pressed his forehead against hers.

"I got in Gilberto's emergency pod. We landed in the Dead Sea and went into Jerusalem. I hitched a ride back here with one of our citizens."

"Jorge," the supreme leader has missiles. "They're going to use them after battling the Maredians and level this whole place, wiping out whoever's left. That is their plan, and the supreme leader agrees with this. Does Emperor Sebastian know?"

"Are you sure Gilberto wasn't playing with you or testing your loyalties?"

"Something very sinister is going to happen. I feel—" She lost her balance and grabbed Jorge's waist.

His voice echoed in her ears, asking her if she was okay. Her head turned out to the sea. In the vastness of the ocean, her Maredian vision saw, moving steadily like demons from hell approaching, tens of thousands of Maredians swimming toward them. Low hums vibrated through the waters, attracting herds of fish and other sea animals to swim nearby, then swim away. The Maredians twisted and turned over and between each other at the bottom of the Mediterranean.

"The drones," Gracie said in a quivering voice. "Are they able to track Maredians?"

"Yes, they have high resolution and infrared capabilities—and sensors. If there was anything moving in the waters, we would know about it."

"Jorge, the Maredians are at the bottom of the sea. They're moving toward this beach. There are thousands of them. I can see them."

"What are you talking about?"

"They're out there, and I have to warn the emperor and the troops."

"How can you see them?"

"I just can. I'm sorry. I never admitted this before. It's another ability they've given me. I can see them. I don't know how. They have gathered and are approaching. They are some miles away. I have a feeling they're going to Jerusalem. Take me to Emperor Sebastian."

CHAPTER 14

The Battle

Emperor Sebastian, General Da Costa, Katrina, and Nuno listened carefully to everything Gracie told them.

"Have the drones reported back any potential threat?" Emperor Sebastian asked.

"None, at all, Your Majesty," General Da Costa said.

"Gracie, you are always full of surprises," the emperor said. "I'm glad you made it down here. I was a bit worried that my prized soldier got left behind on the ship."

Gracie nodded tersely. Now wasn't the time to express her disappointment that they didn't call out for her. She was alive and was there now.

"Gilberto has always been an odd man," Emperor Sebastian said. "He doesn't keep secrets from me. I've known him since I was a young boy. We have long-standing trust between us. He was teasing you. Trying you. He does that from time to time with odd, sensationalist stories—damn him. You're worked up for nothing, and I need you to focus on killing as many Maredians as you can when the time comes. You're going to win this for our empire, aren't you?" He patted her shoulder.

"I'm only telling you, Your Majesty, so you're prepared. Have some kind of ship ready to leave or head to the Solomon Islands to wait out this nuclear catastrophe the Supreme Leader wants to unleash on the city of Jerusalem."

"Your Majesty, the First and Second empire troops have defeated the Maredians along their eastern coastlines," Nuno said.

"Good. Send those emperors a congratulatory message from me."

"I have heard about these new missiles from another emperor, Gracie. If true, they aren't as dangerous as you think. They're filled with Maredian-killing substances and will be used only if we cannot defeat the Maredians. These substances aren't deadly to humans, and they won't cause a devastating nuclear holocaust, as you believe. You were reading too many books on the Cold War during your captivity."

A chuckle from the emperor.

"Your Majesty, I ask that you leave behind a few soldiers and war drones to keep watch on these shores when we move into Jerusalem—in case something terrible rises out of the sea. I want us to defeat these Maredians for our empire. I am with you, sire."

"All right, if it will keep that persistent sentiment in you, Gracie, I will appease your request. General Da Costa, retain some soldiers here as we move out to Jerusalem."

A screech echoed in Gracie's ears, and she clasped her hands over her ears.

"They're coming?" Jorge asked.

Gracie's vision drifted back out toward the horror in the sea. The Maredians had broken from their entwined embrace and swam eerily through the waters, quickly approaching the beach ahead of them. They didn't come on shore; instead, they disappeared under the sand and made their way, at a much slower pace, underneath the Earth. Gracie shivered at the sight.

"They're moving underground. There are thousands of them, crawling inside the warmth of the Earth, like a gush of water, pushing their way through, moving north, deeper into the land. They will eventually encircle the armies that are here."

The last trucks left the beach to head back to Jerusalem. Hundreds of unsuspecting soldiers remained waiting for the next pickup.

Gracie removed the safety from her gun and moved back. Her sight focused on the dark mass approaching them. She held her breath.

Crackling sounds in their helmets, a burst of screams of terror, and shooting.

"Maredians are coming out of the beach on the north side!"

No kidding, Gracie thought. Jorge steadied his gun.

"Turn on the hum at full volume!" The emperor ordered.

A hum vibrated out from their helmets, the drones, and through the speakers in the tent, but the Maredians kept on inching closer.

"They are still moving!" Gracie shouted. "They are still approaching!"

"Damn it. Spread out!" General Da Costa ordered.

The general and the emperor held their weapons and followed the direction of Gracie's gun.

The dark mass shot upwards ahead, behind, and in front of them.

Weapons blasted full force at tornado-like winds. Sand exploded all around them, reducing their visibility to nothing. Gracie's ears filled with the sound of humans screaming and the screech-hums of the Maredians.

Visible through a clearing in the sand cloud, coiled arms snatched up soldiers and shoved them into the ground, crushing them into an explosion of blood, organs, and splintering bones. Gracie turned on her Maredian vision and spotted their moving bodies in the swirling thick sand. She blasted six of them dead. She ignored their screeching as they died and focussed on the horrifying screaming of the humans.

Sudden movement to her right. She blasted another clump of Maredians and a few came underneath her.

She spotted Jorge a few feet away, shooting down Maredians as they moved in between a crevice of rocks. Gracie ran to the other side and shot them down. Through those bursts of sand, their eyes met, and they nodded to each other, communicating that they were okay.

The emperor was thrown over a pile of debris by Maredians as he shot them dead. One of them had grabbed his right arm. The emperor missed that Maredian a few times, but one blast caught enough of it for the Maredian to let go of his torn and bleeding arm. Without a flinch and through clenched teeth, the emperor blasted the Maredian dead. Then, he lay back against the debris and laughed. His face glowed, sprinkled with sweat and smudged sand. By then, the human screams had died down and the screeching of dying Maredians intensified in her ears.

She reached the emperor. His eyes were on fire. He wasn't the least deterred and not shaken by having almost been killed. He was more vivacious and determined than ever.

"Come on Gracie!" he shouted. "This fight is far from over. Let's free the empire!"

He got up and despite his battered arm, raised his weapon to the grey skies and shot upwards, shouting, "Victory will be ours! Come on!"

He bolted ahead into the thick dust and blasted some more Maredians. Gracie lost sight of him and felt something approach her. A human hand touched her wrist.

"Jorge!"

She turned down her gun.

"I have to attend to the injured. We'll meet by the olive tree down the hill afterwards."

Gracie followed his eyes. "Okay," she said. "Stay safe."

They let go of each other's hands as he joined another medic and two medic drones to tend to several injured soldiers who were surrounded by the crisp dead bodies of Maredians.

Gracie kept her focus on creeping Maredians as she walked over a familiar scene: broken bones, body parts, half-broken faces, and viscera. She shuddered when she ran into familiar eyes that stared ahead. It was Katrina. Her legs had been torn off and thrown in a pile nearby.

Gracie held back the sobs in her throat and kept her focus clear. The enemy's presence still put her in imminent danger.

Gracie ran into a group of soldiers moving through the beach as cautiously as she did.

A sudden flash of movement underneath them.

The Earth burst open, and powerful coils wrapped themselves over the soldiers near Gracie. They screamed horrifically as the Maredians' powerful coils crushed their ribs. Their weapons rose upwards into the air and fell out of their hands. Gracie was stunned for a second and this proved disastrous. An arm shot out and grabbed her leg, tearing at the ligaments. She blasted the arm, and as she did this, other arms shot out through the sand and grabbed her waist and neck.

More Maredians burst through the sand, and screams of assaulted humans rose inside her helmet. She blasted shots at the

Maredian and the one creeping behind her. She was thrown like a rag doll onto a heap of sharp debris which punctured the sides of her rib cage. Her helmet was thrown off. Her lungs reacted to the torrent of pain. A burst of air shot through her throat, and the hums began to rise up her throat. They were quickly overwhelmed by Maredians that endlessly whirled out of the sand like weeds on speed.

Maredians grabbed soldiers and twirled and waved them upwards to the skies as if they were on an amusement ride. Blood spurted out from their mouths, the desperate bellowing of the screams cutting through the air.

Gracie stood up to the group of Maredians coming her way and to another group of them behind her and opened her arms. Her hums rang out. Although she was in immense pain, she vibrated her hums as loud as she could.

This time, the Maredians reacted, and trunk arms dropped soldiers out of their strong grips and remained passively by their sides.

The Maredians didn't move, mesmerized by the hums that came out from the depths of Gracie's lungs and not from helmets or other sound systems the army had. It was as if there was an underlying sound in Gracie's hum that the Maredians could distinctively hear and caused them to remain still which could not be replicated through a recording.

Gracie stumbled around them, gathered them together in front of her, and others more that continued to come up from underneath the sand. On and on her hums reverberated through her, pushing the hundreds of Maredians tightly together in one large assembly. The energy in her hums started to break their power. Behind the wall of the Maredians, over the mounds of debris, soldiers arrived, positioning themselves on top of debris, with weapons pointed down at the gathered Maredians. War drones also finally reached them, and in a coordinated effort, someone's voice inside the soldiers' helmets shouted, "Blast these motherfuckers, now!"

Gracie took a step back and held her breath as gelatinous, kerosine-smelling Maredian body parts splattered over her uniform and the side of her face. She wiped away the tissue and stood over the burning bodies of the Maredians, which were quickly dissolving into dried husks. She listened to their hissing as they died. Someone came from behind and stomped a melting Maredian under his boots, reducing it to dust.

"There are more of these bastards down the beach!" Sergeant Valentim said. A line of blood came down his mouth; his helmet was knocked off, exposing dark curls plastered across his forehead. He gripped at a side that a Maredian had attempted to crush.

"Come on, soldier. We're winning!" he said and grabbed her arm. They raced together toward a hill that had a pit full of dead husks of Maredians and a few dead soldiers. A group of soldiers blasted a dozen more Maredians. Gracie grabbed an abandoned helmet and put it on, listening to victorious hollers, "These bastards are all dead! Some have escaped and are heading toward Jerusalem."

General Da Costa and a few of the soldiers were at the bottom of a pit surrounded by soldiers. They lifted their weapons in the air, celebrating their victory. Drones zoomed above them, moving back and forth.

"What of Emperor Sebastian?" Gracie asked General Da Costa. "I lost sight of him back up the hill."

"He may have gone further ahead. We'll send out a drone. Trucks will be here soon to take us to Jerusalem," General Da Costa said.

She didn't listen to him and made her way down a path, her weapon pointed ahead of her, as she rounded mounds of debris.

There was a strong tingling sensation in her leg. Torn ligaments rejuvenated quickly and got stronger. The shooting pain subsided into a faint numbness.

She moved around debris and saw through the crevices that large rats and millions of insects were chewing and feasting on fresh body parts.

Down the side hill of debris and surrounded by heaps and heaps of dead Maredians, a pair of black military boots jutted outwards from the bottom of a hill. She sped down it, ignoring the increased pain from her healing leg.

Around the curve of the debris, Emperor Sebastian lay, his chest rising with each heavy breath. He was thrown against a pile of rocks and held onto his weapon that pointed directly at the burnt Maredians that disintegrated in front of him.

His face perspired, glowing red from the fight. Blood spurted down his chin and from the side of his mouth. Half of a leg was missing and parts of it were shredded. His helmet had been flung off, and a pool of blood formed under the rocks behind his head.

"Emperor Sebastian!"

His eyes moved over Gracie's face. A half smile.

She placed a hand over his. "Sire, hang on. I'll get help right away—"

The emperor gripped her hand, surprisingly strong. "I have been alive long enough and I can't come back from this one," he said weakly. "I want to finally be with God." He coughed up a stream of blood. "I will die along with my brave soldiers in this land where He once walked."

His eyes begged her.

"Don't let them bring me back again."

"Your Majesty, we can get you to the supreme leader's ship. They have the medical facilities to patch you up. You'll be fine."

He tightened his grip. “No Gracie. A long time ago, my pride once brought me low, but he who is lowly in spirit will truly obtain honour. I’ve made my penance.”

He coughed up a spurt of blood.

“My body isn’t to be transported on any ship. They have technologies that will keep my soul entrapped forever in a network. I’d rather live my eternity with Him in true peace. Bury me with no marker so I will never be found. Promise me.”

Just then, General Da Costa, a few soldiers, and Jorge reached her. They saw the horror of the emperor’s state.

“The emperor has requested to not be treated,” she told them.

Their eyes looked down at the emperor.

“The Maredian menace has been cleared out,” General Da Costa said.

“Good.” The emperor’s eyes returned to Gracie.

“Keep your promise ...”

He coughed some more blood, and the weapon dropped from his hand. His eyes moved from Gracie to the skies above as the Sun set, replaced by multitudes of lights that shone out from hundreds of war drones that flew above them.

His chest fell silent as the last spurt of blood escaped his lips.

CHAPTER 15

Reunion

The emperor was buried by an olive tree that had remained unscathed by decades of time and from the initial Maredian attacks. As he wished, no marker was left. He'd be reported lost on the battlefield, MIA.

In the truck, Gracie sat next to Jorge and General Da Costa. Sergeant Valentim sat in front of them. As they made their way to the city of Jerusalem, a crackle inside their helmets sounded as the report came in.

"*200 Maredian ships have landed along the border of Israel and Jordan. Other Empire troops have entered the region. Maredian menace in all other regions defeated. No further sightings.*"

Despite the solemn ride, a disturbance of victorious screams and jeering erupted outside the truck as it neared a group of soldiers. In the distance, hundreds of soldiers encircled a mound of debris. Gracie recognized the light-blue military uniforms. It was the British army of the Fifth Empire. They waved joyfully up to them in the truck, slowing them down, announcing, "The last of the Maredians is caught, and it's a mighty big one. It's almost dead. They're just toying with it now."

The soldier's mouth kept on moving, but no sound came out from it. The sound that Gracie heard, thumping inside her ears was a familiar chirp-hum. Every molecule in her body came alive, her posture stiffened, and her heart pounded madly, as she recognized the hums that unmistakably belonged to Amigo.

Anguish flared up inside her. They were toying with and hurting Amigo as if her own child was being cornered and brutally assaulted.

She let out a horrific scream, "Don't touch Amigo!"

Before anyone could pull her back, Gracie jumped off the truck and ran faster than she ever had, following the hums, until she reached the group of jeering soldiers, laughing over Amigo that was still inside a mound of debris and was partially burnt on one side. A six-foot-tall soldier squirted Amigo with a deadly chemical that turned a once beautifully amber-gold body of swirling lights and fire into crisp cinders. The soldier stood back and let out a hefty laugh along with the others and plunged a spear into the burnt skin.

One of the soldiers was too close, and liquid splattered over his face. He immediately wiped it away with a handkerchief. He brought it to his nose.

"What the hell? Blood? This thing bleeds?"

"Maybe it ate one of ours?"

"There are no signs of soldiers around it. This thing seems to have been hiding inside the debris for some time, waiting for us to find it and turn it into cinders ... as if it's gone defective."

Gracie tore off her helmet, and her locks of hair flew in the wind, against her wet face. She waved her arms at the soldiers and screamed.

"Stop! Leave it alone! Please!"

The tall soldier turned around, stupefied, and with disgust on her face. Stitched on the left side of the uniform, the name T. Bedford.

"Have you lost your mind soldier? This is my piece of meat."

"Don't kill it. I'm begging you, let me come to it."

T. Bedford's blue eyes nearly popped out of her head.

"Are you serious? You're asking me to spare the enemy's life?"

Robust laughter from the other soldiers.

"I know this Maredian," Gracie said, her voice shaking.

T. Bedford leaned down to Gracie.

"So do I, soldier. It's a demonic, murdering son of a bitch, it killed most of our ancestors mercilessly. Its time is up!"

"Its name is Amigo," Gracie said, "and it didn't kill any of your ancestors because, since its birth, it's lived on a ship, far away from Earth. I know this because I was on that ship with it. It spared my life and helped me live. If it killed, it was only today in the war."

The soldiers howled with laughter.

"Gracie?"

A familiar voice.

Wendy stood behind T. Bedford.

"You know this bat-shit crazy soldier?"

"Yeah, I gave her a lift back to Tel Aviv. She's cool."

Amigo's hums rose louder and screeched in pain.

Gracie clamped her hands over her ears.

"Wendy, it won't hurt me. If it does, it's on me, totally on me. I just want to approach it for one minute."

T. Bedford looked at Wendy perplexed.

Gracie walked past them and the other stupefied soldier who kept on smelling the smudged blood on his handkerchief.

Gracie spread open her arms and focused on her lungs, to summon the humming. She stood close to Amigo's withering body. A trunk arm shot out. She saw it coming and didn't move. It coiled around her waist in a painfully tight grip.

She waved at the soldiers behind her. “Don’t shoot! It’s okay!”

General Da Costa, Jorge, Sergeant Valentim, and a few other soldiers reached them.

“Is that your soldier?” T. Bedford said. “She’s completely lost it. That Maredian will crush her in a few seconds.”

“Stand down, General Teresa Bedford,” said General Da Costa. “It’ll be all right.”

Amazed, General Bedford looked at General Da Costa.

The rush of pain flared open Gracie’s lungs, and she willed the pressure to come up her throat quickly. The hums burst through in strong and steady succession. As her hums permeated the air, Amigo’s tight grip loosened, and Gracie dropped slowly to the ground. Trunk arms retracted to Amigo’s body.

She hummed louder and stronger as her mind screamed, “Amigo, it’s Gracie!”

The surrounding soldiers, watched in complete silence and anticipation with guns half lowered.

Chirp-hums responded back in the same rhythm. Tears filled the corner of her eyes. She kept her hums going. Trunk arms reached out for her, their ends flared with sharp teeth, and retracted inward, as they touched Gracie’s forehead and face. She held on to their ends, wrapping them around her neck, getting closer to Amigo.

“Amigo, it’s Gracie,” she said.

Amigo’s hums came faster. Other trunk arms sprouted from the right side of its body, which hadn’t been burnt, and moved behind her, playfully as it had done so many times.

“I’m sorry, Amigo. I can’t save you.”

Amigo let out a long hum and raised its body higher to show a sparkling, swirling golden white light gathering together in the centre of its chest. A dim image of Jimmy appeared, flickering back and forth.

Gracie smiled.

General Bedford's face twitched and said, "Is that an image of a little kid?"

"I'm sorry, Jimmy," Gracie sobbed. "I couldn't save you and be there for you when it happened."

A small head formed on the side of Amigo and dropped down close to her face.

She pushed a cheek against it.

"Thank you for saving me. I'm sorry. I can't save you. I can't," she sobbed.

The image of Jimmy flicking inside Amigo dimmed as Amigo's body started to die. It would be the last image she would have of Jimmy.

She cried against Amigo, who felt cold for the very first time.

Gracie dropped onto her knees and let Amigo's body crawl over hers. She kept Amigo in her arms until the dim amber rivulets remained still and the hums no longer vibrated through Amigo—no longer vibrated through her.

Amigo's body shrank against her, solidified into a burnt cinder, and turned into wisps of smoky tar that blew into the wind. Amigo was no more.

"Goodbye, my dear friend, my beloved Amigo. Goodbye."

CHAPTER 16

The Purity of Love

Gracie! The generous, kind master allowed it to find Gracie. It missed her so much. How content it felt that she was alive and back on her Earth. It had suffered many injuries and would die soon. But it wouldn't die alone. Gracie was here. It would die peacefully, surrounded by the warmth of her body, her hums, and her human voice. She finally hummed back to it, not as beautiful as its own hums, but she hummed back. It could feel her love and her sorrow. This was love for them. It was a beautiful and powerful sentiment. Death would be taking its physical form soon. It would return to the supreme light of the master. It would be one with the powerful master, the creator of all. It would be there to wait for Gracie and be with her again, and those that she'd known.

Right now, it had to endure the pain of physical death. It would die in her arms, peacefully—not surrounded by hatred but with the sadness and happiness of Gracie's pure love.

PART SIX

≈

New World

≈

I am the Alpha and the Omega,
the beginning and the end.

—Revelation 22:13

CHAPTER 1

A New Start

In the distance, the lights of Jerusalem shone and sparkled. It was human against human now ...

Crackling in their helmets.

Maredians approaching the city. Drones are counting about 200,000.

Gracie's Maredian sight turned on.

Through the mounds of debris and dead bodies of the supreme leader's soldiers and of their opponents, who were civilians in plain clothes, distant shadows of twinkling lights that swirled like night flies were the bodies of still Maredians. There was some movement between them.

Gracie held back her breath. Humans, dressed in plain beige and short capes, with familiar broad faces. Some had survived. Gracie couldn't believe it. She wondered why they'd been brought here. The Maredians didn't need them to fight their battle.

The Maredians clumped in long rows together over a high mound of debris, facing the castle of the supreme leader and behind the opposition armies. They didn't attack but kept still. Their hums were low and in sync. A ship rose out from behind the castle, and council members began to get on the ship, including Global Council members, Gilberto, and a row of soldiers.

Gracie's Maredian sight stretched outwards and fell over the army trucks. The missiles were enveloped in clouds of rumbling smoke. Missile heads rose upwards toward the sky, ready to launch and strike their target.

Gracie turned to Jorge.

"I see the missiles. They've activated them and will destroy everything; the Maredians and everyone here that isn't on that ship evacuating to safety. It's what Gilberto said the Supreme Leader would do. We need to get back to our ships in Tel Aviv, or someplace immediately underground."

Jorge shook his head solemnly and was about to respond when a terrifying, vibrating sound blared throughout the skies. It sounded like a horn being blasted. Gracie covered her ears with her hands. Jorge put an arm around her. The terrifying sound continued to blare, four more times as lights in the city, began to flicker off. The engine of the Supreme Leaders' ship fell silent. The drones flying in the skies lost their power and crashed to the ground and over them. Helmets crackled and struggled to keep power.

"What is happening?" Gracie's voice trembled.

Winds picked up. Balls of fire the size of tennis balls, shot down from the skies, hitting partially destroyed buildings, mountains, and roads in the distance.

"Report immediately," General Da Costa spoke into his helmet. "Are Maredian ships approaching the Earth and attacking from above?"

Some static. Then, a voice responded, "General there's nothing on the radar. No ship or anything approaching."

A white light suddenly lit up the night sky. It wasn't a flash; it was a sparkling white light that began to spread over the night skies.

"There is a disturbance over the skies, are you sure it is not a Maredian ship or a cluster of them approaching?" General Da Costa asked with more urgency in his voice.

Crackling in their helmets.

Sergeant Valentim and General Bedford adjusted their helmets and put on magnifying night visors.

"Has everyone gone mad around here?" General Bedford said. "There's nothing up there. What is this light you're seeing?"

A beam of white light, that Gracie had seen in many dreams Amigo gave her, full of multitudes of roaring fires, spread out from the centre of the dark skies and quickly turned them into daylight.

The Maredians remained still, and the humans by their sides were wild-eyed and the only ones full of joyous wide smiles.

Sergeant Valentim's voice rang out. "How am I not able to see this happening? Are you sure you're seeing this?"

Soldiers took off their helmets and knelt before the approaching light. General Da Costa joined them. A few of the soldiers cried softly and others stood solemnly. Most of the soldiers were seized with terror and went into a panic, hearts beating inside them like wild animals, and they pointed their guns up at whatever was approaching Earth.

Horrified voices returned, crackling through the helmets as a strong wind rose around them. "Other empires are reporting this light. What the heck is going on? This light is being witnessed all over Earth. How is that even possible? Is the enemy using some kind of holographic delusion?"

The Earth shook as if a powerful force pounced down on it, sending mounds of debris and rocks flying everywhere.

In the growing chaos, Gracie felt calm and peaceful. Jorge had the same expression, and he brought her closer to him.

A line of elite soldiers stood behind the supreme leader. The insides of whatever dark matter inside the supreme leader churned wildly. His face, twisted in rage as his eyes burned at the approaching light as if he clearly knew who was coming.

With the strong winds spinning around them and the earthquakes rattling the ground, husks of what was left of the Maredians rose from every place, and flew inside the enormous light, disintegrating inside it.

Desperate screams of terror came from the soldiers behind her. "What the heck are you seeing?" they demanded. They weren't able to see the vision but experienced the terrifying winds and the earthquakes that increased in power and yet didn't touch those who were able to see the approaching vision.

Gracie looked inside the incredible beam of light and the outline of a divine master approached. Behind the divine master, a sea of other figures followed.

Gracie heard the chirp hum distinctively. Amigo was there and letting her know. Her eyes followed the sound, and in its centre, a gold fire light emerged to form Jimmy. It wasn't an image of Jimmy. It was Jimmy! She could see his cherub face, large eyes, red lips, and little arms rising toward her. Amigo kept its promise, it found Jimmy and was bringing him to her. Tears filled up her eyes and the words written over a notepad so long ago came to her: *a new start.*

Amigo had told her that the master's important mission would complete and a new start on Earth would begin.

***

A helmet rolled over the ground by the roots of a tree whose branches filled up with multitudes of red flowers. Seeds fell into the rich soil, and other new life quickly began to sprout.

A voice announced through the helmet for the last time ... *unknown entity covering the entire Earth with incredible light. Number 234 signing off on February 22, 2222 at 22:22 hours.*

THE END

If you have enjoyed reading this book, please scan this QR code to leave an honest feedback on Amazon and Goodreads.

Acknowledgment

A special thanks to **Sush Dutta**, and to the team at Global Publishing for assisting me to bring this project to complete fruition.

A sincere thank you to all of my **readers** around the world, who have taken the time to read my debut novel.

And finally, a special thanks to the electric/trance music artists such as **Armin Van Buuren** and Above and Beyond. Your music helped me get through hours and hours of revising emotionally complex scenes and come out of them not so scathed. Keep on producing this incredible music.

About the Author

Susan B. Iris, a talented author hailing from the vibrant city of Toronto, captures the essence of diverse landscapes in her captivating stories. Susan's narratives are rich tapestries of culture and adventure, inspired by her summers spent in Ontario and Portugal, and her love for history.

Susan's excursion as a novelist started at the regarded Humber College in Toronto where she sharpened her art and developed her extraordinary voice by joining the Creative Writing Program. With a voracious enthusiasm for narrating, she has emptied her innovative energy into making her debut novel, "The Maredian," a scholarly diamond that has gathered basic recognition and contacted the hearts of readers all over the planet.

With her immersive storytelling and nuanced characters, Susan B. Iris continues to captivate readers in her second book, The Novelist. Her composing inspires strong feelings, shipping readers to enthralling universes where the creative mind exceeds all rational limitations.

To remain in contact with Susan B. Iris, follow her on her social media platforms. Through these stages, you'll have the chance to stay aware of her most recent composing projects, take part in significant conversations, and leave on abstract excursions that will remain with you long after you turn the last page.

Contact the author at:
www.susanbiris.com

Manufactured by Amazon.ca
Bolton, ON

38079672R00203